11'94

PRAISE FOR
THE SKELETON'S KNEE
AND ARCHER MAYOR

▲▼▲▼▲▼▲▼▲▼▲▼▲▼▲▼▲▼

"There's fine work here. The complicated plot . . . spins with revelation and surprise; the numerous characters are fully developed; and the villain, once revealed, is everything a villain should be."

—*Publishers Weekly*

▲ ▼ ▲

"If you like a good story, don't miss this one. . . . The action is incredible, yet Mayor makes it believable. . . . An exceptional mystery, you can't put down."

—*Chattanooga Times*

▲ ▼ ▲

"A genuinely absorbing page-turner . . . studded with odd pleasures and unexpected sights. . . . To call *The Skeleton's Knee* a roller coaster ride is to underestimate its narrative pyrotechnics."

—*Vermont Times*

▲ ▼ ▲

more . . .

▲ ▼ ▲

"Gunther is an attractive hero. . . . Mayor renders his own complicated approach with a master's craftsmanship, at once fluid, exciting and hooked on a time of trouble."
—*Orange County (CA) Register*

▲ ▼ ▲

"Crisp and intriguing."
—*Kirkus Reviews*

▲ ▼ ▲

"Well-written, fast-paced, and unpredictable."
—*Vermont Life*

▲ ▼ ▲

"A satisfying tale with more twists than a Green Mountain back-country road."
—*Yale Alumni Magazine*

▲ ▼ ▲

"Should please procedural fans and those who enjoy country-cop-in-the-big-city escapades."
—*Library Journal*

▲ ▼ ▲

"One of my favorite detectives."
—*The Poisoned Pen*

▲ ▼ ▲

▲ ▼ ▲

"At ease with the history and maverick social structure of his region (Brattleboro, VT), the author isn't afraid to look on its dark side. As rugged as those mountains in the background, this virile series should only last as long."

—*New York Times Book Review*

▲ ▼ ▲

"It is our good fortune that Mr. Mayor's skills are equal to the vigor of his imagination."

—*The New Yorker*

▲ ▼ ▲

"Mayor has a way with white-knuckle final scenes."

—*Los Angeles Times Book Review*

▲ ▼ ▲

"A believable . . . appealing hero."

—*Cleveland Plain Dealer*

▲ ▼ ▲

"THE SKELETON'S KNEE is mystery writing at its American best."

—*Trenton Times*

▲ ▼ ▲

OTHER BOOKS BY ARCHER MAYOR

FRUITS OF THE POISONOUS TREE
SCENT OF EVIL
BORDERLINES
OPEN SEASON

THE SKELETON'S KNEE

ARCHER MAYOR

THE MYSTERIOUS PRESS

Published by Warner Books

A Time Warner Company

In this book, as in its predecessors, I have used real settings, and, in some cases, real organizations, against which to place my story. This is to add an element of realism, which readers have told me they enjoy. I do not do this, however, either to embarrass or bring discomfort to anyone associated with those settings or organizations, and I wish to stress that any such possible results were purely unintentional.

MYSTERIOUS PRESS EDITION

Copyright © 1993 by Archer Mayer
All rights reserved.

Cover design by Julia Kushnirsky
Cover illustration by Chris Gall

The Mysterious Press name and logo are regestered trademarks of Warner Books, Inc.

 Mysterious Press books are published by
Warner Books, Inc.
1271 Avenue of the Americas
New York, NY 10020

A Time Warner Company

Printed in the United States of America

Originally published in hardcover by The Mysterious Press.

First Printed in Paperback: November, 1994

10 9 8 7 6 5 4 3 2 1

To Ponnie—
for maintaining that life with a writer,
while not normal,
has its merits

Part One

Chapter One

I have a body for you."

The voice on the line—smooth, cultured, and completely serious—was Beverly Hillstrom's, Vermont's chief medical examiner.

I cradled the phone between my shoulder and cheek, and poured several packets of sugar into my coffee. Unlike the larger urban charnel houses of New York or Los Angeles, the Brattleboro, Vermont, Police Department did not export corpses to the ME's office for autopsy every day of the week, nor even once every six months. When we did, it was usually an "unwitnessed death"—an elderly person who'd died alone in bed, and for whose demise the law required an explanation.

Homicides, the only other professional reason for the ME and I to talk, were rarer still, although recently we had given those numbers a boost during a particularly bloodthirsty case. But that was now history; to my knowledge, we hadn't shipped a body from either category since.

I was, therefore, totally baffled. "It came from here?"

She was suddenly, and uncharacteristically, less sure of herself. "It's an adverse-occurrence case, sent to me by Dr. Michael Brook. You know nothing about this?"

"I don't even know what an 'adverse occurrence' is."

"It's when a patient dies of something other than what he's being treated for. For example, a cardiac patient dying of undiagnosed cancer."

"Uh-huh," I muttered, waiting for the inevitable punch line.

"Or an orthopedic patient dying of an aneurysm caused by a bullet."

I let out a little puff of air. "Who are we talking about?"

"Someone named Abraham Fuller, age forty-seven. He was sent to me by Brattleboro Memorial Hospital, where he'd checked in with severe back pain and lower-limb paralysis, which X rays revealed to be acute osteomyelitis. He suddenly up and died in the hospital two days later, and Dr. Brook wanted me to take a look."

"And you found a bullet wound."

"Specifically, I found a traumatic aortic aneurysm caused by a bullet crease some time ago."

I put my feet up on my scarred wooden desk and rocked my chair back, getting comfortable. "Some time ago? How long?"

"I'll give you the long-winded answer to explain why I have to be a little vague on the timing. When a bone is damaged, as part of Mr. Fuller's spine was by the same bullet, it undergoes a series of sequential changes before stabilizing, much as the skin does when it scars over. But the process with the skin occurs rapidly, whereas the bone takes its time, five years generally, from start to finish. Technically, all I could say is that since Mr. Fuller's bone-tissue exhibits having gone through this entire process, his wound is at least five years old."

I caught her inference. "And not so technically?"

"Between you and me, based on my own experience, I'd say it was easily twice that, and maybe more. But I couldn't back that opinion up with one shred of scientific data."

I sighed and closed my eyes. A time-honored policeman's adage has it that with homicides, if you haven't nailed your killer inside a week, your chances of ever doing so divide by half for every subsequent week that passes. "So in a nutshell, you've just given me one very old, cold homicide."

"I'm afraid so."

"The aneurysm could only have been caused by the bullet?"

"I found trace elements of metal and had them sent to Waterbury for analysis under the scanning electron microscope. They were consistent with the lead used in bullets.

Also, I have both an entrance and an exit wound, and internal scarring defining the trajectory within the body. So yes, the aneurysm was caused by a bullet and death was due to the aneurysm.''

''What took the aneurysm so long to burst?''

''That's hard to say. I could venture a few guesses, but none of them would do you any good. Let's just say he'd reached his time.''

I turned all this over in my mind. ''He must have been wounded before he moved to the area. I don't remember any local ending up in a wheelchair from a gunshot wound.''

''He wasn't confined to a wheelchair. The paralysis I mentioned was recent, stemming from a sudden infection that formed around the old bone and lead fragments.''

''A sudden infection? Did he reopen the wound?''

There was a pause at the other end. ''He might have done something to precipitate it; not reopen it, precisely, but perhaps to cause a shifting of sorts. You see, those fragments were not frozen in place. To a certain extent, the ones that weren't encapsulated by the healing bone were free to wander a bit. It was one of the fragments that triggered the osteomyelitis, which in turn led to an abscess—a dumbbell lesion, specifically—that expanded into the spinal canal, put pressure on the lower cord, and thereby cut off the use of his legs. This is not so rare, by the way; it's part of the reason why surgeons are so careful to remove everything they can from a wound. There are dozens of stories of people stepping on shards of glass and having them pop out of the skin years later far from where they entered.''

I paused a few seconds, reviewing the little I had. Over the phone, I could hear the faint strains of the classical music she favored in her office. ''Could you tell if Fuller was treated at the time he was shot? Were there any suture scars, for instance?''

''None, and I looked carefully. Either the attending physician decided to leave well enough alone or Mr. Fuller never sought treatment. If the latter was the case, I'd say he used to be a very lucky man.''

''Would he have required professional home care, at least?''

"Not necessarily. I followed the scar tissue the bullet left behind. It entered between the navel and the left rib cage, missed the liver, spleen, and left kidney, nicked the aorta and the left transverse process of the spine, and exited. It must have been extremely painful at the time, but neither fatal nor permanently debilitating. Aside from the aorta, nothing vital was hit. He had to have been terribly uncomfortable, and it's amazing the wound didn't become infected, but he could have recovered simply by staying put. The irony was that his recovery turned out to be a false one. One millimeter the other way and he would have been dead. As it was, the wound became a time bomb."

"But wouldn't he have had a limp, or chronic back pain?"

"You'll have to confirm this with Dr. Brook, but I doubt Mr. Fuller had much trouble with his spine until recently. His muscular development in the area of the wound indicates a full and normal range of motion. There were also no signs of long-term chronic infection. If I had to guess, I'd say he'd led a perfectly normal life until the abscess developed. In fact, I've rarely examined a healthier specimen. He didn't smoke, wasn't overweight, his stomach and intestinal contents revealed a vegetarian diet, and his liver was so good-looking, I doubt he drank much alcohol."

I smiled at her enthusiasm. Despite the derision it attracted from my colleagues, I, too, enjoyed autopsies for the insights they provided. They reminded me of searches I'd conducted through people's homes, apartments, and luggage, which also were usually rich in personal details.

"You couldn't guess what the caliber was, could you?"

"Not with any precision, but it wasn't large. Say anything from a .32 on down."

I let out a small grunt. "Well, it looks like I better start digging. Could you send me copies of what you've got, especially a shot of his face?"

"I have a courier heading to Rockingham in a couple of hours. I'll ask him to extend his trip a little."

"Thanks. By the way, who has claim on the body?"

"No one. The record shows no next of kin and no claimant."

That surprised me. "What about an address? Could he have been a street person?"

"He had none of the outward signs. His teeth, nails, hair, and general hygiene didn't reflect that kind of life, unless he was new to the street. The hospital probably has all that."

Familiar sensations were beginning to stir in my mind, the first signs of the case taking hold of my imagination. I knew that, like most homicides, this one probably had an easy and reasonable solution. I was fully prepared to discover that Fuller had been shot accidentally by a .22 pistol ten years ago. But until such a possibility metamorphosed into legal fact, I thought I'd better hedge my bets. "Could you put Mr. Fuller on ice for a few days, until I get a better handle on him, or until someone claims him?"

She hesitated. "It's a little unusual. We normally don't do that unless it's a study cadaver. . . . But sure, I don't see why not. I have space. If it causes a problem down the road, I'll let you know. Don't leave me out on a limb for too long, okay?"

"I promise."

I hung up and stared out the window that separated my office from the rest of the detective squad, grateful that this was cropping up when our work load was comparatively light. My cubicle, small but well lit, and recently remodeled, along with the rest of the ancient building, was the sole display of rank I could brag of as chief of detectives.

I got up and opened the door. Off to one side of the central cluster of four desks was a fifth one, facing the entrance to the public corridor outside. This was Harriet Fritter's station, the squad secretary, or clerk, whose frightening efficiency and competence allowed me to duck most of the paperwork that would otherwise have kept me anchored indoors.

"Harriet," I asked her, "could you call Dr. Michael Brook at the hospital and see if he's available for a quick chat? Also, did you see anything from the town clerk's office listing the week's death certificates? I thought we were supposed to get a copy of that as a matter of routine."

She smiled, already dialing the hospital. "We used to, years ago, but when I told them we were throwing the list out, also as a matter of routine, they quit sending them."

She turned back to the phone and I retreated, suitably abashed. Harriet was a grandmother and the leader of an enormous familial clan. That she could run both her family and our office with good humor and no side effects proved she had little tolerance for wasteful habits, and no bashfulness about correcting them.

She buzzed me on the intercom moments later. "You're in luck. He's got a free hour right now. Nine Belmont Avenue, second floor."

Nine Belmont was a remarkably plain redbrick barracks building, attached to the side of the hospital by a narrow corridor like a near-severed limb. A professional building designed to house a variety of medical offices, it had always struck me as the ideal place to receive bad news about a terminal illness: low-slung, cheap-looking, and generally unpromising. I pushed open the glass and aluminum front door, crossed the worn, water-stained foyer carpet, and made for the stairs to the second floor.

Halfway down the dark corridor, I came to a door marked MICHAEL BROOK, M.D.—ORTHOPEDICS. I knocked and walked in.

Brook was standing in his own empty waiting room, leaning on the counter in front of the nurse/receptionist, picking a piece of candy out of a jar to the side of the sliding glass window. He looked up and stuck his free hand out as I approached. "Hi, Joe. I'm test-marketing my reception room. Got to see if I'm invoking the proper element of dread. Want a candy?"

I accepted a blue cellophane-wrapped offering and followed him through the far door and into a hallway lined with suitably soothing calendar art. He led the way to an office at the far end, stumping from side to side like a land-bound sailor. As ironies would have it, Brook was an orthopedist with one artificial leg, the original having been lost to disease as a teenager. He motioned me into one of two guest chairs, settling into the other one himself.

"What can I do for you?" he asked, unwrapping his candy and popping it in his mouth.

He was a big man, in all dimensions, and had always

reminded me of a sheepdog: all bushy gray hair, bearded and uncombed, surrounding two soft brown eyes that hovered above a pair of half glasses like children looking over a fence. I'd met him more than twenty years earlier, when my wife had consulted him for a pain in her shoulder. That hadn't turned out to be his particular expertise—the pain had been cancer, and Ellen had died within a few months—but Michael Brook had kept by both of us, smoothing the introductions to the many doctors we quickly acquired and translating their incantations into the kind of English we could grasp and digest. While I'd never had to use him professionally since, and our paths rarely crossed socially, his compassion back then had forged a friendship I'd never questioned.

"Mike, I just got a call from Beverly Hillstrom about Abraham Fuller."

Brook's face lit up with interest. "Right. What the hell was that, anyway? We were all stunned when he died; didn't make any sense."

"She called it a traumatic aortic aneurysm, caused by the creasing of a bullet years ago."

His mouth fell open and he pulled his glasses off his face. "Damn. That scar he had. He said he got it falling against a tree branch when he was a kid."

"Apparently, there was an entrance wound near his belly button—a small one. Hillstrom guesstimates a .32 caliber at most."

He shook his head in wonder. "Christ. It never even crossed my mind. Did this guy have a record, too?"

I smiled at the imaginative leap. "Not everyone with a bullet scar is a crook, Michael. Although, for all I know so far, you may be right. I'm just starting to look into his past. I thought I'd start with you."

Brook waggled his shaggy eyebrows at me and pushed himself forward in his chair. "You're not going to get too far. He wasn't a great historian." He twisted his phone console around to face him and pushed one of its many buttons. "Bernice? Could you pull everything we have on Abraham Fuller and bring it in? Thanks."

He settled back in his seat with a small grunt. "I was called in by the Emergency Department a few days ago. Rescue,

Inc., had transported a middle-aged male with back pain resulting in paraplegia. The X rays revealed vertebral osteo-myelitis, complicated by an abscess, all stemming, I thought, from the patient's decades-old encounter with a tree branch. . . ."

"Did he pinpoint the time of the injury?"

Mike shook his head. "No. That's what I meant when I said he was a poor historian. He just said it happened when he was a kid. I asked him the usual background questions, so I could rule out any underlying congenital or genetic causes for his problem, but every time I wanted specifics, he got vague. Maybe that's why I thought he was a crook just now."

There was a knock on the door and a nurse handed Brook a slim folder before retiring. Brook leafed through it cursorily and handed it over to me. "No date of birth, no place of birth, no names of parents, no address, no phone number, no Social Security number, no family physician, no prior records at the hospital. No nothin', when you get down to it."

I glanced over the admission sheets at the front, not bothering with the treatment pages, which were indecipherable scrawls, in any case. They were virtually blank. "Hillstrom told me he stayed several days."

"That's right. I wanted to do a biopsy on the abscess, and I was planning surgery regardless." He paused. "If that damned aneurysm had held on a little longer, we might have caught it in surgery and saved his life."

"Why did it blow, after all this time?"

He shrugged, much as I'd guessed Hillstrom had earlier to the same question. "That kind of aneurysm acts like a stretched-out water balloon. If either the pressure inside increases too much or the outer envelope weakens, it goes pow." He retrieved the file from my lap and flipped it open. "His blood pressure was on the high side, probably due to the pain and anxiety. That alone might have been enough to do the trick."

I let my eyes wander across the walls before me, registering but not reading the various diplomas and citations. A secretive man, admitting to no past, is forced by medical necessity to come out of his hole, and then dies. I shook my head. This was turning out darker than I'd feared . . . and more intriguing.

"How did the Accounting Office deal with him? I notice he didn't list any insurance."

Brook chuckled. "Normally, I wouldn't know, since it ain't my department, as they say, but this guy really made history on that one. The whole hospital heard about it—unofficially, of course. He paid cash, and I mean real cash: greenbacks. At some point, after I'd started talking surgery, someone in Accounting got nervous—Fuller didn't even have a Medicaid number, after all—and they went up to talk to him. He asked them how much they needed, told them to leave the room for a minute, and then handed them five thousand bucks. He told them to regard it either as a down payment or an amount to draw on, depending on the final amount due. They didn't argue, and from what I heard, they didn't ask for explanations."

"Where was he keeping it? Did he have a bag or something?"

"Yeah, one of those small backpacks. I think the hospital still has it, along with his clothing and whatever else he left behind, unless somebody's claimed them by now."

My mind was humming with possibilities, most of them far from innocent, but I wanted to play out at least one straightforward angle before assuming the worst. "Maybe he was a hermit. Did you see him clothed, or did the ER staff have him stripped already?"

Michael paused before answering, thinking back. "He was still partly dressed. They were work clothes—standard J. C. Penney–type stuff. His hands were rough; he had the typical working man's suntan—forearms as black as walnut, the rest of him lily-white. I don't know . . . I guess initially I took him for what he looked like. Not a backwoods type, though. His speech didn't fit that at all. He was pretty well educated, beyond high school. When I described what I'd found out about his back, he had no trouble following it, even asked some fairly sophisticated questions. . . ."

"As if he'd had medical training?"

"No, nothing that fancy, but definitely a college background. He was also a health nut. A lot of construction workers and whatnot are tough as nails, but their eating habits are lousy. It usually shows up in their waistlines. This guy was as thin and hard as cable wire. Described himself as a lacto-vegetarian: no eggs, no meat, no fish, and no poultry. He gave strict instructions to the dietitian.''

"You think he took care of himself because he knew he had a touchy back?''

Brook shook his head. "I don't know. He denied it to me—said he'd never had any trouble with it except when he'd fallen on the tree branch years ago, but who's to know? The guy was obviously not too intimate with the truth.''

I thanked him and moments later passed through the umbilical-like corridor between the hospital and the office building, in search of the head of Accounting. I found her beyond a moderately crowded waiting room in a small, windowless, but cheery cubbyhole decorated with framed Georgia O'Keeffe posters and unusually healthy green plants.

She was an angular, white-haired woman with a flame red dress and an animated face. The nameplate on her tidy desk read, KATHY PARKER. She half-rose from her chair as I entered and shook hands. "The receptionist said you're from the police?''

I smiled and placed my credentials before her. "Yes. Lt. Joe Gunther.''

She looked at me carefully then. "Oh, I've heard of you. My goodness, weren't you almost killed a couple of months ago?''

I smiled at the reference to a recent headline-grabbing case. "A dubious claim to fame. Yes, that was me.''

She returned my badge and gestured to me to sit. "Well, it's an honor.'' Her face acquired a carefully neutral cast. "I take it you're here in a professional capacity?''

"Yes. I want to know about a small backpack belonging to a patient who died here a couple of days ago, an Abraham Fuller.''

Kathy Parker's eyebrows shot up. "Oh yes. I inventoried that myself. Would you like it?''

"I'd like to take a look at it.''

She turned toward a small floor safe behind her, opened its

door, and retrieved an old red canvas bag, laying it on her desk. "I'm not surprised you're here, actually. I mean, we're obviously delighted when a patient pays for his treatment on the barrel, but using a bagful of cash did stir up a few comments."

I picked up the knapsack and rested it in my lap for the moment. "Did anyone know him, or about him?"

"Mr. Fuller? Not that I heard. That's what made it even more mysterious; paying cash is the kind of thing you see drug-runners do on TV." She smiled at the soiled, much-used bag between my hands. "Of course, on TV they usually carry it around in a fancy briefcase. I guess that's the Vermont touch."

I smiled and fingered the material. "I know you didn't mean it literally, but was there anything indicating he was into drugs?"

She shook her head emphatically. "No, no, this was all just gossip; you know how it is, especially in a small place like this. People were also asking if Fuller was a pseudonym for an Italian name, as in Mafia. I never even saw the man." She nodded toward the pack. "I didn't get that until after he'd been shipped off to Burlington for autopsy. It was just . . . Well, open it and see for yourself. It is a little weird."

I undid the knot at the throat of the bag and drew it open, taking a look before I reached in. There were some odds and ends: a toothbrush and paste, a comb, a paperback edition of *A Connecticut Yankee in King Arthur's Court*, a balled-up pair of socks, some underwear, and a single change of clothes. But the attention grabbers were the banded bundles of hundred-dollar bills.

I gingerly pulled one out, holding it by the edges. "Did you count it all?"

"Yes. There're five of them, a thousand dollars each."

"And he'd already paid five thousand for his treatment, is that right?"

She nodded. "We deposited part of what he gave us, for services rendered. The difference is still in escrow, pending retrieval by next of kin."

I looked at the bundle in my hand. The inner bills were new and crisp; the outer ones were unwrinkled but grimy, and the edges of all of them were faintly soiled. They also had an odd feel to them—almost slippery. I held it up to my nose and smelled.

"Mildew," Kathy Parker suggested.

"Yeah. I think you're right." I lifted the knapsack to my nose and detected the same pungent odor. I looked at the face side of one of the cover bills and let out a small grunt, flipping through the others for confirmation.

"What?" Parker asked, presumably keen for more gossip.

I hesitated, then dropped the money back into the bag. "Nothing; I was just wondering about the mildew. If you could draw up a receipt, I think I'll take this down to the Municipal Building and lock it in our evidence room."

She did as I requested, half-curious and half-relieved to be rid of a potential headache. By proxy, I was allowing her to jerk her thumb down the line at us, should anyone later ask about the cash.

Not that I was paying much attention to her quandaries, in any case. As I thanked her, took a copy of the receipt and the bag, and worked my way back to my car, I was mulling over what I'd discovered in glancing at those bills. Not all the bundles were of mint notes—in fact, only two of them were— but those two were utterly pristine, with their serial numbers in perfect chronological sequence. The kicker was, new or old, none of them had been printed more recently than 1969, nearly twenty-five years ago.

Chapter Two

Since the Rescue, Inc., ambulance service had delivered Fuller to the hospital, I made them my next stop after depositing the money at police headquarters.

Located off Interstate 91's Exit 1, Rescue, Inc.'s broad, squat building sat on a small knoll overlooking where Canal

Street petered out as a low-rent, commercialized, somewhat seedy urban drag, to be renamed Chicken Coop Hill on the far side of the underpass—a narrow, rural ribbon of tarmac heading toward Guilford and the southern Vermont hinterlands. The abrupt contrast was typical Brattleboro: an aging, turn-of-the-century industrial town, in spots old enough, worn enough, and frail enough to appear threatened by the encroaching countryside. It wasn't true, of course. Brattleboro was expanding, if timidly. It just had the New England sensibility to be subtle about it.

I didn't see anyone around when I got out of my car. All three ambulances and the crash truck were parked on the apron before the two huge, open garage doors, the early-fall air still balmy enough to be welcome inside and out. I stood in the cavernous central truck bay for a moment and listened for voices, hearing a murmur emanating from behind a door far to the back.

I crossed the bay, knocked once, and opened the door to what looked like a classroom, complete with blackboard. Seven people, five of them in uniform, sat side by side at a pair of long tables, stuffing, stamping, licking, and cataloging thousands of envelopes.

Alphonse Duchene, the burly, white-haired president of the company, raised his head and grinned. "Caught us in the act."

"Fund-raising time?"

He rose, stretching his back, and walked over to shake my hand. "Forever and always. Want to join in?"

I looked at the dulled expressions of his colleagues. "Not even maybe. I wanted to ask you about a call you had a few days ago."

His expression, while still genial, became slightly guarded. "We might be able to tell you a little, assuming it doesn't trespass into patient confidentiality."

"The patient's dead."

Now he looked downright nervous. Ambulance personnel, like police officers and fire fighters, have come to fear lawsuits more than personal injury. I quickly took him off the hook.

"Name was Abraham Fuller. You picked him up for back pain and leg paralysis. He died in the hospital two days later of unrelated causes, more or less."

Duchene's face cleared somewhat, but I noticed all activity had stopped at the long table. One of the men in uniform, a paramedic I knew slightly, named John Breen, spoke up. "I was on that one. What killed him?"

"Aneurysm. There's no question of impropriety. You guys did it by the numbers, as did the hospital staff. It was just a long-standing thing that finally let go." I had no interest in revealing too much. We had our own confidentialities to protect.

My answer apparently did the trick, however. Duchene, the happy host once more, escorted me back out the door, calling over his shoulder as he went, "John, why don't you join us in my office?"

The three of us cut across the truck bay to a small glass-walled room in the far corner. Duchene held the door open, made sure we were both settled comfortably, and then planted his considerable hulk behind a cluttered metal desk, locking his hands behind his neck. "So, what's on your mind?"

"Where did you pick him up?"

Breen made a face. "The far side of the moon. About three miles up Sunset Lake Road, out of West Bratt, there's a horseshoe-shaped road."

"Hescock Road," I put in.

"Right; Hescock or Goodall, depending on who you talk to. Well, it leads to an old farmhouse owned by . . ." Breen hesitated a moment, thinking back. "Ed? No, Fred Coyner. He was the one who called us."

"So Fuller lived with Coyner?"

Breen laughed and shook his head. "No, no, it gets worse; it took us over forty minutes to get to this place from the time we got called. Coyner owns the property, but Fuller lived in a small building a half mile behind the main house, deep in the woods. We couldn't drive the rig to it—there was barely a track, much less a road—so we had to hoof it with the cot. Another fifteen minutes."

"What did you find?"

"The patient lying on the floor of a central room—living

room, kitchen, and everything else combined. He was in a lot of pain, had probably been there for several days. He was fully oriented; he'd managed to drag some food off a table nearby to sustain himself, but he was slightly dehydrated.''

"How was he psychologically?"

"He wasn't happy to see us. Coyner had warned us that he'd made the call over Fuller's objections—that happens a lot, and we often end up not transporting—but this was an extreme case. The guy was really furious, accused Coyner of a 'breach of faith,' whatever that meant.''

"But still you transported. You can't do that if the patient doesn't want it, can you?"

"Not unless he's deemed incompetent," Duchene put in.

"He wasn't that," Breen resumed. "This was a highly intelligent man. He was just angry, outraged that we'd invaded his privacy. It took a long time just to get him to talk about why we were there; he kept asking why he couldn't die in peace. I got the impression he'd been living as a hermit, totally cut off from the world around him.''

"He really thought he was dying?"

Breen shrugged. "I don't think he meant that literally—hard to say. Of course, seeing how things turned out, maybe he knew something we didn't. At the time, he was in agony, and I just wrote it off to that. Also, we finally did talk him into going with us, which reinforced my feeling he was being a little overdramatic.''

I didn't fault Breen his seeming callousness. As with cops, lots of people in the rescue business grow numb to some of the subtleties of human anguish; it was less a hardness—although it could be that, too—and more a sense that they'd seen it all before. "Did you notice a dirty red knapsack?"

Breen shook his head. "Not at first. After we'd finally convinced him to come along with us, he made us all go outside for a few minutes. When we came back in, he was holding the pack. Never let go of it all the way to the hospital.''

"He show you what was inside?"

"Nope. And it could have held anything—two hundred toothbrushes, for all I know. Nothing else had been normal about the call.''

"How many minutes were you outside?"

Breen paused, thinking back. "Couldn't have been more than five."

"And you didn't see the knapsack before going back in?"

"I didn't, no. I generally look around quickly when I enter a scene, to check for any danger, or clues to the patient's condition, like pill bottles or needles or whatever. I don't remember seeing the pack, but then it probably wouldn't have registered anyway, since it wouldn't have told me anything."

"But if it had been hanging from a hook on the wall or in a closet, could he have reached it? How helpless was he?"

"He could barely move. Like I said, he'd been there for days, and the only food he'd been able to reach was on a nearby table—a bag of trail food and a bowl of fruit. He'd only gotten that because he'd pulled on the tablecloth and dragged it to within reach. He was lying in his own waste, if that gives you any idea."

It did. Fuller had been a desperate man, torn between a passion for solitude and the need for help. I closed my small notebook and stood up. "Well, I guess that's it for the moment. I'll let you get back to your paper cuts."

I put my hand on the doorknob and then hesitated, looking back at Breen. "How did you convince him to go with you?"

"I think he finally convinced himself. At first, when he was trying to send us away, he kept saying it would pass, as it had before, but I don't think he really believed it. No one wants to live with that much pain if there're people around who can help."

"He said the pain had passed before? Did he explain that?"

"Nope. When I asked him later if this had ever happened before, he denied it. By that point, of course, he didn't have much credibility with us, since he'd also denied having a date of birth, a Social Security number, or even a mailing address."

I thanked them both and headed back to my car. A hermit, Fuller may have been, but not just that. I remembered the contents of the red bag: Aside from the money, there'd been a change of socks and underwear, a few toilet articles, and a book by Mark Twain, all of which, now that I thought back, had been both musty-smelling and brand-new, with the wrappers still on and the back of the book unbroken.

During the Korean War, one of the things I'd learned the hard way was always to have a pack ready at hand, something light and compact, containing the essentials of survival, that could be grabbed at a moment's notice, along with my rifle. Life then had been an uncertain thing, with the Chinese threatening to overrun us at any time. We never knew if our tenuous connection to the rear might not vanish altogether. I couldn't help wondering if Abraham Fuller hadn't acquired the same habit of always having the bare essentials packed and ready by the door, including ten thousand dollars in antique bank notes.

I could blame the Chinese army, but what had been Fuller's dread? One obvious suggestion was the police. But despite his initial resistance, Fuller had finally agreed to go to the hospital, possibly to have his old bullet wound discovered, and therefore be interviewed by us. That risk couldn't have escaped him.

So either the police were not the stimulus that kept him packed and ready to run—which implied that somebody else was—or he was a demented and paranoid reclusive with a fondness for classic American literature.

Chapter Three

My office is located on the first floor of one of the Victorian era's least successful architectural leftovers. The Municipal Building—all red brick, carved stone, and bristling with rooftop spires—is perched threateningly on a steep bank overlooking upper Main Street. It is also as functional as a survivor from a train wreck. Years of remodeling and renovation have introduced elements of modern heating and cooling into its labyrinthine soul, but, like Frankenstein's monster, it seems cursed with a defective mind all its own.

The police department occupies the rear of the first floor and is cut in two by a broad central corridor running the length of the building. After parking my car in the rear lot, I was buzzed through the main entrance by Dispatch—Maxine Paroddy—who waved to me through the tellerlike glass window. The chief's office was located in the far corner of the main reception area.

A visit to Tony Brandt's office was like a trip back in time to when London heated itself with soft coal exclusively and force-fed black lung into all its inhabitants. Tony smoked a pipe. It was a habit he said he took up to cure his addiction to cigarettes, but he smoked so much, and in such airtight circumstances, I never could grasp the advantage of his conversion.

He looked up as I paused on the threshold, letting as much of the fog bank roll by as possible before plunging in. As always, I left the door open, and, as always, he motioned me to shut it. "Rumor has it we have a dead body on our hands."

I settled into one of the guest chairs as he leaned back and locked his hands behind his neck, ignoring the periodic beeps that softly emanated from his glowing computer screen. "So far, that's about all we've got, that and the decades-old bullet wound that killed him. How'd you hear about it?"

"Harriet told me. I was trying to hunt you down for some paperwork. Give me the details."

I told him what I had so far, which took ten minutes at most.

Brandt formed a steeple with his fingers and tapped his lips a couple of times before speaking. "None of this rings any bells concerning unexplained shootings or losses of money in recent years?"

I shook my head. "My immediate guess is that Mr. Fuller brought his problem with him from somewhere else. In fact, the money and the bullet may have nothing in common, and neither one is necessarily a sign of criminal activity. He could have been a wounded Vietnam vet with a mistrust of banks. I wouldn't be surprised if we end up handing it over to some other jurisdiction pretty quick, probably right after the FBI spits out something on his fingerprints."

Brandt was silent a while before asking me, "What do you intend to do now?"

"I'd like to check his residence out. It seems to me that if we're going to get a handle on this guy, that's where we'll find it. Maybe we can pin down a prior address and wash our hands of it even before the FBI stirs itself into action."

In fact, I had my doubts things would be that easy, doubts I was pretty sure Brandt shared. But neither one of us was willing to turn up the political heat just yet, still smarting as we were from the fallout that had followed a recent grisly case involving a fellow officer, an investigation tainted by insider leaks and a lingering distrust among the various agencies involved.

Brandt gently tapped his pipe against his ashtray. "All right. That seems fine to me. You're planning to secure a warrant?"

"Of course," I answered.

"But check it out alone, okay?" Brandt added quickly. "No forensics team. If you find anything, you can call them in later. And I'll let the state's attorney know."

I shrugged. It was a little unconventional, not to mention impractical, but I sympathized with his wishful thinking. "You got it. One tiptoe at a time."

Neither one of us smiled.

Two hours later, a signed search warrant in my pocket, I drove along Route 9 into West Bratt, in the local jargon—a barely separate entity from Brattleboro, segregated by I-91's gray slab of a no-man's-land, which only three streets manage to breach. The fire department has a substation out there, as does the post office, among a small cluster of commercial buildings at the intersection of Greenleaf Street and Route 9, but the sense of it being a community apart is lacking. Despite occasional yearnings to be otherwise, West Bratt remains a commercial tentacle on the map, dangling from downtown.

There is an irony to this, since the village of West Brattleboro cropped up in the late eighteenth century, around the same time Brattleboro, or the "east village," was being settled. In fact, the west village was an independent entity until 1927, catering to the rural trade that found its bustling, more industrialized neighbor largely unapproachable. By then, however, the battle had already been lost, and West Brattleboro fell victim to urban Darwinism.

Seen on a map, it appears like a finger pointing west, the only intrusion on an otherwise-green expanse of forests, meadows, and farm fields. Indeed, once I'd turned off of Route 9 onto Sunset Lake Road, I didn't go more than a third of a mile before I was embraced by almost pristine countryside, making it hard to believe I was only minutes from the fourth-largest town in Vermont.

Sunset Lake Road climbs to the body of water after which it's named—a large, beautiful hilltop pond ringed by rustic cabins and dense woods, but the lake is actually in Marlboro township, which raised a concern in my mind that Coyner's property might be just outside the Brattleboro town line, and therefore outside my jurisdiction.

Along its least civilized stretches, the road has blind corners, intermittent axle-killing ditches, and spots where a storm's runoff reduces it to little more than a stream crossing. But, as I approached the Hescock Road turnoff, the reward proved worth the effort: a view of operatic scale, extending south-southeast into Massachusetts and seemingly forever beyond. Blue-gray hills, spiky with evergreens, mountain passes, and the occasional glimmering pond, all lay before me with the same hopelessly romantic artificiality of a mural-sized landscape painting.

I followed Hescock's semicircle less than halfway around, until I came to an overgrown driveway marked by a mailbox and the rutted passage of years' worth of four-wheel traffic. The driveway—more of a grass-tufted lane—meandered a few hundred yards through the woods to a clearing as spectacular as the one I'd just left, where I found a rambling two-hundred-year-old Greek Revival farmhouse, weather-beaten and in need of paint, but as seemingly solid as the boulders poking through the lawn at its feet. By my calculations, I was still within township lines.

I killed the engine and swung out of the car, automatically slinging the department's 35-mm camera over my shoulder, my eyes irresistibly drawn to the hundred-mile view at my feet. I noticed then that a few leaves had already begun to fall from some of the trees, in reaction to the cool mountain air. In the valleys, early September meant a slight chill at night. Up here, that chill stayed put until midafternoon.

"Who are you?"

I turned at the voice, at once challenging but unthreatening. A tall, stooped, white-haired man had rounded the corner of the house, wearing a red-and-black-checked wool overshirt and holding a rake in his hand.

"Joe Gunther. I'm from the Brattleboro Police Department."

The white-haired man stopped about ten feet from me, his pale eyes still and watchful, glistening like polished stones in a narrow, much-seamed, expressionless face. "What do you want?" He quickly glanced at the camera.

"Are you Fred Coyner?"

"Maybe."

I couldn't suppress a smile. The answer was a parody of how "real" Vermonters speak. "I wanted to ask you about Abraham Fuller. I gather you called the ambulance several days ago that took him to the hospital?"

Coyner remained silent, seemingly uninterested in confirming the obvious.

"Did anyone give you an update on his condition?"

"Nope."

"He died, Mr. Coyner. Of a very old bullet wound."

There was a prolonged silence, offset only by distant bird-calls and the occasional rustle of a few crown-top leaves. Coyner's expression, what there was of it, didn't change, but after a pause, he shifted his gaze from me to the vague and distant horizon.

"Did you know he'd once suffered a gunshot wound?" I asked.

He still refused to answer. After several moments of contemplation, he finally muttered, "What do you want here?"

"I'd like to see where he lived, for starters."

"Follow me." He turned abruptly and began marching off at a surprisingly fast and steady pace, given his age. Having studied him up close, I guessed him to be somewhere in his seventies, lean, leathery, and hard, shaped by the weather and the personal isolation he wore like a mantle.

We walked for about fifteen minutes along a barely discernible path cut through the woods. I noticed to my surprise that running from tree to tree, fastened by bent-over nails or just looped over branches, was a heavy-gauge electrical wire.

"How long did you know Mr. Fuller?" I asked at one point, but the response was much as I'd expected: total silence. We trudged along quietly after that. I began to wonder if I would get any more from Coyner than I might from the surrounding trees.

We eventually came to a large opening in the woods, completely hemmed in by an impenetrable circle of trees and brush, as if a giant's heel had crushed the woods flat in this one spot, leaving the rest of the forest untouched. At the edge of the clearing, across from where we entered, was a small dirt-colored dwelling, a story and a half high, mostly made of logs, with a rusty metal roof, a rough lean-to on one side, and a sturdy homemade greenhouse on the other. A metal chimney poked out of the building's center. It was no thing of beauty, but it looked trim and tight and well tended. It was a shelter rather than an architectural expression, and as such it displayed a certain comforting appeal, like the huts and cottages in an illustrated children's book.

The storybook feeling was heightened by the landscaping before us, in front of the house. Every inch of open space from the front door to the very edge of the woods was under cultivation. Rows of vegetables, banks of berry bushes, arbors, trellises, stepped-up flower beds, and a sinuous, graceful latticework of pathways all combined to form an intricate, soothing display of virtually every form of plant life supportable in this area. The weather had begun to turn cold up here, the first hard frosts were just a few weeks away, and the summer's colorful cloak had begun to fade and unravel. Nevertheless, it was easy to see that this insulated, private spot, jealously tended and walled off from the rest of the world, was a paradise for six months of the year.

"Was Fuller the one with the green thumb, or is all this yours?" I asked my taciturn guide, who had entered the clearing with barely a glance around.

"His."

We marched in single file up to the door of the cabin, where Coyner stepped aside like the bellboy to some hotel room, his job done, eager to be gone. He nodded his head toward the building, lifted the latch to the door, and pushed it open a few inches. "There. All yours."

I called after him as he retreated back down the narrow central path. "You going to be around for a couple of hours? I'd like to ask you a few questions later."

He didn't answer.

I pushed the door wide open and stood there for a few moments, adjusting to the darkness within, taking account of what I could see, smell, and sense. I then took the camera out of its case and checked its settings.

It is a given at the start of a homicide investigation that everything and everybody should be approached fresh and without prejudice, so that no telltale signal, no matter how subtle, can be eclipsed by the investigator's preconceptions. It is a fact, however, that such perfect neutrality is impossible.

Except here.

In my subconscious, ever since I'd first heard of him, I'd been trying to nail Abraham Fuller down. Images had stirred of a rough, back-to-nature man, a product of the sixties, with a secret, violent past. Dr. Brook and the hospital comptroller had introduced the notion of a loony hermit. But now, standing on the threshold to his house, confronted by the pristine, picture-perfect world he'd made for himself, I no longer knew what to think.

The cabin reminded me of the period set pieces found in popular folk museums, where the chairs, tables, rugs, and wall hangings of a specific era are arranged to evoke days long past. The effect usually flops, of course. The human energy is always missing, leaving behind only silence and an overwhelming sense of sterility. In Fuller's place, the theme was contemporary, middle-class, woodsy-rural—and just as hollow.

Something else was missing, too. In every home, no matter how compulsive the owner, there are at least a few signs of life ongoing—bills piled on desks, tables covered with unread magazines, sinks filled with dirty dishes.

This place had none of that. It was as if the entire house had been plucked from a showroom and airlifted into the wilderness.

I stepped inside and closed the door behind me, acutely conscious of my intrusiveness. Shafts of sunlight angled in through the clear windows, reflecting off the pale, scrubbed wood floors and muted oval rag rugs. I took the first shot of a fresh roll of film.

The furniture was spare, old but not antique, solid and comfortable in appearance, obviously belonging to a determinedly single person: one armchair by the wood stove, one chair at the table, one set of eating utensils by the sink. More than the home of a man who lived alone, this was a monument to someone wishing absolute solitude.

As John Breen had described, the cabin consisted of one large room, where the kitchen occupied one end of a combination dining-living area. An overhead platform loft jutted out from one far wall, hovering between the floor where I stood and an overall cathedral ceiling of massive wooden roof beams. A ladder to the loft was attached to the wall and disappeared through a hole above.

The only jarring note to the sparse tidiness rested on the floor near the long harvest-style table. Again, giving substance to Breen's testimony, I could see where Fuller had lain in his own filth for days, surrounded by a half-spilled bag of trail mix, some partially rotted fruit, and the wadded-up table runner that he had used to drag these items over to him. I could also see by the way it was disturbed that the soiled rug had been used as a blanket during the cold nights. Given the oddly impersonal feeling of this otherwise-clean and comfortable home, the remains of Abraham Fuller's agonizing ordeal packed the same emotional punch as a blood-soaked sheet in an aseptic, empty operating room.

I turned away from the spot. I wanted to find out about the man who had ended up on that rug, but to do so, I felt the need to conclude my examination of his house there, rather than begin it. I therefore started with the kitchen area, taking more pictures as I went.

Both Hillstrom and Brook had commented on Fuller's diet. What I found, both in the cabinets and the electric refrigerator—an odd contrast with the hand pump by the sink—was an almost total absence of store-bought food. There were paper bags, glass containers, and tin boxes all carefully stored away by the dozen. None of them was labeled—another sure sign of single living—and all contained an assortment of mostly—to me—unrecognizable beans, flours, herbs, and liquids. For someone whose idea of heaven was boxed, neon-colored macaroni and cheese, I found Fuller's cupboard about as appetizing as a bowlful of grass cuttings.

Nevertheless, I was impressed by the energy and specialized education it must have taken to fill all these shelves. It was, to my professional eye, a rarity, and any rarity in an investigation is also more easily traceable—or so I hoped.

My next stop was the loft, which turned out to be the bedroom. Again, I was struck by the monastic sparseness: a neat twin bed, a small chest of drawers half-filled with nondescript, sturdy clothes, and a simple night table with an electric lamp. The only window was mounted in the end wall, and the only place I could stand fully erect under the sloping roof beams was at the foot of the narrow bed, in the center of the platform. Looking over the balcony to the room below, the shafts of yellow sun highlighting the wool of the rugs and the grain of the wooden floor and furniture, I was briefly caught up by what must have made this place special to its occupant. There was a serenity to it, a hard-won peacefulness. This was a retreat more than a home, a shrine to what life could be away from the hubbub beyond the encircling trees.

I suddenly thought of another reason why such effort had been expended to keep this house so severely neat. It was a tribute to self-discipline—a guide rule by which Fuller could measure his success at maintaining a straight and narrow line. In this light, the aesthetic serenity was not an end in itself, but a reward for personal sacrifice. Not for the first time, I wondered if Fuller might have isolated himself more for practical reasons and less for whimsical ones. Living here, he had only to look around every day to be reminded that being apart from the world was also being safe from the threats it might hold.

Not that I ruled out any whimsical motivations. To live in Brattleboro was to reside in one of the East's more notable respites for aging hippies. I was very familiar with alternate lifestyles, and didn't bat an eye at the usual naturalist trimmings, a good many of which were in evidence in this house. The difference in this case was the cash Fuller had on him, and the fact that it had appeared, bank-banded and moldy, out of a bag. That—and the bullet wound—introduced two distinctly foreign elements, and a suspicion that Fuller's mania for neatness and isolation might be triggered by a self-preserving paranoia.

Downstairs, I'd noticed a wall full of books, but I hadn't seen any photographs, address books, notepads, filing cabinets, or even a desk. There was nothing of a personal nature in the whole house, as far as I'd seen. It made me think of a recovering alcoholic not having booze in the house—because of the temptation it represented.

The one inconsistency with that observation hung over both the bed and the window behind it. It was a chart of some kind, framed and under glass. The chart was circular, its outer band divided into wedges like an old-time carnival money wheel, and parked within some of the wedges were odd symbols, like letters from an ancient foreign alphabet. The blank inner circle was crisscrossed by differently colored lines that connected the mysterious symbols in an overlapping series of triangles. To one side, apart from the circle, was another, much smaller chart, linear in form, with more enigmatic symbols and numbers.

I moved alongside the bed and leaned over to take a closer look. The entire document had been carefully handwritten, and it was not whole. One slightly fuzzy edge indicated that the paper, after much creasing, had been neatly torn across the top.

I hadn't the slightest idea what this was, but I knew in my gut it was something personal to Abraham Fuller, which, in this barren context, made it—along with the obsessive vegetarianism—another rarity. Despite his obvious efforts to leave no trace of himself, I felt I was gaining, just a bit, on my quarry. I adjusted the camera to compensate for the light coming in through the window, then took several shots.

I returned downstairs to investigate the building's two

wings. The lean-to shed was accessible only from the outside, and it was filled with the expected accessories of a major-league organic gardener. In predictably neat rows and piles, I found a specialist's paradise in tools, seeds, and natural fertilizers. Hanging in tidy bundles from the low rafters were mysterious bunches of bulbs, twigs, and dried leaves, all of which might have made sense to my long-dead father, who'd been a farmer, but not to me.

The other wing, the greenhouse, was connected by an inner door to the kitchen area. It was much larger than I'd thought from the outside, wider than the house, and half-buried in the ground, so that I had to climb down a short flight of steps to reach the wood-slatted floor.

The greenhouse was as extreme a contrast to the central part of the house as a flamingo is to a mud hen. Where the first had been almost sterile, this room was tropically wild, pungent with the strong odor of damp earth and sun-warmed vegetation, and blazing with the exotic colors that had already been muted outside by the coming winter's cold.

Rows of slate-walled wooden tables lined the edges of the room, each filled with dark earth and a riot of plants and vegetables, some of which grew in vines up the translucent walls. Nestled in their midst, not far from the foot of the steps, was a large redwood hot tub hooked to a bizarre wood-fueled heating stove that was vented through the glass ceiling. From what I could tell, the stove warmed both the greenhouse and the tub's water, presumably allowing Fuller to soak in near-Mediterranean splendor all through the winter months. I was relieved to find the tub. It not only partially addressed a question I had concerning the lack of a bathroom but it also offset the image I'd been forming of a blighted, driven, paranoid man. Here I could envision both a yearning and an outlet for leisure and comfort, as well as a relief valve for some of the compulsive behavior revealed by the rest of the house.

The other sanitation question I had was answered in a far corner of the greenhouse. Lurking among the overhanging plants, I discovered what functioned as a toilet—an earth-colored, seat-shaped contraption that I guessed was half old-fashioned outhouse and half highly engineered recycling device. Whatever it was, its function was obvious and its setting quite soothing.

I left the greenhouse to go to the bookshelves inside. Having seen how Fuller had pampered himself physically, I was all the more curious to find out how he'd entertained his mind.

Books, unlike health food, were something I could gauge with a certain confidence. Gail Zigman, my friend and lover of the past twelve years, proclaimed my appetite for reading to be as voracious and eclectic as my taste for bad food was predictable and self-destructive. It struck me as ironic, therefore, that the reverse held true for Fuller. His collection of books was surprisingly mundane.

Not that his library consisted of trashy beach novels. In addition to the Mark Twain I'd dug out of the red knapsack earlier, I found several of Twain's other works, along with samplings of Hemingway, Fitzgerald, Faulkner, Wharton, Poe, Hardy, Dostoyevski, and a dozen others, all of whose last names alone were sufficient to identify the authors. But the actual titles were not always representative of the author's best work. *The Adventures of Huckleberry Finn* was missing, for example, and *What Is Man?* and *The Mysterious Stranger* were parked side by side.

Still, the quality and diversity of the books was only part of the collection's oddness. My own books were a jumble of mysteries, histories, novels of dubious merit, a couple of volumes on carpentry, old texts from college, police manuals, and even an abysmally written but stimulating work of pornography I'd once confiscated from a ten-year-old. I suspected my library was like most people's, built over decades, reflecting varying interests.

Abraham Fuller's, by contrast, looked like the offerings of a low-rent book club specializing in high-profile modern novelists, and while some of the volumes were paperbacks, a few bound in leather, and some looked on the verge of collapse, others had never been opened. And all of them were shelved in alphabetical order by author.

Had Fuller been genuinely interested in his reading? Or was this home-built "collection of the masters" another task he'd set himself to keep on the straight and narrow, another form of self-discipline?

I shook my head at the track my own mind was taking. I needed more than an odd assortment of books, a fetish for neatness, and an obsession for gardening and home cooking to draw any accurate conclusions about the man who'd lived here. And that, in fact, was about all I had so far. Aside from the strange chart, I still hadn't discovered a single personal document.

Which brought me back to the last place Fuller had occupied in the house.

I'd thought about his days-long ordeal on the floor quite a bit since I'd first heard Breen describe it. Indeed, my initial curiosity had focused on Fuller's mobility: Could he have crawled somewhere in order to fetch his red bag during the five minutes the Rescue crew was outside? Breen had doubted it—such mobility would have allowed Fuller to avoid lying in his own waste. On the other hand, if a trip to the toilet, far off in another room and down a flight of stairs, might have been impossible, a short slide across the smooth floor—given the proper incentive—might not.

It was a reasonable-enough assumption, I thought, and it implied a hiding place in the immediate vicinity. I pulled the rug away, hoping in vain that a trapdoor would theatrically appear. The boards were tightly joined, and the small cracks between them were packed with the microscopic dirt that even the most dedicated housekeeper can't remove.

I sat back on my heels and looked around. Presumably, Fuller had stayed on the rug, expecting either to die or to recover on his own. The arrival of the ambulance, however, had prompted him to bear the increase in pain, move to where he kept his pack, and then return to the rug in order to cover his tracks.

I didn't want to sell Breen short. He'd been a paramedic for years and had developed a pretty keen eye for other people's pain tolerances. If Fuller had pulled the wool over his eyes, it had been only because the red pack's hiding place was nearby.

My eyes traveled across the floor to the first likely spot: a freestanding counter opposite the kitchen sink, topped by an oversized chopping block that hid a large, now rank-smelling garbage pail. I walked over to it and tried to shift the counter, to no avail. I then moved the pail and examined the floor, checking the interior recesses of the counter. I found no signs of either a hiding place or a secret latch that might reveal one.

Disappointed, I continued on my miniature voyage from where the rug lay in a heap, imagining Fuller pulling himself across the floor, grimacing in pain, intent on his goal. Like a navigator on the sea, I sought out the next available landfall, turning to the kitchen counters lining the wall.

I worked methodically, figuring that Fuller's obvious meticulousness would extend to how well he hid his most private belongings. I pulled out drawers, checked for cavities under the counters, and knocked against the back walls, listening for hollowness, and finally, under the sink counter, I came up with something.

Under normal circumstances, I would have missed it. The bottom of the cabinet under the sink had been lined with tile, presumably to combat the mildew and rot that normally accumulate there. Where most people put down linoleum for the same purpose, Fuller—typically, I now thought—had gone the extra distance. What caught my eye, however, wasn't the craftsmanship but the fact that the sponges, brushes, bottles of biodegradable soap, and whatnot had all been shoved messily to one side, leaving half of the tiled surface clear.

It took me a while to find the catch, back behind the front brace into which the cabinet hinges had been screwed. In fact, I had to crawl half into the narrow space before I could even see it. But once discovered, I found it smooth and easy to operate. With a click, the uncluttered part of the tile flooring swung down like a trapdoor, revealing a damp-smelling black hole.

I pulled out a small penlight from my pocket and shined it into the hiding spot. It was fairly large, about the size of a steamer trunk, extending to the right and left of the opening, and it was lined with what appeared to be cedar, whose odor mixed unpleasantly with the dampness.

This, as far as I knew, was the sanctum sanctorum of Abraham Fuller—the one place on earth a very secretive man had chosen to hide his most personal possessions.

It was also not the cornucopia I'd been hoping for. There were no passports, photo albums, tape recordings, or reams of revealing letters. Instead, I found one mildew-dusted duffel bag and one old and brittle holster, packed not with a gun but with a partially filled box of .32-caliber ammunition, now green with age. The duffel bag, however, was filled with a small fortune in neatly bundled hundred-dollar bills.

Disturbing the cache as little as possible, in the hope that a forensic exam might later find what I could not, I gently poked around, taking more photographs. I found nothing more . . . nor did I find the missing gun.

Everyone holds on to symbols of their past, some more ostentatiously than others. That's what makes locating missing persons a little easier. They maintain contact with their former lives, either through pictures, or mementos, or even a single Mother's Day card sent during a moment's nostalgia.

Abraham Fuller had been more successful than most. He had kept only his money, an indecipherable chart on his wall, a box of bullets, and an empty holster. Eccentric as it all seemed, I could only hope it would eventually speak to me in a voice I could understand.

Chapter Four

The cabin had no phone, so I retraced my steps through the garden, along the overgrown path, and back to my car, where I'd earlier tossed the department's new cellular phone as an afterthought.

Tony Brandt had wanted me to investigate Fuller's place alone to cut as low a profile as possible. It hadn't been an unreasonable request, given the supposition that Fuller had brought his festering wound, and his bagful of money, from far beyond our jurisdiction. Chances were I would find a normal, empty house and nothing more. But I'd been nagged from the start by the thought that this case would not slip from our grasp quite as smoothly as we all seemed to be hoping.

Harriet Fritter answered the detective squad's private line on the first ring.

"Hi, it's Joe. You better send Tyler and the crime kit up here for a search. Who's within easy reach to help him out?"

"Ron and Willy."

I grimaced. As a team, Ron Klesczewski and Willy Kunkle made cats and dogs look mutually compatible.

She caught my hesitation. "Want someone else?"

"No. I don't want to lose time."

"All right. Consider them on the way."

As I stood by the car, I felt rather than heard Fred Coyner behind me. He was standing out in the open, his back to the panoramic view, watching me, his hands empty, hanging loosely by his sides. I had the uncomfortable feeling he'd been there for quite a while.

I was well used to the famous Vermont reticence. My own father considered anything beyond a few sentences a day to be idle chitchat. But that was while he was working, when talking usually meant taking time off to lean on a shovel. During off-hours, with his family or friends, he opened up some and the dormant humor I often saw in his eyes crept out, if only a little.

I saw no such glint in Fred Coyner's eyes. They were as cool and expressionless as water.

"Mind if I ask some questions?" I asked.

"Wouldn't make much difference if I did." He turned his back to me to face the valleys and hills below us. I moved beside him, shoulder-to-shoulder.

"You know Abraham Fuller well?"

He shrugged. "Nope."

"Was that his real name?" The question was purely spontaneous, which I thought was a better approach than some textbook psychological angle he'd spot a mile off.

There was a pause. His expression didn't change, from

what I could see of it, but I sensed he was surprised. "I suppose."

"So you had no personal connection to him."

He shook his head. "Not likely. He rented the place."

"For how long?"

"Twenty years, about."

I resisted doing a double take, but just barely. Instead, I kept my voice as flat as his. "That's quite a while. Looks like he led an exotic life—hot tub, the greenhouse, the garden. Unusual guy. What was he like?"

"Wouldn't know. He was a granola-head; kept to himself, which suited me fine."

"He pay the rent in cash?"

Again, there was a pause, calculating this time. Coyner chewed his lower lip a while before answering. "Wasn't that kind of rent. I didn't use the place. It was being wasted, buried back there."

I guessed at a possible explanation for this incongruous generosity. "If you're worried about the IRS, don't be. I just want to know why Fuller died."

"Don't give a damn about the IRS."

"They might give a damn if you haven't declared his rent as income."

"He bartered—food for the house."

"And the electricity." I remembered the wire looped through the trees between the houses.

"That was my idea. I didn't want him burning the place down with the old oil lamps that were there."

"Did you give him the refrigerator?" I asked, trying to widen the view he'd allowed me of their relationship.

Coyner nodded. "I was getting rid of it."

I couldn't shake the impression that Coyner was not the renting type, unless there'd been some irresistible angle. "How often did you see him?"

"Barely saw him at all."

"Monthly?"

"Not even. He never moved from the place."

"Didn't he ask you what you needed from his garden?"

"He knew, after a while; I'm a man of regular habits. If something special came up, we left notes. Said he wanted to be left alone—no ifs, ands, or buts. So that's what I did. I wasn't interested anyhow. If he wanted to be a hermit, it was fine with me.''

"But you called the ambulance," I insisted

"He was supposed to drop some stuff off. I got to wondering. He had regular habits, too."

"Lucky for him."

"Guess not."

I smiled inwardly. Sentimental he was not, but I suspected that after twenty years, at least an element of predictability had been disrupted by Fuller's death, which had resulted in the closest thing Fred Coyner would ever come to mourning.

"Mr. Coyner, I noticed Fuller had a lot of supplies and equipment to keep his garden going. How did he pay for it?"

"Guess he was a rich guy."

I feigned surprise. "Really? He didn't look it."

"Well, he was." Coyner's face suddenly became stern. I could sense a concern that he'd said too much.

I kept pressing. "Did he pay for fixing the house up, too? A lot of that work doesn't date back twenty years."

"Yeah."

"He did pay for it?"

Coyner's lips were compressed to two thin white lines. He nodded wordlessly.

I shook my head and whistled softly. "I guess he was loaded. You said he never left the place. How did he buy the building materials, the gardening equipment, all the rest of it?"

Coyner was becoming restless; his hands found one another and began unconsciously fidgeting. "I got it. He'd leave a note."

I moved to throw him further off balance. "And a hundred-dollar bill or two."

His back stiffened and he chewed his lower lip for a moment. "I got work to do." He began to walk off.

My voice lost its leisurely tone. "We'll have to finish this sometime. Me or maybe the state's attorney or the state police."

He stopped and glared back at me. "They'll be trespassing."

I shook my head. "No they won't. But they'll drag you into this further than you want to go. It's your choice."

He suddenly grimaced and clenched his fists. "So what if he paid in hundred-dollar bills? Wasn't my business."

"Didn't say it was. What else did you buy for him?"

Coyner shrugged, his fists loosening somewhat. "Supplies—whole wheat, tofu, nuts and berries, and anything else he needed. I'd get most of it in Bratt."

"How did you two first meet?"

His expression remained guarded, but he became a bit freer with what he knew. "He found me. Somebody must've told him about the house. Said he wanted to be left alone, that the world was a shitty place. He also said he'd make it worth my while, and he did, and that's all there was to it. I let him alone and he did likewise."

"There's a lot more food growing around that house than two men can eat. Did he let you sell the surplus?"

The fists closing again was confirmation enough. I moved on quickly. "He ever have visitors?"

"Early on, when he was adding onto the building."

"You never saw who?"

"They came and left at night. I don't know who, or how many, but I do know it stopped."

"When?"

"Same time—'bout twenty years back."

"And nobody since?"

"Nope."

"What about the newer construction? Did he bring people in to help him? Or did you do it?"

"He did it himself—alone."

"And you never saw him leave the place?"

"Only on that ambulance."

"You ever hear a gunshot?"

"Nope."

"And you never suspected he'd been hit by a bullet?"

"Nope."

He was shaking his head almost continuously now, as if trying to throw off where my questions were leading. I doubted at this point if the truth meant a whole lot to him. It was more important to pacify me, to get me off his back.

For the moment, I would play along, although we had more ground to cover. "Mr. Coyner, some of my men'll be coming to join me soon, to look through that house more carefully. We'll try to be as unobtrusive as possible." I reached into my pocket and handed him the search warrant.

He glanced at it and handed it back without a word.

He turned to leave again. I let him go a few feet before I called out a final question. "What did Fuller mean when he accused you of a breach of faith for calling that ambulance?"

The old man looked back at me for a long, measured silence, his face as impenetrable as ever. "Don't know; didn't know what the hell he was talking about most of the time."

I doubted that, just as I doubted his relationship with Fuller was as uncomplicated as he made it out to be. But I had time. We would talk again.

I returned to the cottage in the clearing, pausing this time to absorb fully the uniqueness of the garden. Every inch of its several acres had been manicured in some way, even if only to make it look untouched. Here and there, as if to give the emotions a rest, a patch or strip of ground had been left alone—pauses in a symphony of color and shape. But even those occasional respites were cultured and contoured, free of weeds and distracting blemishes. In their emptiness, they were as complex and satisfying as the horticultural riot around them. I envisioned Fuller spending season after season out here, steeped in the pursuit of perfection, applying a near-fanatical concentration in his efforts.

I reentered the house, still feeling like I was on the wrong side of a glass wall, retracing my steps of a half hour ago. The place was basically as I'd found it, as attractive and sterile as a monastery cell.

There was one difference, however, a change that hit me like a hammer, smashing the tidy myth of a crime long past.

As I stepped away from the ladder after climbing to the sleeping loft, my eyes went to the one item I felt instinctively had the most to offer.

But the chart over the bed had been removed.

Chapter Five

J. P. Tyler, Willy Kunkle, and Ron Klesczewski found me pacing in front of the cottage a half hour later, boiling over with anger and frustration.

"Where the hell have you guys been?"

Each of them reacted true to form at my outburst. Tyler silently raised his eyebrows, Kunkle smirked and ignored me, and Klesczewski looked worried.

"We left as soon as you called," he answered.

"Did you see an old guy in a red-and-black-checked wool shirt when you drove up?"

Tyler answered crisply, "Nope. Is this the place you want checked out?"

I began walking quickly toward Coyner's house. "Yeah, but wait 'til I get back. Ron, come with me. You guys just keep an eye out."

I heard Kunkle's "So much for bustin' our butts to get here" as I led Klesczewski back down the trail.

"What's goin' on?" he asked in a tentative voice. Ron Klesczewski was my second in command, a senior detective sergeant still in his twenties, serious, sober, and hardworking, a little shy of using his authority, and a man in dire need of a good sense of humor.

Not that I would have appreciated one had he chosen to display it now. "While I was using the phone to get you three up here, somebody ripped off a major piece of evidence."

"The guy in the wool shirt?"

"His name's Coyner. He owns this whole place. Did Harriet give you any idea of what's going on here?"

"Pretty much."

By the time I got to the edge of the woods, within sight of Coyner's house, I'd cooled down considerably from my earlier humiliation and had come to realize that I was hunting for a lion with an empty gun. I stopped dead in my tracks, staring at the distant house and breathing heavily, both from exertion and the dregs of my anger.

Klesczewski took a couple of steps farther on and then hesitated. He looked back at me quizzically. "What's wrong?"

"I'm being a horse's ass—again."

"You don't think Coyner took it?"

"I'm sure he took it, but there's not a hell of a lot I can do about it. I have no proof, so I can get no warrant. He could have that damn thing right behind his front door, and there's nothing I can do about it."

"Unless he invites us in."

I smiled at the thought. "He might invite us to drop dead, but that's about it."

We both stood there in silence for a moment, with nothing much to weigh. I finally shrugged. "What the hell; we're here. We might as well knock."

I resumed my course, slower and calmer now, thinking more about what the search of Fuller's house might reveal than about the chances of Fred Coyner undergoing a sudden personality change. If we were lucky during the search, we might even get something to pin Coyner to the theft of the chart.

We walked up to his front door and I pounded on it with my fist, having fruitlessly looked for a bell. There was a pause; I thought I heard something move within the house.

"There he is," Ron muttered.

At a side window, the curtains moved slightly, revealing Fred Coyner's impassive, creased face. He looked at us without expression for several seconds, and then the curtain fell back into place. We could hear footsteps retreating slowly away from the door.

We waited a half minute more, until I finally shrugged and turned my back. "Okay, he screwed us. Off to plan B."

"Search the other house?"

My pace grew stronger as I set my sights ahead, the sharp sting of my earlier embarrassment fading, if not vanishing completely. "That, and have the photographs I took developed. There may be another way around Mr. Coyner."

Back at the cottage, Tyler was loitering in the garden, looking around generally, his technically oriented mind no doubt intrigued by the effort in Fuller's work. Willy Kunkle, by contrast, was lying flat on his back near the front door, staring at the clouds overhead with a cigarette parked in the corner of his mouth.

"Jesus," Ron sighed under his breath as he caught sight of him. Willy Kunkle, the most unique member of our detective squad, had one working arm, a lousy attitude, and a sniper's eye for other people's weak spots. He was also one of the best cops I'd ever worked with. He went after cases like a pit bull after a mailman, when he was inspired, ignoring long hours, hard work, and lousy working conditions, all while staying totally sharp to every new wrinkle around him. He had a feel for the overlooked detail and a nose for his fellow humans' devious ways. But his contemptuous, cynical, and constantly testing attitude gave truth to the cliché that some great cops, given the right spin at the wrong time, had the makings of crooks.

His instincts were as nasty and combative as Ron's were compassionate and hesitant, an outlook not helped by the crippled left arm he'd lost to a rifle bullet several years ago and which he dealt with by stuffing his shriveled hand in his pants pocket so the arm wouldn't flop around. That arm was a symbol to him of adversity overcome and of his own tenacity; it was also a symbol to us of how embittered and unbalanced he could become when his occasional self-pity kicked in and dragged him into the depths. To say he was an emotional roller coaster was to put it lightly, which explained why Ron tended to treat him like unstable dynamite.

The search took the rest of the day. We used a line method, stringing out four abreast and working our way, on hands and knees, across the floor to the kitchen area's far wall. It was a painstaking effort, involving the occasional use of tweezers and a magnifying lens; transparent sticky tape for lifting hair and soil samples; and tiny Ziploc bags for storing minute particles whose origin only a lab analysis could reveal. As one of us located some item of interest, the rest had to stop where we were and wait, so the integrity of the line would be maintained. Traveling twenty-five feet of open floor took over an hour.

Tyler was in his element. This, rather than working street snitches and following up leads, was his idea of police work at its best. Due to our small staff and the mundane quality of most of our cases, however, Tyler's forensic expertise was only rarely called upon.

Four long hours later, J.P. had a cornucopia of hair, dirt, and fiber samples to keep him busy for days, and I had a headache and nothing more to show for our efforts than what I'd discovered earlier on my own.

I also had nothing linking the chart's disappearance to Fred Coyner.

I sent my three colleagues back to the office with the evidence, the film from my camera, and the duffel bag full of money from under the kitchen sink, while I remained behind. All sense that this was a paperwork case destined to pass from our hands to some other agency's had vanished along with the chart on that wall. Its disappearance had served notice that Fuller's crimes, if he had committed any, might not be as remote in time or distance as we'd imagined.

I made my way back to Coyner's house. What warmth there'd been was fading with the day, and an autumnal chill ran down my back and numbed my face. As before, Coyner looked impassively out at me following my knock on his front door. This time, however, the door opened.

"What." It was less a question than a demand, but gently put, as if the old man was resigned to whatever Fuller's death would bring down upon him.

"I wanted to tell you that our investigation into Abraham Fuller is going to be stepped up. Removing that chart from his wall while I was on the portable phone was illegal, and we're going to have to pursue it. That also means we'll be digging into his past and yours, and looking under every rock we come across."

His face didn't change, but I sensed a new tension in the man. "Don't know what you're talking about."

I shrugged. He hadn't invited me in, and while the cold didn't seem to affect him, I was beginning to shiver, which rarely adds to a cop's credibility. "Maybe, but we'll have to figure that out on our own. I think I ought to warn you, though, that cooperating with us might help you in the long run."

He didn't respond. He didn't even blink.

"Left to our own devices, not knowing exactly what we're after, we're going to have to put you under a microscope, and we'll find out things you wouldn't believe. Information like that gets hard to control, once it gets out."

"Look all you want."

The door shut in my face, quietly but firmly. It was apparent that the connection between Coyner and his tenant would have to be uncovered the hard way—if at all.

By the time I got back to my office, the medical examiner's courier had dropped off what little information on Abraham Fuller Beverly Hillstrom had been able to gather, which boiled down to a set of fingerprints, some photographs, and a detailed analysis of her physical findings.

Morgue pictures are hardly the most scintillating of art forms, but in this case I looked them over with keen interest. They showed a tall, slim, clean-cut man, well muscled, with strong facial features. Even with his eyes half-closed in death—a cadaver's typically sleepy drunk appearance—Fuller's angular nose, his hollow cheeks, and powerful chin all told of a driven intensity.

He had taken on a personality for me by now, still vague and elusive, but tinted with enough unusual character traits to capture my imagination. Homicides are generally uncomplicated affairs—brutal, forthright, displaying little planning or subtlety. Most of the time, the investigator doesn't have to look far beyond the victim's immediate circle of acquaintances to find the one with the gun or knife.

But not here. Unless the fingerprint card in my hand had all the answers we needed, this case had the elements of a true mystery.

I carried the card to Harriet Fritter's desk. "Could you have J.P. classify these and forward them on to the FBI? And is Ron in the building?"

She gestured with a nod of the head. "In the conference room."

The conference room was a dead end beyond the cluster of detectives' desks and marked the second half of our office space. It held a long table, some blackboards, a few lockers, and a TV-VCR setup. Some of us used it individually for either private interviews or the extra table space. As I walked in, I saw Ron was taking advantage of the latter; the table's entire surface was covered with the fruits of a paper trail he'd established to nail a local bank embezzler, a case he'd been on for the better part of a month.

"Getting anywhere?"

He looked up and gave a weary smile. "Yeah, but for all the time and effort, I doubt it's worth it. Prosecuting this guy's going to cost a whole lot more than what he stole in the first place."

I nodded at the sheaf of papers still in his hand. "Sorry if this afternoon screwed up your fun here. How much longer before you can hand it over to the state's attorney?"

"Not long—a few days. You got something you want me to do?"

I laughed at his eagerness. "Don't you wish. No, I'll use people with a little less on their plates. There is one thing, though; in your digging through bank statements and whatnot, have you ever run across someone who knows a lot about currency?"

He frowned and knitted his brows, muttering, "Right, the moldy C notes . . ." His face then cleared somewhat. "I don't know the guy personally, but one of the people I'm working with on this case mentioned that one of his colleagues collects money as a hobby. I could give him a call and get a name."

I thanked him, but he stopped me as I turned to leave. "I'm almost wrapped up here, you know. Just waiting for a few more items to come in the mail. The pressure's really off of it."

I smiled at his excess eagerness. There were times when he made me almost as weary as Kunkle did. "I'll keep that in mind, Ron. Thanks again."

I stopped by Harriet's desk on my way back to my corner

cubicle and asked her to get a list of all the bookstores—new and used—in the immediate vicinity. I also asked her to locate the two missing members of the detective squad, Martens and DeFlorio, for a quick meeting in my office in one hour.

I then retrieved the roll of film I'd shot that morning, along with the others that J.P. had taken during the search, and headed for the freedom of the street.

The front door of the Municipal Building gives out onto a sweeping view of a busy intersection to the impartial observer, a Gordian knot to the traffic-pattern expert, and a pain in the butt to anyone in a car. I took the steep stone steps down to street level and turned right to walk downtown.

This particular Main Street is fairly rare in the lexicon of American downtowns. Its industrial heyday having peaked at the end of the previous century, Brattleboro didn't have the money to tear its architectural heart out and rebuild it according to the latest fashions. Businesses came and went, storefronts changed as with the seasons, but the buildings they inhabited remained like ponderous, ancient redwood trees, host to a nonstop stream of temporary inhabitants.

The end result is a quarter-mile stretch of fifty buildings that appear on the National Register of Historic Places— old brick monsters proudly touting their names in embossed granite stonework: Brooks House, Richardson Building, Union Block, and, somewhat incongruously, Amadeus Di Angeles. None of them is particularly graceful, inspiring, or even fanciful. Reflecting the era and the mentality that gave them birth, they are for the most part solid, practical, and businesslike. With the exception of the Brooks House and its Second Empire fifth-floor tower, the heavy, smudged brick and granite buildings standing shoulder-to-shoulder are a perfect reflection of the serious, dogmatic, slightly vainglorious New England industrial spirit.

I headed for Photo 101, a hole-in-the-wall photography store owned by a tall, stooped, skinny chemist named Allen Rogers, whose years of exposure to darkroom fumes and chemicals had stained his hands, affected his eyesight, and damaged his lungs. As the police department didn't have a darkroom, much to J.P.'s distress, Allen had become our primary film processor.

The store, just opposite the Vermont National Bank, was on the first floor of what looked like a brownstone walk-up. Its front room was narrow and high, its ornamental tin ceiling smudged with ancient leaks from the floor above, and its shelves and counters cluttered with archaic photographic paraphernalia so old and dusty, it looked more like a bankrupt museum than a store. The old-fashioned bell above the door tinkled feebly as I entered.

"Be right with you." The voice came from the gloomy rear of the building, beyond a wall partition decorated with photographs of airbrushed prom-night girls with bouffant hairdos, all of whom were well into middle age by now.

"Take your time, Al. It's Joe Gunther."

"Hey, Joe. Come on back."

I began picking my way carefully toward the disembodied voice. Despite appearances, Allen Rogers made a good living. As a darkroom technician, he was a near genius, capable not only of producing beautiful prints from standard negatives but also of salvaging decent results from negatives so poor that most people would have thrown them out. It was a talent he marketed well.

I reached the partition and edged around its side, entering a back room that was half stock area, lined with freestanding metal shelf units, and half closed-off darkroom, the door of which had a red light burning brightly above it. My eyes instinctively scanned the contents of the shelves as I passed them to approach the darkroom door. The other strength of Allen's business was that he mostly served the highbrows of his profession; stacked in neat and orderly piles were papers, chemicals, and films I'd never even heard of, reserved for those whose forays into the darkroom were truly artistic. Indeed, Al had once told me that he kept the front part of his shop in such musty chaos to politely discourage weekend snapshooters.

I knocked on the door. "You want me to come in?"

"Sure; I'm just racking some prints."

I twisted the knob and walked into a brightly lit laboratory as pristine and orderly as an operating room. The shiny steel surfaces of long, deep sinks and circulating equipment contrasted with several looming dark enlargers, the softly glowing eyes of digital timers and thermometers, and the light-absorbing black paint covering the walls and ceiling.

"Never been in here before?" Rogers glanced at me over his shoulder. He was slipping damp oversized prints onto wire mesh racks so they could dry.

"No. Looks like something out of NASA."

"Well, don't tell the IRS; I only tell them about the front. What's on your mind? You usually send J.P. down here."

"Now I know why he takes so long getting back to the office."

Allen laughed as he placed his last print in place. "Yeah—he's got a mind like a vacuum cleaner, always full of questions."

I pulled the rolls of film out of my pocket and held them out to him.

He raised his eyebrows. "That's it?"

"It's a little special. On this one roll, I photographed a piece of evidence that was stolen immediately afterward—a chart hanging on a wall. This is the only copy I've got of it."

He took the roll in question and held it in his palm, as if he could already see its contents. "Cloak and dagger, huh? Great. When do you want it?"

"In an hour?"

He gave me a quick glance. While our business was both appreciated and occasionally intriguing, the police department was not one of Allen's big-spending clients; and rush work out of his shop usually cost a fortune. "You just want prints of the chart, right? The rest of it by tomorrow?"

"That would be great."

He smiled and steered me toward the door. "Okay. I better get cracking. I'll charge you the standard rate and drop it off at your office on my way home. Show yourself out, okay?" He stopped suddenly. "By the way, was there a girl with dirty blond hair out front when you walked in?"

"No. Place was empty."

He shrugged vaguely. "Okay. She must have gone home for the day. Do me a favor and lock the door behind you, will you? Thanks."

I said I would, shaking my head and smiling at his casualness. Brattleboro was hardly crime-free. In fact, the worsening economy, especially in Massachusetts, just a few miles to the south, had caused a surge in criminal activity. But it hadn't gotten very sophisticated, nor was it rampant, and attitudes like Allen Rogers's were only beginning to change.

The light was ebbing as I stepped back onto the sidewalk, dulling the subtle colors in the old masonry walls along the street and transforming the world around me to monochromatic shades of gray and brown. I checked my watch; I had forty minutes before Harriet Fritter would begin getting twitchy.

I was standing where Elliot Street dead-ends into Main, allowing a view up Elliot almost to the central firehouse before the street curves out of sight. It also let me see that the lights were still on at Zigman Realty's second-floor office partway down the block. I crossed at the loudly buzzing WALK sign—one of the town's odd and unique conciliatory gestures toward the visually handicapped—and made my way to the narrow door by the side of an upscale pastry shop.

Gail Zigman's office was located right over the shop, a position imbuing it with the most seductive aroma of any nonbakery in town. Gail—the owner and sole employee— claimed she'd given up working from her home for the convenience of a downtown location. Of course, every time I visited her office, I knew otherwise; it was the smell of fresh bread that had lured her off her hill. Convenience, if there was any of it, had come purely by happenstance.

I knocked on the glass-paneled door and stuck my head in. "Got something with high walls and a moat?"

She was sitting in a huge beanbag chair by the window, framed by the fading light and the drooping leaves of an eight-foot potted plant, reading from a thick manila file. The office was an antique one-room affair with high ceilings, tall sash windows, and ancient, rattling steam heating. She looked over her glasses at me and smiled. "Feeling the need for one?"

A tall, slim, muscular woman, now in her forties, Gail was graced with a dynamic face, both angular and strong, dark, serious eyes, and a complexion molded and tanned by an uncaring exposure to the weather. Most importantly of all, she had in abundance what my mother had always counseled me to look for in my friends: character.

"Not yet. In fact, I'm feeling pretty good." I closed the door behind me and crossed over to her, bending low to give her a kiss.

I pulled her office chair away from the desk and turned it to face her, settling myself comfortably in it, with my feet propped next to hers on the windowsill. She removed her reading glasses and lay back against the beanbag, a smile on her face. "Oh yeah? Stuck another crowbar in some bureaucrat's bicycle wheel?"

It was a pointed remark. I had gathered enough evidence against one of the selectmen during a case two months ago to stimulate both his resignation and an indictment, much to Gail's delight. Still, it had been an uncomfortable time for her, since she, too, was on the board of selectmen.

"Nope, I have myself an old-fashioned mystery."

I told her of my day's activities, from Hillstrom's baffling phone call to my doubts about Coyner and my concerns about the chart's disappearance. Through it all, she listened carefully, her paperwork resting on her stomach, her long blue-jeaned legs stretched out before her, knowing that I wasn't just shooting the breeze but indirectly enlisting her help.

This was by no means unusual. We covered different aspects of this municipality—she the political/business side and I the streets and crooks. But in a small town, these arenas often overlapped, so Gail and I had become comfortable exchanging information. We never quoted each other in public, were sensitive to the potential pitfalls of our sharing, and occasionally were able to defuse a few situations when the police department and the selectmen had locked horns.

My appeal to her this time, however, had more to do with the instincts and interests that had brought her to southern Vermont in the first place. Gail had been part of the hippie communes that had surrounded Brattleboro in the 1960s like dolphins clustering around a friendly boat, and although she'd joined the mainstream long since, many of her friends still followed their own unconventional drummers. I was hoping that she, or someone she could suggest, might shed some light on the stolen chart.

She thought a moment after I'd finished my brief saga. "What did the chart look like?"

I held my hands a yard apart. "What there was of it was about this big; the top edge had been torn off neatly, either from a large drawing pad or to remove one part of the document. The chart itself was like a sundial wheel with the center crisscrossed by connecting straight lines of different colors—"

"How many segments was the dial broken into?" she interrupted.

I closed my eyes to concentrate. "Seemed like about six to a side; twelve overall."

She handed me a pencil and the manila folder from her lap. "Can you scribble one of the symbols on the back of that from memory?"

"I'll have a photograph soon, so I can show you the whole thing, but I do remember three of them. The first two I already knew: the signs for male and female. The third one was a circle with a dot in the middle."

She smiled and nodded. "Mars, Venus, and the Sun. That was an astrological chart, Joe. It didn't have a date or a name anywhere on it?"

I shook my head. "It might have at one point; that may explain the tear. Could you tell anything about it if I showed it to you?"

"Probably not. I could identify most of the symbols, and, given enough time, I might be able to give a very general reading using the few books I've got, but I think Billie Lucas is the person you want to talk to. She's been doing them for years and she's very good. I had lunch with her today, in fact."

I instinctively demurred. Confiding in Gail was one thing, but the idea of officially consulting an astrologer brought out the skeptic in me.

"I don't know. I don't take that stuff too seriously."

She shrugged. "Can't hurt to try. If you don't like what you hear, you can forget it. I've had Billie do my chart—yours, too, in fact. It taught me a few things about myself I hadn't realized."

I was amused at her admission, and curiously touched. "How'd I come out?"

"She said you were one of the most sensible things I'd ever done." She smiled before forging ahead. "There's a lot of shading in astrology, of course, a lot of 'he could be this way, or he could be the other, depending on this or that.' That's why some people use charts to let themselves off the hook. But a good reader like Billie might be useful; it could turn out to be like an artist's sketch—close enough to be handy.

"Besides," she added pointedly, "it sounds like that chart's the only real thing you've got, and it was the only thing that got stolen. It must have something going for it. You want me to call Billie and set something up?"

I stood up, still not convinced. "Yeah, okay—try to tell her diplomatically that I don't want to spend a lot of time on this, though. I agree I ought to check it out, but I still don't have much faith in it. It smacks of voodoo and crystal balls." I checked my watch. "I better run, or Harriet'll have my head. There is one other thing: Outside of the local food co-ops in town, are there any other health-food wholesalers Fuller might have used for his supplies?"

She thought for a moment. "How varied was the garden?"

"Enough that I sure didn't recognize much. Some of it was decorative, but it was mostly produce. And the house was filled with the kind of seeds, grains, nuts, and rabbit pellets you people call food."

She grinned and poked me with her foot. "Did he sell any of it?"

"Coyner did the selling, in exchange for rent; I'm going to have someone look into that end of it."

"But Coyner wouldn't tell you where the supplies were bought?"

"Not yet, and he may not; he's not feeling very friendly right now."

"Let me call around. I won't mention names," she added, anticipating what I was about to say.

I kissed her quickly before heading out the door. "Thanks. I appreciate it."

"My pleasure. There is a price, though: dinner at my place tonight?"

I made a face. "Can I bring my own food?"

"No." She laughed and threw a pencil at the door.

I was just about to climb the long set of stone steps leading from Main Street to the Municipal Building when I heard Allen Rogers call me from across the street. "Hey," he said, waving an oversized envelope out the driver's window of his car. "How's this for service?"

"Great, Al. I appreciate it." I crossed over to him as he backed into a parking space.

"No sweat—I was heading home. By the way, were you alone when you were photographing that chart?"

I looked at him carefully. "Yes. Why?"

He got out of the car and joined me on the sidewalk, an excited smile on his face. "Well, I did the print like you asked, as a close-up of the chart, but the negative included both the chart and the window below it, so I did a full-frame proof first." He handed me the envelope. "Open it."

I did so, spreading the contents out on Allen's car hood. There were three photographs: one of the chart, in high contrast to make it easily legible; one of both the window and the chart above it, in which the exposure had been cut back to favor the latter; and one of just the window, exposed to favor the stronger outside light. In this last picture, badly out of focus and distorted by the window's cheap glass, was the unmistakable figure of a human being, lurking at the edge of the blurry trees.

"Interesting?" Allen asked, his face beaming.

"Very," I muttered.

"You know who it is? I can't even tell if it's a man or a woman."

"I think it's a thief," I answered. "And maybe worse."

Chapter Six

Sammie Martens and Dennis DeFlorio, the two squad members I'd asked Harriet to locate earlier, were waiting for me in my office. I invited Willy Kunkle to join us and sat on the edge of my desk to address them.

I began with Sammie and Dennis. "Have you two been brought up to date?"

"Ron did the honors," Sammie answered, "And we've read the reports."

"Good. Sammie, I'd like you to check out the hospital. Interview everyone who had anything to do with Abraham Fuller, from the nurses and orderlies to the finance people who got the cash from him. Then I'd like you to check out Fred Coyner's records at the tax assessor's office, the county clerk's, and anywhere else he may have left a paper trail."

Samantha Martens, intense, dogged, enthusiastic, occasionally bullheaded, was never going to give anyone cause to use her gender against her. Even Kunkle conceded that she'd never be caught napping. She pulled out her notepad and made a few notes.

DeFlorio, by contrast, was fat, short, sometimes laid-back to a fault, and no candidate for a Ph.D.—but he did what was asked of him with rarely a complaint. On my bad days, that alone could put him higher in my estimation than his brighter colleagues.

"Dennis," I resumed, "I'd like you to contact all police agencies in the New England area with what we've got on Fuller so far and see if you get lucky. Ask them about any old shootings in which Fuller might have played a part. And remember, if he does have a record, chances are that's not his real name. Also, make a list of the serial numbers from Fuller's loot and send it to the Secret Service to see if it's stolen. And get the paperwork started on requests for information from the IRS and Social Security, just to see if there ever was an Abraham Fuller.''

Dennis DeFlorio merely nodded.

The phone rang in the other room.

''Willy, see what you can get on Fred Coyner from his neighbors, old employers, and others; maybe Sammie can locate some of those names from the records. And check out this produce scam he had going with Fuller—where he bought the tools, seeds, and whatnot, and where he unloaded what Fuller grew. I'm curious about how much business we're talking about. Gail Zigman said she'd check into potential sources for Fuller's gardening supplies, on the chance he didn't use mainstream wholesalers or retailers. I'll let you know what she comes up with tomorrow morning. Also, Harriet's put together a list of bookstores that Coyner or Fuller might have used to fill up that library. Poke around and see if anyone remembers either one of them frequenting their business.''

Willy Kunkle, true to form, merely scratched himself and looked out the window.

Harriet stuck her head in. ''Billie Lucas is on the phone. Want to take it?''

I nodded to her. ''I think we're set here. Any questions?'' All three officers prepared to leave.

''By the way, does anyone know if J.P.'s totaled up the money we found in Fuller's house?'' I asked as they began filing out the door.

''About three hundred thousand,'' Sammie answered.

Billie Lucas's voice was low, clear, and oddly soothing, like the archetypal psychiatrist. ''Gail Zigman asked if I wanted to play detective with you. It's an intriguing offer.''

I gave an embarrassed laugh, covering my own mixed feelings about this whole idea. ''I'm not sure if it'll be as much fun as it sounds. I came across an astrological chart in one of my investigations, and Gail mentioned you might be able to give me an idea of the person whose chart it is.''

''I can certainly try. I'd like to have some time alone to examine it before we meet, though. I'll need to consult some reference books, and maybe redo it in my own style. There are a considerable number of variables involved.''

I rolled my eyes at the phone—already the escape clauses were being penciled in. "No problem. Where should I send a copy?"

"I'm guessing you want this done pretty quickly. Why don't you leave it with your dispatcher, and I'll pick it up later tonight. We can meet tomorrow morning. Then I'll have a better idea of how I can help you."

At least her sense of timing was good. "Well, I appreciate your help. You sure it's no trouble?"

"No, no. I'm looking forward to it; this is a first for me. Can you come by my place at around nine? It's on Whipple Street—the house with the picket fence out front."

"You got it. See you at nine." I broke the connection and dialed the extension to the conference room. Ron picked up on the third ring, sounding harassed.

"Did you get anything on that currency collector you mentioned?"

His voice regained some of its usual enthusiasm. "Yeah, I did—Richard Schimke, Rich to his friends. He specializes in American money, mostly Confederate and earlier, but he knows a lot about currency generally and he's easy to get along with. I'd be happy to do it for you."

"How's it going with your paper chase?"

"Almost finished—just a few odds and ends."

"All right, it's a deal. But remember, we don't have enough to get a search warrant for any of Coyner's records right now. You're going to have to be careful finding out where he banks and what he's been up to. Get people to volunteer information to you, okay?"

He sounded like a sailor with a fresh wind in his sails. "You got it."

I finished what was left of my vegetarian lasagna and sat back in my chair, feeling full and content. Gail was mopping up the last of the sauce from her plate with a piece of French bread. She popped it in her mouth and smiled at me. "So, how was it?"

The usual kidding I gave her couldn't compete. "Delicious—you win."

I helped her clear the table and began filling the kitchen

sink with soapy dishwater while she put the leftovers in the fridge.

Gail and I had been a couple for over a decade by now, and yet we still lived apart. Losing a wife to cancer had made me shy of repeating that degree of intimacy. Gail believed that a shared mortgage and the risk of one of us evicting the other in a dispute would undermine the honesty of our relationship. Both arguments had their flaws, but the bottom line was that we both liked things the way they were.

The dishes done, we left the kitchen area and climbed a dizzying, freestanding set of stairs to a loft with a sofa and a picture window overlooking the moonlit tumult of hills where the West River and the Connecticut River valleys converge.

Gail settled in a nest of pillows, leaving the lights off so that the dim blue-gray view could spread into the room like water spilled from a pail. I sat next to her and stretched my stockinged feet across the coffee table before us.

"Did Billie get in touch?" she asked sleepily.

"Yeah. Told me to leave a copy of the chart at the PD so she could check it out tonight, before we meet tomorrow morning."

Gail chuckled. "That's Billie, all right. I'm glad I thought of her; if anyone can decipher that chart, she can."

I was a little surprised. "Why wouldn't you have thought of her? I thought she did it for a living."

"Oh, no. She does get paid for it, but that's just to stop her friends from bugging her for free readings. She's a potter, and a very good one; sells to companies who want to decorate their boardrooms and corner offices. She also has pieces in a museum or two. I met her through VermontGreen; she's our activities coordinator this year."

VermontGreen was a headline-grabbing environmental group that was doing all in its power to keep Vermont rural. It had some good ideas and made effective use of the media, but, like most single-issue groups, it treated its detractors like reactionary industrialists hell-bent on paving the state over. Gail was a member, albeit a moderate one, which made debating the group's merits something I tended to avoid.

I therefore kept my voice strictly neutral. "You say she's very gung ho?"

Gail nodded approvingly. "Oh, yes. This year, it's activities coordinator, but she's always heading up something, plus doing a ton of other things. On top of the pottery, the astrology, and VermontGreen, she also teaches pottery to both adults and children, and runs a kind of halfway house out of her home for just about anyone who needs a shoulder to cry on. Amazing woman, and a good listener. You'll like her."

I didn't answer, and she interpreted my silence accurately.

"Still bugged about the astrology? It's no stranger than some of the other things you've relied on, and she's well trained. She's been doing it for years, and she's a bit of a skeptic herself—avoids the mumbo jumbo. Besides, if you don't like what you hear, I'll find you another left-wing loonie to talk to—maybe someone who's into crystals or pyramids. The boys'll love that."

I conceded defeat. "All right. I've already committed myself. Did you manage to dig up any other natural-foods suppliers?"

"Just one. Who do you have looking into that?"

"Kunkle."

She laughed. "Oh, perfect. Tell him to contact Sunshine Jackson in Guilford. He supplies a lot of people who think the Food Co-op is a subdivision of Dow Chemical."

I pulled my small notebook from my pocket and wrote down Jackson's name, not that I thought I'd easily forget it.

"I take it you still don't know who shot that man, or who stole the chart?"

I rested my head against the pillow behind me and watched the moon between half-closed lids. "Nope. I think Coyner's hiding something, but I don't know what. He may be the beginning and the end of this case, or he may just be a suspicious old woodchuck who resents his property being invaded. Hard to say."

"And all you've got is the chart and some money."

I was silent for a while, thinking about that. "That's the sexy stuff; there is more."

Gail sounded surprised. "What?"

"The house itself, for one—it was like a shrine to his own emptiness." I envisioned the contents of his house slowly parading by in the half-light before me, including those most cherished possessions that he'd hidden away especially. "And there was a holster without a gun . . . and a few old bullets."

She mulled that over, similarly baffled. "Why keep those?"

"I don't know," I answered, "but I think I'll make an effort to find that missing gun."

Chapter Seven

The hunt for Fuller's gun was dependent not only on securing another search warrant but on getting hold of the right tool for the job. I thought I could coax the former from a judge; the latter, in this small state, would take some research.

I was standing by Harriet's desk the following morning when she walked in, impatient to get things rolling. "Do me a favor, would you? Call the state police and ask if we can borrow their metal detector. I think the Rockingham barracks has one, but you might have to dig deeper." I handed her a sheet of paper. "Also, please make sure Willy gets this—it's some homework Gail did for him. And last," I added with an apologetic smile, "I'd appreciate it if you could get either Sammie or Dennis to file for a search warrant for Fuller's missing gun." I handed her the rough draft of an affidavit I'd worked up before her arrival.

She took both sheets of paper. "Will one detector be enough?"

"You think you can get another?"

"We could rent one."

I stared at her nonplussed for a moment, astonished at my own lapse, then broke into a grin. "Great. See what you can find. I'll be at Billie Lucas's house on Whipple in the meantime."

She shook her head slightly as I walked away.

Whipple Street had once been a convenient alleyway in which to leave the garbage for removal, and before then had probably served as a tree-shaded side street for horse-drawn buggies. But in the time-honored tradition of old neighborhoods yielding to technology's endless pushiness, it had been widened, denuded, and paved over. It was now a heavily traveled connector street between Green and High. It was, no doubt, convenient for traffic, but it had turned what once had been an ideal spot for stickball and hopscotch into a potential killing zone.

The house Billie Lucas had described was fairly nondescript—two-storied, clapboarded, in need of paint—but it showed signs of having once been the pride of a burgeoning middle class. The tasteful and frugal use of stained glass here and there and the occasional extravagance of some gingerbread molding at a corner or along a roof edge belied the building's present plight.

The gate didn't work, so I walked around the small picket fence, along the side of the house, and to the garage at the back. Here, the mood was more hopeful. There were cars parked all over, toys scattered about, a basketball hoop bolted to the wall, and a sense that the building had merely turned its back on its troubles.

The rear door obviously now served as the main entrance. I crossed the threshold and into a large room with a desk facing the door. A few chairs and magazine tables lined the walls, and the floor was again littered with toys. I was reminded of a pediatrician's office.

A teenage girl was sitting at the desk. "May I help you?"

I could hear a baby crying somewhere down a hall and the sound of laughter from somewhere else. "Yes. I'm here to see Billie Lucas."

"And your name?"

"Gunther."

She was very poised, despite her torn blue jeans, her acne, and her youth. She rose and disappeared through a far door.

I looked around, aware of more sounds emanating from all corners of the building—typewriters, phones ringing, people talking. The place was obviously bustling. The walls of the reception area were covered with announcements and posters addressing everything from VermontGreen's latest targets to La Leche League workshops.

The young girl reappeared and requested me to follow her. She led me up two flights of stairs; we passed a large room, filled with potter's wheels and an electric kiln, in which a class was in full session. Gail's admiration of Billie Lucas's many interests came back to mind.

I was ushered into a large room with a cathedral ceiling, obviously a converted attic. The beams had been left exposed, and bookshelves along the walls picked up the natural wood tone, as did the old but burnished oak flooring. Color was supplied not by the muted and tasteful prints and furniture but by exotic flowers by the dozens, sprouting from pottery vases all around the room. The smell, however, was neither intoxicating nor suffocating, but surprisingly light and seductive, reminding me of Gail's office. Except where Gail's place was old, blemished, familiar, and embracing, this was clean, sunlit, beautiful, but curiously aseptic.

"Mr. Gunther," my guide announced, and withdrew, closing the door behind her.

The woman seated at the computer rose and came around the desk to greet me. She was tall and slim, dressed in worn jeans and a loose white cotton shirt. Her hair, long, blond, and thick, was piled loosely on top of her head, with strands breaking for freedom in an attractive revolt. She wore a pair of very shiny, round gold-rimmed glasses. The total effect was extraordinarily appealing.

She held her hand out. "Lieutenant Gunther, I'm Billie Lucas. I was just putting the finishing touches on our project." She tilted her head toward the glowing computer. Her hand was cool, smooth, and firm.

"I appreciate your seeing me on such short notice. Looks like you run quite an operation here."

She smiled and returned to the computer, punching a few keys to start the printer. She indicated one of two armchairs placed by a large, sunny window. "Have a seat. Would you like a cup of coffee or tea?"

I moved to the window and sat, comforted by both the overstuffed chair and Lucas's quiet, professional manner. "Coffee'd be fine—milk and sugar if you've got it."

I appreciated her approach, and the lack of paraphernalia I'd assumed an astrologer would be surrounded with. The discomfort I'd felt anticipating this conversation—imagining myself having to smile and nod politely at some off-the-wall, wild-eyed stargazer—began to dissipate.

Lucas poured two cups and crossed over to me with one of them. "Here you go. It sounds like the printer's finished, too." She retired to collect the paperwork and her own cup before settling cross-legged opposite me, both the printout and the copy of the chart I'd left for her the previous evening spread out on her lap.

She adjusted her glasses and looked at me seriously. "Well, I've done what I can—it was a little more complicated because the time and date of birth were missing. I'm also not sure how much you were expecting."

I spread my hands, not wishing to appear antagonistic. "To be honest, not much; but that chart is about all I've got right now."

She smiled slightly. "That's all right; I don't expect many policemen are astrology fans." Her expression switched to a more clinical mien. "So you know nothing at all about this person? Not even their sex?"

I decided to sit on my one speculation that the chart might have been Fuller's. "Not a thing."

She nodded, as if coming to some private conclusion. "All right, then we'll start with the basics. There are two types of information you can derive from a chart; one is very concrete, and very brief—the type I assume you're after—and the second appears just as solid to those of us who believe in astrology, but it has an elusive quality to it, since it's directly affected by the actions of the person involved, which makes not knowing that person a disadvantage."

"Okay," I said noncommittally, having anticipated the disclaimer.

"The concrete information is that this person was born at ten-fifty-five P.M., eastern standard time, on April 7, 1946, which makes him forty-seven years old."

I nodded. That was already more than I'd expected, and, if accurate, a valuable clue.

She continued cautiously. "But that's it. All the rest of

what I have to say depends on how this person has learned to manage him- or herself. And I must admit right off, if this was my chart, I'd be in therapy.''

She turned the chart toward me and indicated the traffic jam of colored lines running from the two o'clock position on the wheel to the five o'clock. ''See how loaded up and lopsided this looks? That's not a bad way of visualizing the owner of this chart. Each one of the twelve wedges on the innermost circle of the wheel is called a 'house.' Each house represents an area of one's life. For example, the fifth house is creative expression; the eighth deals with sex and money; and so on. The house system allows us to connect the signs to the way we live. Now sometimes, the relationships between the houses and the planets in them are very harmonious, and the end result is a person who is happy, normal, and at peace with himself and the world. But a chart like this one is just the opposite. Many of the planets are what we call 'squared' with one another, or in conflict. It's just shy of crippling, in fact.''

''How so?''

''Root causes are often the easiest to pin down. For example, I suspect child abuse here, on the receiving end. I see a very repressed early life, with the Moon, Saturn, and Mars all in the eighth house, which also means sex was a factor.''

''A father abusing a daughter?'' I asked hopefully.

But she wouldn't go that far. ''Perhaps—that's the standard. But there are oddities, things I haven't been able to quite decipher.''

I sighed inwardly, disappointed, and backtracked a bit. ''How about something you can be sure of?''

She pointed to one of the wedges. ''The most prominent is in the fifth house; whoever this is craves solitude and being left alone, even at the cost of personal relationships. And there are a lot of secrets in this chart—secrets, sex, death, and taboos.''

Fuller came back to mind, as did the growing conviction that this whole conversation was going nowhere fast. I tried again, stimulated more by a loyalty to Gail than by any hopes of success. ''But can you tie that in with anything I can use?''

She looked up at the tone in my voice and fixed me with

a cool eye. "Lieutenant, you want this to be a mug shot. It's not. It's a map to somebody's character, and as such, it can be a useful tool. Once you find whoever you're after, you could get him to open up by making him realize you know more about him that he thinks you do. But it won't help you locate some guy out of the blue."

I realized I'd let my antipathy work against me. I stepped back mentally and tried to match my needs more realistically with what she could supply. "You've been at this a long time. Maybe our best approach would be for you to compare this chart with similar ones you've done in the past—ones where you know the people involved. If there are common traits among them, that might help us flesh out whoever's behind the anonymous chart."

She looked doubtful, so I pressed on. "Patterns are bound to be repeated. As you do chart after chart, things come around more than once; they become familiar. You end up knowing what you've got even before you go through the whole routine. That's true for us when we do an investigation."

She was thoughtful for a few moments, looking out the window, and then she let out a small sigh. "There is a risk of the tail wagging the dog—we could end up putting labels on this chart that shouldn't be applied, even to identifying the person's sex."

I was about to argue the point, until I suddenly wondered if she wasn't already way ahead of me. "You've thought of one, haven't you? A chart that fits."

She laughed and pretended to tear her hair in mock exasperation, further loosening the elegant pile on top of her head. "Yes, I do, but I'm extremely reluctant to mention it. It is just a single other chart."

I shook my head. "Look, I know you're trying to be conscientious, but I promise not to take what you tell me as gospel. Let's just try this out, okay?"

"All right. The chart I thought of immediately—even last night—was of a homosexual client I once had."

"A male."

"Right. He had a terribly abusive mother and no father—at least none that he knew of. Now, why he was gay, I don't know, but his chart revealed a lot of anger directed at his mother, just like this one." She tapped the chart in her lap. "And both his chart and this one have the male sex sign over in this spot, with Pluto indicating a definite interest, maybe even a compulsion, for partners of the same sex, and Mars pointing toward that sex being male."

She paused and looked up at me, her expression animated. Despite her earlier hesitation, she'd obviously become intrigued. "That's about it for real similarities, but if, for argument's sake, you do make this chart that of a gay male, other things begin to fall into place. Here's the harshness to his representation of the female, for which you could read the mother figure. Also, you have Neptune highlighting a lot of imagery and flair in the way he expresses himself, like a painter or designer might have. And he has a lot of friends, but no solid partner, and there's an implication of no children, which could fit a member of a male gay community. Some of that's a little clichéd, but there it is."

"Could the painter be a fancy gardener instead?"

She nodded unequivocally. "Oh, sure—there's a strong connection to the earth here—very strong."

"How about the mother—can you give me anything on her?"

At that, Billie Lucas closed her eyes for a moment, and I realized I'd overplayed the game. When she reopened them, she also stood up, placing her paperwork on the floor. Her voice had a new firmness to it. "No, we should stop this. It's not proper, and it's definitely not astrology. I give you high marks for persuasiveness, though."

She took my hand and pulled me to my feet, leaving no doubt that she was throwing me out, albeit pleasantly. "I should have known what I was getting into when you called me last night. Gail had me do your chart some time ago."

"She mentioned that," I said over my shoulder as she gently propelled me toward the door. "She didn't go into details, though."

"You're perfectly suited to your profession."

I stopped on the threshold and faced her, risking the remnants of her good humor. "I've got to ask you one last question: You mentioned a house dealing with money. How does this guy look there?"

She paused and looked reflective. "That's fair enough. There are two houses dealing with money. The second concerns personal finances, the eighth shared income. With Capricorn in the second house, he or she has a hard time getting hold of money. This chart's big emphasis is in the eighth, though."

"What does shared income mean? Do you mean that literally, as in a tax form?"

"It can be, but it means any money not your own in which you have a share, like a business or a marriage."

"Or money you stole."

She stared at me in silence for a couple of seconds, no doubt disappointed with the workings of my mind, and then she nodded. "Yes. Or money you stole."

Chapter Eight

Harriet stopped me as I walked into the office. "Ron called from the SA's office. Everybody's running late, and they've only just started reviewing his evidence on the embezzling case. He's supposed to be meeting Richard Schimke at the bank in ten minutes. Do you want me to put Dennis on it? He's the only one around."

I looked at my watch. "Doesn't Ron have a file or something?"

She patted a folder lying on her desk. "A list of serial numbers, some photos J.P. took of the money, a couple of the bands that were holding the bills together, and a full breakdown of the dates on the bills, plus the names of the Federal Reserve banks that issued them."

I scooped up the file as I headed back out the door. "Guess you know where you can find me."

Vermont National Bank occupies the corner of Main and Elliot, across the street from Allen Rogers's photo store. I asked for Schimke's name at the information desk in the lobby and was told to take the elevator to the third floor.

The man who greeted me there was my idea of the small-town banker's banker: average height, dark blow-dried hair, clean-shaven and pink-cheeked, a little on the chubby side, and blazingly affable. He was wearing an unremarkable dark three-piece suit and sporting an oversized college ring on his right hand and a wedding band on his left. Before I was led to his office, I was sure he'd have a diploma or two on the wall and a photo of his wife and kids on his desk.

But there I was wrong.

His office, at the end of the hall, had been rigged out as a Civil War museum, complete with broadsides, paintings, crossed swords, mounted pistols, and a tattered Confederate battle flag. Interspersed on the walls were framed displays of antique American paper currency—ornate, colorful, and running the gamut from smudged, hand-printed company scrip to lavishly detailed works of art, all dating back to the pregreenback days when banks, states, and territories felt free to issue their own cash almost at will. I was so startled that I came to a dead stop on the threshold.

Rich Schimke looked back at me with a slightly embarrassed grin. "I guess it's a little overwhelming at first. It's just that I had all this stuff at home and never got to see it. I'm still not sure I won't be told to take it all down; I've only had it here a couple of weeks, and I don't think word has leaked upstairs yet."

He shook his head sadly. "It'll be a shame to lose it all again."

I began walking around, looking at the collection more closely. "Hey, this may make you the most popular guy to visit in this bank."

"That'd be nice," he said wistfully.

I looked at him closely, ashamed at having pigeonholed him earlier and sorry to think that he was probably right in foretelling his own fate. I handed him the file I'd brought, hoping to cheer him up. "Well, maybe this'll help. I'm here officially, and if you can throw any light at all on this, I'll make sure the brass hears about it."

He laughed and took the file, parking himself in his own guest chair to look it over. I described the circumstances in which we'd found the loot, how much there'd been, and how it had been bundled. He nodded as I spoke, studying the detailed inventory J.P. had drawn up.

"Well," he finally said, "it certainly is unusual . . . Hey, you don't happen to know whose signatures were on the 1934 notes, do you? You've got several of them listed here."

I looked at him for a second, having forgotten he was a collector as well as a banker. "No; would they be worth a lot?"

"Not a lot—maybe double their face value. You've got some others I'd love to look at, too."

I didn't answer, not willing to make him promises I probably couldn't keep.

He caught the implication and returned to the topic at hand. "I take it you sent the serial numbers to the Secret Service?"

I nodded.

"Considering the amount, they should be back to you pretty quick. If it was stolen, three hundred thousand must've made a dent in somebody's pocket."

"Couldn't this be an aggravated version of stuffing cash into a mattress?"

Schimke looked doubtful. "Not like this. You've got both mint and used money here, but it's all banded with official bank straps, complete with names and addresses. It looks to me like it came out of several banks in lump sums, and not from the tellers, either. They break the bands around the bundles as soon as they get them, to make the money easier to handle, and they rarely have more than one thousand dollars at one time anyhow, for security reasons. If this guy did stick up a series of banks, he didn't go down the counters cleaning out the tills and collecting loose bills. All this came straight from the vaults."

"But not from the same bank?" I asked. I regretted not having had the time to review Tyler's file. My questions sounded foolish even to me.

But Schimke didn't seem to notice or care. He shook his head affably. "Oh no. Any money that comes out of a bank legally is either loose or it's strapped with that bank's band. It doesn't matter if it's old or new money, since no matter where it comes from originally, it's always recounted and rebanded by the receiver, even if it comes from a Fed bank. From what I can see from your list, this money came from banks in Nevada, Colorado, Illinois, California—"

"Nothing from the East?" I interrupted, struck by the regional proximity of the states.

"No, which brings up something else. All mint notes originate from the twelve regional Federal Reserve banks, which then circulate them to surrounding private banks. In this area—in your own pocket, for instance—the really spanking-new money will be from the Fed bank in Boston, since it hasn't had a chance to circulate far from where it was printed."

I pulled a worn five-dollar bill from my wallet and looked at it. Schimke sidled over and pointed at the round emblem to the left of Lincoln's portrait.

"That's from San Francisco, but it's been around a while, which is why you have to focus either on the straps or the mint notes to get a geographical fix on them. An old, loose note won't tell you a thing. My point is that all the mint notes listed in your inventory were printed in the West or the Midwest. What you've got here"—he tapped the file J.P. had put together—"shows me the new money at least made a beeline from the Reserve bank to the local vault to your suspect."

"Which implies," I finished for him, "that he was out west when he collected it."

Schimke's eyes were shining by now. "That's what the mint notes imply, but that's the funny part; it tells you *only* that he was out west. It doesn't even pin down a particular state. I mean, if he had held up one bank, all the bands would be the same. And if he'd hit an armored car, the bands might be different, but they still wouldn't be from banks thousands of miles apart. It's a little hard to make sense of it."

"Unless he robbed a series of banks, like you said, or maybe got cash as payment for something."

"Yeah—like drugs or racketeering."

I remained silent, not wanting to encourage too much speculation in someone outside the department. But I wasn't so sure he hadn't hit on something. In our naïveté, we'd really focused on Fuller only as a bank robber.

Schimke stood up suddenly, struck by something in the file. "I'll be damned; I missed this before." He punched the columns of figures with his fingertip for emphasis. "This might nail down the exact date all this money was collected. Look—while all the older notes are 1963 issues or earlier, only the mint ones are '69s. . . . ."

"Implying that they were taken out of the bank that year."

"Right. I mean, sometimes you can get mint bills from a smaller, low-volume bank up to a year or so after issue, but every one of these is crisp, no matter which bank they came from."

"What percentage of the total is mint in that list?"

He was positively gleeful by now. "That's the whole point; it's very high, like thirty percent or so. That would never happen unless the Fed had just released a new printing to be distributed throughout the system. And the fact that the mint samples come from several banks in different states clinches it. I can't tell you what happened, but it was definitely in 1969."

I thanked Richard Schimke profusely, vowed him to silence concerning our conversation, and encouraged him to hang tough on his office decor.

When I returned to the station, Harriet was looking pleased with herself. "One down, one to go. The state police dropped off their metal detector ten minutes ago, and the rental place said theirs would be available in an hour, guaranteed. I've already told most of the squad to be here by then. Ron, of course, won't be available."

I thanked her, then turned, to find J.P. Tyler standing by my office door, a thick file in his hand. "What's up?"

He handed me the file. "It's a preliminary report on our forensics search. It doesn't have any of the State Crime Lab results yet, but it lists what we found and where we found it. The photographs are arranged from start of search to end, and they're indexed to the report and the map of the place. I'm afraid you won't find much.''

I took the file to my desk and opened it before me. I didn't doubt Tyler's opinion. I'd been through Fuller's place twice by now and was pretty sure it was almost as bare as a clean motel room. Nevertheless, I always valued the search report, since it organized a place according to its tiniest details, ignoring the distracting environmental influences that could make your eye skim over a small but important item.

So it was with a cautious curiosity that I pored over the results of yesterday's hours of crawling with tweezers, sticky tape, and a magnifying glass, seeing for the first time all of our separate findings organized in a logical manner.

I quickly understood what Tyler had meant. Even microscopically, Fuller's place had been pretty sterile. Hair, dirt, and fingerprint samples were all consistent with a house that had sheltered only one person for a long time, and a lot of intruders just recently. Tyler had even gone the extra yard by determining the hair colors of the search team, the ambulance crew, and Fred Coyner, so that any stray samples could be properly accounted for.

Nothing stood out until I got to the wood stove.

Tyler had been the one nearest the stove. I remembered him opening it, checking its contents with a flashlight, and scribbling in his notebook. Now, in the report's terse language, I read: "L-18: cast-iron wood-fired heating stove, found with door slightly open. Contents: small quantity cold wood ash, one partially burned wooden kitchen match.''

I began flipping through both the photographs and the rest of the report, looking for any mention of either a candle or a kerosene lamp. I found both eventually, but as stored items, far from the stove, and obviously not in current use.

I sat back and thought for a moment. I'd been brought up with a wood stove heating the home; in fact, once I was old enough, it had been my job to light it every morning before the rest of the family got up. Assembling the wood in the firebox, the kindling at the bottom, clustered around a heart of tightly crumpled newspaper, had become a habit so inbred, I got so I could do it while still half asleep. It had become totally automatic, including throwing the spent match onto the burgeoning flame. Never had I opened a stove in the morning to find a half-burned match waiting for me. It would have been as incongruous as a rose blooming in February.

I hit the intercom button on my phone and dialed Tyler's extension. "Do you remember looking into Fuller's wood stove?"

"Sure."

"All you saw was cold wood ash and the match; no burned paper or anything else unusual?"

J.P. paused at the other end, never one to dismiss such a question without thought. "There was nothing obvious, Joe, but that's not to say something couldn't have been burned and then destroyed to blend into the regular ash."

"Okay. Thanks."

I pawed over the assorted papers on my desk and finally came up with the report from the medical examiner's office. I flipped it open and went over the section detailing the body's appearance. There was nothing unusual concerning Fuller's hands or fingernails, except a small cut on his forefinger—probably the result of a blood draw at the hospital—and a note that they had obviously been exposed to a lifetime of manual labor and exposure to the soil. There was a footnote that the hospital had cleaned up the patient prior to his death.

I called Rescue, Inc., and asked to talk to John Breen, the paramedic who had initially treated Abraham Fuller. "This is Joe Gunther, from the PD. Do you remember anything unusual about Fuller's hands when you picked him up?"

"His hands?" There was a pause. "What do you mean 'unusual'?"

I didn't want to plant any ideas in his head. "You tell me."

Again he hesitated. "Well, they were workingman's hands. Let's see . . . Yeah, there was one thing. His right hand was sooty—the palm had ash stains all over it. And his fingertip was cut—pricked, actually. It wasn't bleeding much, though. It stopped before I could do anything about it."

So much for blood draws, not that any alternatives leapt to mind. "Did you notice the soot before or after he sent you guys outside for that five minutes?"

"After. He wouldn't let us near him before then."

I was a little disappointed at that. "How about an odor after you went back in?"

Breen chuckled. "There was an odor all right. He was lying in the middle of it."

"No—I meant something else, something new."

"No, sorry. It smelled pretty raw in there. If there'd been another odor, I doubt we would have smelled it, anyhow."

"Okay. Thanks a lot."

I tried to picture what must have happened: Fuller, after deciding to go on the ambulance, sends the crew outside, drags himself to where he's hidden the money, pulls out his emergencies-only red bag, along with some sort of document. He then drags himself back to the stove, near where he was lying to begin with, and burns the document with a match he tosses into the stove. Finally, after the document has been destroyed, he crumples the ashes up in his right hand so they'll mingle with the wood ashes in the stove, and then he crawls back to the rug near the bookcase.

I considered that Coyner, or whoever had stolen the chart, might have also burned something in the stove, maybe even the chart itself, minus the frame and glass. But the first scenario made more sense, especially with Fuller's stained right hand.

It meant that Fuller had taken the precaution of burning the paper, either because he didn't want someone to find it while he was recuperating in the hospital or because he suspected he wasn't going to survive. Initially, after all, he had told Breen and his partner to let him die in peace.

If he hadn't thought he was going to return, burning something self-incriminating wouldn't make much sense. Unless the document—whatever it was—incriminated someone else.

After all, why live in a house for twenty years, eliminating everything that might reveal your past, and yet keep a self-incriminating document for posterity? Whatever it was he'd burned had to have pointed the finger at someone else, someone who posed a threat to him personally and yet whose secret he'd wanted to die with him if necessary.

Had that been the same person who had stolen the chart?

I began studying Tyler's photographs one by one, focusing on every detail, hunting for anything odd. What burned in my mind now was the most banal of revelations: The person who had stolen the chart had to have known it was there to begin with. Did he, therefore, also know about the incriminating document? And if he did, then why wasn't the place torn apart in a desperate search?

I pulled open the file containing my own photographs, the ones including both the chart and the unfocused shadow of someone lurking outside the window. I placed my shots of the building's interior next to Tyler's and compared them, looking for any discrepancies. The chart had vanished in the time between the taking of both sets of photographs; maybe something else had disappeared, too—something that had told the thief his secret was secure and that he had no need to conduct a frantic search.

Tyler had also taken a shot of the bookcase, straight-on, as I had. I laid them side by side and looked from one to the other, back and forth, my eyes aching with the concentration. What finally froze me wasn't a single item but, rather, the absence of one; there was a small gap on the bottom shelf, near the stove, in Tyler's picture. I squinted at my own picture, where the same gap was filled with the spine of a paperback book, the title of which had been circled with a broad band, like a felt-tip pen.

I sat back, curiously satisfied. The photos were in color, but the mark around the book's title merely appeared brown. I was convinced, however, that had the picture been taken earlier, just after Fuller's departure on the ambulance, the circle would have been as red as the blood from his pricked fingertip.

I stared at the now-missing book, smiling at its intended pun and admiring the mind of the man who had brought it to my attention, and to that of the chart thief. It was a copy of Nathaniel Hawthorne's *The Scarlet Letter*.

Chapter Nine

Harriet poked her head around the door to say that the second metal detector was waiting for us at the rental place and that everyone except Ron was either here or would meet us at Fuller's place.

I neatened up my paperwork and crossed over to J.P.'s desk in the middle of the squad room. "I got something extra I'd like you to do when we get to Fuller's."

"Shoot."

"I want you to go over the contents of that stove with a fine-tooth comb. If my hunch is right, you should find at least some trace of newly burned paper mixed in with the wood ash, near the front of the stove door. I think Fuller destroyed a document or a letter just before he was taken to the hospital."

Tyler quietly nodded and crossed over to the closet where he kept his forensics bag of tricks.

The trip back up to Coyner's remote property was made largely in silence. I had Dennis and Tyler with me; Sammie and Willy Kunkle were in separate cars.

At first, I wrote the quiet drive off to the contrasting personalities of my passengers. Dennis DeFlorio was as much a slob as Tyler was neat and precise, and they were not given to idle chats under the best of circumstances. But the farther we drove, the more I began to share their lack of enthusiasm for the search. Looking for the gun would be a long and tiresome procedure, and probably a fruitless one at that. Moreover, if by some miracle we did locate it, what would it prove? It would no longer have any prints on it, and any serial numbers would doubtless lead nowhere; a man of Fuller's intelligence and caution would hardly have left behind a gun so easily traceable. The net result, if this all proved accurate, would be another brick wall, and although our efforts had only just begun, I was already feeling a sense of futility. We'd made some progress on the case, but nothing had brought us any closer to the solution of a more than twenty-year-old homicide.

By the time we arrived at Coyner's house, Kunkle was already there with the rented metal detector, predictably giving voice to all our doubts. "Hey, Joe, we really going to hunt around for this guy's gun?"

"Yeah. Anyone seen Coyner?"

Sammie, sitting in the passenger seat of her car with her legs stretched out toward the breathtaking view of the valleys below, answered, "I knocked—no answer."

I checked my watch. "Okay, let's get moving; we've got about five hours of light left."

Tyler held up a canvas bag he'd brought along, adding without humor, "And flashlights for everybody."

The general mood did not improve much during the afternoon, even with Tyler's discovery, after painstaking work with tweezers and a magnifying glass, of the blackened remains of a letter in the wood stove. Unfortunately, he couldn't tell us more, since his conclusions were based on a few minute scraps of shiny ash.

It was, however, the sole highlight of the afternoon. The rest of our time was spent crisscrossing Fuller's horticultural masterpiece in two teams, one detector apiece, stopping every few feet to investigate whatever set the machines off. Sometimes the reason was an old nail, a lost tool, the remains of a container; other times nothing was found, and when the area was rechecked after some digging, the detector stayed mute. J.P. hypothesized about the effects of iron in the soil; Kunkle was both less charitable and more crude.

At sunset, I feared that morale had dipped so low, I would have to call it quits. Instead, I had Tyler radio for the department's emergency services van, equipped with portable halogen lamps, by whose light we continued along our narrow, predetermined search grids. I kept hopefully silent while the others punctuated their work with increasing complaints about the cold, the equipment, and their fate in general.

Since there were five of us, the odd member of the group sat out a quarter hour while the other four worked on. At around 7:45, the sun long since set, I was sitting on Fuller's front stoop, watching the others shuffling through their paces near the edge of the woods, their shadows sharp-edged by the harsh lights, when for the hundredth time I heard the persistent complaint of one of the detectors. I saw Sammie's diminutive form stop, while Dennis's bulk dropped to all fours and began to scratch the earth's surface with a hand spade he'd borrowed from the toolshed. He sat back on his haunches a few minutes later, a small pile of dirt by his side, and Sammie played the detector across the surface of the shallow hole once more. The chirping reached my ears again.

I got up and walked toward them, hearing Dennis swearing as he bent to his task again, scooping out larger clods, assisting the spade with his other hand now. Once more, Sammie swept over the hole with the detector's broad, flat, horizontal disk. It sounded a third time.

"Goddamn it," Dennis growled, and reached into the hole.

"What'd you think?" I asked Sammie.

She shrugged noncommittally, but her eyes were tightly focused on Dennis's work. "Beats me. First time it's been this deep."

Tyler and Kunkle crossed over to us, having marked their spot with their own machine. Without asking, Willy fell in next to Dennis, his one powerful hand making his own spade work like a miniature steam shovel.

After they'd gone down about two feet, I interrupted them, aware of Dennis's heavy breathing and the gleam of sweat on the back of his neck. "Try it again."

The detector repeated itself, its irritating alarm now egging us on. I switched places with DeFlorio. Kunkle stayed where he was, muttering, "This better be something, or I'm out of here. This is bullshit."

"At least it's easy digging," I commented, half to myself.

"Yeah—I noticed that," Willy said in a voice that made me pause to look up at him.

He grinned back at me. "Kind of makes you wonder."

It was true, I thought. Vermont soil is notoriously "bony"—as rock-strewn as a boulder field—and all afternoon, in response to the detectors' urging, we'd been proving that generality correct. But here, the consistently soft, almost wet earth moved under our spades as in a well-tilled garden—

except that we were far below the level of Fuller's lovingly tended garden soil.

At three and a half feet, Dennis and J.P. were hanging on to us for dear life, trying to keep us from falling into the narrow hole. Each scoop of the spade now had to be followed by a grunting heave back up to the surface so the dirt wouldn't slide back to the bottom, but neither Willy nor I would be relieved. Driven by the detector's persistence, we were now convinced we were close to discovery, although Willy, true to form, disguised his own excitement by muttering, "Probably a fucking Model T under here."

We all knew it as soon as my spade made contact, sending up a single sharp clang that froze us all in position.

"Shine a light in here," I ordered.

Four bright halos cascaded into the hole where I was hanging almost upside down. I stuck the spade into the soft earthen wall around me and used my bare hand to brush the dirt away.

"What the hell is that?" In their craning to see, I felt someone's grip loosen on my legs, then felt myself slide down the hole until my nose was almost flat on the bottom.

"Goddamn it."

When I scooped the earth away, I discovered a bright, shiny stainless-steel globe, about the size of an orange. I carefully worked my fingers to either side of it, trying to gain some definition. It was attached to two darker, grittier objects that extended from it at a forty-five degree angle, like shafts from the apex of some oversized drafting compass. Indeed, now that I could see it better, I knew the metal ball was actually a hinge, beautifully designed, immaculately crafted, and surgically precise.

"Pull me back up."

They dragged me over the edge and went back to staring at our small, twinkling treasure, ignoring me as I tried scraping some of the mud from my stomach and face.

"It's some sort of machine," Dennis said tentatively.

"In a way," I answered. "It's an artificial stainless-steel knee joint, and it's attached to a skeleton."

Chapter Ten

Hello, Lieutenant.''

I turned away from the jumble of people setting up staging and equipment by the roped-off grave site and saw Beverly Hillstrom coming toward me. I had called her right after discovering the skeleton, to ask her advice on how to deal with it. It was now 10:00 A.M. the following morning.

I smiled at her with genuine pleasure and shook her slim, elegant hand. "Doctor. It's wonderful to see you; I thought one of your regional MEs would be attending. I didn't know you were coming."

"I wasn't going to initially, but then I couldn't resist it. Besides, once I'd recommended a forensic archaeologist, I thought the least I could do was to introduce him personally."

She turned and gestured to a short, wiry man whose face was as bushy with black hair as his head was gleamingly bald. His eyes looked enormous behind thick, dark-framed glasses, and he squinted at me slightly as we exchanged formalities, as if considering what a slice of me would look like under a microscope.

Hillstrom beamed between us, the immaculate hostess. "Dr. Boris Leach—Lt. Joe Gunther."

Leach's eyes shifted away from me after a cursory glance, focusing instead on the activities by the hole. His hand was cold and limp in mine and I dropped it as soon as I could.

"Lieutenant, I take it no one has aggravated the hole any further?" He stepped around me and ducked under the yellow Mylar "Police Line" we'd used to surround the site.

Hillstrom patted my arm quickly and smiled, encouraging me to ignore Leach's arrogant tone of voice. I realized then she wasn't here purely out of professional curiosity. When I'd called her about the skeleton, she'd warned me that Leach was no Miss Manners; she'd obviously decided upon reflection to run interference between us.

I lifted the barrier for her and we followed in Leach's wake. "It's just the way we left it last night, except for what your assistant dropped off a while ago."

He stood at the edge of the hole, now illuminated by the bright, cool sunlight. The metal knee joint shone like a white spark, nestled in its pit. He looked around suddenly, "Where's the backhoe? I told Henry specifically to request a backhoe. I can't be expected to remove four feet of dirt by myself. It's idiotic . . . pointless."

I held up my hand to interrupt him. "It's coming, Doctor; it should be here in a few minutes. What about everything else?"

That sidetracked him for a while. He left us to examine the pile of equipment his twitchy, birdlike assistant Henry had brought in a pickup truck some forty-five minutes earlier.

Watching him, I muttered to Hillstrom, "Too many years digging in the Gobi Desert?"

She smiled like an indulgent mother. "Take the bad with the good, Lieutenant. This man is very good."

Leach returned from his inventory and fixed me with his fierce owl-wide eyes. "Who's the forensics man on your team?"

"J. P. Tyler." I shouted over to J.P., who was doing his own surreptitious examination of Leach's assembled hardware.

Rather than waiting for Tyler to join us, Leach marched off and made his own introductions. Both men took hammers and large spikes and set off toward opposite trees near the grave site. Once there, they drove the spikes into the trunks, fastened them to the ends of two reeled measuring tapes, and unrolled the tapes toward the hole, establishing both a double set of fixed surveying points and an accurate triangulation system. From now on, all maps of the site would feature the two trees, and all items on that map would be measured from them. Indeed, even as I was admiring the simple efficiency of the plan, I saw Leach thrust a drawing pad, a pencil, and a ruler into Tyler's hands.

At that point, Leach shouted over to Hillstrom. "You can play photographer now, if you want to earn your keep."

Hillstrom merely chuckled and pulled a camera from the bag hanging off her shoulder. Even considering our friendship, it never would have occurred to me to address her in such a tone.

From that point on, Dr. Leach was like a caricature general in the field, shouting orders to his troops, and doing most of the work himself.

After a quick sketch of the scene as it was, the surface debris of leaves and stray stones was cleared away to reveal the true topography of the land. Shovels were handed out, and slowly, inch by inch, the top layer of soil was removed over about a ten-foot-by-five-foot area, revealing at first a uniform mantle of dark, moist, nutrient-rich dirt.

I wandered near Hillstrom at one point in this drawn-out process and asked how deep we were going to go. She shook her head in shocked amusement. "Not to worry. That's why he was asking for the backhoe. Soil like this is divided into two parts: The upper layer can be about eight inches deep, like it is here, and it tends to be dark and rich. Below it is the lighter-colored, generally sandier layer, which usually goes down until you hit ledge or water or whatever. The premise is that if you dig a grave, you'll punch through the top and burrow into the lower layer, but when you later fill in the hole, the dirt you throw in will be a mixture of both dark and light. So, years later, if you skim the dark topsoil off of a larger surrounding area, chances are you'll discover one spot in the lighter, deeper soil that looks slightly different, because it's been disturbed. That's how you know exactly where your grave is."

"But we know where the grave is," I persisted, unembarrassed to display my archaeological ignorance.

"Yes, but we don't know its orientation or size. People rarely dig nice big, deep rectangular holes for their murder victims. They do what they can in a hurry, crunch their victims up as tightly as possible, and stuff them in. Boris and I have found them headfirst, balled up, and cut into pieces. It's amazing."

Her explanation was right on the mark. At about one foot

down, a barely perceptible darker patch, about three and a half feet around, distinguished itself from its pale surroundings. The hole we'd dug the night before was right at the edge of it.

The backhoe had long since arrived, accompanied but not operated by the high-strung Henry, whom Leach put to work laying out wooden stakes and a grid. Once a cut line was established, the machine was put to work digging a wide, deep trench right next to the grave site.

Leach stood next to me as we watched the backhoe at work. "You ever been to a dig before?" he asked suddenly without looking at me.

"No."

"Well, it's a pain in the ass to dig straight down. The position's uncomfortable, the visibility stinks, and the dirt keeps falling back into the hole. Plus, if the body's still ripe, the stench comes straight up at you. Much easier to put a trench alongside the site and work at it in comfort, directly in front of you. Then it's more like emptying a chest of drawers, from the top one down."

I was about to thank him for this unexpected tidbit when he left as abruptly as he'd come, signaled to the backhoe operator to stop, and jumped over the trench like some bespectacled billy goat, falling to his knees at the point where the light dirt and the mixed dirt met. He used a long knife to cut a cake-sized wedge between them and then signaled to me to join him.

I knelt down by his side and he pointed at the cleavage the wedge had left behind. "Shovel marks left by whoever dug the hole. You can see from the scalloped cut that it was a spade-shaped shovel, about twelve inches wide at the base and slightly curved."

He looked up suddenly. "Beverly—where the hell are you? You want to take possession of this mess fast, you've got to help me out."

Hillstrom, standing nearby, shook her head silently and joined us, focusing her camera on the evidence as Leach laid out a ruler for comparison. In the meantime, I called over to Dennis to check the toolshed for a shovel fitting Leach's description. As I did so, I noticed State's Attorney James

Dunn quietly joining the crowd at the police barrier, as irresistibly drawn to this death scene as he was to all the ones
I'd ever attended during his tenure. I'd realized by now that
we'd be here most of the day; it astounded me that Dunn's
specialized curiosity would allow him to abandon the office
for so long on such short notice. Hard to keep a man from
his personal interests. I gave him a small wave and went back
to being a spectator.

The trench now complete, Leach set to work in earnest,
scraping the side of the dirt wall before him until the faintest
change in color indicated he was right at the wall of the
narrow, vertical, cylindrical grave. Then, as he'd told me he
would, he set to work removing the dirt from the top down.

By the time he'd reached the artificial knee, Dennis had
returned with a shovel, and we took a brief pause to document
that we had indeed found a match for the scars in the dirt.
This was no small matter to me privately, for while everyone
else was narrowly focused on the task at hand, I was still
wondering if the body in the hole had anything at all to do
with Abraham Fuller. The shovel was a comforting bridge
over that gap. It didn't prove culpability; it didn't even point
at Fuller, since it was perfectly possible that the shovel was
Coyner's and that he'd buried Old Kneecap before Fuller had
appeared on the scene. Nevertheless, it was a link, until
something better came along.

The artificial knee, it turned out, was the highest point
of the body, since both upper and lower leg bones angled
downward from where we'd found it. Indeed, as Leach pro-
gressively laid bare the skeleton, we could all see that it rested
upside down on the nape of its neck, its torso curved and
twisted skyward and its heels tucked in so as not to stick out
of the ground.

With that much clear, but with most of the body still encased in dirt, Leach summoned Tyler, Henry, Hillstrom, and
me to his side.

"Okay, this is what we've got so far. You"—he pointed
at Tyler—"take measurements and make a sketch while I
point all this out. Henry, help him out."

Hillstrom had already begun taking photographs, so he left
her alone and focused on me, standing before the half-visible

skeleton as he might have before a blackboard. "We're looking at an adult, probably fully grown—whether male or female, I don't know. It's about six feet in length, which would
statistically indicate a male, but that can be misleading—
there are a lot of tall women around.

"He or she was dressed at the time of death in what looks
to be a nylon shirt and a pair of blue jeans, but he wasn't
wearing any shoes. If he was wearing a sweater, all traces of
it have long since vanished, but I'm pretty sure he was not
wearing a coat of any kind. The only buttons here are consistent with the shirt alone."

I bent forward and put my eyes a few inches away from
where the skeleton was held by the dirt like a bug on flypaper.
All I could see was skeleton. I didn't know what the hell he
was talking about.

My body language gave me away. With a sigh of impatience, he began pointing out the telltale signs. "Blue jeans,
see? The zipper and the copper stress-point tabs they use to
secure the pocket corners have all left telltale green stains on
the bone. The nylon shirt"—he pointed at a small shred of
rotted material—"is the only material that might survive this
long; cotton and wool vanish very quickly. And here, see the
plastic buttons? Also, look at the feet: no lace grommets, no
leather or rubber sole, no boot nails, no nothing. Therefore,
no shoes."

I was beginning to see what he saw. I pointed to a mass of
tiny confetti-sized fragments that seemed to surround the entire outline of the body. "And that?"

"Plastic. He was wrapped in it—or she was; I'm just
saying *he* for convenience. Don't forget that." He pulled a
small trowel from his back pocket and scratched away at his
exhibit. "Look, see those round plastic circles, like Life
Savers? Those are the reinforced holes running along the top
of a shower curtain. You'll notice they're all bunched together, as if they were gathered in a knot. And just below
them, see that? Rope strands, indicating that the curtain had
been tied off above the head, to make it a container for the
body."

He shifted to the feet. "Same thing here, see? No little
circles, of course, since this is the bottom of the curtain, but

you can see where there are more plastic fragments from where the curtain has been bunched together, and again, here are the rope strands.''

''So he was wrapped in the curtain, which was tied off at both ends with rope, and dragged to the hole.''

''From inside the house,'' Leach finished.

''Because of the lack of shoes?''

''Possibly, although it was apparently warm weather—no jacket, remember—so he might have been running around barefoot. But the shower curtain also implies an interior death. If he died outside, why tear down the curtain from inside? Why not just dig the hole and dump him in? If he died inside, possibly pouring out a lot of blood, then you'd be more inclined to wrap him in something both handy and waterproof, like a shower curtain.''

A slow smile spread across my face, which he seemed to take as an affront, adding, ''Of course, all that's utterly meaningless with a body this old—just a little magic show to entertain the unwashed masses.''

He turned to Henry and Tyler. ''You finished yet? I'd like to get this over with before next summer. Set up the rocker screens over there and filter the dirt I've already removed.''

The next stage of Leach's ''magic show'' took on the more traditional appearance of a documentary on digging up dinosaurs. The backhoe was retired, the shovels stacked, and even the hand trowels put away. Now Hillstrom's cranky little expert was down to dental tools and toothbrushes. The fact that he was toiling over an upside-down corpse with a metal knee instead of bits and pieces of a brontosaurus gradually lost its impact. As the hours went by, most of us lost sight of the overall horror of what had led us here. Like Leach, we became locked onto one minute patch of bone and dirt after another, cataloging with him the retrieval of each button, belt buckle, scrap of cloth, and wristwatch that gradually was pried from the hard-packed damp earth.

Also, the skeleton itself lost its ghoulish powers as it was slowly dismantled and laid in an open body bag spread out on a stretcher, the soil supporting it having been removed and sifted through the fine-mesh rocker screens that Henry and J.P. steadily shook back and forth. James Dunn, despite his own peculiar enthusiasm, began looking distracted, glancing at his watch more and more frequently, no doubt ruing his decision not to have sent an assistant in his place.

The care and time finally paid off, however, when Leach quietly gestured to Hillstrom to take a photograph of the area just below the skeleton's inverted rib cage. Looking over her shoulder as she focused for the shot, I saw the recognizable remains of a small-caliber bullet resting in the dirt, where presumably it had settled after the flesh holding it in place had rotted away.

That was all James Dunn needed. With a satisfied grunt, he rose from the rock he'd claimed as his chair for the past several hours and headed back to his office, the proud owner of another felony.

My own emotions were more complicated, since we were the ones who'd have to name the skeleton, as well as the person who'd placed him in his pit. Though not disproved by this latest discovery, any chances that Abraham Fuller had acquired his lethal wound through an accidental shooting had become microscopic.

Beverly Hillstrom stood beside me, watching as Leach carefully removed the rib cage and placed it on the stretcher, leaving only the skull in place. Her voice was very soft. "I feel like apologizing."

"For what?"

"Ever since I called you about Mr. Fuller, your job seems to be getting increasingly difficult."

I let out a little sigh. "Looks that way now. Maybe once you get this guy on your examining table in Burlington, things'll improve."

She shook her head. "I don't see how. I might be able to trace the bullet's trajectory, get a little more precise about his sex, age, and race, but there's a limit, and that's about it."

"What about the knee?"

"Yes—I was thinking about that. A complete data search might yield something, especially if we can locate a serial number. If this fellow's been in here too long, though, chances are the prosthesis originated in Europe, and that'll open up a whole new set of problems . . . and expenses."

I remained glum and silent.

"There is one thing, though . . ." she added tentatively, revealing that terrierlike inability to let go that I so valued in her.

"What?"

"I have a friend—a forensic anthropologist—who might be interested in taking a look. She's very good, and bones are her specialty."

"So what's the catch?"

"Money. If I bring her in, my office has to pay."

"And you're as broke as everybody else."

She didn't answer at first, but a slow smile crossed her face as she abstractly watched Leach remove the last of the skeleton from its grave, destined for the nearby hearse that would carry it to Burlington. Finally, she turned to me. "Look, let me get back to my office and make a couple of phone calls. There might be a way around this. Will you be available tomorrow?"

"Absolutely," I answered without hesitation.

She gave my forearm a squeeze and began walking toward the slope leading out of the trench. "We'll get this fellow to talk one way or the other."

Chapter Eleven

Five hours had been spent disinterring our nameless skeleton, and in that time, an inordinate number of haphazardly parked cars, trucks, and other vehicles had washed up on Fred Coyner's front lawn, like debris left over from a flash flood.

It took twenty minutes or more in the rapidly fading light to sort this mess out, a period in which Hillstrom, Leach, the hearse driver, and several other early birds—now all buried in the back of the pack—had to sit in their cars or stand around and wait. I, too, wanted to leave so I could attend the postponed squad meeting at the office, but I spent the enforced delay coordinating the conclusion of our search for the gun, which we still hadn't found. At this point, I was none too optimistic about our chances, so I put a couple of experienced patrolmen to the task, rather than members of my own team.

When I finally emerged from the woods, the driveway was almost clear. Coyner's house, in contrast to the bustle of moving vehicles, was as dark and still as it had been all day, seemingly abandoned by its owner in the face of overwhelming odds.

"You talk to him about the body yet?" a quiet voice asked me as I stood alone near the edge of the lawn that overlooked the darkening valleys below.

I turned from the house, surprised both by the gentle tone and by the fact that its owner had never been known to use one. Stanley Katz, abrasive, cynical, ambitious, and unrelenting, covered the cops-and-courts beat for the local daily *Brattleboro Reformer*. He was also, I had to reluctantly admit, one of the best reporters they had; for all his obnoxious ways and superior manner, he went after a story with grim determination, not caring who might be injured, so long as the facts were considered accurate up to deadline time. On the sliding scale of Truth, he sometimes hit lower than midpoint, but not because of any lack of integrity. The nature of his job was to report a story often before it was finished, a handicap that almost guaranteed an occasional shot in the foot.

Not that any of this meant I liked him. Like everyone else I knew who'd suffered at his hands in print, I thought the man was a pain in the ass.

I therefore took my time responding to his question, weighing the pros and cons of a simple "no comment" versus a running dialogue about Fred Coyner, whom I wasn't even sure Katz knew about. I finally hedged my bets and reacted solely and specifically to the question: "No."

Katz, small, narrow, and perpetually pale, merely nodded. "That was a bullet Leach found, wasn't it?"

"It looked like one, but that may not mean much."

He raised his eyebrows.

"There're quite a few people running around with old bullets in them."

I expected an incredulous outburst at that, which is partly why I brought it up, but again he merely nodded, his hands still nonchalantly buried in his pockets, as if he was merely passing the time of day, instead of pursuing a story.

I finally turned to face him fully. "You all right, Stan? You seem a little under the weather."

He gave me an echo of the shifty-eyed leer that had often made my blood boil in the past. "Why? Because I haven't given you the third degree? You shouldn't hold yourself so high, Joe. While you've been sitting in a hole for the past five hours, I've been grilling almost everyone here, including members of your illustrious profession. Besides, you don't talk to me much, anyway."

"That never stopped you in the past," I persisted, sensing something else.

He shrugged and glanced toward the hundred-mile panorama facing Coyner's house. It was almost dark by now, the distant, broken horizon a thin crimson line fading to dim starlight high above. As if mirroring the sky, pinpoints of light had appeared in the shadowy valleys beneath us, leading me to wonder, as I often did at night, what all those people were up to and whether their activities would eventually cause our paths to cross.

"I resigned today," Katz murmured, half as explanation and half, I thought, as confession. "Effective next week."

I was stunned. Katz and the *Reformer* had been one and the same for years, as inseparable, some would have said, as death and the plague. His announcement, therefore, left me groping among several emotional responses. I was sad for the paper, which would only suffer from his departure; happy for us, from whose back he would finally be plucked; and curious about the community's response, which, like most small towns, viewed any and all change with an initial burst of befuddlement.

I decided to let him be my guide. "Jesus, Stan, I hope that's good news for you."

Now his grin returned with most of the familiar malevolence in place. "Well, Joe, if it is, it ain't going to change much for you. I've already sold my talents to the *Rutland*

Herald, which, as you know, is just over the mountains. Which means," he added, with a condescending pat on my shoulder, "that I'll still be as tight on you as a tick on a dog."

So much for the lessening of our burden, not that I actually believed him. Rutland was a large town, quite capable of keeping his exclusive interest. "That's nice, Stanley. I hope you starve to death."

I was halfway to my car, seeing that the traffic jam had finally untangled itself and that both Hillstrom and the hearse driver had started their cars, when I heard Katz swear loudly behind me. I turned, to see him staring openmouthed at a small, hatchback vanishing down the driveway.

"Miss your ride back?" I asked.

"Yeah—that son of a bitch—I told him to wait."

"That'll teach you to jump ship." I continued toward my car.

I could hear him running after me. "Hey, Joe, wait a minute. Can you give me a lift?"

I opened my door. "I don't know, Stanley. You were a little hostile a few minutes ago. Didn't leave me in a great mood to do you any favors."

He stopped and looked around, checking his options. But aside from the hearse and the medical examiner, I was it. He was now looking downright peeved. "Come on, goddamn it, don't jerk me around."

I shook my head. "Get in."

We were the last of the caravan, and as I reached the first curve of the driveway, I glanced into my dark rearview mirror, half-expecting to see Coyner climb out of the woods to return home. There was nothing.

"Thanks, by the way," Katz muttered.

"No problem. So why the big change?"

"It was just time," he answered carelessly, and immediately switched subjects. "What's your angle on our bony friend with the flashy kneecap?"

I ignored him. "Was it the new midwestern bosses and their bite-sized news?" The *Reformer* had been purchased several months ago by a minor *USA Today* clone, which had promptly changed the page-one banner to bright red and had reduced its articles to ten column inches maximum, with no overruns to other pages. It was now peppy, perky, and pointless to read. Katz's articles had been among the few to make the blood circulate, and the only ones allowed occasionally to extend the length limitation.

"Something like that," he answered. "So are you treating this as a homicide?"

"You should've been happier than a hog in heaven—chief investigative reporter, or whatever they named you."

Stanley looked out the window at the tenebrous, flashing shadows of passing trees, his neck rigid with irritation. After a few venomously silent moments, during which I smiled happily in the dark at Hillstrom's taillights before me, Katz finally let out a long sigh.

"All right, although I don't know why you give a damn. I left because of the politics, the paperwork, and the pissing contests—not unlike this one."

"Worse than before?"

His voice rose an octave. "Before was a picnic. Compared to this bullshit, it was like turning out a newsletter for the Brownies. Now you use one hand to type and the other to check your back for knife handles."

I settled back to listen, only half-interested in his complaints, delighted instead that I wouldn't have to play informational footsie with him anymore.

I'd agreed to drive Stan back to his office, just off Exit 3, before returning downtown. I therefore followed both Hillstrom and the hearse onto the interstate at Exit 2, amused that Hillstrom was probably thinking my eagerness to have the skeleton analyzed had gotten the better of me and that I was going to follow her all the way to Burlington.

What happened instead bordered on the surreal. We had barely picked up speed off the entry ramp when a horizontal spray of red tracers spat out of the darkness from the low ridge to our right. It engulfed the hearse just ahead of Hillstrom's car and caused both vehicles to swerve violently.

"What the hell is that?" Katz shouted in alarm.

The deadly flashes of light kept lashing out at the hearse in short spurts, forcing it to brake sharply.

"Gunfire," I answered, swinging my own car over to the

left breakdown lane. I threw open the door and dragged Katz out after me, sliding into the median-strip ditch that separated the northbound lane from the southbound. I quickly raised Dispatch on my portable radio. "M-eighty from 0-three. We're under machine-gun fire on I-91 northbound, just above Exit Two. Repeat: We're under machine-gun fire. The shots are coming from the east side, about due west of the Frog Pond behind Harris Hill. Send everyone available to seal off the area and close off the interstate, north and south."

I began running in a low crouch toward the two cars ahead of me, both of which were also haphazardly parked in the breakdown lane. The machine-gun bursts continued in deadly earnest, brief, controlled, and aimed exclusively at the hearse. In the lights from Hillstrom's car, I could see steam rising from the hearse's engine, and I could smell gas from the ruptured tank.

I reached the driver's side of the medical examiner's car, pulled open the door, and found her staring at me from a prone position on the front seat, her eyes wide with terror.

"You hit?"

"No."

I reached in, grabbed her hands, and pulled her out into the ditch's shallow shelter next to Katz, who had followed me, muttering obscenities.

Only then, knowing I couldn't reach the hearse's driver, did I direct my attention to the source of the machine-gun fire. I drew my pistol, steadied it on the hood of Hillstrom's car, and fired three shots at the stuttering red-hot bull's-eye that hovered in the distant blackness.

My mind was no longer in Brattleboro, Vermont, but somewhere in the mountains of Korea, where night after night I'd lain still and silent behind my rifle, straining to pierce the darkness of the night, a box of grenades by my side. In Korea, too, they'd used incendiaries at times, hoping to hit an ammo dump or a pile of gas tanks, and we'd taken advantage of the one major drawback of using such ammunition: You can follow it right back to the muzzle that fired it.

The machine-gun fire suddenly stopped, just in time. Despite the now-overpowering reek of gas from the hearse, it hadn't yet burst into flame.

I circled the front of Hillstrom's car, paused for an incongruous bit of traffic, and sprinted across the road, yelling, "Stay put—don't check out the driver 'til I give the all clear." The absurdity that I might be hit by a car on the interstate while trying to take out a machine-gun nest rattled in the back of my mind.

I slid up against the far guardrail, expecting another burst of fire to catch me at any moment, but all remained quiet. I paused a moment to catch my breath, then vaulted over the protective guardrail and made for the grassy slope ahead. I could hear a growing chorus of siren wails approaching from all sides.

The bank led up to a short wall of trees, beyond which was an undeveloped low ridge overlooking the interstate. As I reached the tree line, the first squad car squealed to a showy stop below me. Two patrolmen jumped out, guns drawn.

"Lieutenant, you get him?"

I took cover behind a small tree. "I don't know, but he'll sure as hell get you if you don't move."

They did an embarrassed double take and scrambled for the trees to either side of me, climbing the slope like two cats with their tails on fire.

"Who's coordinating you guys? You were right in the line of fire."

They looked sheepishly at each other. The one named Hartley, a relative newcomer to the force, balefully admitted, "We didn't check in. We just heard you needed help and responded."

I shook my head and used my radio again. "M-eighty from 0-three; who's coordinating on the shooter?"

"0-three from 0-two," I heard Assistant Chief Billy Manierre's reassuring growl. "I got it. Where are you?"

"Tree line east of the interstate, with two backup. I returned fire and haven't heard anything since. He may be on the run."

"All right. We've almost got the area boxed in. Give me five minutes and I'll call you back."

I sent Hartley and his partner far out to either side, to better intercept anyone coming off the ridge and to reduce the chance of all three of us being caught in a single burst of fire. I looked over my shoulder at the three cars and saw Katz following my footsteps in a hunched-over hundred-yard dash. The interstate was now mercifully empty of traffic.

He reached my side barely able to speak. "See anything?"

"I see someone who shouldn't be here. You willing to die to get a story?"

He shrugged. "Sure—what the hell."

That made it a hard point to argue, and I wasn't going to test it by sending him back across the shooting gallery. "Then I guess today's your lucky day. Stick right behind me, all right? If you don't, I'll shoot you myself."

"0-three from 0-two."

I keyed the radio mike. "Go ahead."

"Ready to close in from all four sides."

"Okay, let's go."

The area we were slowly hemming in belonged mostly to the Retreat, Brattleboro's largest landowner, and its second-largest employer. A substance-abuse and mental-rehabilitation facility founded over a century and a half ago, the Retreat had turned its real estate holdings into farmland, woodlots, and recreational areas, giving Brattleboro much of its rustic flavor.

That was of little comfort to us now, however, confronted with a half-mile square of hilly, pitch-black wilderness instead of an easily patrolled grid of residential streets.

Our problems were compounded by the haste needed to contain the area. Over the radio, I heard Manierre coordinating, in addition to our own men, several responding state troopers, Windham County deputies, a state Motor Vehicles inspector, and even two patrolmen from Hinsdale, New Hampshire, just across the river.

The three of us, with Katz nervously dogging my heels, left the comfort of the interstate's openess for a claustrophobic tangle of dense, dark, and disorienting underbrush. The noise we made, stumbling and pushing our way past the enveloping branches, added to the dread that we, and not some disembodied sniper, were the ones increasingly at risk. To either side of me, I could hear the two patrolmen cursing and talking to themselves, doing their best to sustain their courage, praying the next shadowy clump of trees ahead wouldn't suddenly come alive with a crimson burst of machine-gun fire.

It wasn't easy. The farther we buried ourselves in this wilderness, the more the tension became punctuated by sounds far off, the flickering of half-seen flashlights, and the incessant urgent mutterings of our portable radios. As the four sides of this roughly coordinated search grid converged, the danger increased that one of us might mistake the other for a target and convert this well-intentioned effort into tragedy.

This very point was driven home when Katz, slightly to my right, stepped on a rabbit, which immediately bolted into the bush, causing him to shout out in alarm and Hartley—just barely visible on the flank—to swing toward us, gun raised.

"It's okay," I shouted, freezing in midstep, half-dropped into a crouch.

"Who's there?" came a voice from off to the side, reinforced by the nervously flitting beam of a powerful flashlight.

"Joe Gunther and three others. You the other flank?" Instinctively, I and the other two officers also waved our lights about. I could feel the relief flooding the air among us, thick in Katz's voice as he muttered, "Thank God."

We found Billy Manierre in a small clearing near the Frog Pond five minutes later. A large, white-haired, avuncular man, representing, along with Brandt and myself, the old guard of the department, he was always dressed in uniform—a recruiting poster testament to how high a patrolman could go.

He was holding a map in one hand and a flashlight in the other, grilling one of his team leaders on their coverage of the scene. Greenhill Parkway, a seldom-used, isolated residential street, had not been blocked off.

The young officer wilting under Manierre's questioning tried his best to explain, but his stammered excuses could never address the root of the problem, as both Billy and I well knew. We were a "full service" department, which meant we offered everything a big city department did. But while every branch of a major metropolitan police force was fully funded and staffed, ours were sometimes represented by a single individual, often one with several other hats to wear. As tonight's efforts had amply demonstrated, our lofty aims, combined with our lack of personnel and experience, sometimes fell a little short of the mark.

Greenhill Parkway was a dead-end street paralleling the interstate and leading off Route 9. It didn't even border the area we'd just searched, but, rather, pointed like a finger into its heart. Billy was by now convinced that leaving it open had allowed the shooter to jump calmly into his car and join the backed-up traffic on Route 9 while we were noisily setting up our dragnet.

I returned to the interstate, to find Beverly Hillstrom in the company of Ron Klesczewski, a tow truck crew, and a fire engine company that was hosing down the punctured hearse. Farther off, several state troopers were beginning to direct the newly released traffic.

"No luck, I take it?" Ron asked.

I shook my head. "How's the driver?"

"Serious but stable," Hillstrom answered. "He was hit twice in the leg. Why was someone trying to kill us?"

"I don't think he was necessarily trying to kill anyone. I think he was after our friend here." I peered through the remains of the hearse's back window at the black plastic body bag on the stretcher. "You had a chance to check him out yet?"

Ron, no doubt still smarting from his day-long ordeal at the state's attorney's office, muttered, "You'd think he was dead enough already."

Hillstrom opened the back of the wounded station wagon and climbed in. "He's dead enough, Sergeant, but he may have things to tell us yet. Lieutenant, if you had any worries earlier about my bringing in a specialist to examine these bones, you can relax. It will be done."

She carefully checked the body bag for bullet holes. "There's one near the head, and another lower down. If there's any damage, it shouldn't be difficult differentiating it from any older trauma. For all that gunfire, I'd say the sniper wasn't a very good shot."

"He was aiming for the gas tank," I replied.

She nodded soberly, realizing that by mere proximity, had

the hearse exploded, her car would have been burned to a crisp. "Well, if you'll help me get this fellow into my back-seat, I'd like to get to work on this as soon as possible."

I looked at her and smiled, wondering if she'd been as rattled as I, and knowing I'd never find out. "You mind if I arrange a state police escort?"

She smiled back a little tiredly. "No. I think I'd like that."

Chapter Twelve

It was ten o'clock before various members of the squad began filtering back into the office, slightly stunned at being catapulted from a low-profile, twenty-year-old brain-teaser of a murder case to a headline-grabbing machine-gun attack by a maniac on a national interstate highway.

We had conducted the postambush follow-up by the numbers, including using Red, our narcotics tracking dog, to see if the shooter had left a scent from the place where Billy Manierre and his ragtag crew had found a handful of spent cartridge shells. There'd actually been a moment of hope when the dog had taken off in a beeline—but the scent had dried up at the top of Greenhill Parkway, confirming Billy's pessimistic oracle that the shooter had not overlooked the same obvious escape route we had.

Brandt had made an appearance, something he rarely did, to invoke his famous GOYA and KOD maxim, which stood for "Get Off Your Asses and Knock on Doors." It was good advice, if indelicately phrased, and had already been put in motion. But nothing had come of it. No one in the entire neighborhood had seen or heard a thing, with the exception of a few who'd confused the actual gunfire for a truck mal-functioning on the interstate.

There was a feeling hovering over all of us, as palpable as smog, that we'd just been given a proper mugging.

Nevertheless, I figured I'd better start with the only physical evidence we had so far, and so I went to visit Tyler in his tiny corner laboratory—a converted broom closet.

He was standing at one of two narrow counters, looking up something in a thick reference book.

"Any luck?" I asked, leaning against the doorjamb.

He jotted down a quick note, then emptied a manila envelope onto the counter. Some fifteen brass shells rolled and spun out into a semicircle before him. ".223 caliber, consistent with ammunition they were putting into M-16s over twenty years ago."

He reached out and picked one up at random. "No prints on any of them, and they're all stamped 'LC 67,' which I just found out stands for the Lake City Arsenal, Independence, Missouri, 1967—the year they were manufactured. Lake City had a contract with the military to churn these out during the Vietnam War."

He stopped, took off his reading glasses, and looked at me.

"Anything else?" I asked him.

"That's it."

I now understood why he hadn't come running into my office earlier. "And you don't have anything new from yesterday?"

He shook his head. "Not enough time yet."

I thanked him and crossed the squad room to seek out Sammie Martens, whom I could hear pounding away on her typewriter. She was sitting in one of the cubicles we'd formed by erecting several interconnecting soundproof panels.

"How 'bout you? Any encouraging news?"

She sat back in her chair and made a face at me. "If you mean about tonight, forget it." But then she smiled. "I do have something on Fred Coyner, though."

She consulted a sheet of notes next to the typewriter. "Frederick Mills Coyner was born here in Brattleboro on August 4, 1917, the only child of a couple who died within three years of each other when Fred was a teenager. He inherited the house off Hescock Road, along with about five thousand dollars and some two hundred acres surrounding the house.

"He dropped out of high school after his mother died, and from then on pretty much made his living off the land. On various forms over the years, he's listed his occupation as logger, sugarman, farmer, and contract mechanic. He never made much money, but apparently he stayed solvent and kept his nose clean with both the local police and the IRS.

"He married Hannah Wilcox in 1940, when he was twenty-three. They had two children over the next few years, both of which died as infants."

"Anything suspicious in the kids' deaths?"

"None that I could see. The death records indicate birth defects in both children. The Coyners lived on Hescock Road with no fanfare and no troubles until January 1967, when Fred sold off his first piece of land."

The mention of 1967, right after my conversation with J.P., added a sudden extra weight to her biography.

"Why did he sell the land?" I asked.

"It took me a while to nail that down. Fred's wife died of cancer in 1970, but I found out she'd been diagnosed about four years earlier, just before he began selling off property."

"So he was paying for her medical treatments," I muttered.

"As far as I can tell, yes. Of the two hundred original acres, he unloaded all but ten, and finally took out a mortgage on the house. In late 1969, we busted him for being drunk and disorderly, but he was driven home instead of spending the night in the tank when we found out he had an invalid wife at home with no one to take care of her. By the time Hannah died in 1970, Coyner's delinquent tax bill totaled almost twenty thousand dollars and papers had been filed to sell his property at a tax sale."

I remembered my own wife's battle with cancer just a few years later. We, too, had been childless, and despite my own job security, finances had played no small part in adding to the stress. It had been a lonely, desperate time. Alcohol had helped me through a couple of the toughest stretches, until I'd given it up for good, fearful of its appeal.

"Later that same year," Sammie continued, "out of the blue and almost fresh from the funeral, Fred settled all his bills. A note at the tax assessor's says the settlement was made in cash. And from that time on, he's listed his profession as produce farmer, although the only part of his land that's agricultural is located around Fuller's place.''

She put her crib notes back down, but she wasn't finished. "I asked Ron if he'd discovered anything about Coyner's banking habits, but all he's been able to get so far is that the bank is First Vermont and that the guy is living comfortably.''

Willy Kunkle appeared from around the panel separating Sammie's desk from his. "There's your rat, if you ask me.''

I turned to him. "What'd you find out?''

"That there's no way Coyner could make a comfortable living from what he was dealing in produce. He could only grow stuff for three or four months out of the year at most, and he didn't bust his ass even then. According to your fruity friend Sunshine Jackson, Coyner was more of a recreational grower. I asked Jackson if maybe the old guy was growing dope. He just wiggled his eyebrows at me. Weird son of a bitch.''

"How long has Coyner been doing business with him?''

"Years, apparently, but they aren't buddy-buddy. Sunshine said I reminded him of Coyner, and I don't think he was making a run up my leg. Thought Coyner was a crook of some kind, 'cause he usually paid in hundred-dollar bills.''

"Jackson only sells seeds and fertilizer and whatever, right? Where did Coyner unload the produce?''

"Farmer's Market, Food Co-op, various fairs around the area. Pretty low-key. I talked to other people who do the same thing. None of them knows Coyner real well, no more than to say hello and get nothing in return.''

"Did you talk to any neighbors?'' I asked.

"Yeah. Seems pretty clear that Coyner only likes his own company. I got more gossip about the time his wife was sick, though. According to the Sunset Lake Road crowd—the year-round people, that is, which come to about twelve—the time we nailed Fred for D&D wasn't the only time he flew off the handle. He'd get lit on a regular basis toward the end—1970, I guess—and tear around the neighborhood raising hell.''

"Nobody complained?''

"They knew what was up, and he didn't do any harm—scared the dogs, shot up a few road signs. Most of the time, someone would either steer him back home or he'd head that way himself eventually. There was one time when he went down to Hippie Hollow and started blowing out the bus windows with a shotgun. A few people got pissed then.''

"Hippie Hollow?" Sammie asked.

"About halfway between Coyner's place and Route Nine," I answered. "There's a road heading west. Twenty years ago, there was a sort of commune up there—they all lived out of five or six old yellow school buses." I paused and thought back a moment. "You know, our own state's attorney defended them in a couple of cases before he switched hats. I'll have to give him a call and ask him about that.''

I turned back to Willy. "No one pressed charges after the incident with the shotgun?"

"Nope. Once his situation was explained to them, they decided to let it slide. And after his wife died, he went back to being the invisible man of the neighborhood.''

"By the way," Kunkle added, "I told Dennis to hold up on faxing Fuller's photograph to everyone. I figured if we had the Boston PD's forensic guys take twenty years off Fuller's face by running the picture through their imaging computer, we could fax before and after pictures and maybe improve our chances.''

I moved to the center of the room to address them all, since Ron Klesczewski had just entered the office and I could now hold an impromptu staff meeting. "Apparently, we've stirred up somebody who's hell-bent on erasing the past, and since the skeleton may give us an explanation, I'll be headng up to Burlington tomorrow to see what Hillstrom has found out.

"In the meantime, we should circulate the recent and early portraits of Fuller as soon as we get them back. Maybe someone will remember him and give us a fresh lead. Also, since we know the shooter used an M-16, we need to find out what we can about the local availability of Vietnam-vintage weapons. Check with bartenders, club owners, gun shop and sports store operators, and your snitches to find out if there's been any unusual activity concerning M-16s or .223 ammo, either preceding or following tonight's pyrotechnics.

"Finally, although there's no sign I hit this guy when I fired at him, let's check the hospitals, both here and in Keene,

Greenfield, and Townshend, as well as the local doctors' offices and pharmacies for anyone buying either painkillers or trauma dressing. Ron, you coordinate with everyone."

Ron nodded without comment.

"Okay. Let's meet officially tomorrow at sixteen hundred hours to compare notes. By then, I should know something about that skeleton."

Chapter Thirteen

The trip to Burlington took a shade over three hours. I left Gail's house just before dawn and had settled into the soothing monotony of long-distance travel by the time the sun spread its pallor across the eastern hills of New Hampshire. In that short period between total darkness and when the burgeoning monochromatic daylight reveals a world beyond the headlamps, my mind floated away from the troublesome details surrounding Fred Coyner and Abraham Fuller, focusing instead on the beauty around me.

Interstate 91 is one of only two such roads in Vermont. It shoots straight north toward Canada, paralleling the Connecticut River border with New Hampshire until just below St. Johnsbury, where the border veers off to the northeast. At White River Junction, some sixty miles south, 91 intersects I-89, which takes a diagonal path to Burlington, in the northwest corner of the state.

Combined, the two roads offer one of the best time-compressed tours of Vermont I know of, taking one from the "banana belt" of Brattleboro, through the low hills and river views of the southern valley, along the dramatic forested gaps of the Green Mountains, and finally out onto the rich, flat plains of the Lake Champlain valley. It amounts to a seamless succession of picture-perfect postcards.

Beverly Hillstrom's lab was located at the rear of the University of Vermont's Medical Center Hospital, off Colchester

Avenue, in an inconspicuous corner not far from the loading docks. I had a little difficulty finding it, even knowing which entrance to use—autopsy areas don't tend to advertise, especially within hospitals—and the first person I saw when I finally did walk through the metal double doors looked at me as if I'd lost my way. Only my badge and my using Dr. Hillstrom's name changed his mind.

I was ushered into a small white lab room lined with cabinets, mounted light boxes for X rays, and several freestanding bulletin boards covered with the photographs Hillstrom had taken the day before. Hillstrom herself was deep in conversation with a small dark-haired woman with half glasses, periodically referring to the mottled dark brown pelvis of the skeleton on which I was pinning so much hope. He—or she— was stretched out on a porcelain table in the middle of the room, looking like a rejected medical-school model that needed reassembling.

Hillstrom looked away from her companion and gave me a wide grin—the most expansive greeting she'd ever bestowed on me. "Lieutenant, good to see you. You must have left at the crack of dawn. I'd like you to meet Dr. Nora Gold, forensic anthropologist. She's not only agreed to help us out with this case—she's kept us at it through most of the night."

Nora Gold and I shook hands. Her warm brown eyes were surrounded by clusters of radiating laugh lines, and she had an engaging, almost mischievous smile. I guessed her to be somewhere in her fifties.

I nodded toward the bones. "Has he confessed yet?"

Dr. Gold chuckled. "To some things, he has."

I looked at her for a moment, hoping for some good news at last. "How much can he tell us?"

"Have you ever dealt with forensic anthropology before, or someone practicing its particular form of witchcraft?"

"No, but I've read or heard about some of the things you can do."

"Well, one of the things that lots of people find frustrating is the amount we have to equivocate. They think the Ph.D. and the lab coat make us purveyors of the truth. We aren't. Forensic anthropology is more an interpretive art than it is an exact science. It depends almost entirely on statistical analysis and probability—number crunching, to put it simply. For example, when I say this fellow is a male, I actually mean I'm eighty percent sure of it. There's an outside chance it's a female.''

I pushed out my lower lip and sighed gently. The Ph.D. and lab coat had certainly gotten me to expect more.

Nora Gold patted my arm and looked up at me, still smiling. I noticed then that Hillstrom was looking amused, as well. ''Lieutenant, that was the limited-warranty speech. I actually do think we can help you out here, but I didn't want you taking everything you hear from me as gospel. Okay?''

''Okay,'' I agreed tentatively.

She gave my arm one last squeeze and then rubbed her hands together, turning toward the photographs and the X rays covering the wall-mounted light boxes. ''Here we go, then. There are six things we can evaluate when we have a specimen as complete as this one: sex, age, height, weight, race, and handedness. Some of those, we can nail down pretty well; others are almost flights of fancy. Sex,'' she added pointedly, ''is pretty solid.

''Now, I won't give you a postgraduate lecture, but I think you ought to know that the validity of some of these conclusions is based on a massive amount of previous data. A few people over the past hundred years have measured thousands of skeletons they already knew a good deal about. The point of the exercise was that if they could find a set of common physical denominators in skeletons they knew were female, or black, or left-handed, or forty-five years old, or whatever, then later they could apply those denominators to skeletons they knew nothing about.'' She turned to the neat pile of bones on the table. ''Like our friend here.''

It was nice to hear. ''So he's a male, according to your guidelines.''

She smiled and rested the tips of her fingers on the darkened skeleton, as if feeling for a telltale pulse. ''Yes. What Bev and I were doing half the night was measuring almost every square inch of this poor man, taking X rays and tissue samples, even slicing him here and there to look at him under the microscope. What I can tell you with as much certainty as possible is that he was also Caucasian, almost exactly six feet tall, left-handed, and in his late twenties."

I understood the amount of effort both these people had put into this case. Not only was their homework decorating the walls all around us but I could see it in their tired faces. They had brought both their professional and personal interest to bear. And yet, despite that, I was disappointed. The description they'd furnished me could have fit a sizable percentage of the population.

I did my best to keep my ambivalence to myself. "Interesting. What makes you think he's left-handed?"

"The long bones. Actually, you hit on one of the lesser strengths of this science. A lot of the study skeletons I mentioned came from military conflicts, in which official records supplied the comparative data. Unfortunately, handedness is not recorded as a relevant vital statistic, so we've had to establish a standard through other means, mostly by comparing the number of living right- and left-handers to a similar mathematical discrepancy among skeletons. What we found was that living left-handers make up the same percentage of the overall population as the percentage of skeletons with elongated, more torsioned left humerus bones, who also have a distinct beveling of the dorsal margin of the glenoid cavity in their left clavicles.

"Translated into English, it means that if you spend your life throwing balls with one arm instead of the other, the bones and the shoulder blade of that arm show the effects."

I nodded without comment, causing Dr. Gold to suggest, with the friendliest of smiles, "You expected much more, didn't you?"

"No, no. I mean, I had nothing before—"

She interrupted me. "Well, there is more. I wouldn't say that in a courtroom, but Bev's spent half the night singing your praises, so I think I can trust you."

I laughed and shook my head, realizing I was being thoroughly manipulated. On the other hand, if they did have more to offer, having it fed to me in bits and pieces was a small price to pay for their satisfaction.

"In addition to the six categories of physical appearance I

described to you, there are also two other factors that leave their marks on a person's anatomy—environmental influences and historical landmarks. Examples of each would be a man who worked in a granite quarry all his life, and whose teeth were therefore evenly worn by the stone dust he'd been unconsciously grinding all his life, or a person whose case of childhood rickets left him with a pair of permanently curved legs.''

She moved to the end of the table and picked up a femur. ''What we found trespasses into both those areas, although I'd weight it more as historical in origin.'' She pointed to a rough rippling at the bottom end of the femur. ''See this? It's where the gastrocnemius—the calf muscle—attaches to the distal head of the femur, or thighbone, just above the knee joint. That muscle, as you know, tightens up when you stand on your toes. In fact, its major function is to help us pushing off, as you would at the start of a sprint. Of course, all the other muscles of the upper and lower leg play a part, too, but that tiptoe gesture plays most heavily in the calf. Well, over the years, we've discovered that a certain repetitive muscular movement sometimes irritates the proximal end of the gastrocnemius, to where it finally scars the bone at the point of attachment.''

''What do you mean?'' I asked, a little lost, ''Bouncing around on . . .'' I paused and smiled. ''A ballet dancer?''

She laughed at my amazement but cautioned me with a hand gesture. ''Maybe. I can show you the evidence and I can tell you how we've linked it to a certain activity in the past, but it's up to you to draw the conclusions.''

She pointed to one of the skeleton's heels. ''There's something else. Notice how this small bony ledge extends forward from the calcaneus, the heel bone? That's a spur. He has one on each heel. They don't look serious, so it's very possible he never knew he had them, but they are suggestive of another kind of chronic activity.''

''But not ballet?''

''No—remember, the stress there occurs when the dancer's on his toes. This comes about more often from pounding the heel repetitively.''

''Jogging?''

She straightened with a pleased expression on her face. "Excellent, although the 'buyer beware' warning still applies. Other things can cause the same spur to develop."

"But you've connected this thing to jogging more than to anything else," I persisted.

"I have, and so have others. There definitely is a pattern."

"Okay. You mentioned you could establish how much he weighed." There was no longer any need to control the tone of my voice. Even with her repeated caveats, Nora Gold had done a good deal to rekindle my spirits. As ghostly as his identity still was, the man on the table was beginning to fill out in my mind.

Beverly Hillstrom, who had been sitting on a stool throughout our conversation, wagged a finger at her friend. "I told you he'd hold you to that."

"All right, all right," Gold conceded. "You picked the weakest of my magic tricks. I can mutter about probabilities and sliding scales and margins of error on all the rest of this, but I can't call my estimate of his weight anything other than a pure guess." She then gave me a theatrically imperious look. "A highly educated guess, of course. It boils down to this: How many fat ballet dancers do you know? None, right? Here was a man in his late twenties, with two historic landmarks indicating strenuous physical activity. I have a tough time imagining him as anything other than fit and muscular, which, if true, would then put him in the one-eighty to two-hundred-pound category, more or less. That's the full extent of the science on that one."

"Reasonable enough, though," I murmured.

"See?" Gold turned to her friend, "I told you he'd buy it. I have to admit, though, there was another factor that led me to guess that weight, but it has only to do with ego—his, not mine."

She picked up the skull without the jawbone and held it out to me upside down, so that I was looking down at the upper row of perfectly aligned, even teeth. "Look at the right incisor, from the inside."

I did so, and noticed a faint diagonal line separating the crown of the tooth from its base.

"It's been broken, mostly from the back of the tooth, and replaced with a sort of dental modeling epoxy—a plastic resin that can be molded right on the break, and shaped and colored to look just like the real McCoy. From the front, it's a perfect match, but dentists usually don't put the same effort into fixing the posterior side, for obvious reasons."

"I thought they capped broken teeth."

"They often do, but this tooth wasn't so much broken as seriously chipped. It wasn't dead, and the chip hadn't exposed its roots to decay. In fact, he might have wandered around with a chipped tooth for years before getting it fixed. The point I'm getting at is that the dentistry is purely cosmetic, and that it was done to an otherwise-perfect set of teeth—there's not a single filling here. That's both very rare and a natural source of pride in a perfection-driven society."

I looked at her quizzically, never having given teeth much social significance before, unless they were moss-covered and stinking of rot.

"Remember who we have here: an athlete, who runs enough to cause bone spurs; a dancer, who, despite a recurring muscle tenderness, persists in his art; and a man with perfect teeth, who goes to the trouble of fixing a chipped tooth. I think our friend here kept one eye on the mirror. That's the other reason I think he was slim and muscular—his ego demanded it of him."

"What about the metal knee?" I asked finally. "He couldn't have been a ballet dancer with that."

"That's true. I think he was dead before he had a chance to get the knee back to full operational order."

That sent a tingle down my back. "He died right after surgery?"

"Within a couple of months of it. Bone is dynamic tissue, remodeling itself over the years. That's how we can gauge things like age—cranial sutures continue to close until we're eighty years old. That's what explains how we can recover from a broken leg or arm: The bone reunites, growing back together sometimes to form a bond that's stronger than before. When a surgeon puts in an artificial knee, he removes the ends of the bones to each side of the joint with a saw, exposing the marrow-filled hollow shaft that he partially fills with bone cement—like predrilling screw holes in wood before mounting a door hinge.

"With a door, though, nothing happens where the metal hinge touches the wood. The metal might rust a bit, and the wood might swell in the dampness, but they remain two separate entities, as does the sawdust, unless you or a breeze removes it. With bone, it's different; over time, it begins to heal over, removing the rough edges of the cut, along with any residual blood, and also reabsorbing the minute shards of bone dust that were created by the surgeon's saw blade.

"Here, however, there was very little healing. The line where the bone ends and the metal begins is only a couple of months old at the most. The residual blood has been reabsorbed, which takes a few weeks, but microscopic remnants of bone dust remain. Also, I could still see the striations left behind by the surgeon's saw—not fresh, but again, not very old."

I shook my head, amazed at my luck. "There's no way you could know why the knee was replaced?"

She smiled regretfully. " 'Fraid not, Lieutenant. Could have been any number of things. There was one additional aspect I thought was odd, though."

I looked at her carefully. "What was that?"

For the first time, she seemed slightly hesitant. "Well, it's trespassing into an area I really know nothing about, so there's probably a perfectly mundane explanation for it, but one last indicator that this surgery took place slightly before his death is the amount of leachate surrounding the bone cement. Normally, after an operation like this, the cement, as it sets, leaches out somewhat over the next few months. The leachate is carried away and cleansed by the circulatory system."

"And here you found some leachate still hanging around?"

I could tell by her tone that there was a little more to it. "Yes, that's true, and it helped corroborate my time estimate based on the bone fragments, but it was the leachate itself that caught my eye. It looked different from what I'm used to. Now, I admit, it's not every day that I have a skeleton with a prosthesis implanted, so I'm hardly an expert in the field, but still, it made me wonder. So I did a scraping and had the cement analyzed. The results came back just before you got here. It turns out the cement was a slurry of sorts, heavily impregnated with antibiotics.''

"And that's not normal?'' I asked.

She gave me a rueful smiled and shrugged. "That's just it. I don't know, and I haven't had time to check around. Bev's the only physician I had immediately available, but she didn't know, either.''

I immediately thought of Michael Brook, Ellen's old doctor, and the man who had hoped to operate on Abraham Fuller. He was both old enough to have been practicing back in the sixties and experienced enough to at least get me started in the right direction. "Were there any markings on the knee? Something I could use to trace it?''

She pulled a piece of paper out of her lab coat and gave it to me. "Two separate numbers. I have to admit, though, I'm not sure how useful they'll be. I don't know if they're serial numbers or not.''

I glanced at them, one with four digits, a dash, and two more, the other starting with a letter, followed by three digits. I shoved the paper into my pocket; that would make another question to ask Brook. "How about the way he looked? Can't you reconstruct a face from the skull?''

She shrugged. "You can. Some of the same people who spent their lives measuring bones also took fresh cadavers and stuck pins into their faces, trying to determine if there were any common denominators between peoples' skin thicknesses. There are reams of figures for chins and foreheads and cheekbones and upper and lower lips. The cadavers must have been wonderful to look at afterward. Needless to say, this was done in the good old days, and not to the aristocracy, either.''

She grabbed a stool at this point and sat, giving a small shrug. "In answer to your question, I can't really answer. I don't think much of the technique myself, but others have had success with it. Clyde Snow, one of the giants in the business, once tested how accurate reconstructions could be. He had one done of a male skull, took a photograph of it, and then placed that photo on a poster with seven other head shots, one of which was actually the real guy. People were asked to match the clay reconstruction to the original. Of two hundred guesses, one hundred and thirty-five were right. Pretty good numbers.''

"So why don't you like the system?"

"How often have you seen two faces that really look the same? Like twins? It's pretty rare. But can you say the same about two skulls? Even to us, they look pretty similar—we have to work hard just to tell the girls from the boys. I don't know how you can slap some clay on a bone and make it look like the original; there're just too many variables, from scars to fat to facial hair. I've always felt that reconstructions are expensive and time-consuming shots in the dark.''

I smiled at her conviction. ''I guess I won't ask you to recommend a sculptor.''

She chuckled then. ''Oh, I wouldn't mind. It's just that you can get so much solid information from remains like these, and still people jump up and down for the Hollywood special effects.''

I waved my hands in protest. ''Not me. I'm quite content. I do have to ask the big question, though. What killed him?''

''At last,'' Hillstrom exclaimed, throwing up her hands.

Nora Gold began to laugh.

I stared at both of them, nonplussed.

''Nora promised me that if you asked for the cause of death,'' Hillstrom explained, ''I, as medical examiner, could have the honors. Otherwise, I'd never get to say anything.''

I looked at them both quizzically.

''You'll have to excuse us. We are old, old friends. . . .''

''And very, very tired,'' Gold added.

Over the years, I had become genuinely fond of Beverly Hillstrom, despite a professional coolness that I took merely as her style but that others often misinterpreted as barely veiled hostility. Seeing her cutting up with her small dynamo of a friend reinforced my appreciation of her and marked, I thought, a small turning point in our friendship. I doubted she would have let many people see her so relaxed.

Hillstrom moved to the skeleton's chest, putting her finger on a neat hole slightly below the center of the sternum. ''In my opinion, Lieutenant, a single bullet killed him, or at least could have. This hole fits the bullet we recovered to a tee, and the breakout pattern on the inside is entirely consistent with a bullet wound. Also, bone growth stopped at the time trauma was inflicted; none of the remodeling Nora mentioned earlier happened here. However, since we don't actually have any soft tissue to consult, I can't swear that the bullet hit his heart in a lethal fashion. But that's what I think happened.''

I pointed to several broken ribs. ''What about these?''

She pursed her lips. ''Those are from last night's ambush. We didn't find a single indication of any old trauma beyond the one bullet hole, which encourages me to think the cardiac wound was the culprit. But who can tell? He could have had half his midsection removed by a simultaneous shotgun blast without a scratch left on his skeleton.''

''But you're not saying he might have died of pneumonia or scarlet fever or something nonhomicidal, are you?''

''My opinion is homicide, and that's what's going on the certificate. But anything's possible when you have this little to work on.''

I turned to Dr. Gold. ''How long would you guess he'd been underground?''

She made a face at that. ''That's a tough one—it depends so much on the burial site. Quite a few years, certainly.''

''Closer to five, or twenty-five?''

''Longer rather than shorter. Fifteen to twenty years wouldn't be out of line—possibly more.''

There was a long pause as we all found ourselves staring at the remains of our now certified murder victim, the stillness of his tarnished bones in violent contradiction to the manner of his death.

Dr. Gold laid her hand on my arm gently. ''We've told you everything we can. We'll be giving you the photos and the X rays and whatever else you need and you'll be on your own; so I was wondering if I could ask you a favor.''

''Sure—anything.''

''Tell me what happened—tell me who he was.''

I squeezed her hand and looked back at the skeleton, realizing for the first time the bonds she established with each of her ''patients'' in order to do her work well. It was a startling glimpse at the humanity that underlay professions like hers and Beverly Hillstrom's—occupations that were at best regarded with ghoulish curiosity.

"If I ever find out, I will."

Chapter Fourteen

I drove straight from Burlington to Brattleboro Memorial Hospital, not bothering to check in at the office. What Nora Gold and Beverly Hillstrom had given me was the breakthrough I'd been hungering for—tangible evidence linking the skeleton, and therefore Abraham Fuller, to a concrete historical event. If I was lucky, the metal knee would not only lead to the surgeon who'd implanted it but to the identity of the skeleton, and possibly that of last night's sniper, whose desperate attempt to destroy the knee had given my hopes a boost.

I found Michael Brook where his nurse said I would, in the hospital cafeteria—a small, pleasant, sunlit room with one window looking out on the parking lot and another overseeing the front lobby. It was one of the town's best-kept secrets: a low-priced, high-quality, friendly place to eat that was rarely crowded.

Mike was sitting by the outside window, his artificial leg stuck straight under the chair opposite him, finishing up a chicken-salad sandwich. It was well beyond the lunch hour, and there were only two other people in the place, sitting together in a far corner.

"Joe," he called out, "you've been grabbing headlines again."

He pulled a rolled up newspaper from his lab coat pocket and slapped it on the table. CARS RIDDLED BY SNIPER ON I-91, the headline screamed. There were pictures of the burial scene, a shot of the hearse on the interstate, and one of Red, our tracker dog, sitting on his butt, looking bored.

Mike hoisted his leg out of the way and I sat across the small table from him. "You got a couple of minutes?"

"Sure. This is my afternoon off. I was about to get rid of some paperwork. This about Fuller again?"

I shook my head and tapped the picture of the burial scene. "This."

His eyes widened. "The skeleton? Who was it?"

"I've just spent the morning with Hillstrom and a forensic anthropologist friend of hers, trying to find out. I got an amazing amount of information from them, but a couple of things came up I was hoping you could help me with."

He finished off his Coke and sat back. "Shoot."

"The skeleton was outfitted with an artificial knee."

An interested grin appeared between the mustache and the beard. "So I read."

"Well, the anthropologist figures the guy died within a few months of getting that knee. . . ."

"Of an infection?"

"No, no. He was shot; as far as I know, the operation went fine. But Nora Gold, the anthropologist, thought the leachate from the bone cement looked a little odd, so she had it analyzed. Turns out it was heavily laced with antibiotics."

Brook stared at me for a long moment without moving. "Why was the knee put in?" he finally asked.

"We don't know yet."

He turned his gaze toward the window and scratched his whiskered cheek absentmindedly. "Huh. Did Nora Gold— or Hillstrom, for that matter—notice if any other kind of surgical procedure had been done on the leg?"

"They didn't mention it if they did. I looked at the thing and it seemed clean as a whistle, except for the fancy metalwork. Why?"

"Just kicking a few ideas around in my head. What about the general condition of the guy. Could they tell if he'd been healthy, or suffering from hemophilia or TB?"

"No; in fact, Gold's guess was he was a jock—a runner, a ballet dancer. She even hypothesized he'd had a bit of an ego, which further helped to keep him trim."

He chuckled at that. "So, the ego's in the bones. I always wondered. Look, let's assume she's right—that he was a perfectly healthy, normal specimen. That means the knee was a result of trauma. Now, normally, a patient comes in with his knee shattered, we open it up, clean it out, and let it sit for a few days, watching and treating for infection, which is almost a given in those cases. Then, we might even fuse the joint temporarily while we scratch our heads about the next move. To make a long story short, the guy's left dangling for quite a while before we finally decide to slip him a metal knee, assuming that's what we opt for. Then, we cut a little here, drill a little there, dab on a bunch of cement, and put the whole thing together.

"The point is, by the time that happens, the infection-fighting stage—as a result of the wound, that is—is over, so there's no need for antibiotics in the cement."

He crossed his arms over his chest and gave me a satisfied look.

"That may mean something to you, Mike, but it don't mean squat to me."

He laughed loudly, drawing stares from the other table and giggles from the counter servers. "Right, right. I guess it wouldn't. The point is, the only justification for a surgeon to apply a cement mixed with antibiotics is because he slapped the joint in right off the bat, with the wound still fresh. Very jazzy thing to do—also a bit foolish, for my money. Nowdays, with all those hungry lawyers running around, you'd have to have your head examined."

"Those bones were twenty years old."

He grew animated with interest. "The bonanza years. Between 1965 and 1975, there were about two hundred and fifty different knee designs out there. Everybody with a slide rule and a lathe was cranking them out. Then the FDA got twitchy and brought down the hammer. You wouldn't have a picture of the thing, would you?"

I smiled at his enthusiasm, and my own good fortune. I opened the manila envelope Nora Gold had prepared for me and slid out the glossies of the knee assembly.

Brook studied them intently. "Can't say I recognize it; probably built by one of the companies that went under. Big son of a gun—no wonder the metal detector sniffed it out."

I was going to ask him how he knew about the detector,

then remembered the newspaper. ''They don't make them that big anymore?''

''They do—I'm not crazy about the hinged style, but there're plenty of 'em around, mostly made of a cobalt, chrome, molybdenum alloy.'' He put the photos down. ''They used to make airplane turbine blades out of that stuff in the late forties.''

I pulled the slip of paper Nora Gold had given me out of my pocket. ''These numbers were on the knee. They mean anything to you?''

He glanced at them. ''Not offhand; probably a catalog number followed by a lot number. Companies put these on for their own benefit, using patients as guinea pigs, in a way. If the implant fails, they get it back, check those two numbers, and trace it back to its origin to find out why it crapped out. They're always fooling with one aspect or another, changing alloy mixes or designs.''

''Can you tell who the manufacturer was?'' I asked hopefully.

He stuck a lower lip out and I expected the worst. ''Don't see why not,'' he said, surprising me. ''See the first number, the one with the 03 after the hyphen? That's probably the catalog number. Generally, the first digit or two of the catalog number identifies the product—in this case an artificial-knee assembly. Each company has a different product identifier, so their device won't be confused with another company's. All we need to do is find the manufacturer's catalog in which this number stands for knee assemblies.''

I couldn't keep the skepticism from my voice. ''Won't that mean locating the twenty-year-old catalogs of all two hundred and fifty manufacturers?''

He pushed himself up out of his chair, completely unruffled. ''No problem. I've got 'em all—all the way back to 1948.''

I stood also. ''Every catalog?''

He laughed at my expression. ''Yup. Knees, hips, elbows, wrists, ankles—you name it. They're just like any other catalog you get in the mail. Don't ask me why, but I never throw 'em away—kept every one I ever received.''

He led the way down the hall, detailing the mania that had

driven him to save volume upon volume of useless literature, but I was only half-listening. My mind was already leaping ahead to petitioning Brandt for travel papers for wherever this kneecap factory might be.

I should have curbed my enthusiasm. Michael Brook's description of his collection paled by comparison to the real thing. He had an entire room dedicated to it, lined with bookcases and piled with cardboard boxes. There were medical journals, books, magazines, and ream upon ream of catalogs for everything under the medical sun.

I froze on the threshold, daunted by the number of days I thought I'd be spending here, and already convinced the search would be fruitless.

Brook, however, didn't even pause. He went straight to a particular shelf and beckoned me to join him. "All right, this shelf holds catalogs from about twenty years ago, give or take five. You start from one end and I'll start from the other. The trick is to check the contents for knee replacements, or anything having to do with knees, go to that part of the catalog, and see if the first two digits of the first item match what you've got. If they don't, then you know you've got the wrong company. If you get a match, then all we have to do is concentrate on that one company's catalogs. Shouldn't take over half an hour."

To my relief, he was right—even pessimistic. Twenty minutes later, he slapped a single catalog on the wooden table in the center of the room. "There you go—Articu-Tech, 1969, located in Boston. Course that's good news/bad news."

"Why?" I asked as I opened the catalog and flipped to the right page.

"Because while Boston's nearby, Articu-Tech's out of business. Has been for years."

I pulled Nora Gold's photo back out of the manila envelope and laid it next to the glossy black-and-white illustration before me. They were one and the same. The sense of victory I felt completely obliterated any gloom I might have felt from Michael's "bad news." To me, seeing that knee assembly was like finding a long-lost murder weapon. I felt I was on a roll, as I had since I'd left Burlington, and, indeed, as I'd been hoping I would be since we'd found the unmarked grave.

I flipped back to the front of the catalog and looked at the masthead. There was an address, along with the names of three people: the CEO/president, the vice president in charge of sales, and the treasurer. I looked up at Brook, who was beaming like a proud parent. "All right, assuming I find one of these people, or someone else who could help me, and assuming they still have all their records, would the lot number show me who bought this particular knee?" I tapped the photo Gold had taken.

Michael shrugged. "Maybe, but probably not. It might tell you who sold it, though. Articu-Tech was pretty big in its day and had its own sales force. The lot-number files should indicate which direction the knee went. Then you'd probably have to canvass the hospitals or surgeon's offices that particular salesman covered to find your specific knee. It shouldn't be all that bad, though. Remember, with all those assemblies flooding the market, no one of them was a runaway bestseller. Individual lot numbers usually covered only a few units."

I closed the catalog and straightened my back. "You've been a scholar and a gentleman, Michael. Can I borrow this?"

"Sure—you kidding? You've just justified my keeping the whole mess."

I went home first, instead of back to the office. Although it was only midafternoon and I needed to know if the dozen or so feelers we had out had snagged anything, I needed a little peace and quiet and the chance to see if I could make any headway on the Articu-Tech lead.

I sat down in a lumpy, ancient, but very comfortable leather armchair nestled in the embrace of one of the apartment's three bay windows. Besides my bed, this is where I spent the majority of my time at home. The light was good, the curved enclosure allowed me to surround myself with a table, a bookcase, a reading lamp, and a phone, all within equal reach, and I could also look up when the whim required and cast an eye across most of my domain.

I'd lived in this apartment for more years than I could recall. It was old and not dressed up by any means, but with the odd grace note that told of an earlier splendor: panes of leaded glass here and there, dark wood wainscoting throughout, slightly uneven, trowel-applied plaster on the walls. From the outside, these subtleties had been flattened into submission by a long-gone remodeler with little money and no taste, who'd converted a once-majestic Victorian into a three-floor apartment building. Presumably, the gingerbread, the fancy ironwork, and the broad, shady porches that had once given the building its flair had been condemned as too much to keep up. Their removal had left a forlorn blandness behind.

But the innards—especially the top floor, where I lived, and which had been the least touched of all—had retained the soul of that earlier gentility. I'd done little to help the situation, admittedly. I had no interest in interior decorating. But over the years, the house and I had blended somewhat, so that my garage-sale furnishings probably fitted in better than the antiques that had once lived here. Also, there were my books and the shelves that supported them, both of which helped bridge the cultural gap between the building's highborn beginnings and my own humble tastes. Reflecting a lifetime of eclectic interests, the books rested everywhere, from proper bookcases that lined almost every wall, to tabletops and counters, windowsills and closets. Among them all was a battered portable television set that was turned on during my gloomiest moments, when other mental support systems had crashed; but the books were my best company, along with the classical music I would play gently in the background when I read.

I parked Michael Brook's catalog on my lap, open at the masthead, and placed the phone before me.

Simply dialing the number listed as the Articu-Tech headquarters proved too optimistic by far, as Michael had warned me it would be. The receptionist answering identified the company as a computer software company, stated she'd never heard of Articu-Tech, and maintained she'd been answering this number for the past ten years.

At first, Directory Assistance was no help, either. They

didn't list the company or the man identified in the catalog as its CEO and president. They also had nothing for the vice president. The treasurer, however, was listed, or at least someone with the same name.

It was not a man's voice, though, that answered the phone, but a woman's, tired and blurry. The treasurer was known to her—in fact, he'd walked out on her eighteen years earlier, right after the company had gone belly-up. That had left her with a big house, a fancy car, and a lot of unpaid bills. She had no idea where he was, but it was far enough away that they'd never been able to slap a subpoena on him, and she'd didn't give a damn any more, anyhow.

I commiserated with her, lending an ear to her tale of economic disintegration, before gently turning the conversation to the people he'd worked with. It was a long time ago, she stressed, but there had been one guy—Hank Broca—she still saw on the street every once in a blue moon. Maybe I could find him.

I did, again through the operator—or more precisely, I found his wife, who gave me his work number.

"Articu-Tech?" Broca repeated back to me. "Wow. I haven't heard that name in a while. I worked for 'em, all right—more like a summer job, for the amount of time it lasted."

"Oh?" I said, trying to sound as encouraging as possible.

But Hank Broca didn't need much prompting. "Well, all right, maybe it was a year, but time flies when you're playing fast and loose, the way they did. Not that I knew that when I joined up. But, you know, fresh out of graduate school, full of hopes—Christ, I had no idea what they were up to."

"What was that, Mr. Broca?"

"Hank. I still don't know everything. I just know it put us all out of work. You gotta remember, of course, it was the go-go sixties. Companies like Articu-Tech were a dime a dozen; every engineer with a design for a hip, knee, wrist, or whatever hung out a shingle and made a grab for a million bucks. No surprise most of the companies went broke, and no surprise most of the designs didn't hold up and that the feds came down hard."

"Was the Articu-Tech knee any good?"

There was a stunned silence, and I immediately regretted my question. "Which one?"

I flipped to the right page and read the catalog number to him.

"Oh. That one was okay. That was more an adaptation than a true design; the Germans had put one out like it years before."

"What did you do for Articu-Tech?"

"I'm a mechanical engineer—was for them, too, a cheap one. I ain't so cheap no more." He laughed with great self-contentment.

"Did you work on this particular knee?"

For the first time, I sensed caution on his part. He had not, so far, even asked me why I was calling, nor had I had a real chance to tell him. "Why do you want to know?"

"I'm a policeman up in Vermont. We've just dug up a twenty-year-old skeleton with that particular knee implant, and I need to put a name to the skeleton."

The caution vanished as quickly as it had arrived. "No shit. Really? That's amazing. You know what I thought at first?"

"What's that?"

"I thought you were a lawyer representing some poor slob with a sour implant. You know how people get: As soon as something like that goes wrong, they forget about the ten years of pain-free activity it gave them, and they try to sue you because they jumped off a ladder one too many times and screwed up the works. It ain't like a real knee—we tell 'em that from the start. You got to take care of it."

"Mr. Broca, I don't want to tie you up too long, but I was wondering how I could find out who bought that particular knee."

"Please—Hank. Boy, that's a tall order."

I waited for more, but nothing came. "Did you keep in touch with any of the people you worked with back then? Maybe someone in sales?"

He laughed again. "Hey, I know. Give me that lot number again. There was one guy—a lawyer. I always thought he was about the only straight shooter among them. He was real twitchy about lawsuits, although I never heard of one being filed against Articu-Tech. I'll give him a buzz and see what I can find out. You got a phone number?"

"I'm calling from home at the moment. Maybe I better give you my office number."

"No, no. Sit tight. This'll only take a few minutes. We're not great friends, but I know where to find this guy. I'll call you right back."

I gave him the number and waited. He was true to his word; ten minutes later, he called back.

"Told you—back in a flash. There were three pieces in that lot, and all of 'em were sold in Chicago."

I was amazed. "The lawyer knew that?"

His laugh almost deafened my ear. "Hah. Pretty good, huh? I told you he was twitchy? He kept all the files—there weren't that many, anyhow. See, he went with the firm that bought most of the bits and pieces of Articu-Tech after they folded. I don't know if that meant they also bought the liability if something went wrong with an implant, but I figured this guy was the type to think that way, just to be on the safe side. I mean, we're talking major compulsive here, right? I gave him the number and he pulled the file, like he had it right under his hand. Must be weird being married to a mind like that, huh?"

"He didn't say where in Chicago, or who, did he?"

"Oh, no—I could've told you that. They didn't give a damn about that part of it. The records only reflected what was interesting to them—the design evolution, the alloy mixes used, stuff like that. They didn't track who bought 'em. I asked who the sales rep was, just for laughs—I mean, you never know, right? But he drew a blank. Chicago's the best I can tell you, and all three of 'em sold, so it shouldn't be too hard to locate who put the one in your skeleton. Hey, tell me something. What did your guy die of?"

It was obviously payoff time, which he had richly deserved. It made me sad not only to disappoint him but to mislead him, as well. "Can't say. We think he died of a heart attack, hunting in the woods. We just have to get an ID on him. Pretty routine, I'm afraid. By the way, do you have an approximate date when the implants were delivered to the Chicago area?"

"Yeah, early '69."

"Would that mean that the knee was put in around the same time? Or can things like that sit on the shelf for a long time?"

"Beats me. You may have to go to Chicago to find that out."

Chapter Fifteen

I found Tony Brandt where his secretary said he would be, sitting alone on the glassed-in second-floor balcony of the Common Ground Restaurant, overlooking Elliot Street. It was just after 4:30 in the afternoon, and the place was officially closed, except for the odd tea drinker who could serve himself from a side counter lined with a wide variety of leaf-filled jars. The Common Ground was a perfectly preserved throwback to the 1960s, serving a full line of Indian-influenced vegetarian meals sporting strange names and sometimes stranger appearances. It was an unusual place for a cop—which partially explained Brandt's presence. He was rarely one to do the expected.

He was sitting at a small corner table, where he could watch the street below, holding a mug in both hands, just below his chin, so he could fully catch the aroma. "Hi, Joe," he said without surprise.

I pulled out the chair opposite him and sat down. "Hi, yourself. What're you drinking?"

He glanced down at the mug. "Don't know. The label was too long to read; tastes good, though. How was Burlington?"

"I think it's given me the only strong lead we've got."

"Will it give us last night's shooter?"

"Maybe, in a roundabout way."

"How roundabout?" His eyes were still on the street, which I could see reflected in his rimless glasses.

"Chicago in the late sixties."

He looked at me and smiled thinly. "Time travel? They'll love the voucher on that one."

He finally put the cup down and sat back in his chair, his arms crossed. "All right, give me the guided tour."

"Fred Coyner's wife died in 1970, after her cancer wiped out the family finances."

Brandt nodded, having read the updated reports.

"But right after her death, Coyner settled all his debts, from what we can tell, just about the time Abraham Fuller set up camp in his back forty. Considering the amount of money we found at Fuller's, it seems likely he paid off Coyner to hide him. I think that's what Fuller meant when he accused Coyner of a 'breach of faith' for calling the ambulance."

"All right."

"There are more people involved in this than just Fuller, as our little encounter with the machine gunner made clear. . . ."

Brandt shook his head. "Hold it; couldn't that have been Coyner? Didn't you think he'd taken the chart?"

"Yes, yes, but bear with me, okay? There are a lot of coincidences involving 1969 that go well beyond Coyner. Coyner, after all, we can account for up to 1970. The money in Fuller's possession, thanks to the bank bands, can be dated back to '69, and so can the artificial knee. Hillstrom and her anthropologist pal swear the guy wearing it died within a few months of the operation. Also, the ammunition used in the ambush last night was made in 1967, and while Hillstrom can't swear that Fuller's original wound is older than five years, she did say that, based on her experience, she'd guess it was much older. Long story short, an amazing amount of shit was hitting the fan back then, and I don't think Fred Coyner played a bigger role than landlord in any of it."

Brandt merely shrugged.

I leaned forward. "All right. Why would Coyner steal the chart? It's not his—the birth date is all wrong—and the astrologer I consulted pegged the chart owner as a neurotic loner, and maybe a homosexual male. Coyner was married for decades and almost flipped out when his wife died. If the chart was Fuller's, which does sound more likely, it still makes no sense, 'cause he's already dead and there'd be no point stealing it, unless, of course, it either meant a great deal to somebody—like a grieving lover, maybe—or it implicated someone.

"In any case, all three of those possibilities point to a missing person—the same person Fuller left a message for when he circled the title of *The Scarlet Letter* with blood from his fingertip."

"All right," Brandt conceded, "maybe there is a missing player; why Chicago?"

"I just came from the office. So far there's been no feedback on the bank notes, or on Fuller's face and prints, or on any unsolved twenty-year-old shootings. Nor have we found any medical facility or doctor who admits treating a wound like Fuller's back then. On the prints, we haven't heard from the FBI officially yet, but I called a contact there and he told me to forget it. And the Secret Service came up blank on the money—as far as they're concerned, it's clean.

"Now, Richard Schimke—he's the money expert I talked to at the bank—says those hundred-dollar bills came from the West and the Midwest, not from around here, and we confirmed that with the Secret Service. Finally, I traced that skeleton's metal knee to a company called Articu-Tech, which sold three like it in the Chicago area in 1969. It seems reasonable to me that at least some of the answers to this case are out there. It was pretty obvious that whoever took those shots at us last night wanted to destroy the skeleton; I think it's because he was afraid the knee would point us to Chicago. If nothing else, I ought to be able to come up with an I.D. for the guy in the grave."

Brandt thought all that over for a few moments, gently sliding his cup back and forth on the table before him. "What about the search for the shooter?"

I shook my head. "Nothing. Kunkle's the best on that kind of digging, and he warned us to expect little or less. He says there aren't even ripples out on the street—his contacts are as curious as we are about it."

Brandt made a face, rose to his feet, and began heading

for the door. "Okay, you got it—one trip to Chicago. I'll give you a week to match that kneecap to a name."

Gail rested against the headboard of my bed, sitting cross-legged on both pillows, watching me as I packed. "Chicago. I've always wanted to go there. It's supposed to be wonderful."

"I doubt I'll get to enjoy the highlights. With my luck, I'll be stuck pawing through hospital medical records."

"I wish we could go together." Her voice was soft and wistful.

I paused to squeeze her foot. "I'll keep my eye peeled for hot spots. If it looks like a fun town, maybe we could go there on vacation sometime."

She smiled doubtfully and changed the subject, knowing from experience it never led anywhere. A small-town boy with a penchant for confusing work with pleasure, I didn't yearn for time off, nor did I feel comfortable far from home. It was a provincialism she often worked to erode, although not this time. "What ever happened with Billie? You never told me."

I made a disappointed face. "Not much. Apparently, a chart reveals more when you can compare it to the owner. She did spend a lot of time on it, though, especially tracing the birth date, but all I got was that we're looking for a screwed-up gay loner who was abused as a child by a mother he hated."

Gail looked startled, so I quickly covered for her friend. "I admit, I coerced most of that out of her. I got her to admit she'd seen the same kind of thing with a gay client of hers. She stressed you couldn't do that, but I was getting frustrated. To be honest, I think she was as glad to see the back of me as I was to give up on that chart."

She was obviously disappointed. "Do you still have it?"

Somewhat sheepishly, I pulled a folder out from the bottom of my suitcase and flipped it open. "Yeah. I thought I'd take it with me just in case. Maybe it was done out there." I located the colorful document and handed it to her.

She looked at it a long time. "It is a stressful chart. You

know, she's been at it a long time. Just because you were pushy doesn't mean you forced her to say things she didn't partly believe. Do you have a copy of this?''

"That is a copy. I had Harriet run off several color copies across the street, just in case I had to spread them around. Keep that one if you like."

"Thanks. Maybe I'll hit the books while you're gone. I love doing these things."

I smiled at her enthusiasm, and at her ability to pull herself out of the blues. I leaned over and kissed her. "Don't stop reading travel brochures."

Part Two

Part Two

Chapter Sixteen

I never realized how big Lake Michigan was until the plane's lowering wheels shook me awake. I instinctively glanced out the window. All I could see, clear to the razor-sharp horizon, was water.

The shoreline, when it did come into view, was verdant, well tended, and littered with golf courses—hardly the image I'd harbored of Carl Sandburg's famed "City of the Big Shoulders," which a glance out the opposite windows would have revealed stretching out to the south.

All of it quickly vanished, however, replaced by O'Hare's black-streaked pale runway shooting into view. Now the horizon consisted solely of chain-link fences, parking lots, and commercial buildings with bland fronts. There was no longer a tree in sight, nor an unsullied blade of grass.

The plane's approach, made over Chicago's affluent northern suburbs, slipped from me, half-remembered, leaving only wonder and a twinge of homesickness—this was as different from Vermont as I could imagine.

It was hard shrugging off an otherworldly sense as I drove along the interstate toward the center of town. The unusual flatness of my surroundings made the approaching city center, spiraling up toward the distant sky, seem unreal, like some gargantuan glass and metal stalagmite around which everything revolved. The Sears Tower, with its dramatically over-built twin antennae, was the aspiring apex, encircled by a cluster of increasingly stunted attendants, each supported by its slightly shorter neighbor until the outer ring faded into the horizontal landscape. It was a heroic image—bold, thrusting, heaven-bound and new—but at the same time strangely futile, encased as it was by that impassive, impenetrable, dismissively vast blue sky.

The sensation didn't last. The expressway came within reach and then broke free of downtown's gravitational pull, continuing south and away, eventually letting me peel off onto the side streets near South State, where the Chicago Police Department had its headquarters.

Here was a different environment entirely. Just beyond the city's grandiose and gaudy downtown, but several miles outside the reach of the old, abandoned stockyards and the notorious high-rise projects to the south, the police department held sway over a borderline demilitarized zone that appeared neither blighted nor truly viable. Whole buildings stood empty, their windows intact but blank, their smeared brick walls touting hand-painted advertisements of companies thirty years out of business. A rusted elevated railway roared and rattled with the rhythmic passing of commuter trains heading elsewhere. And yet there was some commerce—parking lots, a few small shops, a tired motel here and there—leftovers from what had obviously once been a much more muscular, healthy, but now-forgotten, section of town.

I parked my car on the wide, lightly traveled street and walked up the sidewalk toward my destination. The police headquarters building was a curious reflection of its surroundings. Its street-facing facade was a smooth, almost sleek, pale cement slab, regularly punctured by severe rectangular windows, looking like one of those old computer punch cards standing up on end. The rest of the building—most of its sides and its back—was old white-painted brick, bristling with air conditioners and a rusty fire escape zigzagging down to the parking lot. It was incongruous in appearance—half a face-lift—and made me wonder whether, like the neighborhood, the building was coming or going.

As I stood across the street from the building, waiting for a bus to pass, I was struck not only by the number of assertive-looking, cheaply dressed men who were using the front door but also by the number of parked cars that had that familiar lived-in look about them—paperbacks and windbreakers or hats on the rear seat, Styrofoam cups, sunglasses, and mashed cigarette packs littering the dashboards and floors. They looked like what they were: places where people sat for hours on end, observing, waiting, struggling to keep awake, as worn and familiar as the offices I was about to visit. It was like having my own provincial policeman's experience expanded and multiplied a hundredfold. It reminded me with a jolt just how enormous the contrast was between my own department and Chicago's, and yet how deep the similarities ran.

The lobby reminded me of the airport—barren, harsh, with signs and arrows, a uniformed officer at an information booth, and, to his right, a roped-off area corralling people through two metal detectors. There was an instant feeling of hostility and paranoia in the air.

I went to the patrolman in the booth and introduced myself, mentioning that I was supposed to meet with Chief of Detectives Donahue.

The cop stared at my shield and identity card as if they were poor forgeries, his wrinkled, vein-mapped face impassive. "Donahue, huh?"

"That's what I was told. My chief made the arrangements."

Finally, he handed back the ID, grinning. "Okay. Straight to the back, through those double glass doors. Didn't know they had cops in Vermont. You ski?"

"No," I lied, "I just shovel the stuff."

It hadn't been unfriendly, but it also hadn't been the fraternal embrace I'd hoped for in my heart. Of course, the man had been an older patrolman, set in his prejudices against detectives, no doubt, and he was part of a police force that had more cops in it than the entire state of Vermont. Still, it was a bit of a dampener, a reminder that a single Brattleboro policeman chasing down a twenty-year-old lead was not going to move anyone here to the edge of their chair.

I paused by the detector, uncertain whether to wait docilely in line or to flash my badge and go through the opening that was obviously reserved for cops.

The man ahead of me was a tourist, camera in hand, asking about public tours of the police department. The uniformed man opposite him, younger and more jovial than the one in the booth, shook his head. "Wouldn't know nothin' about it. Talk to PR, but you can't take the camera in."

The visitor stared at the camera, a small Instamatic. "Okay. Can I leave it with you while I ask?"

"Uh-uh. Might be a bomb."

The man's mouth fell open.

The cop smiled. "Sorry. If you came in your car, why don't you put it there and come back?"

The tourist left, shaking his head. I showed my badge and was waved through.

The receptionist beyond the advertised double doors gave me directions with a friendliness that quieted some of the "stranger in a strange land" qualms that had been nagging me, and set me off on my quest.

I found Donahue, or at least his secretary, four floors above; an hour later, I was ushered into his office. The wait hadn't bothered me. The secretary, as pleasant as her colleague downstairs, told me it would be a long time and urged me to poke around discreetly. This I did, wandering the halls and studying the bulletin boards. What I came away with, and took with me into Donahue's office, was an appreciation of the work load these people wrestled with. Never before had I seen such piles of case files, distributed among so many desks, being worked on by so many exhausted-looking people. Nor had I ever seen so many phones used simultaneously. By the time I was ushered over the chief's threshold, I was eternally grateful to be the small-town cop I was—despite the laughter and the familiar corridor high jinks that I'd also witnessed, the supposed allure of the "big time" just wasn't there.

Chief of Detectives Donahue was a short, gray-haired, burly man who smoked a cigar and sported a large Marine Corps ring. He was seated at an overloaded desk in an office decorated with calendars, roster sheets, and a row of clipboards hanging from nails in the wall.

"Lieutenant Gunther." It had been a statement of fact.

I nodded without speaking, which brought a thin smile to his lips. He stuck his hand out. "Glad to meet you. Have a seat. Your chief says you're checking out a metal knee on a twenty-year-old skeleton.''

"That's about it."

"You got any more than that?"

"Nope. I don't know who the skeleton is, I don't know when the knee was put in, and I don't know who might have put it in. I'm not even sure the procedure was done in Chicago, although I have been told the knee was sold here by the manufacturer.''

Donahue nodded. "You know where to look?"

"I figured I'd start asking around at the big hospitals.''

He frowned and shook his head, dropping the sheet of paper back onto his desk. "Well, good luck. You'll need it. I'm assigning you to Area Six—that's Commander Jeffers. You know the city at all?''

"I've got a good map.''

He handed me a small slip of note paper. "Belmont and Western. 2452 West Belmont, to be precise—that's about twenty blocks west of Wrigley Field and a little south. I'll tell him to expect you.''

He stood up and shook hands. The interview was over. I left without having the slightest idea what the system was I was obviously being plugged into or why my particular address within it was almost halfway back to the airport. Presumably, Commander Jeffers would be the enlightener on those subjects. As I crossed the street to get back to my car, I felt like a freshman on his first day on campus, being shuttled from office to office, accumulating scraps of information from a bureaucracy in full tilt that could just barely give me a few moments of its time. Still, I thought hopefully, he had known who I was.

According to the map, the quickest route to Area 6 was to retrace my way back up the Kennedy Expressway. But having already done that once, I decided to expand my horizons. I headed east toward the lake and took Lake Shore Drive north.

The contrast to my drive into Chicago was startling. Going up alongside Grant Park, by the Navy Pier, and through Lincoln Park above that, I was dazzled by how well the city met the shore. Paralleling a pristine, tree-filled no-man's-land between the distant serried ranks of downtown's elegant turn-of-the-century buildings and the enormous, dizzying, oceanlike emptiness of Lake Michigan, Lake Shore Drive affords a tourist's-eye view of urban development at its most beautiful. The vague sense I'd had earlier at the airport of infiltrating fresh air—a hint of nature's struggle against the spread of concrete—was here given full rein. The sky and water utterly dominated the scene, and yet the city—with its older, lower, more graceful buildings facing Grant Park and the taller, more futuristic obelisks of gleaming glass and metal just behind them and north of the river—held its own. From this theatrical angle, Chicago flaunted its own majesty. Unsheltered by the lee of a nearby friendly mountain range, as was Los Angeles, or tucked among the islands, rivers, and bays of New York, Chicago was merely there, on center stage, arrogantly exposed to the elements it had set out to challenge. It reminded me of Dallas—another city that existed solely because of the aggressive business drive of a country hell-bent on achievement.

I fought the allure of the many parking lots at the water's edge, and, leaving North Shore Drive, disappeared instead back into the city, impressed by how many times, in such a short time span, Chicago had shown me some totally different aspect of its character.

Behind Lincoln Park, away from the lake, I found the process continuing. From traveling between high rises on one side and sailboats and yachts on the other, I was now surrounded by buildings that for the most part seemed plucked from another town entirely. Rarely over three or four stories high, many of them hovering near a hundred years old, the landmarks of this neighborhood looked complacently ignorant of being surrounded by a far larger city. The variety of shops and restaurants, movie theaters and bars all pointed to a self-sustaining, thriving independence.

I continued west, losing some of that isolated security. The buildings became coarser, newer, more functional, and less gentrified. At the corners of Belmont, Western, and Clybourn, I paused before a small confusion of roads, cement buildings, and a shopping mall parking lot. Looming overhead, ominously omnipotent, a red-and-white radio tower stared down on us all. Near its foot, its low-slung, bland, modern brick walls absurdly set off by a hulking red-white-and-blue metal monstrosity of a sculpture, was the address I was seeking: Police Headquarters, Area 6, 19th District.

For the second time today, I parked and prepared to meet my hosts. There was a better feeling to it this time, though. For one thing, the neighborhood seemed friendlier—at least alive if not aesthetic—and for another, I was hoping that this might become my surrogate office, the launching pad for what I'd come to do here. Driving around Chicago from police station to police station had been educational, but it did nothing to answer the questions posed by those two bodies in Vermont.

The entrance to 2452 West Belmont was a lot less imposing than its big brother downtown. The metal detector was still there, but the atmosphere was more pleasant, and there were no comments about skiing.

As befitted the newer building, Commander Jeffers's office was also more user-friendly, as was its occupant, who actually came out to the reception area to greet me before I'd had a chance to sit down and who escorted me inside.

"Don't think we've ever had a police officer from Vermont before. Want some coffee?"

"No thanks."

He poured himself a cup from a counter behind his desk. "Donahue tells me you're chasing down an old kneecap—that you got squat to go on."

I laughed at the way my ambitions were being miniaturized and filled Jeffers in on the whole story, from Fuller's blown aneurysm to the machine-gun nest above I-91.

But by the end of it, like his State Street boss, Jeffers wasn't overly impressed. "So, you're basically here for a name and an address, both of which may be history by now."

"I'm also hoping to get a handle on what happened—the cash, the guns."

"But only if you're lucky."

I conceded the point. "Right."

That obviously pleased him, apparently settling some private, unvoiced question. He leaned forward and stabbed a button on his intercom. "Get me Norm Runnion."

He then stood up, encouraging me to do likewise, and wandered slowly toward the door, talking as he went. "I'm assigning you one of my men, primarily as a contact and resource person. If you feel the need, you can have him accompany you on your rounds, but from what you've told me, it sounds like you can do most of the legwork on your own. It's your choice, though."

I saw where he was headed. "I don't mind going it alone."

"Fine. You armed?"

"Yes—it's in my luggage right now."

"Okay. We're pretty relaxed. Donahue tells me you're your department's chief of detectives?

"That's right."

"I wouldn't worry about it, then. Course, if your nosing around goes beyond just that—if you think you're onto something that might interest us—we'd like to know."

"Sure."

The door opened and a tall, stooped man with a full beard and glasses stepped in. He reminded me instantly of some disheveled English professor who'd just been interrupted in midchapter. I guessed, both from the gray in his beard and the bags under his eyes, that he was somewhere in his mid-fifties.

Jeffers introduced us. "Lieutenant Gunther—Detective Runnion. The lieutenant is chasing after a twenty-year-old metal kneecap from Vermont. Here's the file. Right now, he just needs a liaison man." He handed Runnion a thin folder I hadn't noticed earlier, welcomed me to the department once more, and closed his door in our faces.

Runnion looked down at the folder in his hand without opening it. He then stared at me for a moment and gave me a wan, bushy smile. "Looks like you've been reduced to a couple of pieces of paper. Follow me and I'll read about you. You can tell me later what they fucked up."

I trailed him through part of the building, until we came to a large room with a dozen desks scattered about, each one looking like someone's private camping place, with decorative postcards, assorted memorabilia, and the usual piles of paperwork. About half the desks were manned by people either typing or talking on the phone. One man was leaning back in his chair, staring at the ceiling, and slowly, meditatively scratching his balls.

Runnion motioned me to a chair and slumped into his own, already reading the file. After a few minutes, still reading, he grunted and muttered, " '67 ammo—I'll be damned. Too bad there were no prints on the shells."

I'd never mentioned the absence of prints, which made me suddenly realize that the merry-go-round I'd been following with Donahue, Jeffers, and now Runnion had been far less arbitrary or bureaucratic than I'd thought. Runnion was reading about my case—with details only Brandt or I could have supplied—on a fax paper flimsy, which presumably had originated in Brattleboro and been passed along by Donahue. Apparently, while both Jeffers and Donahue had played ignorant, they'd already read what was now in Runnion's hands. I'd therefore been given the official once-over . . . twice. That Jeffers had ushered me out the door with such little concern obviously proved that I'd come up to snuff, but it still made me feel somehow processed, like a side of beef passing inspection.

Runnion finally tossed the file onto his cluttered desk, his face and demeanor noncommittal. "You got yourself a real mystery. How're you going to solve it?"

I pointed at the folder. "Does that mention the Articu-Tech angle?"

He nodded.

"Well, they apparently sold the three knees with that particular lot number in Chicago sometime in early 1969. So I thought I'd start with the major hospitals around here—the ones that were doing that kind of operation back then—and see if I get lucky."

Runnion grunted again but didn't react with Donahue's dismissiveness. "That's probably why they put you here. Area Six includes Northwestern. They've been doing hotshot procedures for years."

"Who else?"

"Right offhand? University of Chicago. In fact, I would've thought of them first. There's also Cook County Hospital, Rush Presbyterian, and a bunch of others."

"What area is the University of Chicago in?"

Runnion looked surprised. "One, but that doesn't matter—you can work out of here regardless of where you're poking around, unless you and I develop marital problems, of course."

"What is this area thing, anyway?"

Runnion brushed it off. "Oh, it's like precincts. Chicago has twenty-five police districts for the patrol division and six detective areas, with each area covering several districts, but that's all organizational. If you need me to help you out on any of this, it won't matter where it is, as long as we're within city limits."

I nodded and checked my watch. "Great, then I guess I'll start with Northwestern tomorrow morning and see where I end up." I stood up. "And as for us developing marital problems, I won't throw the first dish if you won't."

An appealing grin appeared through the thick beard. "Deal. Where're you staying?"

"The La Salle Motor Court."

He nodded and smiled. "Tight budget, huh? It's an okay place."

He got up and walked me to the building's lobby, handing me a business card at the door, his earlier reserve replaced, I thought, by relief that I wasn't going to be much of a burden. "Enjoy yourself. Normally, I'd have to baby-sit you, so they obviously think you're okay on your own. But don't get lonely, okay? If you need help, whether it's pushing a bureaucrat around or something bigger, call me. This city can get a little unruly sometimes—real quick."

I shook his hand. "Thanks. Shouldn't be too tough."

Runnion gave me a long, quiet look, his soft brown eyes world-weary and wise, which made me half-regret my cynicism of a moment ago. "Don't go in thinking like that."

The drive back into town on Lake Shore Drive—an impractical, roundabout route I chose out of pure prejudice—was considerably less enjoyable the second time around. Rush hour had kicked in, and while the heaviest traffic was headed north, for the great suburban escape, the combination of quitting time and an inordinate amount of road repair work—with the attending barricades and single-lane detours—made my side of the street just as slow. For well over an hour, I crawled along, still enjoying the sights, especially as the sun set and the lights came on, but by the time I arrived at the hotel—located within a long walk of the Northwestern campus, as it turned out—all I wanted to do was to grab a sandwich and turn in.

The La Salle Motor Court was not as bad as I'd feared from Runnion's lackluster endorsement. It was a standard-issue motel—two floors, flat roof, exterior staircases, all wrapped around an open-sided parking lot. Although it was old and slightly battle-scarred, it was clean and, for the moment at least, relatively quiet, barring the expected traffic noise. Given my personal habits, I was as happy here—especially with the fast-food restaurant I'd noticed at the corner—as I might be in downtown Brattleboro.

Much later, unable to sleep, I stood by the window, with all the lights off, looking down across the parking lot at the street. There was no view to speak of—just the traffic and the buildings opposite—but the activity was impressive. At a time when most people in Brattleboro were either heading for bed or groping for a midnight snack, this street was humming with twenty-four hour, round-the-clock energy.

I'd read in some old guidebook that Chicago had 3 million residents—six times the population of Vermont. It made me wonder just how many of them were out there now, walking, driving, working, partying, breaking and entering, or just breaking—the law and each other's heads—and how many of those I might get to meet personally.

Norm Runnion's parting words of caution came back clearly to mind.

Chapter Seventeen

Northwestern's Memorial Hospital was half a block away from the city's flamboyant old Water Tower, a bright yellow stone survivor of the famous 1871 fire, and, at one point, the tallest structure around. That distinction was downright quaint now, since the tower had all the impact of an overdesigned Lego castle next to its flashy, looming, monstrous neighbors.

The hospital, by contrast, was a nondescript urban box, wedged between two busy streets, across from the university's Chicago campus. I entered the front lobby, looked for the Orthopedic Department, and headed for the elevators.

I'd thought about the various approaches I could take at this early stage, including dragging Runnion along with all his vested authority. But I'd opted for a quieter angle first. Doctors, I'd discovered, have an unusual empathy for what plainclothes policemen do. Perhaps there's a shared conservatism there, or a sense that we're both investigators of a sort, or that we play sympathetic roles in the standard human tragedies, but whatever the link, I've often found them to be interested and responsive to most low-key inquiries.

My problems, however, were not only that I was a fish out of water, holding a badge with all the impact of a costume prop, but that I was pursuing ancient history. I walked up to the registration counter in Orthopedics and leaned in close to speak quietly with a young nurse who was flipping through a thick file.

She looked up with a slightly pasted-on smile. "Do you have your card?"

"No. I'm not a patient." I quickly showed her my badge, covering the clearly written *Brattleboro* across its top with my fingers. "I was wondering if I could speak with either the

head of the department or one of its surgeons who was working here, or at least in Chicago, in 1969.''

She stared at me as if I'd just spoken in Latin. "1969?"

"Yes, that's right. We're investigating an old case that has
recently been reopened, and I'm looking for some expert
advice from someone who was working back then.''

I kept my most pleasant smile in place as I watched her
blink a couple of times and scratch her head. "Well, this is
a first. Let me ask around. What's your name?''

"Lt. Joe Gunther.''

"Wait here.'' She rose and vanished through a back door,
leaving me to prop my elbow on the counter and gaze across
the room of waiting patients.

She returned a few minutes later, ushered me to a small
office down the hallway, and asked me to wait. I did so,
reading the framed diplomas and wondering if their owner
was the man I was supposed to be meeting. He was certainly
of the right vintage—Milton Yancy, Northwestern University
Medical School, 1965.

A very short, round, pink-faced man with bristly white hair
and a flowered tie bustled through the door and stood looking
up at me with a bemused expression on his face. He stuck
out a pudgy hand. "Lieutenant? Dr. Yancy at your service.
You've caused quite a bit of tittering up and down the hallway.''

"Sorry. I tried to be discreet.''

He laughed and sat on the narrow examination table pushed
up against the wall, his feet dangling. "Don't worry about
it. I haven't seen them this animated in quite a while. I hope
I'll be allowed to satisfy their curiosity later.''

I smiled back, pleased by his relaxed manner. "I'll leave
that to you—it's not confidential.'' I opened the oversized
manila envelope I'd been carrying and extracted the X rays
and photographs. "These are of a skeleton buried approxi-
mately twenty years ago, which we just recently discovered.
He had an artificial knee implanted shortly before he died.
We think the implant was sold in Chicago in early 1969, but
we don't know who bought it, nor do we know who did the
surgery.''

"But it was done at Northwestern."

I hesitated, sorry to disappoint him. "We don't know that, either."

His eyes narrowed and he looked up from the documents I'd handed him. "You said the implant was sold in '69. Does that mean you're not even sure the surgery was done that year?"

"I'm afraid not."

He shook his head. "Good Lord. Are you planning to talk to every orthopedist who was practicing in Chicago back then?"

I put on a brave smile. "I'm hoping to get lucky."

He looked back at the X rays and held one up against the light from the window. "Who made this device?"

"Articu-Tech," I said hopefully.

"Never heard of them. Decent knee, though—a little on the heavy side; European influence."

"The medical examiner in Vermont found that the cement was impregnated with antibiotics, which an orthopedist friend of mine said implied a hasty operation—one that most likely took place immediately following the trauma. They both agreed that was a sign of a real hotshot, a maverick."

"Gambling with somebody else's money," Yancy muttered, studying the X ray with renewed interest. "Any idea what kind of trauma it was?"

"No." Although I was tempted to theorize.

Dr. Yancy finally slid all the pictures back into the envelope and returned them to me. "I can't help you specifically. The knee's not familiar, nor is any scenario that might have promoted such haste with the implantation. I was here in 1969, at this hospital, in fact, and I'm pretty sure I would remember such a case."

I nodded, resigned to hitting the road again.

But Yancy wasn't quite finished. "I am intrigued by the possible motivations behind such a procedure. Your friend was correct, of course—the surgeon was a hotshot, and there weren't too many of them around in '69. For that matter, there aren't too many of them around now. It's rarely rewarding to stick your neck out in practice without a lot of previous homework. Someone sure did this time, though."

There was a moment's silence, during which I murmured, "We think a significant amount of money might have played a part in this."

Yancy grunted. "It's possible. Someone who was underpaid, underrecognized, and rash might have found some under-the-counter cash rewarding in several ways, but I wouldn't downplay the psychological aspects here. We're a careful, cautious, sometimes even paranoid profession when the risk of a lawsuit drifts our way. We can also be tied to stifling traditional and conventional philosophies. And all this was even truer twenty years ago.

"Many a young surgeon has been known to champ at the bit. That can cause the institution that employs him to bear down and the individual to become sullen and resentful."

I tapped the envelope with my fingertip. "And you think this might have been the case here?"

He stuck his lower lip out meditatively. "It's purely hypothetical, but it fits. Medically, there's no reason to justify the kind of speed that was demonstrated here, which means the motivation lies not with the patient's medical needs but perhaps with the surgeon's and the patient's emotional needs working in tandem. That would more fully explain why the surgeon took the risk—along with the money, it would have been a double revenge against a repressive system."

I liked it, but, as Yancy had implied, it didn't mean much without a cast of characters. "So where does that leave me?"

He snapped out of his reverie and smiled, spreading his hands. "It leaves me wishing you good luck." He hopped off the table and opened the door, ushering me out. "I recommend that you go next to the University of Chicago campus, however. Talk to Dr. Philip Hoolihan in Orthopedics. He's as old as Moses, been in the business forever, and is a homegrown Chicago boy. What you've got in that envelope amounts to a passport photo in this business. Hoolihan might recognize it. I'll give him a call and warm him up a little—he's not quite as approachable as I am."

I thanked Dr. Yancy and returned to where I'd parked my car, considerably more hopeful than I'd been an hour ago. Much of it was the comfort of simply getting back to work, instead of acting like a tourist; but it also had something to do with Yancy's thoughtful meditation. His sending me to Hoolihan was no casual suggestion—it was a definite direction, but given, for reasons of his own, with discretion.

The University of Chicago is built in Old English Gothic style, swarming with rampant gargoyles, crenellations, iron-spiked stone spires, and offset by clusters of tree-shaded quadrangles and a field-sized midway similar in scope to the Mall in downtown Washington, D.C. The whole thing is as incongruous as a Rolls-Royce at a bicycle convention. With more or less fire-gutted, violence-torn, poor neighborhoods all around it, Hyde Park—the area to which the university is overlord—looks captive, besieged, and yet stubbornly wishful, perhaps realizing it has little choice but to hang on.

The broad, courtly, almost royal facade of the school's medical center further added to the fantasy. I forgot for a moment where I was, so convincing was the allusion to a long-gone Europe, and I slowly entered the building's courtyard embrace thoroughly impressed by what enough Rockefeller money could do.

Several minutes later, and several floors higher up, I didn't even have to see Philip Hoolihan to understand Dr. Yancy's subtle warning about his ineffability. His secretary's attitude was enough.

"You have no appointment," she stated flatly, her cold blue eyes contrasting sharply with a soft and luxuriant snow-white hairdo.

I had purposefully announced my name only, not my profession, hoping a show of diplomacy might stand me in good stead. "Dr. Milton Yancy just called. Perhaps Dr. Hoolihan hasn't had a chance to tell you."

She resisted using the phone to confirm that. "I seriously doubt it. What is the purpose of your visit?"

"I'm conducting a police investigation," I reluctantly admitted, utterly convinced of where we were leading with this.

"You're a policeman?" Her tone let me know just how pathetic she thought my plight to be.

"Yes."

"May I see some identification?"

I inwardly sighed. Flashing an out-of-state badge was definitely not going to work here, meaning some twenty more minutes would be wasted while Norm Runnion was located and my Valkyrie interrogator satisfied. I decided to use her own methods against her. "I'll present those to Dr. Hoolihan himself, who is waiting for me, no matter what you've been told."

There was a long, electrically charged pause, during which I impassively returned her ice-cold glare. Finally, no doubt wishing it was my right eye, she stabbed a button on her intercom with the eraser end of her pencil. "Doctor, were you expecting a visit from the police?"

"Send him in."

Her face darkened and she pointed to a door behind her, without an additional word.

Hoolihan's office fit the architecture that surrounded it: vast, high-ceilinged, with dark wood-paneled walls and a long stretch of tall diamond-paned windows that reminded me of a captain's cabin in an ancient man-of-war. The furniture was burnished mahogany, the desk lamp Tiffany, and the drapes and rugs enough to make Scarlett O'Hara weep with envy.

Parked behind the aircraft carrier–sized desk was the man himself—big, bald, and broad across the shoulders, with a craggy, impenetrably hard face, overshadowed by a pair of run-amuck tufted white eyebrows.

"Show me the X rays," he ordered, indicating the gleaming field of wood before him.

I pulled them out silently and laid them out before him.

He picked them up one by one, swiveled around in his chair, and held them up to the windows behind him. Eventually, he laid the last one down and fixed me with a hard, angry look. "What did this man die of?"

"A gunshot wound to the chest."

His eyes wavered, but only for a second. "You're not a Chicago cop." It wasn't a question.

"No, sir—I'm from Vermont." I began to dig for my credentials, wondering what had tipped him off.

He waved me to be still. "I don't care. Go see Kevin Shilly."

I leaned over the desk and gathered up the negatives. "Who's he?"

Hoolihan bristled. "Who are you looking for?"

"He's the surgeon who did this?"

"Ask him."

I refilled my large manila envelope. "Can you tell me—"

The old man placed both his hands on the desk, as if he was about to vault out of his chair. His face was red with fury. "No, I cannot. What Dr. Shilly may or may not have done is between you and him. He is no longer associated with this facility or this university, and is, therefore, not my responsibility."

"There was bad blood about his departure?"

Hoolihan turned to face the windows. "Good day."

"Thank you, Doctor," I said to the back of his head, and left the office.

Normally, I would have chatted with the secretary a bit, trying to get a handle on Kevin Shilly's obviously turbulent history here. But her loyalty to her boss had been made clear a mere three minutes earlier, and I wasn't too hopeful. Other options would have been to drop by the administrative offices or to find another friendly face in the Orthopedic Department, but Milton Yancy's words about medical hierarchies came back to me as if in warning. Chances were good that with a man like Hoolihan at the top, people would not be as free-spoken as I needed.

I took the elevator down to the lobby and located a pay phone instead.

"Runnion."

"Hi, this is Joe Gunther."

There was a chuckle at the other end. "Been mugged yet?"

"Only by bureaucrats. Can you put a name into your computer and see what comes up?"

"Sure. You hit something?"

"Maybe. Dr. Kevin Shilly—orthopedic surgeon."

"Hold on."

I waited ten minutes. Runnion's voice, when he came back on, was almost apologetic. "We don't have a thing. I found him in the phone book, though—office only; residence is unlisted." He gave me an address on North Michigan Avenue.

"Would your files go back twenty years or more?"

"No, but there would've been a note to check the archives, along with a reference number."

I thanked him, promising to give him an update as soon as I could, and then dialed Northwestern Memorial Hospital.

It took twenty minutes to get Dr. Yancy on the line, during which I received several malevolent mutterings for hogging the phone.

"Sorry—I was with a patient. Any luck with the affable Dr. Hoolihan?"

"You weren't kidding. He gave me one name, without actually saying it was the guy I'm after. Kevin Shilly. Does that ring a bell?"

There was a long pause. I remembered wondering earlier if Yancy had pointed me to Hoolihan in the hopes the old man would say what Yancy could only silently suspect. I knew now I'd been right.

"I know of him," he finally admitted.

"How?"

"It wasn't front-page news or anything. He didn't get in trouble legally. But he did get in trouble. Hoolihan threw him out, from what we heard through the grapevine."

"He was the one you were thinking about when you mentioned young doctors chafing at the bit?"

"Yes, but I was only guessing."

"So what else did the grapevine say?"

"He did something like what you described—collected some extra money for a risky procedure that didn't pan out. I guess that was around '72 or '73. Hoolihan and the others at the top had ordered him not to do it, so they had just cause, but there was history there, too. I guess it wasn't the first time—just the first time he got caught."

"Shilly didn't lose his license or get reprimanded?"

"Almost. That's another reason Hoolihan still bears a grudge. Shilly was pretty political back then, trying to socialize medicine, kick over the old traditions, open the place up to poor neighborhood blacks. And he wasn't publicity-shy; he had good contacts in the media. When he got canned, a deal was made. Hoolihan was to let it go; Shilly was to keep his mouth shut. End of story. It helped that the patient wasn't one of the complainers, despite the operation's failure. Shilly had totally charmed the old lady—so they say.''

''What did he do afterward?''

''In terms of gossip, he pretty much disappeared after his run-in with Hoolihan—did the storefront-practice bit for the disadvantaged for a couple of years, I guess, then decided to hang it up and go for the money. I hear he's got a high-class private practice north of the river.''

''But no more scandal?''

''Not that I heard. I always thought the entire episode was a little pathetic—basically two good people refusing to bend, to the detriment of everyone. A big waste, especially there. That's one of the best medical outfits around, except for here,'' he added with natural pride. ''And Shilly could've been one of their stars.''

The address Runnion had given me over the phone put me back in the vicinity of Northwestern Memorial, but far from its comforting atmosphere of institutionalized caring. Indeed, the tall modern steel building I entered forty-five minutes later smacked more of wealth, commerce, and business deals than of medicine. Nevertheless, on the thirtieth floor, attached to an elegant hardwood door, was an ornate brass plaque boasting the name KEVIN SHILLY, M.D.—ORTHOPEDIC SPECIALIST.

Beyond this door was no iron-spined harridan ready to throw me out like Hoolihan's secretary, nor a white-clad nurse asking if I had an appointment. Instead, I was greeted like a guest by an elegant young woman in a business suit who hovered in style between classy receptionist and upscale therapist.

She rose from her desk and escorted me to a ponderous antique table with two ornate chairs, gesturing for me to sit, explaining all the while that her name was Giovanna, that she was delighted to meet me, and that she'd like to know exactly what my problem was and how Dr. Shilly might be of service.

I knew it was so much shellac—a justification for what was obviously the Oscar of medical fees—but it was soothing, flattering, and unique, guaranteed to make the wealthy lame feel they had finally found their proper healer.

I took my seat, therefore, and gazed placidly into Giovanna's large hazel eyes. "I was wondering what made Dr. Shilly any different from any other orthopedist."

For all her grace, Giovanna had been drilled with all the zeal of a hard-nosed encyclopedia salesman. "Years ago, Dr. Shilly became aware of how shoddily many patients were being treated by the average hospital staff. Despite their pain and anxiety, they were being reduced to mere numbers on an admission form. Often, they were not assigned fully trained physicians, but residents and even interns. They were used as guinea pigs for medical students and exposed to needless embarrassment and harassment as a result. . . ."

"So Dr. Shilly offers something a little more refined," I interrupted pleasantly.

She smiled. "That's well put. However, the fact that Dr. Shilly's service is more supportive and encouraging is a small thing in itself; what he offers above all is possibly the best orthopedic care available in the city."

"He's that good, is he?"

She tilted her head to one side and smiled with irrepressible enthusiasm. "He's wonderful—the most caring man I've ever met."

It was a great show, improved, no doubt, by Giovanna's conviction that most of it was true.

"I heard he was thrown out of the University of Chicago for playing fast and loose with the rules."

Her smile froze.

"I'm a policeman, Giovanna—Lieutenant Gunther. I wonder if you could tell Dr. Shilly that I'd like to speak with him?"

She got to her feet awkwardly, her sales pitch forgotten. "Well, I . . . Does he . . . ? No, I guess not. Could you wait here a sec?" Scratching her head, disturbing that perfectly brushed hair, she left the reception area.

It didn't take long. Both the message and the messenger were alarming enough to grant me almost instant gratification. Giovanna returned in five minutes and stiffly asked me to follow her down a short hallway to a pleasant and spacious examining room, complete with more antique furniture. There, I was told to wait.

Using a hostile approach had been a calculated gamble, and not one I'd planned before crossing the threshold. But the exclusive layout of Shilly's practice, combined with what I knew of his past, suggested a man in a permanent dilemma, hanging between an angry, idealistic youth and a crassly exploitative middle age that had made him what he'd hated years ago: a complicated man who deserved a complicated approach.

He entered quickly, nervously, his tanned, urbane, well-tended face a cross between anger and confusion. He looked beautiful otherwise. His clothes were immaculate, the shoes soft Italian leather, the French cuffs of his shirt peeking out just the right amount from beneath a fashionable jacket. He looked like a Neiman Marcus store manager—better than the customers but dependent upon their cash.

His tone did not match his attire. "What do you want?" he asked brusquely.

I emptied my well-traveled envelope and showed him the X rays. "This knee implant was done twenty-four years ago." I paused. "Remember it?"

He snapped the pictures into a wall-mounted light box and peered at them in stony silence for a long time. His face, already tense, was otherwise unreadable to me. "Why do you want to know? What's this about?"

Interesting side step, I thought. "Do you remember the operation?"

He hedged again. "Do you have any idea how many of these I do every year? Multiply that times twenty-four."

"It was done fast—the cement was mixed with antibiotics so you wouldn't have to wait for the wound to stabilize. It was the type of showy stunt you became infamous for at the University of Chicago."

His face reddened. "That's total crap. I had new techniques they weren't willing to try, techniques that are common today. I was good and I was right. They threw me out because they couldn't admit that."

I nodded my head toward the X rays. "That's not a common technique even today; it's still a risky shortcut. Why'd you take it?"

He hesitated, watching me. This was the break point; he

either went for the bluff or he came up with one of his own. "I didn't," he finally said, his voice back under control. "I've never seen those before."

I didn't show my disappointment, although I shouldn't have been surprised; I should have known that while a risk taker might age gracefully, he's not one to deny his own nature. Shilly had just won his bet that I had no proof connecting him to the negatives.

I shook my head, trying a different angle. "That's too bad. We know your connection to this guy—but we were hoping you'd just been in the wrong place at the wrong time. Obviously not." I stood up and collected the X rays off the light box. "I guess we'll make you a part of the full investigation." I looked at our opulent surroundings. "And then we'll see where we all end up."

I gave him plenty of time to reconsider, slowly stuffing the X rays back into the envelope, but he held firm, if none too steadily. The sweat on his forehead told me that. I finally headed for the door, opened it, and looked back at him. "You decide to come clean, call Norm Runnion at Area Six headquarters." I gestured at the expensive furnishings of the room. "Be a shame to jeopardize all this for such a little thing."

His eyes widened slightly at the last two words, but he kept silent.

"Good-bye, Dr. Shilly—for now."

I checked my watch on the elevator, trying to be philosophical about this snag. For some reason, while I knew my mysterious skeleton's surgeon had played it fast and loose, I'd never actually thought he'd played a criminal role. Now I wasn't sure. Shilly's behavior was either the response of a natural gambler, hoping that a denial would be all that was necessary, or he was more involved than I'd thought. A third possibility—that he hadn't performed the surgery—was no longer feasible. His body language, Hoolihan's and Yancy's suspicions, and my own experience had all killed that one.

I reached the lobby and sought out the guard I'd seen stationed at a TV set–equipped console earlier. A pleasant young black man in his twenties, he smiled as I approached. "Can I help you?"

I pulled out my badge and flashed it at him quickly, doing the fingers-over-the-top gag that had worked once before. "Yeah, I was wondering if you could tell me where the residents of this building park their cars."

He sat back, the smile spreading to a grin. "And why would you like to know that?"

That threw me off slightly. "Police business—we're conducting an investigation."

He nodded affably. "Sounds real good—for who?"

I paused, weighing my options, knowing he'd nailed me. Finally, I just shrugged, pulled out the badge again, and dropped it in front of him. "Sorry—trying to cut corners. For the Brattleboro Police Department, in Vermont. I'm on assignment, working with your local police."

The smile crystallized somewhat. "I work with the local police, too. I just moonlight here."

"Call Norm Runnion in Area Six and ask about me."

I said this with as much joviality as I could muster, since I sensed my interrogator was losing his humor fast. If I didn't become legitimate quickly, I suspected I'd be a host of the city in a whole new way.

He dialed the phone before him and spoke into it briefly, eventually hanging up with a doubtful expression. "Okay—he says you're straight." The emphasis was on the *he*.

I leaned over and retrieved my disreputable credentials.

He gestured at them as I did so. "I wouldn't pull that stunt again. You want to know where they park, right?"

"Yeah—I just want to keep an eye on someone here."

"Who?"

He had me there. It was a question I didn't need to answer, and another phone call would have made that clear, but the unwritten rules said differently—he'd caught me red-handed, and I owed him one. "Dr. Kevin Shilly."

He raised his eyebrows and grunted, checking a three-ring binder by the phone. "Mr. Beautiful. Take the elevator to the second basement—slot 2-318. It's a brown Mercedes—two-seater. There's enough empty slots that you can park pretty near and keep an eye on it."

"Thanks."

He stopped me as I turned to go. "What's Vermont like?"

"Lots of mountains, lots of trees, lots of bullshitters like me."

He laughed and waved me off.

The parking basement was typical of its kind—gray, low-ceilinged, with drumlike acoustics, spotty fluorescent lighting, and a regularly spaced army of squatty cement pillars holding the roof up. The Mercedes was where the guard said it would be, and I was able to park my rental behind one of the pillars, but in clear view of slot 2-318.

Why I did so was another matter, and it underlined the uneasy vagueness that had plagued this case from the start.

I had nothing on "Mr. Beautiful." He, and Fred Coyner, and the defunct Abraham Fuller, and even the left-handed skeleton with the all but perfect teeth could have played different roles from the ones we'd ascribed them, simply because we had no solid proof to make ours the unchallenged truth.

So for now they remained in an orderly row—Shilly, for all his denials, being merely the latest one in line. But sooner or later, with enough encouragement, I knew one of them would break ranks and lead us in the right direction, and then the entire line, as if by the wave on parade, would follow. It was just a matter of time and perseverance—and maybe a little encouragement.

Chapter Eighteen

I hadn't been waiting for more than half an hour before I heard footsteps echoing through the garage, approaching from the elevator bank. I slid down in my seat, waiting for whoever it was to pass by.

The sounds stopped opposite my front bumper. I waited for a minute longer, feeling increasingly foolish, and finally lifted myself up just enough to peer over the dash. Norm

Runnion was standing there, a grin on his face, wiggling the fingers of one hand at me in greeting.

With all the dignity of an embarrassed eight-year-old, I struggled to straighten up nonchalantly.

Runnion came around to the side door and slid in next to me. "Catch any bad guys yet?" He pulled a half-empty bag of Fig Newtons from his pocket and handed it over.

"What're you doing here?" I asked, gratefully biting into one of the cookies.

He chuckled. "I think you got Jeffers nervous. When I told him you were waving funny credentials in front of building guards, he had visions of a country cowboy running amok. We waiting for Shilly?"

"Yeah." I liked his approach—relaxed, friendly, one of the boys, and yet very sharp. That he had traced my whereabouts was no remarkable feat, but that he had apparently taken the time to watch me after I'd left his office to see what kind of car I was driving—just for future reference—struck me as the workings of a careful, calculating mind.

"What'd you have on him?"

I told him, along with how I'd gathered my information. I finished with a question I'd been planning to ask him later. "Do you have any contacts inside the University of Chicago hospital?"

"Sure."

"Could they get us a look at Shilly's old files there?"

He was quiet for a time, bouncing a thumbnail against his lower lip. I was worried he'd end by downplaying my interest in Shilly, claiming I was grabbing at straws. But either he saw no harm in examining straws—especially when we had little else—or he was homesick for a good chase, because he finally said, "Maybe. We'd have to watch out for patient confidentiality, though, unless we got someone similar to your Dr. Yancy. My connection's more on the administrative side."

I thought of another angle. "How about tracing the metal knee? That's administrative—pure inventory. I have the make and model number; we connect that to a specific operation, then maybe we can get a warrant if we need it—the knee does connect to a homicide, after all."

That made him much happier. "Okay. Let's go."

I checked my watch, reluctant to abandon my planned tail of Shilly. "Your contact still there? It's almost quittin' time."

"Yup—staggered shifts. Besides, I hate stakeouts—bad for my butt. We can find out where Shilly lives from the tax assessor's office in the morning."

I headed out into traffic, following Runnion's advice on which streets to take. It was nice having him along—he was open and conversational, totally lacking in the inbred mistrust many of my Vermont colleagues might have displayed had the roles been reversed.

I began asking him about his background—where'd he'd been born, where he'd gone to school, whether he was married. He'd attended Chicago City College night school, he'd informed me, and yes, he was married, with two kids. His replies came in elliptical, anecdotal, humorous monologues that blended his biography with those of thousands of others like him who'd spent their entire lives helping to make the city what it had become.

"Chicago's different. It's neighborhoods, family ties, and the Catholic Church—at least for people like me. That's the old-style Chicago. There're lots of new people, new trends, but the old ways—the politics, the who-knows-who way of doing business, that sense of everybody knowing the other guy's roots—that's still real strong."

He spoke of the ward politics, the old Daley Machine, the huge black and ethnic populations, the hapless Cubs, supported with the exaggerated weariness of fatalistic in-laws. He spoke of the city's energy, its raw nerve, the source of its renowned, almost belligerent self-confidence, and he talked of the bars, restaurants, and music clubs, examples of which he pointed out now and then as we drove.

It was a rambling, disjointed, free-for-all tour, fueled by questions I fed him to keep it going. It made the long, traffic-clogged trip go more quickly and helped me to understand both my new and sometimes-overwhelming environment and my affable, temporary host.

Norm Runnion, it turned out, was three months shy of retirement. At age fifty-five, he had spent thirty years on the force; he had been disappointed in promotions after making detective ten years back—late in life by modern hyperactive standards—and now was resigned to spending the rest of his life on pension, taking on odd jobs to keep himself sane.

"That's one of the reasons I'm glad you came along," he explained. "They won't let me out on the street anymore—not officially. Afraid I'll screw up 'cause I won't give a damn anymore, as if I could just turn it all off after thirty years. Typical of the brass, I suppose; they think all this time you been faking it—doing it just for the money and not really caring." He looked out the window at the endless blur of buildings and people, each half mile exhibiting enough sights, sounds, and energy to fuel the entire state of Vermont.

"They've had me doing paperwork for the past six months," he concluded with a murmur.

I glanced over at him, his eyes glued to the scenery, and saw the loneliness that his words had been struggling to suppress. I remembered then Captain Jeffers's questioning me about how little help I'd need before he'd rung for Runnion, and the memory angered me. I wasn't that far from retirement myself, and I, too, wondered what life would be like afterwards—from the outside, looking in.

When we finally got to the University of Chicago, we didn't enter the medical complex by the front door, as I had earlier. The entrance we did use was so far from that gloriously self-indulgent entrance—and so modest in appearance—that I doubted we were in the same building.

Runnion led me along a baffling maze of hallways and back stairs, finally stopping at the door of a room containing several young women sitting at computer terminals, one of whom looked up with a broad, crooked-toothed smile and called out, "Norm—long time no see."

Norm introduced me and waved to the others, all of whom seemed well used to him. "Leslie's one of my favorite deep-cover operatives. She's a great cook, has a husband who likes to beat on my car, works at the right job, and is something like a cousin forty-three times removed. None of which matters," he added after she'd given him a friendly punch in the stomach, "since I'd love her, anyway."

Leslie rolled her eyes. "I guess I know why you're here."

Runnion gave her a hug where she sat. "Cynical, but true.

How're you at checking ancient inventory on that thing?'' He nodded at the computer.

She looked surprised. "Inventory? Like what?"

"A metal knee, bought in early '69—we think.''

She didn't seem surprised. "You'd have to have the exact numbers.''

Runnion glanced at me as I dug into my pocket for the catalog and lot numbers and handed it to Leslie.

She stuck the information on the edge of her computer screen with a bit of tape and began tapping away at the keyboard.

I looked on, amazed as always at both the depth of information passing before me and at the trust people put in these machines. As undeniably useful as they were, I still put more faith in huge, badly lit rooms stuffed with generations of lovingly filed, dusty archives. It wasn't the fear of loss that put me off computer-stored information—I recognized that a good fire could wipe out a storeroom as easily as a bolt of lightning could fry a hard disc. It was more a longing for the hands-on experience. Pawing through reams of old files gave me a feel for when they were amassed. A computer screen was always the same, regardless of how old the information it was disgorging.

Nevertheless, this computer had been well fed. After some fifteen minutes of back-filing and cross-checking, Leslie let out a little grunt of satisfaction and sat back in her chair. "I wasn't going to admit it, but I wasn't so sure these files went back that far. But there it is.''

Runnion and I both craned our necks over her shoulder to see what she'd found, but while I recognized Shilly's name, it was surrounded by clusters of numbers that meant absolutely nothing to me.

"Translate, Les," Runnion muttered.

She stabbed the screen with a slightly pudgy, nail-bitten finger. "Okay, here you've got your friend's numbers. There's our purchase number; there's the purchase date, and our own inventory number, and the assignment bin so we'd know where to find it. These are cross-references to manufacturer, salesman, type and style of prosthesis, and basic material—like plastic, metal, wood, what have you. . . .''

"What was the purchase date?" I asked.

She looked up at me, surprised that I'd spoken. "February 8, 1969."

Runnion eased her back to the screen. "So when did it move off the shelf?"

"October tenth, same year. Dr. Shilly used it. Payment was routed . . ." She hesitated and tapped in a couple more commands. "Huh—that's unusual. Looks like it was a cash transaction—not insurance."

"Who got the knee?" Runnion asked gently.

She turned on him in genuine alarm. "You know I can't give you that. I'd get in enough trouble just for doing this."

He patted her shoulder. "I know, I know. Don't worry about it. Just give me the case number and we'll go through channels."

"Maybe we can do even better than that," I muttered, looking around. "You have a phone directory—for this building?"

"Sure." Leslie pulled open a drawer near her leg and handed me a softcover phone book about the same thickness as Brattleboro's. "The phone's over there."

I crossed over to the counter she'd indicated, leafing through the directory until I found Hoolihan's name. I dialed the number and reintroduced myself to his secretary's familiar protective voice. She hedged at first but finally admitted he was in. I told her I'd be right up.

Just as with regular phone books, this one had a limited address opposite the names. "Know how to find that?" I asked Runnion.

He was eyeing me with keen interest. "I thought Hoolihan had you right up there with root canal work."

I shrugged. "He gave me Shilly's name. I doubt he thought that would be the end of it."

We left Leslie with many thanks and a promise from Runnion to bring a one-pound bag of peanut M&M's for everyone next time, then rode the elevator up to the top floor. Hoolihan's acerbic secretary merely stared at us as I took the lead and ushered Runnion into the cavernous office beyond.

Hoolihan was sitting where I'd found him before, still

looking like a crouchy gnome behind a too-large desk. "You found Shilly."

I passed on introducing Runnion, who, in any case, hadn't received so much as a glance. "Yes. He denied doing the operation."

"Then I have no other suggestions." Hoolihan began his dismissal trick of swiveling toward the window.

"But your records indicate otherwise."

The swivel stopped. "Our records?"

"We traced the prosthesis. Shilly took it off the shelf and used it in October 1969. It was paid for in cash. I'd like to look at the files concerning that operation."

Hoolihan didn't move or immediately respond. In profile, I could see his lips compressing and relaxing, as if he was slowly grinding out an answer between his teeth. Finally, he turned back to face us, for the first time addressing Norm Runnion. "I take it you have enough for a warrant in any case."

Despite the doubtfulness of that statement, Runnion didn't equivocate. "We do."

"What do I get for being cooperative?"

I knew what he wanted. "You and the university get left out of it, at least as far as we can control things."

He nodded. "Fair enough. What's the case number?"

The low-ceilinged basement vault, jammed with tightly serried rows of metal shelf units, which in turn bulged with thousands of compressed medical files, was much more my element. Just walking the length of the aisles, I could sense the energy that had created this room's contents—the agonies, ordeals, triumphs, and failures that could be extruded from the batches of hastily scrawled notes and reports that mark every patient's stay in a hospital.

Runnion and I were following a diminutive gray-haired woman whose stature had been inflated with anger. She fairly hummed ahead of us, bitterly muttering to herself about the thoughtlessness of others and of the sacredness of quitting time, the latter of which we'd trampled upon with our arrival on her doorstep, complete with an authoritative note from Dr. Hoolihan.

She finally came to a spot about halfway down one of the aisles, wrenched a file from its place with undisguised viciousness, and thrust it like a sword toward Runnion's chest. "You can use the tables at the back. I'll be waiting."

The venom of those last three words swirled in the air like smoke as she stalked rigidly back to her post. Runnion wiggled his eyebrows at me in mock horror and set a course in the opposite direction.

We sat side by side, the file open before us, trying to nail down a chronological sequence of events. I was holding an Emergency Room admittance sheet, struggling to make the hieroglyphic scrawl become English. From prior experience, I'd discovered that doctors, nurses, EMTs, and just about everyone else who learns how to take a blood pressure not only lose their penmanship in the process but also a large chunk of the English language.

"What the hell does CAO × 3 c/o mean?"

Runnion looked up and took the form from me. "Okay, you got the Admit. That's 'conscious, alert, and oriented to time, place, and date'—that's pretty good, considering the injury." He scanned the sheet generally, seemingly unstumped by the jargon.

"I'll translate—I've gotten pretty good at this garbage."

I pulled my notepad from my pocket and opened it flat on the table.

Runnion spoke slowly, occasionally turning to other pages to fill in the blanks. "Okay—bottom lines first. Name: Robert Shattuck; date of birth: 9/11/38; address: transient; physician: doctor on call, meaning he took what they gave him. Apparently, he was a 'walk-in'—I have a hard time believing that. . . ."

"Does it say who helped him walk in?"

He flipped through several pages. "Nope, just that; no more. He was suffering from a gunshot wound to the knee. . . ."

Runnion looked up suddenly. "That would have been reported—or it should have been. We can run Shattuck through our computer later and see what we come up with; maybe that'll identify whoever helped him get to the ER."

He returned to his scrutiny. "Says here the wound was

self-inflicted and accidental—with a .45 semiautomatic. Jesus—that explains the damage. There's a note here further on—could be from Shilly himself—that says the damage fits the story. There're a couple of other reports from other docs—I can't really tell what they're about. Here's a comment by one of them saying, 'The large-caliber missile caused only transient nontraumatic bruising.' That sounds like bullshit.''

"Is there anything there that explains why Shilly moved so fast?"

Runnion was clearly distracted, having latched onto yet another scrap of officialese. "I don't know yet—but here is something. Apparently Mr. Shattuck checked himself out five days later, in the middle of the night."

"Legitimately?"

Runnion shook his head. "Not hardly. Reading between the lines here, I'd say there were a lot of red faces the next day. Physical therapy was supposed to start the following morning, so they obviously didn't think he was mobile; the nurses' patient-care log shows he was still using a bedpan. I guess he was faking how weak he was."

"No one went after him?"

"No reason to. The bill was paid. . . ."

"With hundred-dollar bills, no doubt," I muttered.

Runnion paused, obviously recalling the case history he'd read at his office. "Just like your guy with the aneurysm. Well, they don't say what denominations, but he's labeled 'self-pay,' which means no insurance, and 'Paid in Full' is stamped across the bottom." He showed me the page.

I leaned back in my chair and stared at the ceiling. "When did Shilly get pulled into the case?"

Runnion checked. "That night, about five minutes after admit. He was the orthopedist on duty."

I smiled at that. "The workings of fate maybe."

"Makes you wonder what happened to make Shattuck so eager to disappear. I can check our files to see if somewhere in the city a large amount of money changed hands with a bang that night."

I was still mulling over Shilly's appearance in all this. Shilly might have cut corners for fortune and spite, but the fact that his patient vanished immediately afterward must have looked pretty suspicious—like he knew from the start Shattuck was somehow on the lam. "Makes you wonder why nobody asked any questions."

Runnion was very still next to me. "Which says what?"

I was suddenly aware of how he was looking at me. My focus in that hypothesis had been the possibility that Shilly had known Shattuck before the shooting. But Runnion had looked up Shilly's name in his computer just a few hours earlier at my request, and the fact that he wasn't there made it clear that Shilly had no history with the police, which he would have had if they'd investigated a case as suspicious as this. Without intending to, I'd turned the searchlight we were both tending onto the Chicago Police Department itself. I lamely murmured an answer to his question, "Maybe nothing."

"Assuming our computer—or the archives—spit out an explanation I can live with," he finished for me.

There was a long silence. Runnion broke the ice by letting out a small laugh and standing up. "I think if either one of us is going to get a good night's sleep, we'd better do a little checking." He nodded toward my small notebook. "You got enough of the pertinent details? We'll probably be back here at some point, anyway."

We didn't drive all the way back to his office, but, rather, a mere couple of blocks to South Wentworth Avenue and the Area 1 headquarters building. Runnion was obviously in no mood to let his impatience fester.

He found us an empty computer-equipped office and arranged two chairs side by side in front of the smudged and battle-scarred terminal.

"Okay," he said, directing his erratically jabbing fingers across the keyboard, "we know Shilly's not on board, so let's see about Robert Shattuck. Maybe we'll get lucky. What was the DOB?"

I checked my notes and read him the birth date.

He typed it in and we watched as the screen slowly filled with information. "Holy shit. This guy's been around."

Runnion scrolled the screen by slowly so we could follow

the itemized arrests one by one. The top of the list was promising enough—a series of civil-unrest complaints dating back to the period I was interested in—but as the data marched on, my spirits began to sag. Year by year, with occasional gaps here and there, Robert Shattuck's activities drove a wedge between the old skeleton I was tracing and the identity I'd hoped we'd pinned to it. Shattuck's career of political disturbances petered out in the mid-1980s, but it was already clear to both of us that he and the man with the metal knee were not the same.

Runnion finally sat back in his chair with a sigh. "Well, that kills that theory. Let's see what kind of intelligence we've got on him."

He called up another file and we read the opinions the Chicago Police Department had formed from its years-long relationship with Shattuck. It was a study in evolutionary radicalism, from peripheral involvement in mid-sixties protest marches, in which he was occasionally rounded up as part of an antiwar group, to more prominent roles within increasingly hard-core militant leftist cells, suspected of far more than sit-ins and peace demonstrations. There was some jail time now and then, but the tone of the intelligence report made clear the frustration at never catching Shattuck at the kind of gun-running and bomb manufacturing the police suspected him of.

And it was a frustration they would never get to satisfy. As with most of the rock-ribbed radicals of those days, Shattuck's career eventually hit its inevitable downward curve, caving in to a nation's growing disinterest, to the war petering out, and perhaps to the weariness of encroaching middle age. Like a storm reaching full cycle, Shattuck returned to the gentler forms of protest that had marked his early years, finally sliding altogether from the police department's spotlight. The report listed a last known address, which I dutifully took down.

Runnion rubbed his eyes with both palms. "You notice the same thing I did?"

"No mention of Shilly or the hospital or anything criminal around the time of the operation."

"Right. Of course, this isn't the whole intelligence file—just a synopsis. We don't put the nitty-gritty on the network, in case somebody ever breaks in. Later, maybe we can pull his file at Central and get some details, as well as double check on Shilly.''

I nodded and pointed at the screen. ''Could you do me a favor?''

''Sure.''

''See if you have the name Abraham Fuller in there.''

Runnion entered the name and waited for a response. He merely raised his eyebrows at the blinking NO ENTRY FOUND message.

''Thanks,'' I muttered. ''It was a long shot.''

He stretched his arms, cracked his knuckles, and prepared to type again. ''Okay. Let's get into the archives and access the police log for that night.''

I watched him pecking away, a graceless typist but a master at getting what he wanted out of the machine, his keenness further fueled by the smell of something amiss. I sympathized with his pursuit, but I didn't share his enthusiasm. Maybe the absence of a gunshot report and a visit to the hospital by a patrol unit that night did implicate the police. More likely, Shilly had simply agreed, maybe for a little extra on top, to run interference with the ER staff. I doubted the police had ever been called.

Runnion dropped his hands to his lap and straightened his back, sighing. ''Guess I'll have to go at it the hard way. There's not enough in here to give me what I want—too far back. I need to find the actual dispatch transcripts to see if a unit was even sent to investigate. Incidentally, while I was at it, I did check to see if any big money scam went down that night.'' He shook his head. ''Nothin'—no banks, no armored cars, no illegal bookie joints—at least nothing we responded to, which probably amounts to about ten percent of all the shit that goes down in this town.''

He leaned forward and switched off the computer. ''I guess we can give it a rest 'til tomorrow. You want to drop by my office in the morning, we can go over to city hall and get a home address and whatever other information there is on Kevin Shilly. See if we can shake him up a little.''

He led the way outside to his car so he could drive me back to where I'd left my rental. ''We can work on Shattuck, too, assuming he's still in the area, but I think Shilly's our best bet. He put the knee in, after all, and he's obviously not bragging about it for some reason.''

We drove north in easy traffic, catching the lights just right, heading up State Street at a steady clip toward the piled-up building blocks of downtown, whose streets—usually the informational garden for most cultivating detectives—were as barren to me as the asphalt they were made of.

I was disappointed. When Bob Shattuck's criminal report had first flickered up on that computer screen, I'd felt the satisfaction of a hunt well conducted. I'd followed the evidence, had gone with my instincts, and had landed the prize— or so I'd thought.

Now I just had a surgeon who wasn't talking, the name of a burned-out radical that had probably been borrowed for the occasion, and my still-nameless pile of bones back home.

I knew Runnion's case load would soon be knocking at his conscience, especially once his own interest in all this had been satisfied. He'd still help me open a few bureaucratic doors, partially to be helpful and partially out of nostalgia, but the piles of paper on his desk were beckoning.

I needed to regain the steam I'd thought I had earlier, but my options were either limited or diplomatically risky. I'd either have to follow in Runnion's wake, hoping to get lucky very soon, or I'd have to become more independent, a little less circumspect, and perhaps stimulate a few people's interest. To start with, I wasn't at all sure that going back to Shilly was the reasonable next step. I'd challenged him once, after all, and he'd outbluffed me fair and square. I didn't see where harassing him would better my prospects. But Shattuck interested me. Assuming he hadn't been at the hospital that night, I wanted to know why his name had been used.

''You going to turn in or sample a little of the nightlife?'' Runnion asked, negotiating the thicker traffic of the bustling city's heart, his face reflecting the garish colors of its clustered neon life signs.

I hedged my response. ''I might wander around a bit.''

Chapter Nineteen

I sat in my car for a good twenty minutes, watching the last known address of Robert Shattuck. It was an odd building, tall, bland, and gray, its first floor blatantly commercial—with a sandwich shop and a shoe-repair place, both closed now that it was long after hours—while its upper floors remained noncommittal. Some windows were lit, most were not. It was hard to tell what the place was used for.

The neighborhood appeared similarly ambiguous. From my vantage point in the deserted parking lot across the street, I was conscious of emptiness and silence, despite the fact that I was within walking distance of where the Chicago River's north, east, and south branches converge, right across the water from the famed Chicago Loop. None of that was readily apparent, however—the looming clifflike mass of the darkened Merchandise Mart just behind me blocked all sights and sounds of anything lying beyond it.

Indeed, it was perhaps the stultifying influence of that one building, second only to the Pentagon in sheer mass, that affected the entire area around it. There were few people on the sidewalks, few cars passing by. Only the occasional rumbling of the elevated train around the corner disturbed what appeared to be the sole grave-still pocket in this otherwise-teeming city.

I'd been waiting for signs of life either entering or leaving the building, if only to locate which of several unpromising candidates was the building's front door. I was finally rewarded by a small, bent-over man coaxing a small dog on a leash, who briefly appeared under the streetlight near the middle of the building's west wall before shambling off into the gloom.

I slowly got out of my car, looking around, sensitive to the echo that greeted my slammed door. I'd been expecting something entirely different after reading Shattuck's rap sheet. Knowing nothing of the address at the time, I'd envisioned him as the only white holdout in a ghetto slum, true to his reformist soul; or, alternatively, in a not uncommon about-face, inhabiting the quintessential suburban home, complete with an aged Volvo bedecked with environmental bumper stickers. This austere gray huddling of faceless concrete walls, as hospitable as an abandoned factory, fitted neither image and left me nothing to go on.

I crossed the dark, empty street, my eyes warily on the windows above me, and entered the side street into which the old man had stepped with his dog. Opposite the streetlight that had briefly caught him, almost flush with the cement wall, was a metal fire door, one of several I'd noticed. I turned the knob, expecting resistance, and instead stepped into a half-lit hallway, lined on one side with copper-colored mailboxes and blocked at the far end by a locked glass door with a speaker by its side.

I studied the rows of mailboxes, each one of which, under its keyhole, had a nameplate slot and a buzzer to gain admittance. Many of the boxes had no names, others were obviously businesses, their official cards substituting for hand-lettered nameplates, and the rest were presumably what I was after—apartments.

I had just located the name Shattuck in a red ink scrawl when the front door opened behind me. I swung around to face the old man with the dog, startling him.

"Just me," he said nervously. "Come on, Butch."

The dog, as wide as it was long, reluctantly waddled into the lobby, looking around like some dispirited, overgrown, ancient rodent. Nevertheless, despite his anemic charisma, Butch was obviously a bolster to his master's courage, who now nodded knowingly but mistakenly at the car keys I was inexplicably still holding in my hand, and commented, "No mail today, huh? Me, neither. Not even junk."

I smiled and shrugged my shoulders.

He shuffled over to the glass door, inserted his key, and swung it open. "You comin'?"

I yielded to temptation, pocketed my own keys, and followed him in. "Maybe I'll have better luck tomorrow."

"Probably just get bills," he muttered, half to me and half to Butch.

I headed up the cement stairs to the upper floors as the old man kept on going down the dark hallway, until all I could hear of either of them was the shuffle of his shoes and the light clittering of Butch's nails.

The number over Shattuck's name had been 46, implying the fourth floor. I climbed slowly and quietly, but the crunching of the grit underfoot still reverberated off the hard, plain walls with the brittle harshness of a maximum-security prison. I had rarely been in a dwelling so utterly devoid of any soothing human touch. There wasn't even any graffiti on the walls.

I still wasn't sure why I'd taken the old man up on his offer to bypass the security system. My interest in Shattuck was purely informational—on the surface, at least. But there was something nagging me about all this, like a tune I couldn't quite bring to mind. Chicago was to have been the place where the puzzle pieces would make sense—where the bones would be given a name, and their appearance in Vermont an explanation. Sitting out in that parking lot, waiting, I'd had time to question that notion. Shilly's denial had nothing to do with some ethical misbehavior from the past. His reticence— perhaps his fear—had struck me as being as fresh as the shots that had perforated the hearse back in Brattleboro.

The bones, and the money, and the wound in Abraham Fuller's back may have all had their birth in the late sixties, but none of them had stopped there. Indeed, they may have been only the beginning.

That was the thought that made me cautious now.

Shattuck's door was at the end of the hallway. I listened for a few seconds, hoping again for some small insight into the man I was pursuing—the kind of music he liked, or the TV show he preferred to watch at this hour—but there was no sound. I knocked loudly and waited.

"Who is it?"

I started at the soft voice, from both its proximity and the fact that I'd heard no footsteps announcing its arrival. It was like a disembodied entity of its own, hanging at eye level on the other side of the door.

"Mr. Shattuck?"

"Who is it?" The tone hadn't changed. It was still light, flat, and without noticeable interest.

"My name's Gunther. I've come a long way to talk to you. From Vermont."

"Why?"

I hesitated, not wanting to give him enough to turn me down before he'd even opened the door. "Can we do this face-to-face? It's kind of a long story."

The flatness was replaced by either suspicion or curiosity— I couldn't tell which. "Who are you?"

This was where suspicion would keep the door shut or curiosity would open it up. "I'm a policeman."

The door opened. "From Vermont? No kidding."

The man before me, only half-visible in the dim hallway light, was tall and thin, with a tangled gray beard and long hair tied back in a ponytail. He was wearing blue jeans and a faded T-shirt with FARM AID emblazoned across a stylized guitar. "Come in; watch your step—it's a little dark."

In fact, it was almost pitch-black, the only source of light being a single guttering candle planted in the middle of the floor ahead of me. Shattuck led the way, pointing to the vague outline of a pillow. "Have a seat. I was meditating."

I lowered myself awkwardly to the floor, moving the pillow back a little so I could prop myself against the wall.

"So what's going on in Vermont?" He was more of a ghost than a living being, with only the white highlights of his clothing and hair visible in the gloom. But his voice was now open and friendly, and while the lighting was unconventional, it was also curiously soothing.

"We found a skeleton that we've traced back to Chicago, and we just tagged your name to it."

"My name? To a skeleton? Far out. How old a skeleton?"

"About twenty years—a little more. Do you—or did you ever—know anyone in Vermont?"

The shadowy head shook from side to side. "No—never even been there. I don't understand, though—how did you connect my name to a bunch of bones?"

"Do you know a Dr. Shilly?" I asked instead.

"Shilly? Doesn't ring a bell. What kind of doctor?"

"Orthopedic surgeon."

"Bones again. No—never heard of him."

"You were here in Chicago in the late sixties?"

"I've always been here—born and bred."

"Pretty active in the protest movement and such?"

There was a pause, and I felt the genial atmosphere chill by several degrees. "I guess by that you've already seen my sheet. What's your point?"

I tried to defuse the tension slightly with a friendlier approach. "Sorry, bad habit. I didn't mean to give you the third degree. I really am just trying to put a name to this body. I did see your record, but that's when I thought you were the skeleton. The implication was that you became quite radical—had maybe even become one of the leaders. . . ."

His gentle laughter interrupted me. "Leaders? Not hardly. Look, I don't know how you run things in ol' Vermont, but here—especially back in those days—the cops were making paranoids look mellow. They saw a conspiracy every time two hippies shook hands. We didn't have rank—we had beliefs. We worked together for a common cause—"

This time, I interrupted. "Yes, but not all those causes saw eye-to-eye. The Weathermen were hardly the peaceniks."

Shattuck seemed to reflect on that for a moment. "And you want to know which one I was." His voice became guarded. "What's your interest?"

It wasn't the ideal interview of a potentially hostile witness. Usually, I was prearmed with facts that merely needed confirmation or clarification. Here, I was after raw data, and didn't know if the witness was hostile or not. It tended to throw most of the rules of interrogation right out the window.

I decided to backtrack a little. "This body—or what's left of it—might have been involved in a fairly violent branch of the protest movement around here."

I reached into my inside jacket pocket and pulled out one of the composite five-by-sevens I'd made of Abraham Fuller's face, both as a corpse and with twenty years taken off it and the eyes airbrushed in, open and lifelike. "Does this man look familiar?"

Shattuck leaned far forward, holding the photo almost directly in the timid candle's flame. He spent a long time studying it. "I thought you said he was a skeleton."

"This is somebody else. Do you know him?"

He shook his head. "No. Are these two different shots? The one with the eyes open looks strange."

"It's been touched up to make him look younger."

Shattuck looked up at me, the candlelight making his eyes shine. "So he just died? You never got to talk to him?"

I looked at him closely, interested by the precision of his last question. "You sure you don't know him?"

He returned the photo and receded into the dark, his voice casual again. "Sure I'm sure; I was just a little confused by the chronology. I didn't know you also had a fresh body on your hands. You think he's connected to the skeleton?"

"You ever hear the name Abraham Fuller?"

He sounded more comfortable again. "Nope—sounds vaguely biblical. Was that his name?"

I switched tacks slightly. "You still keep in touch with anyone from the old days?"

"A few—not many. A lot's changed."

"Bobby Seale in a three-piece suit?"

I could almost see the rueful smile—and I could hear it in his voice. "Yeah, I guess so."

"Could you give me the name of anyone else who might be able to help me out?"

He shifted his weight, recrossing his legs. "I don't know; giving references to cops isn't a great way to keep friends in this group."

"It's all ancient history," I lied.

He caught that immediately. "That's not what that photograph says."

"The only thing he did recently was die."

"Of natural causes?"

I stood up, ready to leave, knowing I'd gotten all I would get and that Shattuck was now trying to turn the tables. "Natural to him, I think."

Chapter Twenty

What was he like?'' Runnion asked as we waited for the crosswalk signal to staunch the early-morning downtown traffic.

I'd been thinking about Shattuck half the night, lying in bed, listening to the sounds of the unfamiliar city around me. "Seemingly a pleasant, slightly off-the-wall retired peace protester—just as advertised in your files.''

Runnion looked at me with a smile. "Seemingly?''

"Call it my own paranoia, but I was pretty sure he knew more than he was letting on. When I showed him Abraham Fuller's photograph, I felt like I'd handed him a gold coin—not that he showed it much.''

Runnion was unimpressed. "Oh, hell, that happens sometimes. Maybe something'll come of it.''

We were standing across from Chicago's City Hall and Cook County Building, a heavy, squared-off, flat-roofed monster. With an army of six-story-tall pale stone Corinthian columns on the outside and turn-of-the-century metal-encased windows peeking out in between them, the whole structure looked like a hundred-year-old office building that had been swallowed up by an ancient Greek temple

We crossed Randolph Street and walked through the building's north entrance, taking the stairs down from the first floor's vaulted grandeur to the conventional modern basement below. Runnion pushed through a pair of glass double doors marked COUNTY CLERK—BUREAU OF VITAL STATISTICS—BIRTH, MARRIAGE, DEATH. Ignoring the rows of plastic chairs in the waiting area, already half full of depressed-looking people, he waved to a heavyset black woman sitting at a desk beyond the counter clerks.

She gave him a small smile, which I took as a form of professional supervisory reserve, and met him at the far end of the counter, where her enthusiasm rose more clearly, albeit quietly, to the surface. "Hey, Norman. What you been up to?"

"Hi, Flo. Not much—waiting for the pension. This is a friend of mine—Joe Gunther—lieutenant from Vermont."

Flo's eyes widened. "Vermont? Long way from home."

I shook hands with her. "Don't I know it."

She smiled broadly, then shifted her attention to Runnion. "So, what's on your mind, Norman? Who do you want the goods on?"

Runnion slipped her a piece of paper with Kevin Shilly's name on it. "He's white, rich, and uncooperative."

She laughed and took the paper with her, disappearing through a door behind the desks.

Runnion pushed himself away from the counter, heading back toward the door. "That'll take her a few minutes; let's see what else we can dig up."

He turned right out the door and headed down the hall to a distant door marked MARRIAGE BUREAU, NOTARY & BUSINESS REGISTRATION. "Maybe we can get something on his practice."

His request for information at the Business Registration desk roughly mirrored his chat with Flo, as did similar requests upstairs at the county treasurer's office, the county assessor's office, and a number of other places throughout the building. At every stop, he had a friendly acquaintance, an exchange of pleasantries, and parted with another person digging on our behalf. At the end of the tour, he returned to Flo's counter to collect what she'd discovered, then continued to each office in turn, reaping what he'd sowed.

We were back on the sidewalk some two hours later, clutching a fistful of copied documents. "Let's get some coffee and look this stuff over."

There was a doughnut shop nearby, narrow and long, almost empty during the midmorning lull. We took a booth at the very back.

"So how did you build up all those contacts?" I asked as we doctored our coffee. "That can't be typical of every cop in this town."

He grinned, pleased that I'd recognized his prowess.

"Took me years. Even so, I'm not sure I could have done it anywhere else. I visited New York once, on assignment like you, and was led through their version of the paper chase. Lasted forever. Amazing number of cranky people. Chicago's a whole lot friendlier."

He took a sip of his coffee. "Takes work, of course. I get to know these people, their families. I help 'em out when I can—keep them up to date on friends or relatives in jail. I buy 'em presents sometimes, or spring for a meal. Mostly, I make myself available. I become their own private police-man—the guy who can cut through the red tape. It's a 'you help me, I help you' kind of thing."

He pushed his cup to one side and began laying out his treasure on the table between us. "Let's see what we've got."

What we had was a fairly complete portrait of the capitalist system at its most rewarding: a luxury apartment in a glisten-ing tower overlooking the lake; a yacht; a Mercedes-Benz and an Alfa-Romeo; a wife born of one of the city's prominent families; two boys now in exclusive prep schools; and a cumulative estate assessed by the county at about $5 million.

Whatever it was Kevin Shilly was hiding, it was pretty obvious what the stakes were. I hoped I could use that to my advantage when I went to pay him a second call.

I entered Shilly's office building off Michigan Avenue and waved to the security guard who'd helped me the day before. He returned the salute and added, "He's not in."

I hesitated, and the guard added, "Never showed this morning."

I thanked him and headed for the elevator bank. Maybe Giovanna knew what was up.

I was without Runnion by now, who'd begun to feel the gravitational pull of his paperwork. He was still chewing over the mysteriously absent gunshot report—he'd found no mention of it anywhere in the files. His assumption now was that the hospital had never called it in, and agreed with me that Shilly had probably run interference. That was one ques-tion he'd asked me to add to my own list.

Giovanna was distinctly less delighted to see me. "He's not here," she said as I crossed the threshold.

"So I gather. Off playing golf?"

"He doesn't play golf." She looked as immaculate as before, in a different suit this time, wearing a silky-looking blue blouse with an enormous droopy bow that hung down the front. Her expression, however, wore more than just her displeasure with me.

"What's up? You look worried."

She seemed surprised by the question, and touched her cheek with her fingertips as if to brush away a blemish. "He was supposed to be here. I've been canceling appointments all morning."

"You call his home?" A faint chill began to trickle down my spine.

"Of course. There's no answer."

"How about his wife?"

"She's in Europe."

"He ever done this before?" The chill was now becoming a dread that I'd just committed a tremendous blunder.

"No."

"Did he go home last night?"

"I think so. He sometimes spends the night on his boat, but that number doesn't answer, either."

"Call his apartment building," I said as I stepped back into the hallway. "Tell security I'm coming and to let me up to his apartment. But they are not to move a muscle before I get there, understand? And call Detective Norman Runnion at Area Six headquarters and tell him to meet me at Shilly's right away."

Shilly's apartment tower was a ten-minute drive from North Michigan on Lake Shore Drive—a sixty-story black glass and steel cylinder standing alone, almost directly opposite the Navy Pier. Ordinarily, I wouldn't have had Giovanna call ahead, but I was hoping it would convince the building's rent-a-cops to let me in without asking questions.

I parked in the NO PARKING zone directly in front of the doorman, whom I addressed with a hurried but authoritative, "Police business."

The man behind the half-round desk in the lobby was less startled, rising as I announced myself and indicating a second armed guard who was standing by the elevator bank. "One of our men will go with you.'' In the background, bolstering my credibility, we could all hear an approaching siren.

''Can he get inside the apartment?''

''Yes, sir.''

The tall black security cop and I rode up in silence. He stood with his back to the far wall of the elevator, his right hand nervously rubbing his holstered gun butt, his eyes fixed on the row of floor numbers, no doubt wondering what kind of mess I was about to get him in.

On the forty-fifth floor, the doors whispered open. ''Which one is it?''

The guard nodded silently at the door opposite us. I rang the doorbell and waited.

''When did you come on this morning?''

''Six.''

''See this guy at all?''

''No, sir.''

''Would you know him if you did?''

''No, but Will checked the log. He left last night.''

That surprised me. ''You mean late?''

'' 'Bout midnight.''

''And he hasn't been back?''

''No, sir.''

I pondered that for a moment, ringing the bell again. ''Did he have any visitors?''

''One, just before. He left with him.''

''You get a name?''

''Will told it to me—'case you asked. Name was Gunther.''

I felt like a mild electrical jolt had hit the base of my skull. ''You better unlock this.''

We were greeted by total silence, punctuated only by the ticking of a distant clock and the steady faint hum of the building's circulatory system. We stood, the guard slightly behind me, in the front hallway of a huge apartment, its acreage of living room stretching out before us. It was not the apartment, however, that caught the eye, but what extended beyond it. Through the wall-to-wall, floor-to-ceiling bank of windows, Lake Michigan reached as far as the eye could see—a solid blue sheet, as clear and featureless as the sky above it, giving me the giddy feeling of somehow being in flight, high over the earth.

I turned back to the guard. "Why don't you stay here? I want to look the place over."

The kitchen, dining room, guest bedroom, even the bathrooms all had spectacular vistas, either out onto the lake or along its shore. And all of them were appointed in the latest modern spaceship fashions, with an excess of tubular steel, glass, and synthetic marble. It occurred to me that Shilly had decorated his home much like an operating room.

I located the master bedroom last—again huge, sterile, and expensive, but not pristine. The bed had been slept in—one side only—and there were clothes on the floor, a pair of pajamas draped messily over the foot of the bed. One of the closets was open and a single drawer of a gigantic recessed chest gaped wide open. The one jarring note was the delicate, rhythmic, melodious pulse of the alarm clock by the side of the bed—designed, no doubt, to drag you ever so comfortably away from your dreams.

I stood in the middle of the room, taking my time, ignoring the alarm. Indeed, it was helpful—it and the pajamas and the clothes on the floor all told me he'd been in bed when his midnight caller had come visiting.

There was a slight sound behind me and I turned, to see Norm Runnion standing in the doorway, as attuned as I was that something had gone wrong here.

"This may not be exactly legal," he said.

"If I'm right, it won't matter much. You see the log downstairs?"

He nodded. "I take it that wasn't you."

"I think it was Shattuck—right after I told him about Shilly."

My tone of voice told him what I thought of myself at the moment. He pursed his lips. "I'll call in a lab team. You check the place out already?"

"Not completely." Nor would I be able to, now that the locals were here.

But he surprised me. He smiled thinly and muttered, "Well, finish up—I won't be long."

With that reprieve, I moved swiftly to the kitchen and then

to the bar just off the living room, all my senses focusing on the fastest search of my career.

Apparently, Shilly had eaten dinner out, which his dishwasher, pantry, and fridge told me he did regularly, and he hadn't entertained his late-night guest with a cocktail—no dirty glasses, no melted water in the ice bucket.

I returned to the bedroom, playing back Shilly's activities here according to the evidence. So, a normal evening, finished when he sets the alarm and goes to bed. The desk then rings from downstairs. Shilly answers from the box by the bedroom door. Gunther again. No doubt cursing the name but not daring to refuse him, Shilly lets him up and opens the front door. There is no peephole—the building has armed guards, after all, and his visitor is a cop.

I made a mental note to get a description of "Gunther" from the night deskman later. Maybe the guy's holding a gun, or maybe he's just the holder of Shilly's secret—enough to get him out of his pajamas and into . . . what?

I moved over to the open closet and the drawer, hearing Runnion's distant voice on the phone down the hall. Casual clothing only—blue jeans, windbreakers, sweaters, T-shirts. I continued searching, finding the suit he'd worn the day before inside another closet filled with suits and dress shirts. It was on a special counter, to be taken out and cleaned. No doubt people came and did things like that for him every day—clean and wash and tidy up.

So, dressed casually, Shilly leaves with Mr. Gunther. But maybe not quite yet. I went into the bathroom. If I'd been under duress, I'd use the bathroom to leave a sign of some sort—the one place I could have a moment's privacy before being forced out the door. Hollywood stuff, but that's what people fall back on when they have no personal experience to guide them.

I got close to the mirror—ten feet long and half again as high, looming over two marble sinks. The surface over one of them was smeared, slightly greasy, and vaguely pink, over about a two-foot-square area. I shook my head, muttered, "Christ," and poked carefully in the trash basket near the toilet. There was a thick wad of toilet paper covered with red, and a flat-nosed lipstick, its usual perfect tip crushed like the end of a crayon.

On the floor, near the corner, was a broken glass with a toothbrush nearby, and a rack where the towel was so skewed, it was barely hanging on. I faked the motions, pretending to write on the mirror, being hip-checked by someone coming through the door, being thrown across the room, knocking the glass off its perch and disturbing the towel below it. On the floor, near the glass, barely discernible except from my hands and knees, I found a single half-wiped drop of blood. A cut hand? A lip? Maybe a nose? Again, something to ask the night crew in the lobby.

Kevin Shilly had been snatched—just a few hours after I'd given his name to Bob Shattuck. Small-town cop in the big city helps prominent local citizen get abducted—or worse.

"Why would Shattuck grab Shilly?" Runnion asked from the door.

I got up. "I don't know. When we talked, he was all innocence. He'd even been meditating when I knocked on his door. . . . Son of a bitch."

Runnion mulled that over for a few moments before finally saying, "I have to wait here for the lab crew, but I can have a unit meet you at his place so you'll be a little more official. What's the address?"

I gave it to him. "Is this going to get your butt in a sling?"

He shrugged. "It's a little unorthodox, that's all. No problem, as long as you don't go inside without an invite or a warrant."

I gave him a quick smile. "Thanks."

"Sure." He looked vaguely wistful as I headed for the elevator, as if he envied me. I couldn't see the attraction myself, considering how hard I was kicking myself in the ass.

Downstairs, I thanked the deskman for his help and asked him how the security worked in the building.

"This is the public entrance—the only way outsiders get in or out. They check in at the desk, give their name and maybe the company if they're delivering somethin', then we call the tenant. When they leave, we log 'em out."

"How about when a client comes and goes? Isn't there a garage under here?"

"Yeah, and another desk, right by the elevators. Same thing: They go in or out, we log 'em. And the garage has a remote gate—you can't get in without a door opener, and an alarm goes off if a second car tries to piggyback in. There's a camera, too, so the guard can see who's coming. Plus, we got a roamer—J.J. there, who went up with you—who mostly just keeps an eye out."

"You better see if you can get the night crew here. People'll want to talk to them." Especially, I thought, about the use of the name Gunther.

The deskman gave me a pissed-off, weary look, realizing all his cooperation had just been turned against him.

Bob Shattuck's neighborhood didn't look much livelier by day. Both the shoe-repair store and the sandwich shop were open but empty. The temporary quarters of the Chicago Public Library, which I hadn't realized occupied one end of the parking lot, was the only door that had people going in and out.

I was standing on the sidewalk, looking up at Shattuck's building, when a patrol car slid to a stop opposite.

The driver stuck his elbow out the window. "You Gunther?"

I nodded and crossed over as they both swung heavily out of the car—one, an overweight white man; the other, a small, wiry guy with Hispanic features and careful, watchful eyes.

I led the way to the unobtrusive front door and pushed it open for them. They entered, looking around, casually cautious, always aware of what a city like this might tuck behind its doors. They had an animal sharpness to them, even the fat one, which made me think of my own squad back home— less wary, not used to being targets.

The small patrolman looked at me. "You got a key?"

"No."

He grunted softly and pushed the intercom button to the superintendent's apartment. A squawky voice asked who it was.

"Chicago Police."

"What the hell do you guys want?"

"Just checking on one of your tenants."

"They ain't my tenants."

"Open the door, please."

"Open it yourself."

There was a loud buzzing and the electric lock on the double glass doors sprang open. The big cop pushed it open. "So much for security."

I preceded them up the stairs, our shoes making a horrendous clatter against the cement. "You know," the wiry one said, "if nobody's home, that's it. We don't got a warrant."

"I know."

On the fourth floor, as dark as in the middle of the night, I paused, looking down the length of the landing.

"At the end?"

I looked at the big one—Ross, according to his nameplate. "Yeah."

He cleared his flashlight from his belt and switched it on. As he did, his companion—Diaz—instinctively moved to the other side of the hall, slightly in the lee of a door frame.

The flashlight's brilliant halogen glare catapulted to the end of the hallway, through the open, gaping door, and flattened against a distant interior wall.

"Guess we won't have to worry about knockin'," Ross muttered.

We moved toward the distant doorway, my companions no longer disinterested—on the balls of their feet, their hands on their gun butts. We positioned ourselves to both sides of the entrance and waited briefly, listening to the interior of the dark apartment. I didn't know what they knew of me, except that I was obviously a "suit," and therefore the asshole who would probably get their tails shot off. I decided I'd better lead the charge.

I reached around and hammered on the open door with my fist. "Shattuck? It's Joe Gunther."

Nothing came back. I thought of Shilly's apartment—that same stillness. Only here, there was something—a feeling of someone waiting.

"Shattuck? Come on out."

Again, nothing. I gestured for Ross's light and shined it around inside, keeping myself behind the door frame. The room, with the extinct candle still sitting in its dish on the floor, was empty. I stepped inside, moving along the wall.

I felt Ross and Diaz hesitate behind me, no doubt silently debating the legality of my actions, before pulling their weapons and following me in.

I hadn't seen a thing the night before, but I'd sensed what I saw now—spareness, almost emptiness: a few pillows on the floor, a few posters on the wall. All the windows had been covered with tinfoil; not a sliver of daylight got through.

Ross stayed in the entrance hall; Diaz moved across the room to the kitchenette, quickly checking the open closet as he went. I waited for them to position themselves before I approached the only other door, presumably to the bedroom and bath beyond.

Again, I stood to one side and knocked, calling out Shattuck's name; still, I got nothing in response.

I leaned over, twisted the doorknob, and pushed. The door swung back with a faint protest and hung open. I poked the flashlight around the corner and took a quick look.

Sitting in a wooden chair facing me, naked, covered with cuts and cigarette-sized welts, his mouth taped shut to stifle his screams, was Kevin Shilly. There was a neat black hole in his forehead.

The rest of the room and the bathroom were empty.

Diaz and Ross stood at the bedroom door, watching me, their arms limp but still holding their guns. Diaz's eyes were hard on the corpse.

Mr. Beautiful, Shilly's office guard had called him. No longer.

Chapter Twenty-one

I shut my eyes gratefully at the sound of Gail's cheerful voice, letting it, like the motel bed beneath me, act on my mind like a balm.

"I was hoping you'd call soon. How're things going?"

"They could be better."

"Oh, oh."

I smiled wanly. "That's one way to put it."

"Are you all right, Joe?"

"I'm okay." Having initiated the call, I was now suddenly reluctant—even slightly embarrassed—to turn it into a confessional. "I just got off the phone with Brandt and Klesczewski. Apparently, nothing new on our sniper. Ron said they're looking for new angles, but Brandt's obviously pretty anxious for me to come home with the goods."

"I noticed there hasn't been anything on the news."

There was a small pause. "So tell me what's really wrong. You sound totally flattened."

I let out a sigh and told her. "I probably played a direct role in getting a man killed over here—tortured and killed, to be accurate."

"My God. Who?"

"No one you know, but he was doing fine until I mentioned his name to somebody I was questioning. I've never felt like a such a jerk."

"Who were you questioning?"

"His name is Shattuck—supposedly a retired peace freak turned radical, but now I don't know . . . and probably never will." The last four words were delivered in a flat tone.

Gail picked up on it. "Did the local cops pull the rug out from under you?"

I laughed, although without much pleasure. Leave it to Gail to grasp the political reality immediately. "It's their case now, and they made it pretty clear they don't see some woodchuck from Vermont as an asset. In fact, they put me through a four-hour grilling. Pretty hostile session; they don't make any bones about my having screwed up. One of them's okay—Norm Runnion—he's my baby-sitter. But he's a few months shy of retirement and he stuck his neck out by giving me more leash than he should've, so now he's almost as much on the outs as I am."

"But he's still your local contact, right? With access to their computers and whatnot?"

I saw where she was headed. "True, except that if the guys running the homicide investigation catch either one of us snooping around their case, there'll be hell to pay. Besides, why would Runnion risk it? He told me earlier that Chicago averages nine hundred and fifty homicides every year, not to mention a few thousand unsuccessful shootings and stabbings."

There was silence at the other end: Gail running out of suggestions. "Does that mean you'll be coming home?"

But suggestions, or at least questions, were finally beginning to stir in my tired brain, despite my own pessimism. "Remember Abraham Fuller?"

"What about him?"

"I'm pretty sure Shattuck knew him. It was the one thing he really focused on during our interview."

"Who is Shattuck, anyway?"

I explained to her about finding Kevin Shilly, tracing the metal knee through inventory, discovering Shattuck's name on the hospital records, and what I'd found out about him through the police files. I told in detail of the conversation by candlelight.

"And you're sure it was Shattuck who killed Shilly?"

I hesitated a moment. "Pretty sure. It was Shattuck who removed him from his apartment building. He used my name at the desk, assuming that would grab Shilly's attention, and when they finally located the night deskman, his description of 'Gunther' fit Shattuck like a glove."

"But why would Shattuck take Shilly back to his own place to kill him, and even leave the door open? Why kill Shilly at all, for that matter? Shattuck had been so innocuous before this."

I'd thought a lot about that over the past several hours. "I can't prove it yet, but I think my telling Shattuck about what we found in Vermont changed everything for him, like I guess it did for whoever machine-gunned us in Brattleboro. We're looking at all this dispassionately—connecting old bones to old money and trying to make sense of it. But something violent and angry is brewing here, something involving more people than we thought. I think I hit Shattuck's button without knowing it and set him off like a rocket.

"He used my name because it was efficient and practical to do so; he used his place to torture Shilly for the same reason; and he killed him either out of pent-up frustration or because he feels he has nothing more to lose. Whether it was consciously done or not, leaving that front door open served notice to everyone that he's come out from under a peaceful-looking twenty-four-year-old rock.

"All of which," I concluded, "also helps explain the paranoia that made whoever it was shoot at the hearse on I-91."

Gail played devil's advocate. "Wasn't that because the shooter wanted to protect his new life? You said yourself that he did it to stop you from tracing the knee."

"I know, but setting up a machine gun and firing at the local police seems a little drastic. It would've made more sense to liquidate his assets quickly and quietly and then disappear without a trace—just like he'd done once before. Having seen what happened to Shilly, I no longer think the Brattleboro Police Department was this guy's biggest concern."

"You think he did it to stop Shattuck from finding out?" Gail said, her voice slightly incredulous.

"Why not? There were three people at the very least who were involved in all this—Fuller, the guy with the knee, and the person who both stole the astrological chart and opened fire on us on the interstate. If I'm right that showing Fuller's picture was enough to get Shilly killed, then our local shooter has bigger reasons than the police to stay hidden. It's got to make you think the money alone is not the issue here."

"Revenge, then? Setting an example?"

"It sounds right, judging from what I've seen."

There was a long pause while I mulled that over. Unfortunately, that was about all I could do.

Gail apparently sensed that impasse. "None of which gets you anywhere if they've frozen you out of the investigation."

But I was no longer feeling so hopeless. Our conversation had kindled an enthusiasm that this afternoon's third degree had almost extinguished. "Maybe not. The investigation is on who killed Shilly—or maybe just on locating Shattuck. But it's not concerned with putting a name to that goddamn metal knee. I might still be able to do that without getting in their way."

"Isn't that a little like sharing a meal with lions?"

"Maybe, but with a routinely high homicide rate, you go for the obvious solutions. Assuming Shattuck did knock off Shilly, and that the local Mounties get their man, that's where it'll end, and it still has nothing directly to do with why I came here."

Gail's silence was skepticism itself.

"Hey—wish me luck."

"I wish for you to stay out of prison, or at least alive."

The woman guarding the archives room in the basement of the University of Chicago medical center was less than thrilled to see me, even though I'd made sure to appear just after opening time.

"Again?" was all she said as I smiled and walked by, hoping that Hoolihan's order to cooperate was still in place.

"You don't need me to show you where that file is again, do you?" she added, establishing her conscientiousness for the record.

"No, ma'am. All set."

In fact, it took me quite a while to ferret it out again, the rows of shelves being similar and the files themselves all but identical to one another. I took it to the same table we'd used before and, page by page, photographed its contents with a secondhand camera I'd bought an hour before at a pawnshop.

What I was doing was more a threat to the case than to my liberty; in legal parlance, Hoolihan's grumpy blessing the first time had amounted to a consent search, and this second visit was, in essence, riding the coattails of the first. Indeed, the archivist, by letting me in, had implied consent. Still, Hoolihan didn't know about this second visit, nor had he ever agreed to our removing the files, which I was in the process of doing photographically.

But I was running out of time, Brandt was running out of patience back home, and this was the only clue I had in this city that might get me beyond a single metal knee and the dead surgeon who'd implanted it.

Two hours later, after spending a reasonable sum at a While-U-Wait processing lab getting my roll of film developed, and a small fortune having eight-by-ten enlargements made, I was parked once again in Dr. Milton Yancy's office at Northwestern, hoping he could shoehorn me in between patients.

"Lieutenant," he said, his expression beaming and his hand outstretched. "Nice to see you again. Is the plot thickening?"

"You could say that. You read the papers today?"

"No. I wait until I get home for that, assuming the rest of the family has left any of it intact." He made a scissors motion with his two fingers.

"Kevin Shilly was found murdered yesterday."

Yancy's face fell. "Oh, my Lord." He unconsciously groped for a chair and sat down heavily. "Did it have anything to do with what you're investigating?"

"I think so, yes."

He shook his head. "How sad. Was he shot?"

"Yes," I said without elaboration. Given Yancy's sensitivity, I saw no point in becoming more graphic. I handed him the pile of photographs. "I was wondering if you could look these over and help me decipher them a bit. They're the patient file on that skeleton I introduced you to the other day."

He spread them across his examining table, shaking his head. "First the skeletal X rays, now the patient file. It's like seeing a life in reverse. You do this a lot, I suppose. . . ."

His voice drifted off as he read, so I saw no need to respond. It was an interesting point, though, and one I'd never thought about. "I was reading this with a colleague earlier," I said to the back of his head. "He mentioned something about reports from other doctors?"

Yancy's voice was back to normal, the shock of Shilly's death having yielded to professional curiosity. "Oh yes." He pawed through a few of the photos. "Doctors Butterworth and Yamani; vascular surgeon and neurosurgeon, respectively. I met Yamani, actually, a few years ago. I think he's in California now."

"Why did Shilly bring them in?"

Yancy straightened suddenly and gave me a large conspiratorial grin. "To cover his ass. Proceeding the way he was, he knew the risks, so he brought in the other two during surgery to back up his opinion and get more names in the file. It's just the kind of thing that eventually landed him in hot water."

He turned back to the pages. "Not in this case, though. The wound was straightforward. Butterworth reports no traumatic damage to the major vessels posterior to the knee, and Yamani says roughly the same thing about the tibial, the peroneal, and the saphenous nerves."

"So only the bone was damaged? Isn't that a little unlikely?"

Yancy shook his head. "Not particularly. They usually don't get away scot-free—there is commonly some bruising of the nerves, as there is here—but that takes care of itself. Mr."—here he referred back to the ER sheet to find the patient's name—"Shattuck was a lucky man, comparatively speaking."

"My understanding is that he disappeared five days after the surgery—faked being dependent on the bedpan so nobody would realize he could get around."

Yancy returned to the file. "Really? I hadn't gotten to that yet."

"My question is, Could he have done that without help? I mean, he did just have his entire knee replaced."

"Oh, he could have done it. The pain would be excruciating—no doubt about that—and he'd have had the stitches to worry about later, but it's certainly possible." He waved his hand at the photos. "There's the proof, after all."

"True, but that doesn't say he walked out on his own. He could have been rolled out in a wheelchair by someone else."

Yancy's eyes widened. "Oh, I see what you're saying. Well, he could have left the hospital on his own. There's a physical write-up on him somewhere in here—they do that to see how fit a patient is for surgery—and he passes that with flying colors: athletic build, no medical problems, good chemistry. . . . Apparently as healthy as a horse, barring the leg, of course.:"

"Does it say whether he was right- or left-handed?"

Yancy looked surprised. "No. Why do you ask?"

"The skeleton was a lefty. How about any other personal information?"

He picked up a single sheet of the file, offering it to me doubtfully. "You didn't see this? The Social Services report?"

I took it from him, remembering how Runnion and I had become sidetracked by the question of a gunshot wound being reported to the police. We'd never gotten this far into the file. I found myself reddening slightly as I looked it over now.

Yancy had the sensitivity to cover my awkwardness. He pointed to midway down the sheet. "It's not complete—barely filled out, actually—but it has a couple of things you might find handy. These forms are usually done when more time is allowed before surgery; in fact, if I interpret this correctly, Social Services started the process without Shilly's okay. See where it says 'incomplete per phys'? Shilly obviously shut them down when he found they'd started the form; that's his signature underneath the notation."

"Why not just throw it out?"

"Turf. Social Services obviously didn't want to catch flak later for failing to do their job, so they forced him to take responsibility. I can almost smell the animosity when I read something like this."

"That's not unusual?"

"Oh yes—the Social Services report is standard and useful, and it can sometimes be quite extensive. Depending on the physician, they'll go so far as getting the names of pets and favorite pastimes, favorite vacation spots, all sorts of things."

"What's the point?" I asked, ruing Shilly's interruption.

"The primary questions are medically relevant—possibly inherited conditions, like hemophilia, or an allergy to some drug, or a family history of stroke, or whatever. The secondary details are mostly so the various docs can be friendly with the patient. A crude example would be my checking a patient's chart before visitation, finding out he had three collie dogs, and opening my conversation with him by alluding to my love of collies. It's a fast and easy way of breaking the ice with people. Sounds a little cynical when I put it that way, but the intention's honorable."

I was still a little mystified, staring at the form. "This has virtually nothing on it. Wouldn't Shilly have needed to know some of this?"

"He probably had most of it verbally. Patients are asked half a dozen times whether they have any past medical history or allergies. If I were to play at your job for a moment, I'd guess that this incomplete form is another indication that something was going on under the table between patient and doctor."

I looked at the mostly blank sheet. Shattuck's name appeared again, along with "no current address" and "deceased" under "next of kin." "A. Salierno" was written next to "in case of emergency, contact," with an address. I showed it to Yancy.

"That ring a bell?"

He raised his eyebrows. "No, but that doesn't say much; I'm hardly a man about town. Give him—or her, I guess—a call; maybe you'll get lucky."

After my encounter with Shattuck, I was a little shy about dropping by people's homes without researching them first. I did use the phone book in the lobby, though, just to see if A. Salierno was listed. I drew a blank.

I was, however, within walking distance of both the *Chicago Tribune*, and its chief competitor, the *Sun-Times*, both of which flanked the two-winged Wrigley Building, making the latter look like a spread-armed referee, keeping two fighters apart.

Not that they were difficult to distinguish architecturally, one being as extreme as the other. But where the Tribune Tower looked like a keep without a castle or a Gothic spire in search of a nave, the Sun-Times Building, its southern wall almost flush with the riverbank, was reminiscent of a huge submarine with squared-off corners. I chose the Trib simply because my route down Michigan Avenue delivered it to me first.

Two hours later, I sat back in the plastic chair I'd been furnished and ground my aching eyes against the heels of both hands, glorying in the brief darkness following endless streams of flickering microfilm.

A—for Angelo—Salierno, it turned out, had acquired a bit more than a clipping here and there. In fact, as thirty-year head of the local Mafia, he and his family—blood-related and otherwise—had earned enough coverage to merit a decent-sized encyclopedia. I had read hundreds of column inches linking the "Dour Don," as the press had dubbed the unsmiling Salierno, to everything from racketeering in Cook County and all its neighbors to playing a major role in the creation of the Vegas mob. The don, who for years had worked out of a sealed and guarded compound in upscale River Forest—the same address listed in "Shattuck's" hospital file—was apparently a cautious, reserved, publicity-shy, traditional leader from the old school.

Presumably, his antique style of leadership owed its endurance to an almost corporate stolidity, which served it well in times of crisis. Despite its 1920s machine gun–toting reputation, the Outfit, as the mob was called in Chicago, had come a long way when it came to discretion.

The low-key style, however, had not fitted all the Saliernos so comfortably. Angelo's eldest son, Tomaso, predictably nicknamed "Tommy," had strained at his father's conservative leash. Indeed, it was Tommy and his private guard of henchmen who had usually landed the Salierno name on the front page, either by getting involved in deals of their own, which had a propensity for going sour, or simply by doing the wrong thing in the wrong place, as when Tommy took a bar stool to a window just as a free-lance photographer happened by. From my reading of his activities, Tommy Salierno was short-tempered, mean-spirited, egotistical, and ambitious. He was also neither smart nor lucky. He ended up facedown in a back alley with a bullet in his chest, the apparent victim of some inner-gang rivalry. The police nailed a minor family functionary for the crime—a numbers runner who'd reportedly lost his wife's affections to Tommy. Angelo retreated even further into his heavily guarded shell, and the Salierno name slid from the headlines, gaining a mention only now and then in articles dealing with the Mafia in general. Angelo himself hadn't been seen outside the River Forest compound in over twenty years, although he was reported to be still very much in charge. On the rare occasions that the *Tribune* was able to give a titillating glimpse of the Salierno hierarchy, it was invariably in the shape of Alfredo Bonatto, Angelo's "adviser." Balding, paunchy, slightly stooped, and wearing thick glasses and dark suits, Bonatto—who was also a lawyer—had become the inglorious image of an organization most people still connected in their minds to the likes of Al Capone.

To my mind, that was precisely what Angelo Salierno had been after all along—to become too outwardly boring to warrant much media attention, and too insulated legally to be touchable by the police.

That he had finally come to my attention, therefore, shouldn't normally have been of great interest to the Dour Don. No single hovering police officer, even from such a metropolitan hot spot as Brattleboro, was worth the time of day, especially without a warrant.

Unless that officer had a hook.

The street Salierno lived on in River Forest was predictably impressive—broad, silent, smelling of flower beds and closely cropped grass. The homes were different in style—English Tudor, fake Southern Plantation, Modern Confused—and more or less discreet, running from totally walled estates to five-thousand-square-foot architectural wedding cakes perched on huge weedless green patches for all the world to see.

The address I was after was predictably retiring: an ivy-covered brick wall, topped by broken glass—along with less visible, more lethal deterrents, no doubt. It was pierced by a single large wrought-iron gate, guarded by a gray intercom perched on a pole.

I parked in front of the gate, feeling self-conscious, convinced that everyone was watching me, although the street to my back looked perfectly normal.

I leaned out the window and stabbed the button under the speaker grille.

"Who is it?" The voice was male and unfriendly.

"My name is Joe Gunther. I'm a lieutenant with the police department in Brattleboro, Vermont." I figured honesty might suit me best, considering the people I was addressing.

"Got a warrant?"

"No, but I know why Tommy Salierno was killed."

There was a long pause. "Wait."

I stood there, feeling the sun gentle on my left shoulder, aware of a lawn mower working steadily some distance away and the sounds of songbirds in the trees lining the street. Ten minutes later, a broad-shouldered man in a tight dark suit walked down what I could see of the drive. He stopped on the other side of the massive gate, his eyes in constant motion, taking in as much of the surroundings as possible—a habit I'd seen in Secret Service agents.

"Got any credentials?"

I exited the car, pulled my badge and ID from my inner pocket, and handed them over.

He took his eyes off the scenery long enough to scrutinize my paperwork with an intensity worthy of an art expert. He finally handed them back. "Go to the coffeehouse six blocks that way and two blocks left and wait." He jerked a thumb up the street, turned on his heel, and marched back out of sight.

I did as I was told, finding a parking place diagonally across the street from the Cup-N-Saucer, which looked like a typical gathering spot for regulars, located on a standard version of a small-town main street. Like other sections of Chicago, this area had blocks that looked transplanted from central Iowa, right next to others that rivaled Beverly Hills.

There'd been no indication of how long I should wait, so I figured I'd better make myself comfortable. I chose a rear booth, sat so I could watch the front door, and ordered a hamburger and a milk shake for lunch.

Over the next two and a half hours, nursing a countless string of coffees, I watched people come and go—mostly go, after the noontime rush—never seeing anybody who struck me as unusual. I pegged most of them to be either retired people, traveling reps on break, or the rarer local office worker running in for a quick cup of something hot and stimulating.

It was therefore pretty obvious when the first of my expected company walked in. Not only was he built like a wrestler in a loose-fitting, untucked sports shirt—which conveniently hid anything tucked underneath—but he appeared from the hallway behind me, leading to the rest rooms and the storage room beyond. He, too, had those shifty, watchful eyes. He parked himself in a booth not too far away.

A second man, thinner, with a light jacket, entered the front and sat at the counter. A third walked to the only occupied booth not far from me, spoke inaudibly to the two old men who were chatting there, and apparently asked them to leave, which they did without comment. Finally, a last one appeared, gestured to the short-order cook and the sole waitress, muttered a few words to them, and escorted them out the door, flipping the CLOSED sign around and drawing the shade as he did so.

By this time, the hair on the back of my neck was rigid. Nobody spoke to anyone. The guards stayed at their posts. My coffee and my confidence began getting cold.

Finally, a shadow appeared at the front door, there was a gentle knock, and the last man in opened up, ushered in an older man wearing a dark three-piece suit, and locked the door again.

The newcomer I recognized by his newspaper photos—he was a little more stooped, the face a touch heavier and more lined, but the eyes were still sharp behind the thick glasses. He walked down the center of the coffee shop and stopped in front of my table. I stayed put, my hands on either side of my cup.

"May I see some identification?"

I pulled out my credentials again and he read them carefully before handing them back. "Gunther doesn't sound like a Vermont name."

"I was born there, as were my father and grandfather."

He nodded like a thoughtful banker. "The melting pot, of course." He finally slid onto the bench opposite mine. "My name is Bonatto; I am Mr. Salierno's adviser. Why have you come to see us?"

I knew—unlike when I'd been with Shattuck—that I was of value to this man. His presence here proved that. My strength, therefore, would come from carefully fanning those embers I'd inadvertently brought back to life, letting their energy do most of my work for me.

I decided to stay away from Tommy Salierno for openers. "Mr. Salierno's name has been connected to a double homicide in Vermont."

Bonatto played along. "Mr. Salierno has never been to Vermont."

"The connection was made in Chicago. One of the victims I'm referring to had an operation here over twenty years ago, before being killed shortly thereafter in Vermont. He listed Mr. Salierno as the one to contact in case of an emergency."

Bonatto's eyes were very still, in contrast to his men's, and looked directly into mine. "Over twenty years ago? What kind of operation?"

"Knee surgery."

"What was this man's name?"

"We don't know. He used an alias."

A flicker of impatience crossed the older man's face. He tried a bluff. "Well, Lieutenant, I don't see where any of this concerns us. . . ."

"The surgery was to repair a massive gunshot wound— from a .45"

The caliber seemed to mean something to him. "When was this operation?"

"October 10, 1969, twenty-four hours before Tommy Salierno was reportedly found dead."

He looked at me hard for a moment, then smiled, ignoring the reference to Tommy. "I must admit, I find all this very confusing. Do you think Mr. Salierno's name was used as a joke of some kind?"

I let him go with it. "Why would that be a joke?"

Bonatto spread his hands. "Because we haven't the slightest idea what this is all about. Perhaps your homicide victim with the anonymous name picked Mr. Salierno at random." He paused. "I am curious, though. . . . How does a shooting and some surgery in Chicago concern a policeman from Vermont, especially after such a long time?"

I shrugged, pleased at his interest. "One thing leads to another."

Bonatto absorbed that for a few seconds. "You mentioned a double homicide."

I rose to my feet, acutely aware of Fuller's photograph in my pocket and of the fact that I didn't want to go too far into such details with this man—at least not yet. My purpose here had been to see if I could stimulate any interest—and that had been achieved. "Yes, that's right. It's a complicated case—the double homicide is only part of it. There's a third person, still alive, who took a few shots at me a while back. Which maybe makes him the killer, and maybe not. But since you and Mr. Salierno are apparently uninvolved, I might as well leave it at that." I got up, causing every shifty eye in the place to lock on me—especially my hands—which I kept clearly in the open. "Good-bye." I walked to the door, and was blocked unobtrusively by the bodyguard at the counter sliding off his stool and standing in my way.

Bonatto hadn't risen, but he turned his head and looked at me. "If we should hear of something, where might we get in touch with you, Lieutenant?"

"Call Norm Runnion at Area Six headquarters. He'll pass on any messages."

The man at my shoulder smiled quietly at that.

"We don't work it that way, Lieutenant. Where will *you* be?"

I gave him the address of my motel.

Bonatto nodded, those cool eyes unblinking. "Thank you. Good luck."

Chapter Twenty-two

Norm Runnion sat back in his office chair and looked at me over the tops of his glasses. "You talked to Angelo Salierno?" His voice was tinged with amazement.

"His adviser, Bonatto."

He shook his head. "Are you this crazy back home?"

"I didn't feel there was any great risk."

He looked like he'd bitten into something sour and muttered, "Not to you, maybe." And then, more directly, he said, "Why? You were almost handed your plane ticket home yesterday." Amazement had quickly yielded to irritation.

I pulled the hospital's now creased and folded Social Services form from my pocket. "Because of this."

He studied the form, chewing on his lip. "Christ, this is getting strange. So the man with the knee was an Outfit guy?"

"I don't think so. Both Shattuck and Bonatto were very interested in what I had to say, but judging from the way they reacted—or pretended not to—I think that whoever had his knee repaired put down Shattuck and Salierno's names to stick their noses in it."

"In what?"

"I don't know, but at some point the three of them shared something in common. The Social Services report was the mystery man's way of flipping the finger at the other two."

Runnion raised both bushy eyebrows high. "How did he know that report would ever surface again?"

I hadn't actually thought any of this out in detail, but as the words came out, they began to gain credibility. "He didn't, any more than any kid does when he throws a bottle into the ocean with a message in it. This guy, whoever he was, was about to disappear forever. It was a gesture, pure and simple—a last chance to write 'Kilroy was here,' or even

'Up yours.' It didn't matter if no one saw it, because he did it for himself.''

"So maybe he ripped off Salierno back when and retired to Vermont with his collection of hundred-dollar bills?''

"Could be—there're a lot of blanks to fill in.''

"Yeah, like where does Shattuck fit in?'' Runnion was looking doubtful. "He couldn't have been a button man for the Outfit; they hate people like him—they're superconservative red-white-and-blue types, in a twisted kind of way.'' He shifted suddenly in his chair and looked at me with a renewed keenness. "How did you get Bonatto to talk to you?''

"It turns out Tommy Salierno died—or more likely was declared dead—twenty-four hours after 'Shattuck's' knee operation.''

Runnion's brow furrowed. "I remember hearing about Tommy,'' he said vaguely.

I pulled a copy I'd made of the article from my pocket and handed it over. He read it carefully, his brain obviously teeming with possibilities. "You think Tommy's death was faked?''

"I think the time of death was faked. According to the papers, Tommy had a history of striking out on his own, of setting up operations independent of his father. Old man Salierno and his bunch might not have touched the likes of Shattuck with a ten-foot pole, but Tommy could have. He was always breaking convention, screwing things up in the process. If he'd been up to his ears in something with Shattuck and this other guy and gotten himself killed, it stands to reason that Salierno would try to tidy things up. He couldn't hide his son's death altogether, but he could make it look more presentable to his peers.''

Runnion was quiet for a long time, mulling it all over. Finally, he took off his glasses, rubbed the corner of one eye, and asked, "So you just drove up to Salierno's front door and dropped all this in their lap, adding your face to the Chicago PD candid-camera collection in the process.''

I felt like a complete rube, not having thought of any potential police surveillance. "You have a team on Salierno?''

Runnion snorted. "You kidding? We have a whole division

that does nothing but eat junk food and squint through camera lenses, all so a bunch of college boys back at headquarters can build files of how many times the don orders out pizza or goes to see his girlfriend. I worked there myself a few years back.'' His voice trailed off.

I remembered his initial alarm when I'd told him of my visit to Salierno's—his questioning my sanity. "And since you're my baby-sitter, you're now in deep shit, too," I finished for him softly. I was both sympathetic and embarrassed that I'd repaid his kindnesses by threatening his livelihood, just a few months shy of retirement.

He just looked at me in silence. His expression, however, wasn't disapproving or even distressed; it was merely thoughtful, which prompted me to ask, after a full minute of this, "Are you okay?"

A slow smile spread across his face, mystifying me. "You know what it's like to hear yourself talk sometimes? When you're thinking things that never would have crossed your mind just a couple of years back?"

I went with it, although I was no longer following him. "You mean you're not in deep shit?"

"Deep enough—nothing terminal. I was just wondering how much that mattered."

Something cathartic was happening here, something I was pretty sure I'd caused but didn't understand. Runnion and I had been friendly enough from the start; we were similarly aged, with similar dispositions. We'd fitted together casually without much effort. I sensed now, however, that our relationship was about to undergo a fundamental change.

"What're your plans now?" he asked, seemingly out of the blue.

"I'm not sure you'll like them. You may not even want to know."

"Try me."

"I was thinking of diving back into the newspaper morgues and digging up everything I could on Shattuck."

"Why?" His tone was interested—unalarmed that I might be coming close to trespassing into the ongoing Shilly case.

"To see if I can identify some of his fellow travelers from the sixties. From what we know of him so far, he was part of a big crowd. I was hoping that through photo captions or feature articles I might be able to find a handful of people that I could chase down—people who knew him well enough to still be helpful.''

I was pretty certain of Runnion's reaction, but he surprised me by simply nodding. ''I might have a better idea,'' he said, ''one that'll give us more information.''

He reached for his phone and for what appeared to be an inner-agency directory. ''But first I better throw a little water on the flames.''

He dialed and asked for a name I didn't catch. ''Hi Walt; it's Norm Runnion in Area Six. I just got something I thought you'd be interested in—in fact, your field boys'll probably be bringing it in soon all hot and excited. It's about Angelo Salierno. I'm baby-sitting some hick cop from Vermont. . . .'' Here he gave me a conspiratorial look. ''Yeah, Vermont. . . . He waltzed up to Salierno's front door today and got an audience with Bonatto. Name's Joe Gunther, lieutenant. . . . yeah, he's chasing down some twenty-year-plus homicide from his side of the mountains. The point is, if I bring him in to talk to you guys, I don't think you'll get much—he's not what you'd call too sophisticated—very suspicious of us city folk. Let me work on him for a couple of days, soften him up, and I'll let you know what he's up to, okay? Sure. . . . No, it's no problem; I'm stuck with him, anyway—might as well make it worthwhile. . . . Yeah, okay. Bye.''

He hung up and smiled—half to himself, I thought. ''That ought to hold 'em off for a while.''

''You make them sound like the Hounds from Hell.''

''Don't laugh; I think they've been studying Outfit types for so long, they've started to act like 'em.''

''You used to work with them?''

He waved his hand. ''Yeah, but a while back. There was less technology and more street work—it was more personal.''

He reached for his phone again.

''So who's next?''

''Intelligence again, only now it's to one of the good guys.'' He paused, his hand still on the receiver. ''There are almost thirteen thousand uniformed police officers in Chicago, not counting secretaries, janitors, and what have you.''

"That's the size of Brattleboro," I muttered, suitably impressed.

"Well, there you go. The trick is to make the system work for you, to set up your own channels. So, while the Outfit surveillance boys are happily thinking I'm slowly loosening your tongue, we'll be digging through their own files. There is a certain charm to it, you got to admit."

I listened to him set up a meeting with his Intelligence contact, remembering Leslie, the helpful computer operator at the University of Chicago, and all the people I'd met at the Cook County Building. Establishing contacts within a department and having a good stable of street snitches was almost a must among policemen, but Norm Runnion was obviously a master at it.

The question was, why was he sticking his neck out, lying to his own people and working behind their backs? Previously, I'd thought of him as a man at peace with himself, resigned to biding his time pushing papers until retirement. Now, all caution seemed thrown to the wind—which made me more concerned about the risks he was taking than he was.

He hung up and chuckled slightly. "Okay, time for a little subterfuge. Want to go for a ride?"

"Sure." I stood up with him as he slipped into his jacket.

"This guy's name is Miles Stoddard," he told me as we made our way out to the parking lot. "He's like a historian, or a librarian—been gathering information on gangs, cults, groups, and the Outfit for over fifteen years. It's funny, in a way; I don't think he's ever seen any action, except maybe right when he was starting off. As long as I've known him, he's been like a hermit, locked away with his files and records, but he knows everything about everybody. Pretty incredible."

As I opened the car door, my eyes idly took in the commercial neighborhood around the police station. People were going about their business—loading up delivery vans, pushing grocery carts to their cars, entering and exiting the numerous stores. The only odd note was a large dark four-door sedan parked across West Belmont, with two men in the front. They weren't looking in our direction; in fact, the one I could see best had eyes only for an attractive young woman walking up the sidewalk in a miniskirt. His companion, half-obscured by the sun reflecting off the windshield, was reading a newspaper I could see propped up against the steering wheel.

"You coming?" Runnion asked.

I slid into the car next to him, saying nothing about the two men across the street. As we moved into traffic and pulled away, I looked back over my shoulder to see the young woman stopped by the side of the car, her hand resting on its roof, talking and laughing.

We headed south, passing through seamlessly abutting neighborhoods that by nature should have been separated by either miles or barbed-wire fencing. Teeming commercial streets festooned with Asiatic signs yielded to neighborhoods lined with BMWs, leafy trees, and decorous wooden town houses, which abruptly bordered scarred and barren combat zones dominated by grim cement housing projects.

"So what did you mean when you said it didn't matter if all this got you in trouble?" I asked after some ten minutes of silence.

He took a long time before answering, his eyes sweeping the street ahead of him. I couldn't decide if he was trying to choose the right words or merely wondering how much he should tell me. "When they yanked me out of Intelligence, where I'd been covering the Outfit, and put me in Area Six, we hadn't won that war and we hadn't lost it—I was just out of it. That really bugged me, after all I'd put into it. Those were the best years I'd ever had in the department, when I thought what I was doing really amounted to something."

He turned to me suddenly, taking his eye briefly off the road. "When we first met, I thought you were a pretty good guy, not just goofing off on company time, and you gave me a chance to get out a little and catch some air—practice the craft a bit. But until this Salierno angle cropped up, I was pretty happy to just let you do your thing and watch you leave town . . . the sooner the better after Shilly got popped."

He returned his attention to the road. "I don't know how to explain it exactly, but this Salierno angle got me to thinking. I don't know if we can do anything with what you got—the Outfit's a tough nut to crack—but I wouldn't mind trying one last time. It would give me a better feeling about calling it quits.''

There was a short pause before he added, ''And it'd make me feel better about those assholes looking down their noses at me yesterday for letting you go haywire.''

He chuckled and nodded to himself.

''What about the fallout when we get caught?''

His smile merely broadened. ''Humor me.''

Miles Stoddard worked in the same building I'd visited upon my arrival in Chicago—police headquarters on South State Street. The only difference was that this time, instead of going upstairs to visit the brass, Runnion took me down to the uppermost of two basement levels.

Being under the same roof as the people who could ruin Runnion and chase me out of town made me a little uneasy—for Norm's sake, if not mine. ''What are Miles's obligations to his bosses?'' I asked diplomatically as we shared an otherwise-empty elevator.

Runnion grinned ruefully. ''Will he squeal on us? No—we go pretty far back, and we've covered for each other before. Besides, I don't think we're heading out on thin ice yet.''

I didn't respond, which he took as encouragement to explain further. ''The investigation of Shilly's murder is being done in the here and now—neighbors are being interviewed, coworkers, relatives, friends, what have you. Shilly's place will be taken apart inch by inch, and so will Shattuck's. It'll take 'em days before they start thinking of going further back in time, and if they get lucky and find Shattuck early, they won't even do that. It's the standard routine, especially when you've got as many homicides as we have every week, and it usually gets results. I don't think we'll bump into each other.''

We found Miles Stoddard in a room from bygone times—an anachronism in the age of the computer. It was long, low, windowless, lit by a variety of overhead fixtures, and stuffed with an odd assortment of shelves, bookcases, freestanding metal bracket units, and even boards on bricks—anything that could possibly be used to carry the reams of files, books, reports, and folders that lurked in untidy ranks on almost every horizontal surface. It made the University of Chicago's medical archives look sterile by comparison. Just seeing how the pages tended to stick out messily from their manila restraints, I could tell this massive library was in constant use, not simply being preserved.

Like a shepherd in the midst of his silent, bedded flock, Stoddard was seated in the middle of the room at a battered old wooden desk, under a shaded lamp that hung from a wire from the gloom overhead.

He looked up as we approached along a narrow central aisle, giving Norm Runnion a beaming smile. "My God—there's a face from the past."

He rose to greet us, Norm making the introductions. He wasn't what I'd expected—no thinning white hair, sallow skin, and Coke-bottle glasses. Instead, he looked like a barely over-the-hill football hero: clear-eyed, athletic, suntanned, the very image of someone who wouldn't be caught dead in a mausoleum like this.

Catching my skepticism, he spread his arms wide to encompass his realm and grinned. "Welcome to the hole of holes—the ultimate in job security."

I shook my head, remembering the intelligence files Runnion and I had reviewed on the computer. "What is all this?"

"History, pretty much pure and simple—a lot more than any flatfoot wants to know when he calls up a name on his console, which is why we keep it off the central network. I don't have current rap sheets or addresses or DMV information down here; it's all deep background. If you have a problem understanding the relationship between two street gangs, or why it is that a certain ward or alderman behaves in a certain way, you come here. The only catch, of course, is that something criminal has to play a part. There are definitely no saints down here." He looked fondly over the rows and rows all around him. "Also, it's got to be older than yesterday's headlines—current intelligence files are kept on Maxwell Street."

"Which is what brings us here," Norm joined in. "What can you tell us about a sixties radical named Robert Shattuck?

We're looking for people he may have formed special connections with."

Stoddard gave him a half-dreamy look, the smile still on his face. "Let's look him up."

He stepped away from his desk and we followed him farther back into the shadows, wending our way down various pathways until we came to a distant wall, lined, as usual, with shelves. A glowing computer was parked there at chest level.

I let out a small grunt of surprise, which Stoddard obviously found amusing. "What did Norm tell you? That I was some gnome sitting in a damp cellar with all this crap in my head? Forget it. It may look old and messy, but it's organized. And I'm just the head of the section; there're a half dozen guys like me who wander around this place. I'd be swamped otherwise. Okay, let's see where our friend is hiding."

He typed in Shattuck's name, along with a few commands. A nearby printer spit out a location list of all references. Only then, list in hand, did Stoddard do the expected and begin ferreting among his informational gold mine. I noticed, here and there, there were indeed other desks and other archivists, tucked away in their private corners like secretive monks. It pleased me, for some perverse reason, to know that an enclave like this was alive and well in a bureaucracy given over to uniformity, strip lighting, and doing away with the "old."

It took over an hour. He set us up at a work table under a hanging fluorescent light and began feeding us with bits and pieces, periodically appearing with memos, captioned intelligence photos, old arrest records, FBI inter-service data sheets, even magazine and newspaper articles that either dealt with Shattuck directly or with aspects of the causes he'd espoused over the years.

Runnion and I went through it all, taking notes, building lists of names, addresses, dates, and events, trying both to establish a chronology of Shattuck's political life and to gain an insight to his personal relations. As we went along, we also kept a separate list of those names that moved with our quarry in his successive shifts toward the radical militant left, pegging them as the true inner circle and the most likely to have kept in touch with him up to the present.

That list was not long, for Shattuck had explored well

beyond the political extremes we'd found on his rap sheet. There were connections to the Weather Underground and to other, more violent splinter groups, although nothing for which he'd ever been arrested, which explained the relative tameness of our first official view of his activities.

Near the end, Norm tapped the list with his finger. "You know, it occurs to me that if any of these hard-core people are still around, they're not likely to be too friendly to us."

I pulled my notepad from somewhere under the growing pile and waved it at him. "I've been scribbling down a few names of those who went only so far with him. Whether they broke ranks or just left town, I don't know, but I'm hoping at least one or two of them grew disenchanted enough to tell us why."

We had also made a separate pile of all the photographs Stoddard had delivered, which included mug shots of 80 percent of everyone on our lists. Getting booked back then had been the unintentionally ironic equivalent of a battlefield promotion. I pulled the pile toward me now and leafed through the rebellious young faces, putting Shattuck's off to one side.

Runnion watched me, smiling sometimes at the extreme Afros and love beads. "So what do you think of Mr. Shattuck now?"

I laid the pictures down, thinking back to my conversation with Gail the night before. "His killing Shilly seems a lot more in character. He was obviously a lot more than a radical protester, at least by the early seventies. Some of the people he hung out with were robbing banks, grabbing hostages, and blowing up buildings. Seems the only difference was, he didn't get caught."

I reached into my pocket and pulled out Abraham Fuller's picture. "I am disappointed, though, that this guy hasn't surfaced. I know goddamn well Shattuck recognized him."

"You run his prints through our files yet?" Stoddard asked from behind us.

"Yeah, when I was still in Brattleboro." I waved my hand across the assembled mug shots. "He either never made the A-team or he was a lot more clever than they were." I placed Fuller on the table next to Shattuck. "It makes me wonder if the guy with the metal knee is here, staring at us right now, or if he's as lost as Mr. Fuller.''

That thought made me dig into my pocket once more, and pull out the birth date Billie Lucas had deciphered from the astrological chart, an item I'd almost forgotten about. I handed it to Stoddard. ''Can you run a check just on a date of birth?''

He took the slip of paper from me. ''Sure.''

Runnion cleared his throat, obviously sensitive of overstaying our welcome here, despite Stoddard's continued affability. ''I have one more favor to ask, too, Miles.''

Stoddard let him off the hook. ''Shoot.''

''What can you tell us about Tommy Salierno—the night he died, and any connections he might have had with any of these folks? That was before my time in Intelligence.''

Stoddard suddenly looked doubtful and checked his watch. ''Angie's boy? The first part of that maybe I can handle, if you can accept a verbal report, but connecting Tommy to the radicals will take some time—more than we've got left today. The Outfit takes up more shelf space than anyone—besides the politicians,'' he added with a laugh. ''Hang on a sec; let me get you the resident expert.''

He disappeared for a few minutes and returned with a man I thought far better suited physically to this environment— wispy white hair, thick glasses, and not built like a quarterback. ''This is Ray—Mr. Mafia. You see Tommy Salierno tied in with a bunch of radical hippies, Ray?''

I held up my hand to interrupt. ''Not tied in necessarily; let's say having any interactions with them.''

Ray ran his hand up and across the top of his bald head, pausing to scratch the back of his neck. ''It's possible—he did things just to drive the old man crazy. I don't remember anything specific, though. The politics sure don't line up. Tommy was as right-wing as his father—most of them are.''

''What do you remember about his death?'' Runnion asked. ''Was there anything suspicious or unusual about it?''

Ray looked surprised. ''Suspicious? It seemed straightforward enough—bad-boy mobster crosses one husband too many.''

''You emphasized *seemed*.''

"Yeah. Well, he had been a pain in Angelo's neck, from when he was a teenager. People talked about how maybe he got to be too much, but I don't think so. Despite the movies, you don't see much of that kind of activity in the Outfit. They tend to be stoics about blood family—good or bad, they figure they're stuck with them. Especially an old-timer like Angelo—blood ties are sacred to him."

"You think Tommy died the same day he was found?" I asked.

Ray's eyes widened slightly. "Like did he die some other day or something? Interesting . . . He could have."

"Why?"

"Only because there's no proof he didn't. All the autopsy files disappeared. About twelve or fifteen years ago, some reporter was doing a story on the local Mafia—a routine feature piece—and he decided to check Tommy's autopsy report. I think just to show what a hotshot he was. It wasn't there. A small article appeared about it, the medical examiner acknowledged that sometimes files wandered, and the system was revamped. No one made much of it."

"What about the doc who did the autopsy?"

"Dead end. He'd moved on, and he died a couple of years later . . . natural causes," he added to our collective but unstated question.

"Still," Runnion persisted, "Tommy's death being vague like that sure is curious." He gathered together the lists of names and handed them to Stoddard. "I know you said it would take a while, but could you copy these and see if any of them connect to Tommy?"

Stoddard shrugged, passed them to Ray with a nod, and Ray turned to get back to work.

I reached out and touched his elbow before he left. "One last question."

He looked back at me, his face expectant. "What's that?"

"Mafia types—the Outfit, I mean—they favor small-caliber weapons for the most part, don't they?"

"Depends. The button men like .22s or .32s 'cause they're small and quiet. Those boys tend to work up close. But some of the others—the general bodyguards, the soldiers—they might carry anything, especially nowadays."

That wasn't what I was hoping for. I tried a different, more specific angle. "What about Tommy Salierno? Did he use something special?"

Ray nodded with a smile. "Oh yeah. Typical, really, given his attitude. He had a nickel-plated, ivory-handled Colt automatic, just as showy as he was."

"A .45?" I asked.

"Yup—big enough to blow your head off."

"Or your knee," I muttered, and one more piece of the puzzle—hypothetical, unsubstantiated, and utterly compelling—fell into place.

Chapter Twenty-three

I got a hit," Norm Runnion said as he approached my desk.

We were still in the basement, in separate vacant office cubbyholes, each equipped with a phone book, a phone, and a computer terminal, on which Norm had taught me how to look up current addresses of anyone with a recent record. We'd been chasing down some of the names we'd accumulated for over an hour and a half without success—until now.

He sat on the corner of the desk, his face slightly quizzical. "Brandon Huff—he was on the hard-core list—an ex–Black Panther, currently at Carruthers, McBride."

"A law firm?"

"Yeah—sounds pretty Waspy, don't it? Actually, it's the kind of place William Kunstler would call home—big on defending the poor and the oppressed, as they say; drives the state's attorney's office nuts on a regular basis. He's agreeable to a meet, but on a Wendella—a tour boat—in less than an hour. We're supposed to stand by the flag at the stern and wait."

I'd noticed the colorful boats plying the Chicago River earlier that day when I'd visited the Tribune Tower; I'd thought they looked as incongruous against Chicago's sophisticated backdrop as a pair of sandals on a three-piece-suited executive. "What'd you think? Any reason to be nervous?"

Norm turned both palms heavenward. "Don't guess so—two of us, one of him. . . . Maybe."

It wasn't quite dark when we acquired our spot at the boat's stern. The sky overhead was tinged bloodred, orange, and yellow by the setting sun, the cirrus clouds looking like rippled, burning lava. The city's towering, sparkling buildings were hard-edged and brittle by comparison—black steel and glittering glass and pale, unyielding stone, flashing with electrical might. Despite the wealth and power bristling beneath it, the sky remained as placid, soothing, and unconcerned as I'd noticed before.

Norm, unlike me, was watching the gangplank. "Hard to tell; there've been a few black guys, but none of them looks right. I wonder if we've just been jerked around."

I was having a hard time sharing his concerns. As corny as these boats had seemed to me earlier, boarding one had proved to be a distinctly odd experience, as if the single step from dock to deck had transported me beyond Chicago's urban grasp. I was suddenly part of the river and the lake nearby, safe from the concrete human meat grinder that crowded both shores. The sounds around me were of softly lapping water, laughter, and clicking cameras. I couldn't bring myself to feel in peril.

The smile that sensation evoked died, however, as soon as I spotted the two men leaning over the bridge railing above us. Both were well built, in their thirties or forties, wearing dark glasses and baseball caps. They were also dressed in colorful T-shirts, and sharing popcorn out of a single big bag, like lots of other people who were out enjoying the early evening. The popcorn vendor, whose umbrella I could just see over the top of the stone balustrade lining the quay, was obviously doing quite a business. Over a dozen of his customers had taken advantage of the setting to loiter by the bridge and eat while staring at the water traffic below.

Was one of the men the same guy I'd seen eyeing the miniskirted girl across from Norm's office? I couldn't be sure, and while I watched, one of the men turned, stretched, slapped his buddy on the back, and they both disappeared from view, presumably to continue their stroll.

I had acted impulsively twice in this case—once when I'd gone to interview Bob Shattuck and again when I'd poked at the local mob. Both had been catalytic, stimulating a response; Shattuck had killed Shilly, and Bonatto, curious, had emerged from his cave to talk. It seemed entirely reasonable to me that either or both had extended their interest enough to pin a tail on me by now.

And there was another possibility. If my visit to the Salierno home had been recorded by the police department's surveillance team, had their bosses been content to swallow Runnion's stall? Or had they put a tail on, anyway? Norm hadn't told me the reason for his abrupt departure from that branch, and I'd assumed the decision had been purely bureaucratic. Maybe I'd been wrong.

The deck began to rumble with the engine's thrust, and dockhands threw off the mooring ropes and pushed at the boat's side with their feet. Runnion sighed next to me and shoved his hands into his pockets. "Oh well, I guess we can see the sights, if nothing else. Never thought I'd take one of these."

I looked at him in surprise. "You've never done this before?"

"Nope. You ever take a bus tour of Vermont?"

I laughed, acknowledging his point.

"You wished to see me?"

The speaker was so near, we both snapped around fast, finding a black man in a sports shirt and slacks standing before us, his hands on his hips. He was of medium height and build but seemed to carry an enormous amount of power within him. His face was impassive, his eyes hard and penetrating, his voice almost theatrically cultured and precise—an English teacher's dream.

Norm cleared his throat. "Yeah, hi. You Brandon Huff?"

Huff ignored the obvious, the distrust apparent in his voice. "You said you had some questions concerning the 1960s."

"Yeah. Didn't I see you come on board with a woman and two kids?"

Huff frowned slightly. "My family, which is why I'd like to get this over with quickly."

I tried to clear the air somewhat. "Sorry—I'm really the cause of all this. My name is Joe Gunther; I'm a policeman from Vermont and I'm trying to pin a name to an old skeleton we uncovered back home."

Huff merely raised his eyebrows, but I sensed some of the tension had eased from his face.

"We believe this man was active politically in the late sixties, around the same time you were."

"I still am."

"Well, you get the idea. Did you know Bob Shattuck?"

A crease appeared between his eyes. "He's not dead, not that I heard."

"When did you last hear?" Runnion asked.

Huff looked slightly scornful. "It's what I didn't hear I'm referring to. My interactions with Shattuck were minimal, even back then. Still, if he'd died, word would have gotten out. I doubt he's your man."

He looked about ready to leave. I said, "We know Shattuck is alive, but he and the skeleton were connected somehow. We don't have much to go on, but if you could tell us a bit about him, it might get us headed in the right direction."

He considered that for a moment, apparently thinking back. "Bob Shattuck . . . What do you have on him?"

I ran down a quick synopsis of the police department rap sheet, omitting any mention of Shattuck's latest activities. I could tell Norm was uncomfortable volunteering so much information—it ran counter to a cop's natural disposition— but I was fairly convinced that if Huff felt we were treating him as anything other than an ally, the conversation would end right there.

Huff glanced at the boat's wake as I finished, a white-foamed cluster of reflected fireflies—all the city's lights bobbing in captured frenzy. "That's it?"

"We suspect more."

"Like what?"

Norm sighed next to me.

"The rap sheet only reflects the times he got caught. We think that in the late sixties, early seventies, he may have been linked to extremist radicals—Weatherman splinter groups and the like.''

"The Panthers?"

I looked at him straight. "No. They never came up."

He nodded slightly. "You suspect violence?"

"Definitely."

Huff addressed Norm. "You're Runnion, right?"

Norm was slightly startled. "Yeah—sorry—should've introduced myself." He made to reach for his credentials, but Huff stopped him with a shake of the head.

"Don't worry about it. I checked you out after you called. That's why I'm here."

He paused, but not for any response from us. He moved slightly, leaning against the railing, his eyes, like ours earlier, on the passing cityscape. "I knew Shattuck back then, but not well. Some of his causes and ours overlapped, or so we believed at first. Not that it mattered much; we were a force unto ourselves and our race, and on that level, he was as much whitey as the police. Still, there were a few activities where some sort of vague cooperation existed . . . for a while."

"What happened?"

"Nothing dramatic. But we began to suspect his motives. We were used to some of that—the wanna-be syndrome—guilty whites hoping to become cool by proximity."

He shook his head, not so much scornful as philosophical. "They tried to be blacker than us—hating more, protesting too much, running around wearing African robes and claw necklaces. Pathetic."

"Shattuck was like that?" I asked, not bothering to hide the incredulity.

"No. I think the stimulus was similar, but he demonstrated it differently. Under a charming, almost obsequious exterior, he was a very violent, unstable man—vengeful. I sensed he wanted more than to be black—he wanted to be a leader of blacks. We soon made it clear we didn't want him within sight."

There was a pause, which Runnion clearly understood. "You're not going to get more specific, are you?"

Huff glanced at him and merely smiled.

I pulled Abraham Fuller's dog-eared photograph out of my pocket and handed it over. "This face ring a bell?"

Huff tilted it so the lights off the boat shone on it. He finally shook his head and handed it back, a gesture I was becoming used to. "No; I'm afraid not."

"One last one; the skeleton I mentioned's been described as a white male, about one hundred and ninety pounds, left-handed, probably a ballet dancer and a runner. Had a chipped front tooth that was fixed and no cavities—something he may have bragged about."

He chuckled and shook his head slightly. "No cavities, huh?" He glanced at his watch and then along the length of the boat. "I need to return to my family."

"Thanks for your help," I said.

He nodded at me quickly but then looked at Norm again closely. "I understand you're retiring soon."

Runnion was impressed. "Not too many people know that."

He paused, obviously considering something, but all he said was, "Too bad" before he turned on his heel and left us.

"I met my first Black Panther tonight."

Gail chuckled over the phone. "What was he like?"

"Talked better than me, dressed better than me, and was smarter than hell."

"No black leather gloves and dark glasses? Didn't call you 'pig'?"

"All right, all right, so I'm culturally deprived."

She laughed and then asked, "What else have you been up to?"

I told her about my meeting with Salierno.

She was no longer amused. "Joe, do you really know what you're doing?"

I knew from the concern in her voice that she wasn't being offensive—it was a serious question, and certainly one I'd been asking myself a lot lately.

"On one level, I do." I hesitated, again remembering the two men in the car, the couple at the bridge. "But it's a little like poking a sleeping dog with a stick. You need to wake him up, but there's no telling what the reaction might be.''

She sighed but didn't pursue the point. "I might have some good news. I've been fooling around with that astrology chart, calling a few people I know, checking some books out of the library. . . . I think it might be possible to get a latitude and longitude on the birthplace.''

''You're kidding me.''

''No. Supposedly, there are dozens of mathematical steps to it, along with a strict procedure, and it only works if the chart is very accurate to begin with. I talked to Billie about it; she wasn't very hopeful. She'd never done it herself and had never heard of it being done—usually there's no call for it. She did agree that it would take a 'real hotshot,' as she put it, to figure it out. She called the person who taught her— some man in California—but he'd never done it, either.''

''So what makes you think it's possible?'' I asked, fighting to keep the skepticism from my voice.

''It was in one of the books. Anyway, I'm going to keep on it—maybe we'll find it pinpoints a single tiny hospital in the middle of the boonies.''

''Or six huge ones in downtown L.A.''

We talked for a while, about other, unrelated topics. She told me of a deal she was closing, and about the latest political scrap among the selectmen. By the time we were done, I was longing to be back home. Part of that was the lingering pleasure of hearing Gail's voice, but another part was being in Chicago. It was just too big for me, too crowded, too complicated, with too many levels to its social structure.

Also, while Brattleboro had its proportion of crazies and hopheads, whose attention was often best grabbed with the working end of a two-by-four, we didn't have the Mafia, or slums that covered several square miles, or nine hundred homicides every year. I was a mere blip among millions in this city, and my being extinguished probably wouldn't even make the front page, assuming someone didn't arrange to make me vanish without a trace.

My thoughts returned to Shattuck and Bonatto, and to the forces they could conceivably control—and which I had so blithely stirred into motion.

It made me wonder how many bodies were anchored to the bottom of that conveniently located ocean-sized lake.

Chapter Twenty-four

Norm Runnion picked me up the next morning, an irrepressible smile on his face.

"What are you so pleased about?"

He slid the car into traffic. "Miles called me last night. He got nowhere on that astrology birth date you had, but after we'd left, he did land a couple of current addresses for our list, one of which was Penny Nivens." He paused for theatrical effect. "She teaches ballet. I thought we could make her our first stop of the day."

The boost this news gave me was almost immediately dampened by the dormant paranoia that had been dogging me for almost the last twenty-four hours.

I peered out the back window, looking in vain for the large dark four-door of the day before. "Pull over, Norm."

Norm stopped opposite a fire hydrant and put the car in park. "What're we looking for?"

I straightened in my seat, quickly debating how to present my fears in a way he would accept. "If you were Bonatto, and I dropped a twenty-four-year-old bomb in your lap and walked away, having dared you to do something about it, how would you react?"

Runnion understood instantly. "We have a tail?"

"We might. I saw two guys in a car opposite your office yesterday afternoon, and I may have seen either the same guys or two others from the tour boat."

"You didn't tell me?"

"I wasn't sure—I'm still not. The two in the car were chatting with a girl passing by, and the others were eating popcorn on the bridge with a crowd of other people. They didn't do anything suspicious; I never saw them looking in our direction, and the car—when we left your office—stayed put."

"What about the two on the bridge?"

"They walked away before we shoved off."

"So they didn't see us meet Huff?"

I sighed, as if hearing what he was thinking. "I don't think so—but others may have."

"Sure," he muttered matter-of-factly, "Two- or three-man teams. Hard to spot."

I looked at him in surprise, relieved by his ready acceptance, and added, "Assuming they're there at all."

He thought about it for a moment, put the car back into gear, and rejoined the flow of traffic. "Let's find out."

He continued up La Salle to North Avenue and turned left. "I'm going to take us out to the expressway, where the traffic is thinner—maybe get a fix on whoever might be out there. What kind of car was it last time?"

"Dark four-door sedan—typical narc car, really." I planted that last idea on purpose, just to see how he'd react.

He picked it up, but cautiously. "You think they were cops?"

"They could be, especially if your Intelligence pals didn't quite swallow your story about me."

He absorbed that without comment.

"The other possibility is Shattuck. If Shilly couldn't give him the answers he wanted, I'd be his only other option, and he certainly knows enough people to pull it off."

Runnion shook his head slightly. "Christ, you sounded like such a milk run when I first met you."

I climbed into the backseat so I could get a better view out the rear window, leaving Norm to search for cars that might be "tailing" us from the front. The traffic on North, however, was cluttered enough to make any discrimination virtually impossible. I scanned the weaving flock of cars behind us, looking for either the same one I'd seen before or the two burly men. But I saw nothing familiar—just a twisting, flowing stream of vehicles, a good half of which might have been following us.

The expressway, however, promised better results.

"You all set?" Norm called back over his shoulder. He hit

the accelerator hard but held his speed at sixty-five, as any jackrabbit driver might. I studied the pattern to our rear—several cars stuck with us.

"How many?" he asked.

"About half a dozen, unless the guy is being real subtle."

"Okay." Norm slowed back down, activated his turn indicator, and pulled off into the breakdown lane, coming to a full stop. "We'll give 'em five minutes, enough to force 'em either to take the next exit or pull over themselves. If they have a two-car team, that'll probably get rid of one of 'em."

We waited a couple of those minutes in silence, our eyes fixed on opposite horizons. "I wish to hell you hadn't planted that 'they might be cops' idea in my head," Norm finally muttered.

Now I was the one to sound surprised. "Why? You think they might be?"

"They're capable of it. What bugs me right now is that I could call in extra units to help us out here, maybe box in whoever it is you think is out there, but I don't want to do it 'til I know who they are."

I didn't respond, and he didn't call Dispatch for help.

When we did roll again, it was at a snail's pace. This time, I couldn't separate anyone from the crowd. They all seemed unanimously irritated at having to negotiate around us—until we crept past the next entrance ramp.

"Bingo. One just got on. He's way back and doesn't seem to know what to do. He's straddling the breakdown line."

"All right, here goes." Norm punched the gas pedal and we catapulted forward to eighty miles an hour. Far behind us, almost blocked by the other traffic, I could see a nondescript beige model lurch away from the emergency lane, its rear tires smoking.

"They bit—they're coming."

Norm risked a glance into his rearview mirror, although they were still quite a ways back. "They just keeping pace, or trying to close the distance?"

"Keeping pace."

He accelerated more, taking some risks now that we were without doubt the fastest car in any lane. He weaved right and left, using his horn, once or twice swinging out into the breakdown lane to maintain speed. Staying as far back as they could afford, our pursuers maintained the distance.

"Still there?" Norm shouted, his voice rising above the engine's howl.

I glanced at him to answer, and wished I hadn't. We were passing cars like they were mere pylons in a suicidal obstacle course. I saw a station wagon just ahead move to get out of our way, realize we were coming on too fast, and switch back jerkily. Norm corrected his direction at the last moment and flew past within inches of the other car's bumper. My hands were gripping the back of the seat so tightly, my fingernails hurt.

"Still there?" he repeated.

I looked back. "Yes."

"Okay. Hang on."

I stared at my white-knuckled fists, wondering how I could do any better. He wrenched the wheel right, slewed across two lanes to an outburst of car horns, and launched us through the air over the top lip of an off ramp. We landed with a sickening, swerving, tire-squealing thump, and Norm pumped the brakes just enough for us to half-turn, half-slide our way into a cross street.

"They comin'?"

I looked out the rear window and saw no beige car. "Nothing yet, but they were pretty far back."

"Okay." He pulled a magnetically mounted blue light from under his seat, slapped it onto the dashboard, and stuck its dangling umbilical into the car's cigarette lighter. He then cranked the wheel hard to the left, hit a switch on his dash that started his siren howling, and proceeded as quickly as possible against the traffic of a curving one-way residential street. Several blocks later, he killed both the light and the siren, turned right, and rejoined the normal flow of cars.

"How 'bout now?"

I checked again. "Clean as a whistle."

Penny Nivens, it turned out, did not teach ballet to the city's up-and-coming prima ballerinas, nor had she opted to bring the arts to the South Side disadvantaged. Instead, Norm Runnion took me north, out of Skokie, where his careening, subsonic trajectory had landed us, and into the lush green embrace of Lake Forest.

A few hundred yards off the Deerpath Avenue exit from Highway 41, the standard tacky commercial clusters yielded almost instantaneously to a rarefied—and artificial—ruralism, the kind I'd experienced at top-drawer country clubs and upscale modern zoos. Everything natural had been sculpted by experts to make it look "better"—no weeds, no dead branches, no rotting clumps of vegetation. The concessions to modern living had been tastefully blended in—the road smooth and gently curving to enhance that unhurried, country feeling; the sidewalks immaculate and free of cracks. Even the low-key police department, located like a discreet sentry along the main corridor to the violent wastelands, had all the bearing of a bland, retiring, almost embarrassed municipal office block.

Runnion drove through the center of town, past expensive inns, designer retail shops, and the only Ferrari car dealership I'd ever set eyes on, and continued into a vast, intricate, mazelike preserve of trees, lawns, and mind-numbingly gigantic houses.

Neither one of us spoke, our thoughts dulled by the massiveness of the wealth all around us, and it was in silence that Runnion finally parked the car under the protective shade of an ancient gnarled tree by the side of the road. Ahead of us was an ivy-swathed, slate-roofed series of redbrick buildings, surrounded by the playing fields of an exclusive private school.

"She teaches here?" I asked.

Runnion opened his door and swung his legs out. "So I'm told."

We asked for Penny Nivens at the reception desk. A teenage girl, prim in a navy uniform and white blouse, her hair pulled back in a flawless ponytail, nodded gravely and used the phone by her side to summon a similarly dressed but slightly more disheveled schoolmate, who merely stood by the entrance to the inner hallway and waited.

There was a moment's awkwardness before an unsmiling portly man in a three-piece suit stepped into the lobby from a side office. Obviously, this was not a place where one just ambled around at will.

"May I help you gentlemen?"

Runnion moved so the two girls couldn't see his hand as he showed the man his badge. "Yes. We're here to see Penny Nivens."

Our challenger's smile became strained, but he kept his poise. "Why don't you come into my office and I'll find out where Miss Nivens is." He looked over to the girl at the hallway entrance. "Mary, why don't you just wait there for a few moments?"

He led us through the door he'd appeared from and shut it behind us, his voice gaining a worried edge. "Is there some trouble?"

Runnion was his affable best. "We just have a couple of questions for Miss Nivens."

"She hasn't done anything wrong?" The question was asked skeptically.

"Not a thing. We're just like any other visitors," Norm suggested.

"Right." He opened the door and smiled rigidly at Mary. "Okay—could you escort these gentlemen to Miss Nivens's classroom, please? Thank you."

He retreated behind his door with a slam, no doubt to swallow something for his stomach. I wondered how long it would take word of our visit to spread throughout the school, based on the fat man's performance alone.

The girl named Mary led us down carpeted, quiet hallways, taking me back to my own high school—a drafty barnlike building with wood stoves, art-covered walls, and the restless hurly-burly of too many cooped-up children. This place was like being in a bank building, where any juvenile excess would be met with baleful glares.

Our guide stopped at a heavy wooden door, knocked quickly, and opened it without waiting for a response. She ushered us in and closed the door behind us.

We were left standing in an enormous, well-lit rectangular room, empty, with a highly polished wooden floor. The wall opposite us was lined with floor-to-ceiling mirrors, so that the first people we saw were ourselves, looking slightly startled.

"Over here."

We both turned toward the clear female voice. In a corner at the far end of the room was a wooden desk, behind which was seated a slim dark-haired woman wearing a black tank-top jersey. She rose as we crossed to greet her, our shoes clattering noisily on the gleaming floorboards. She was dressed in leotards and was shaped like a young woman in her twenties, muscular and athletic. It made me wonder if we hadn't come up with the wrong name somehow.

"Penny Nivens?" Runnion asked as we approached.

"Yes." She came out from behind the desk to greet us. I studied her face, which was friendly and open but gently lined and tugged at by at least forty-odd years of living. My doubts evaporated.

"Can I help you?" she asked.

"I think so," I started. "I'm Joe Gunther; this is Norm Runnion. We're police officers, and we were wondering if we could ask you a few questions."

The smile didn't vanish; there was no sudden watchfulness in the eyes. Instead, she motioned to the single guest chair next to the desk and brought her own out to the front. "I only have two chairs, I'm afraid. I'll sit here." She lithely perched on the desk and drew her legs up underneath her.

I sat, but Runnion wandered off a few paces and leaned against the wall, putting me in the position of authority.

"Are you here about one of the kids?" she asked.

"It's about Bob Shattuck," I said, watching for a reaction.

Her brows furrowed and she frowned quizzically. "Bob Shattuck? I haven't seen him in years—decades even."

"When was the last time?"

"God." She rubbed her forehead. "It must have been 1970 or something like that, right after the trial of the Chicago Seven, at some rally. Is he in trouble?"

"Why do you ask?"

Penny Nivens laughed. "Because you're here. I didn't even know he was still alive."

"He was doing things back then that could have gotten him killed."

She stared at me, her smile fading. "Those were violent times."

"I had a conversation with Bob a couple of nights ago, asking him about the old days. The next morning, one of the people we discussed was found dead in Bob's apartment. He'd been tortured and we're pretty sure Bob did the honors."

Penny Nivens passed her hand across her mouth, visibly confused. "I don't understand. What would I know about this?"

"You and Shattuck were together for several years in the late sixties, but then you seemed to have disappeared. What happened? Was he becoming too radical?"

Anger began to creep into her face.

"Miss Nivens, I've got no bone to pick with you. I'm investigating a twenty-year-old case that started when you and Bob Shattuck and Abraham Fuller were in the revolutionary front lines."

"Abraham Fuller?"

I pulled Fuller's photo out and handed it over.

She stared at it for a long time. "He's dead?"

"Yes." Hope flickered inside me, but only briefly.

She shuddered and returned the picture. "I'm sorry. I don't know him."

"Did you split up with Shattuck?"

"Yes."

"Why?"

Her face now downcast, she let out a long sigh. "Bobby and I were lovers for a while, not that that was anything special back then. He really believed in what we were doing, not like some of them who just wanted to say they got tear-gassed. Bobby was a teacher—a group leader—committed to changing all that shit we were against. . . ."

She suddenly looked up, her eyes passing over my head at the large room behind me, a bitter half smile on her face. "And now I'm teaching rich brats to dance so they can grow up and act superior when they visit the ballet. . . . Christ."

"So what happened with Bobby?" I kept my voice gentle.

"I thought he'd lost his way, that after years of fighting violence, he'd finally been corrupted by it and had ended up embracing it. But now I don't think so; now I think maybe he was more honest than the rest of us. He saw it wasn't working. He knew that Tom Hayden would end up marrying a movie star and selling out. He knew the only real revolution had to be a violent one, that by shunning violence, we were shunning reality—getting ready to go back to our middle-class comforts . . . or to this.'' She waved her hand toward the mirrored wall.

Her anguish seemed to be feeding on itself, expanding now that it had been allowed the space. ''Who did he hook up with?''

She shrugged. ''He didn't tell us—we'd all sold out, in his eyes. He didn't trust us anymore, and we weren't too comfortable around him, either. He was so angry toward the end, he scared me. I wondered sometimes if he wouldn't just take us all out—us and the pigs—one and the same.''

''Did anyone go with him when he left?''

She shook her head, half-baffled, half-lost in the past and her own confusion. ''Who knows? They weren't going to tell *us*.''

I took a shot in the dark, based on the lead that had drawn us to this woman in the first place. ''What about your fellow ballet dancer?''

She stared at me with her mouth open. ''You mean David? David Pendergast?''

''I don't know. I have a description without a name.''

She hugged her arms across her narrow chest, looking smaller and frailer than before. She was silent for a while, breathing deeply, fighting with her emotions. When she finally spoke, she looked grieved, and much older. ''David could have gone with Bobby. He's another one I never heard from again.'' A single large tear broke loose from her eye and coursed unchecked down her cheek.

''You and David were close?''

Her smile was tired and without joy. ''I thought we were all close. Those people were the best friends I ever had, or will ever have. My time with them burns bright in my heart.'' She tapped her chest lightly with her fist, her intensity utterly erasing any hint of theatricality.

I let the silence persist, sensing there was more to come. After a minute or so, she added, ''David and I danced together. We slept together, for a while. I thought I loved him. But he was dangerous. . . . He scared me—like Bobby ended up scaring me."

"And you think they might have joined a more violent element of the movement together?"

She nodded without comment.

I rose from my chair and looked down at her, her shoulders slumped, her head bowed, no longer the pixie. She sat on her desk now like something fragile and ailing, drooping from the pain, the loss, and a sense of bewilderment.

I had one last question to ask: "You mentioned you haven't seen Pendergast since the late sixties; do you know where he was from originally?"

She looked up, her face troubled and tear-stained. "What I remember best about David was his dancing—hard, risky, sometimes beautiful and sometimes scary. He'd throw me high in the air with no warm-up, no practice runs—for the spontaneity, he said. We didn't talk about where we were from—we talked about where we were going."

Her voice drifted off. I waited for more, then finally gave it up. I joined Norm as we made our way back to the hallway door. I noticed, however, that he, like I, stepped more lightly than we had upon entering, as if preserving the sanctity of some funereal occasion. On the threshold, I glanced back at Penny Nivens, utterly reduced by the enormity of her ornate, empty surroundings. She was looking across the expanse of floor at the wall of mirrors, as if mystified by her own reflection.

Chapter Twenty-five

Runnion hung up the phone with a satisfied grunt. "Miles says Pendergast is presumed out of the area. There's no current address in the file, and the last entry on our books was exactly twenty-four years ago."

I held a mug shot labeled "David Pendergast" in my hand, studying the handsome broad face—the square Hollywood chin, the straight, almost Greek nose, the clear, widely set pale eyes—trying to see in his features some hint of the skeletal remains I'd seen on Beverly Hillstrom's autopsy table.

"Can I use your phone?" I asked.

Norm pushed it across to me and I dialed Vermont.

"Medical examiner's office."

"This is Lieutenant Joe Gunther calling from Chicago. Is Dr. Hillstrom available?"

The next voice was Hillstrom's. "Chicago? What are you doing there?"

"I think I've got a name for your skeleton. What would you need to make it stick legally? And please don't say X rays."

There was a long pause. "Do you have a photograph?"

I smiled, sensing victory in the air. "Yeah—head shot."

"Is he grinning?"

The smile died. "Grinning? It's a mug shot."

"If we can get a picture of him with his teeth showing, we might be able to superimpose the photograph on a same-size X ray of the skull and make a match, but we need the skeletal landmarks to lock in the alignment and the sizing of the superimposition—the bigger the grin, the better."

I sighed. "I'll see what I can come up with."

"There is something else," she added quickly before I could hang up. "If you can find some member of his family, see if you can get the location of his old dentist. His dental files might still be around."

"I'll give it a shot."

I hung up and reached for the one sheet of paper we had on David Pendergast. He'd been booked just once in his political career—for civil disturbance, in 1967. The home address listed then had been torn down twelve years ago for a mall. All we had left was a birthplace: Marquette, Michigan.

The phone rang while I was reading, and Norm picked it up, muttered a few monosyllabic responses, and hung up, looking depressed. "That was Intelligence, wondering how I was faring in softening you up for an interview about Salierno."

I looked at him carefully. "Any hints that they might have been tailing us this morning?"

"None—they're either good poker players or it wasn't them."

"Leaving Bonatto and Shattuck."

Much later in the day, I was sitting in a de Havilland Otter—a boxy, rugged twin-engine commuter aircraft—headed for Marquette, in Michigan's remote Upper Peninsula. My departure had been delayed several hours, not through any fault of the airline but because Norm had orchestrated a "tailproof" way out of the city.

He had taken our chase on the expressway very seriously. On the off chance that our tail was still in place, he had outlined a detailed route for me to follow to the airport. I was to use several taxis, and to catch each one only after having ducked through a variety of specific buildings or alleyways. His hope was that even if I couldn't shake a tail, I'd at least be able to spot one on my side trips from cab to cab. In the meantime, Norm checked me out of my motel and returned my rental car.

I followed his plan to the letter, but with mixed feelings. Despite what had happened to Shilly, I was still convinced that I personally ran little risk of harm. As I saw it, I was a bird dog for Bonatto and Shattuck both. They were depending on me to flush out the quarry—or information—whoever or whatever that might be; it wouldn't benefit either one of them if they stopped me before I'd done the job.

The only problem was that my privileged position could change at any time, and for reasons I wouldn't understand. For while my goals were to positively connect David Pendergast to the pile of bones in Hillstrom's morgue, find out why and by whom he'd been buried in Abraham Fuller's backyard, and to nail whoever it was who'd turned I-91 into a shooting gallery, Shattuck and Bonatto already knew most of that—or at least a hell of lot more than I did. That meant that at some point there was a real possibility I might uncover some fact, or somebody, which would mean far more to one of them than it would to me, at which point the rules would change—I could become superfluous, even expendable.

I stared out the plane's window at the distant greenery below. The effort I'd expended so far and the guilt I carried for Shilly's death were driving me as hard as my legal obligations. I wanted to know who had done what, and to whom, and why.

Marquette lies along the southern shore of Lake Superior; with the town to one's back, the watery vastness stretching out to the horizon is reminiscent of the bland blue oblivion that borders Chicago. But somehow, Superior is more threatening than Lake Michigan. Although calm upon my arrival, it felt wilder, colder, and ominous.

Marquette also is less oblivious to its neighbor than is Chicago to its. A far smaller town, it is more respectful of its lake, and more dependent upon it. Here there are few leisure boats and yachts, and more crafts of industry. The city's history as a shipping center for ore and lumber is still strong in the low, dark, turn-of-the-century industrial architecture. It is not a beautiful place, nor an inspiring one, but it speaks much of effort and toil, and of endurance.

It was late afternoon when I landed at the small airport outside of town, so I took a cab directly to city hall to see what luck I would have in chasing down anyone named Pendergast.

Forty minutes later, thanks to both the rarity of the name and the willingness of the various personnel who passed me from office to office with a familiar small-town eagerness to please, I ended up back on the sidewalk with the address of Lucius and Pamela Pendergast, deceased, parents of David, Susan, Elizabeth, and Megan.

The address was northeast of downtown, on a ridge of older buildings overlooking the deep-water port and the imposing, almost quarter-mile-long ore-loading dock to the south. It was a view at once muscular and utilitarian.

The house had been titled to Agnes and Bernard Nilsson in the mid-sixties. It was one of the older, more statuesque buildings on the street. But while built in a quasi-Victorian style of faded dark wood, it had exchanged whatever splendor it once had for a brooding, neglected, weather-stained misery. The paint was half gone, the roof haphazardly patched, the steps leading to the precarious porch rotten and sagging, and one of the bay windows was propped up on an endangered-looking sawhorse.

Still, it retained a grip on its former glory—the gap-toothed gingerbread, the fancy molding, the leaded windows and stained glass, the solid oak door with the heavy brass knocker—all bygone clarions to wealth and status and social propriety.

The woman who eventually opened that heavy door shared many of the same qualities. She was very old—white-haired, bent, skinny as a stick, supporting herself on two metal half crutches whose upper bands encircled her bony forearms. She was nevertheless bright-eyed, clear-spoken, and obviously in full control of her faculties.

"May I help you?" she asked.

I smiled instinctively at her lively face, as full of hopeful anticipation as her house was not. "Mrs. Nilsson? I'm Lieutenant Gunther, from Brattleboro, Vermont." I showed her my credentials, which she peered at with great interest.

"All the way from Vermont. It must be very important."

"We think so, but I don't wish to alarm you. I'm here because this house once belonged to the Pendergasts. They're the ones I'm actually interested in."

She opened the door wider and motioned me inside. "That's quite right. This was their house—their son, David, gave it to my husband and me many years ago."

"Gave it to you?" I stepped into a large dark-walled foyer.

My hostess shuffled toward one of two glass inner doors leading off to opposite corners of the house, speaking over her shoulder. "That's right. It was a gift. The most extraordinary thing. My husband and I worked for the Pendergasts. I was David's nanny."

She opened the door and led the way down a gloomy hallway to a huge living room at the far end. The air smelled sour—of cooking, mustiness, and decay.

"Where are his parents?"

"Long dead—thirty years or more. They died in a boating accident, right out there." We had reached the living room—

long, low, wood-paneled, and crammed with heavy, ornate overstuffed furniture, none of which looked like it had been touched in years. The entire place felt like an abandoned museum—left to rot in mildew under layers of fine dust. Through the dim bay windows, I could see the leaden mass of the lake, undulating ever so gently, like the belly of something fast asleep and inconceivably gigantic.

"So the children were left in your care?"

"Oh, no. Megan died as a young child, Beth has been institutionalized almost since birth, and Susan ran away to Alaska when she was fourteen and hasn't been seen since. Only David was left by the time their parents died, and he was twenty-two and already in college."

She was standing in the middle of the room, looking a little uneasy. I sensed she'd led me here for social reasons—to receive me properly—but that she actually spent so little time here, surrounded by all this musty, forgotten elegance, that she was now at a loss as to what to do next.

"And your husband has also passed away?"

She nodded, her eyes on the floor, where she'd left tracks in the dust across the rug.

I cleared my throat. "Mrs. Nilsson, I appreciate your showing me the view, and it's a lovely room, but to be honest, I was wondering if we could sit in the kitchen or someplace a little less formal?"

She looked up then and smiled, patting my forearm. "Like a funeral parlor, isn't it? I never liked it, even when the place was full of people. This was Colonel Pendergast's room. Follow me."

She took the lead once more, through another door, down another hallway, closer to the smell of cooking I'd noticed earlier.

"What was he a colonel of?"

"Marines—retired."

"He didn't work?"

She pushed open a swinging door and the smell overtook us both—sauerkraut, cheap sausage, and overboiled potatoes, bathed in vinegar. But it was a familiar odor, and not unappealing.

"No. Mrs. Pendergast came from a wealthy family. Her

parents built this house when she was very little. The Colonel 'managed' the money, although he obviously didn't do it very well. The will consisted of this house and nothing else. Would you like to stay for supper?''

I stopped my visual inspection of the ancient, massive kitchen and stared at her back as she checked the pot on the World War II–vintage gas stove. Normally, I would have passed on such an invitation out of professional habit. But I was hungry, and she'd been open and cooperative from the start. I didn't see any point in refusing.

''Thank you—only if you have enough.''

She smiled at me with those perfect yellow store-bought teeth. ''I've got plenty. Sit down.'' She motioned to the metal, enamel-topped table in the middle of the room.

I pulled out a chair and watched her as she puttered around the room, fetching bowls, glasses, and a limp plastic-wrapped log of white bread. She filled a bowl from the stovetop and placed it before me.

''It was nice of David to give you the house,'' I said.

She laughed. ''It only happened because he wanted to wash his hands of it. He didn't remove a single item from it, either, not even his own things.''

''What was he like?''

''As a little boy, before the others were born, he could be wonderful. I often wished later I could have stolen him then and taken him away and given him the love and support he needed. I think he would have turned into a fine man. But I didn't, and he didn't, which I suppose was inevitable. It probably wouldn't have worked out, anyway. Bernie used to say it was in the genes, and maybe he was right.''

''I take it David didn't turn out to be a model citizen.''

She chuckled again. Despite her long-standing ties to the family, she obviously suffered from no sentimental delusions. ''Oh, my goodness, no. He could charm you out of your socks, of course, and as a little boy, that was real. But after he grew up, it didn't mean a thing. He became his father, in a way—a modern version. Just as cold and calculating and manipulative.''

''How did father and son get along?''

''They hated each other, but David was better at it than his father, and eventually he got the Colonel to think he loved him. That's how David got the house, and why he didn't want it later.''

She paused in her eating and placed her thin blue-veined hand to her cheek. "Bernie kept wanting us to leave—Let them murder each other in peace, he'd say—but I couldn't do it.''

"Where was David's mother in all this?"

"Mrs. Pendergast stayed in her garden or in her own bed-room, listening to music and reading, barely speaking to anyone, taking her meals alone, always dressed in her Sunday best. For all intents and purposes, none of the rest of us existed for her.''

"Was David ever violent?"

She took a few bites before answering. "Yes, in a manipulative kind of way. He could get people to do nasty things. It got to be a problem at school.''

I was recalling the anthropologist's description of the skeleton on Beverly Hillstrom's autopsy table. "He was left-handed?''

"Yes, that's right.''

"With perfect teeth—no cavities?"

"No cavities, but he had a chipped front tooth from a football accident. He had it capped by the dentist so it looked like new, but he stopped playing after that.''

I remembered Hillstrom's request. "Is the dentist still around?"

She shook her head several times. "Oh, Lord, no. He died years and years ago and the business closed.''

We had both finished eating by now. "Do you have any pictures of David?"

She rose slowly to her feet. "Come with me. I'll show you what I've got. It isn't much.''

We left the kitchen for a short back hallway and entered a tiny living room with a wooden chair facing a television set. An armchair sat in the corner near the window and the walls were lined with shelves stuffed with odds and ends—boxes, bundles, some books, lots of knickknacks.

"Sit there," she ordered, pointing to the armchair. "I can't use it, anyway.'' She grinned suddenly. ''Couldn't get up if I did.''

I took my place and she began slowly checking the shelves, muttering to herself. She stopped at one point and warned me, ''It's not an album. None of them was very big on picture taking, but I do have a shot or two of David . . . If I could just find the right box.''

''You wouldn't have one of him grinning, would you?''

She paused in her excavation and looked down at me, her face quizzical. ''Why would you want that?''

It would have been perfectly all right to tell her the truth. There was nothing confidential about the skeleton we'd found back in Vermont, but somehow I felt it would have been grossly inappropriate—even gratuitous—to do so. The fact that she hadn't asked a single question about why I was here indicated to me that despite her seeming flat-footedness, Agnes Nilsson had been as much a victim of this disastrous family as any one of its members, perhaps more so, since she had chosen to remain in its midst, even over her husband's objections.

So I shrugged at her question and responded lightly, ''Pictures of people grinning are usually more helpful. The face looks more animated, more like what people are used to.''

She nodded, as if that made perfect sense to her. ''I think I have a couple of him at a fair we had here. I can't remember if he's smiling or not . . .''

Suddenly, she looked up. ''Of course. There's a perfect shot of him in his college yearbook.'' She handed a shoe box to me and rose to attack the shelves once more.

I cradled the box on my lap and began flipping through the slim collection, catching glimpses of landscapes and pets and Bernie and small sailboats. I found the half dozen taken at the fair and scrutinized them, trying to locate the handsome young man with the chipped front tooth. What I found froze me in place.

''Here we go,'' Mrs. Nilsson finally announced, pulling out a book and flipping through it. ''I never liked this picture much—looked much too phony to me—but maybe it'll suit you; it does look like him.''

She thrust the book at me, open to a large, clear, full-face shot of David Pendergast, his mouth wide in a toothy grin. I looked at it absentmindedly, knowing it was exactly what I was after but suddenly finding it of only minor interest.

I nodded agreeably and put the book aside, showing her the picture I'd found in the box. "When was this taken? I mean, how old would David have been?"

She sidled over next to me so we could both look at it together. "Well, he was in college in Chicago, at the University of Illinois. It was shortly after his parents died, so that would put him in his early twenties. He'd come up on vacation."

I pointed to a figure standing to one side and slightly behind David. "Do you know who this is?"

She peered more closely at the picture. "That was a friend of his, I think—a boy he'd brought up with him from college." She straightened and stared off into space. "They stayed here a week. You'd think I'd remember his name."

"How about Abraham Fuller?"

Chapter Twenty-six

Agnes Nilsson hadn't reacted to Abraham Fuller's name, nor had she remembered anything else about him, except that he, like everyone David gathered about him, had seemed diminished somehow in his presence. Nevertheless, my satisfaction at having finally linked Fuller to Pendergast remained complete. The nagging uncertainty that had come with everyone's inability to recognize Fuller from his picture was finally quieted, along with some of my own frustration at producing so little for the time and money I had spent on this case.

Which is why, after checking into a motel on the highway heading back to the Marquette airport, I called Brandt and gave him a full report.

"Have you found anything at your end?" I asked after I'd finished.

"Yeah, actually, we have. We've been concentrating on Coyner, since he's the only one we can actually lay our hands on. Kunkle remembered that when Sammie gave you her account of Coyner's life history, she said his fortunes made an upturn 'fresh from the funeral.' That started him wondering about who'd paid for the funeral, since Coyner was supposedly up to his ears in debt.

"Kunkle can be a little heavy-handed, so I sent Sammie to interview the mortician. Turns out he's ancient—at the Retreat now and a little out of it. After some head scratching, he remembered that Coyner did have a couple of unusual friends hanging around, helping with the arrangements, including the financial end."

"Unusual how?"

"Long hair, bell-bottoms, weird smell. She showed him Fuller's photograph, but it was too long ago and the old man's eyes aren't what they used to be. He said he was struck more by the clothes than the faces, anyhow. They seemed odd companions for Coyner to have. Still, it sounds right."

"And he said there were definitely two of them?"

"Yup."

"I'll mail you a copy of Pendergast's mug shot. Maybe that'll jar his memory."

"I doubt it. He's half blind. Send the picture, though, 'cause there's more. Ron started wondering how Coyner would've wound up connected to two mysterious hippies. Remember Coyner shooting the bus windows at Hippie Hollow? We're hoping to find out who was living there back then and show them Fuller's—now Pendergast's—pictures. If the people we're after were hiding out with the bus crowd, and providence suddenly came knocking in the shape of an alcoholic recluse with a shotgun, financial problems, and a shack out back, it might give us a lead on the machine gunner."

I recalled that the state's attorney had once represented the denizens of Hippie Hollow. "You get Dunn to cooperate?"

Brandt laughed. "Yeah. He's digging through his files right now. It was a pretty transient crowd, but maybe a few of them are still around. So how soon do you think you'll be able to wrap things up out there?''

''Shouldn't be too much longer. I'm going back to Chicago tomorrow. There're still a few loose ends I hope to clear up fast.''

I knew that wasn't what he wanted to hear, but he paid me the courtesy of merely muttering, ''The sooner the better.''

I called Norm Runnion next, but not, as it turned out, to share my good news.

''Where are you?'' he demanded, his voice sharp and excited.

The hairs on the back of my neck began to tingle. ''Still in Marquette. Why?''

''How soon can you get back here?''

I grabbed an airline schedule out of my back pocket, where I'd shoved it absentmindedly. ''There's a flight in ten minutes, but I won't be able to make it.''

''Catch the one in ten minutes. I'll call the airport and tell 'em to wait.''

''What's happening?''

''Someone complained about the high-speed number we did on the expressway. They got the number of the guy who was tailing us. I'm about to stake his place out.''

''Is he mob-connected?''

''No—which means it has to be Shattuck. Come on, move it. I'll make the call. Take a cab to the corner of Montana and Sheffield when you hit town and walk west on Montana. I'll find you.''

The line went dead. It had begun to rain outside.

It was a rough flight back, especially as we neared Chicago. The small plane bucked and shuddered in the night and the pilot came on at one point to say that an alternate airport might be necessary. I stared out the window and saw nothing besides the rain streaking by at a sharp angle.

I was worried about Norm. It was he, after all, who'd read me the rules of the game concerning the Shattuck investigation: The here and now was Homicide's concern; past history was ours. It seemed to me that his eagerness to retire in glory might get us in some serious trouble.

We did land at Chicago, although I wished we hadn't tried. The buffeting from the wind had turned violent, and I saw lightning from the cabin's window as the city's lights lurched and bounced into view. Leaning out of my seat and looking down the length of the tiny cabin, I could see the pilot and copilot through the half-curtained cockpit, their shoulders hunched to the task. The pilot was holding the wheel in a death grip, jerking it spastically to correct the small plane's wild leaps and bounds. The copilot kept wiping his hand against his trouser leg.

The landing was by no means feather-smooth, accompanied as it was by the simultaneous crashing of several items in the galley and at least three pieces of hand luggage, but it was successful, and instantly followed by a spontaneous burst of applause from everybody on board, including, I noted glumly, the stewardess, sitting alone at the back.

The cab ride into town reemphasized why our plane should have landed elsewhere. Through near-deserted, half-flooded streets littered with debris, we drove in the midst of a near hurricane.

At Montana and Sheffield, almost directly under the elevated subway tracks, the cabbie pulled to a stop, and looked over his shoulder at me with a pity reserved for the deranged. I handed him the seventy-five dollars that had been his absolute minimum for venturing out in this filth, then struggled against the wind to open the door.

The effect of finally stepping into the storm, instead of just watching it through various windows, had a strange and contradictory impact. In one sense, it became more real because I was instantly drenched to the skin, yet in another, the threat of it lessened when I found that the wind, though both ferocious and quirky, was not enough to lift me off my feet. It was of a staggering intensity, however, and its erratic gusts, affected by the buildings all around, made progress down Montana a real effort.

I was walking near the buildings, one hand outstretched for stability, the other still hanging on to my overnight case, when I heard a loud, deep rumbling behind me, as of metal against metal. To my amazement, it was the elevated subway, still running despite the weather. Squinting against the driving, lashing rain, I could see the train's row of brightly lit windows passing serenely by, almost all of them empty.

"Joe. In the car, goddamn it." I looked around, trying to locate who'd called me. The street was totally deserted—dark, gleaming wet, the few lights blurred and ineffectual.

I stared stupidly down and saw Norm peering out above his barely opened window. I lurched out into the street, around the car, and half-fell into the front seat, almost losing the door to the gale.

He looked at me, both amused and slightly embarrassed. "I guess you caught the plane."

I wiped my face with my hand. "This better be worth it."

He pursed his lips and wiped the foggy windshield with a rag from the glove compartment. "It's that brownstone over there."

I caught the flatness in his voice. "But you haven't seen a thing yet."

"Nope."

I looked down at myself, sitting in a puddle, and concentrated on lowering the adrenaline that had fueled me all the way here. "Great. So who's supposed to be living there?" I asked.

"Guy named Russell Grange—old-time radical, according to Stoddard, although no direct link to Shattuck that we know."

"You tell Homicide?"

He paused a moment, renewing my fears about his motives. "No. I don't really have anything to tell 'em, except that someone from this address tailed us, which then begs the question of what we were up to at the time."

I mulled that over. If this did turn out to be nothing, and he had told his colleagues of it, he would lose two ways, by both tipping his hand and having nothing to show for his efforts.

"Something else," Runnion added. "I got twitchy after sending you out of town the way I did, so I decided to call Penny Nivens, just to see how she was. She'd had a visit a few hours after we left her—at her home."

A cold wave spread down my spine. "Who?"

"I'd say Outfit boys. Two of 'em, polite but tough, scared her without lifting a finger. She told 'em what she told us."

"How the hell did they get to her?" My question was mostly rhetorical, but Runnion's self-conscious stillness made me look at him more closely.

He frowned and a crease appeared between his eyes, which stayed glued to the house down the street. "We . . . I wasn't as clever as I thought. This guy—or whoever borrowed his car—wasn't our only tail. My car had one of those direction-finding gizmos stuck to it—a transmitter."

I stared dumbfounded for a few seconds, realizing only then that Norm's sharpened interest in being here tonight had less to do with going out in glory and more to do with wounded professional pride.

"There," he suddenly said, interrupting my reflections.

I sat forward and peered through the murky gloom. A figure had appeared in the doorway of the house, dressed in a raincoat and droopy hat.

"Check him out." Norm thrust a pair of binoculars at me.

I brought the binoculars to bear, trying to overcome the blurring effects of the windshield, the rain, and the darkness.

"Is it Shattuck?"

"I don't know yet."

I saw the figure in the coat pull his hat farther down and his coat collar up. He kept his face pointed up the street, toward the Elevated's dark, ugly overhead roadway. As he stepped from the building's shelter and began walking away, braced as if he was on a ship's tilting deck, I saw a gray ponytail break free of the hat and string out in the wind.

"I think it is. I can see his hair."

Norm started his engine, but stayed put. "Russell Grange's car is parked near the end of the block. I'll wait 'til he gets in."

The seconds ticked by, exposing an additional disadvantage to the weather. No matter if he walked or drove, this man and we would be the only ones moving on the street tonight, as conspicuous as dancers in a morgue.

"Shit, he walked past it."

The man in the raincoat reached the corner, instinctively

looked both ways, one hand holding his hat on his head, and crossed the street, now walking directly into the wind and leaning forward at a sharp angle.

"Where's the son of a bitch going?" Norm waited until our quarry had vanished from view, going south on Sheffield, before pulling the car out of its parking place and rolling slowly up to the corner. The El now loomed overhead, mysterious and vaguely threatening.

I wiped the mist from my side window, but the rain was like a waterfall against the outside. "I can't see. Pull around so we can get the wipers working for us."

Norm gunned the accelerator a bit, turned left, and we both scanned the sidewalk ahead.

We didn't get a chance to focus, however. Without warning, like lightning bursting from nowhere, the entire windshield exploded before us. The car was transformed from a dry, warm cocoon into a screaming, glass-filled, rain-soaked bedlam before either one of us could so much as flinch. Appearing between us as if by magic, slicing the top of Norm's head with a burst of blood, was a metal road sign, still attached to its thick javelinlike steel post.

It took me a couple of seconds to recover, to check that I was still all in one piece. I had nicks and cuts across both hands, and I assumed on my face, but both eyes were free of glass, and I could feel no pain. My major problem was simply breathing against the direct onslaught of wind and rain.

I twisted in my seat, trying to move the street sign out of the way enough so I could get a clear look at Norm. He lay slouched against the far door, his mouth open and gasping, his hands feebly moving about, as if groping in the dark. Blood covered the entire right side of his face and ran down his shirt collar.

He blinked at me a couple of times, his eyes refocusing. "Holy shit. I thought he'd shot us."

"How are you?" I shouted over the noise. "You're covered with blood."

He touched his head then and looked at his red-tinged fingers, almost instantly cleansed by the rain. "It doesn't feel too bad." He felt again, less gingerly. "It's just a cut."

I could see better now, having shoved the sign back out the window. Norm had a good six-inch laceration to his scalp, cut down to the bone.

But he was back to watching the street. "I can see him. He's headed for the El. Christ, he didn't even notice us."

I followed his stare and saw the man we'd been following slowly working his way up the stairs leading to the platform above, locked in his own capsule of rain, wind, and noise. He was just over a block away.

"Go for him," Norm shouted at me. "He'll get away."

"You need help."

"I can radio for it, and I'll get troops for the stations down the line, but you got to go after him."

"You don't know how badly you're hurt."

He grabbed the rag he'd used earlier on the windshield and pushed it against the slice in his head. "There—that's as much as you could do. Now go after Shattuck."

I threw my weight against my door to get out, then began to run as fast I could for the station, bent double, slipping and falling constantly, peeling off my coat to cut down on wind resistance, and finally reaching the stairs, gasping for air. As I stumbled up the steps, I heard the deep rumble of a train pulling in.

I half-fell into the last car, just as the doors were closing. It was empty. I paused briefly to get my bearings and began heading for the front. I didn't know which car Shattuck had boarded, but I knew he was ahead somewhere and that it would be a miracle if he still hadn't noticed I was after him.

The far door opened without problem, as did the entrance to the next car, which was also empty. I had my gun out and kept ducking down every once in a while to look under the seats, checking for someone waiting in ambush. I was moving as quickly as possible, almost at a run, hoping to beat the train to the next station. I knew that wherever Shattuck was, he couldn't leave the train until it stopped moving.

I found him in the next car. Thinking it as empty as its predecessor, I pulled the door open just as the train went from above ground to below with a burst of roaring, screaming noise. The change was so sudden, so unexpected, that I instinctively dropped to the floor. Shattuck's first shot smacked into the wall high above my head.

I could see his feet, far at the other end, and fired twice. He shot back as I rolled between two seats, and then he retreated to the next car.

I paused, replaced my spent shells with two of the six extra bullets I always kept in my jacket pocket, and quickly worked my way up to the far door.

Any doubts about the identity of my quarry were gone now. I'd seen him clearly in that brief moment—the same face and eyes that had smiled at me in the glow of a single candle so long ago. But just as I was sure it was Bob Shattuck, I was also quite sure I had no strategy to bring him under control. I was now in a simple running gunfight, which I could safely abandon now or risk seeing through to the finish.

Considering what I'd done to get this far, however, the debate barely flickered in my brain. I opened the door and stepped out between the cars, knowing he'd be waiting for me inside the next car.

I backed as far as I could into the gap between the cars, turned the door handle with my free hand, and kicked the door open with my foot, staying clear of the opening. As I did so, the train slowed and banked into a curve to the protesting shriek of all its wheels, throwing me off balance.

But no bullet came sailing through the open door.

Fighting the centrifugal force of the train, I pulled myself to the opening and peered inside. Far ahead, on the right side, Bob Shattuck was halfway out one of the broad windows. Outside, dimly lit, I could see in that split second that we were gliding nonstop through a darkened, closed station.

Then Shattuck fired again, sending me ducking back for cover.

When I looked out a second time, he was gone.

I quickly stepped into the car, saw the "North & Clybourn" station signs drifting past as the train finished grinding out of the curve before picking up speed once more. The dark, distant curved tile walls of the station slid by, quite slowly now, or so I thought.

As if by some act of unconscious will, everything seemed

to begin moving slowly. In the passing split seconds, my gun hand came up and squeezed off three rounds at the window opposite me, reducing it to a blanched crazy quilt of cracked glass.

Without thought or apprehension, instinct having totally snuffed out common sense, I leapt off one of the benches, curled into a ball with my arms wrapped around my head, and crashed through the weakened glass window onto the platform beyond.

Chapter Twenty-seven

The landing was brutal—and not in slow motion. It was a chaotic, painful jumble of hurt and terror, compounded by the sick last-second realization of just how big an idiot I'd been to try it. My head stayed well protected, with my arms locked tightly in place, but the rest of me took a high toll in bruises, twists, abrasions, and cuts. I rolled, tumbled, crashed, and finally came to a stop spread-eagle on my face, surrounded by broken safety glass, too stunned and racked by pain to move.

The raucous noise of the train was quickly sucked into the far end of the tunnel, and I was left on the platform, wet, bleeding, stunned, and alone. I was only about five feet shy of the station's far wall.

I rolled painfully onto my side and surveyed my surroundings. I was resting on the platform of a large tile-covered vaulted room with two tracks, a platform on either side, and a single concrete wall running lengthwise down the middle, holding up the ceiling. The wall had openings in it every twelve feet or so—three-foot gaps that allowed me to see the station's northbound side. The whole place was dark and quiet, lit only by exit lights and a few odd bare bulbs.

Shattuck was nowhere to be seen, which was just as well

for me. Had he been here, waiting, I now recognized ruefully, it would have been a simple matter to put an executioner's bullet through my head.

I carefully straightened to a sitting position. The fact that he was not here either meant he was lying dead on the tracks out of sight or he'd assumed no sane man would jump out of the train after him.

I got to my feet gingerly, half-surprised to find my gun still clenched in my bloody fist, and moved quietly on the balls of my feet toward the north end of the station. I kept my eyes on the three-foot gaps in the wall next to the tracks, watching the narrow views they afforded of the platform parallel to mine.

Shattuck had known this station was coming up, he'd known the train wouldn't stop, and he'd seemed quite comfortable straddling that window—as if he'd done it before. Also, he wasn't in the station—I was sure of that by now. It all suggested the possibility that he'd had this place in mind from the start.

I continued softly to the end of the platform and stood just by the wall, out of sight from the dark, dank-smelling tunnel, listening.

There was a less appealing explanation, of course, albeit a little farfetched: Shattuck had poised himself on the window ledge, taken a shot at me to make me duck, and then had dropped to the floor of the car and let me assume he'd jumped, hoping I'd oblige him by following suit.

A single small sound, as of someone stumbling in the dark, settled the issue for me. I slipped quietly off the edge of the platform and began walking as quickly and silently as possible away from the station, painfully aware that its lights, as feeble as they were, still made it easy for others to see me.

Now inside the tunnel, where each sound reverberated off the cement walls, I could plainly hear someone walking ahead of me—which meant the reverse would hold true if I wasn't careful. I discovered the only way I could avoid crunching the gravel railbed underfoot was to straddle the outermost rail and step cautiously from cross tie to cross tie.

The concentration this took, however, especially in my

present battered state, made me inattentive to the slow and gradual approach of another southbound train, just beginning to hit the outer reaches of the long curve that led into the station. By the time I looked up, aware of the growing noise and searching out a hiding spot among the indentations in the wall, I suddenly realized I was visible in the subway's single bright headlamp, as was the distant figure of Robert Shattuck, ahead and away on the other side of the tracks.

I jumped away from the rails, no longer worried about any sound I might make, but as I did, Shattuck turned toward me, as if drawn by my own panic. I saw the shock register on his distant face, and finally, just as the train was about to come between us, his gun flew up and spat a flame in my direction, its explosion muffled by the screaming of the subway's wheels. A chunk of cement splattered to the left of me as I ducked into an alcove and the train blew by in a deafening, shrieking roar.

I readied my own weapon, steadying my arm against the edge of the shallow alcove, and was sighting where Shattuck had last been when the train pulled clear. But the tracks were empty.

I stayed where I was, straining to regain my night vision, trying to hear anything at all over the receding rumble of the cars. What I heard, or thought I heard, was the rhythmic pounding of feet running away from me.

I separated from my shelter and began jogging along the track, bent low, moving as fast as I could, no longer worrying about the crunch of gravel. Coming abreast of where I'd seen Shattuck, I slowed, crossed the tracks quietly, and began tracing his steps north. Both the noise of the train and the sound of Shattuck's footfalls had vanished. Sweat began to trickle down my sides.

I came to an opening in the curved wall—a small secondary tunnel with a cement floor—obviously the source of the running sounds I'd heard earlier. It was straight for some one hundred feet and then turned out of sight to the left. A single anemic light was suspended from the domed eight-foot ceiling. The walls were smooth and bare, free of any hiding places—a shooting gallery custom-made for an ambush.

I opened the cylinder of my revolver, extracted the three spent shells, and replaced them with the extras from my pocket, leaving me one in reserve.

In a calmer, more rational setting, logic and caution would have dictated the obvious course to take. By all rights, I should have stayed there, bottling up the exit, waiting for Norm's backup to arrive, which they were bound to do once they found the train with the shattered window and the debris I'd left behind on the platform. But if, as I suspected, this tunnel was merely the front door to a hideaway that Shattuck had harbored for some time, then it undoubtedly had a back door. That didn't leave me much of an alternative, at least not a sane one.

Sanity, of course, is in the mind of the beholder, and what I was beginning to formulate didn't seem too far off-the-wall. The tunnel's blandness, as I saw it, cut two ways. It did expose me to fire, but it also allowed an ambush from a single spot only—the distant inside curve to the left. It was the only cover available, and was as easily assailable by me as I was from it.

I wiped my hand on my pants, took a firm grip on my gun, and bolted from my hiding place, running as fast as I could in a zigzag pattern directly toward the curve in the tunnel. I was startled to hear, echoing all around me and mixing with the pounding of my feet, the sound of my own voice shouting.

About halfway there, I saw a flash of movement from the inside corner, a glimmer of something metallic. I fired, still running for all I was worth, my aches and pains temporarily replaced by a frantic, pounding euphoria.

The gamble paid off. The glimpse of face and arm I'd shot at vanished, and I poured on more speed for the remaining fifty feet.

At the corner, I paused, poked my head around quickly, and saw a large dark room filled with ventilation machinery and odd pieces of track-repair equipment—squat, ugly, gloomily vague. At the far side was another entrance, animated ever so briefly by the blur of a pale shadow disappearing. I ran through the equipment room, almost without pause, risking exposure so I could keep up the pressure.

That was a mistake. The adrenaline that had served me

well during the hundred-foot dash of moments earlier now made me careless. I entered the far exit too fast, sliding past the corner that might have given me protection, and was met by the eruption of a point-blank muzzle flash. Momentarily blinded, deafened, and feeling the sear of burning gunpowder along the right side of my head, I plunged on, hoping pure physical momentum might stifle a second, more accurate shot.

I crashed headlong into Bob Shattuck's chest, sending him staggering backward. His gun, with which he tried to fracture my skull in a crossward blow, almost missed, its front sight slicing a furrow over both my eyes. It was bad enough, however, to send me reeling to the floor, dazed, my eyesight clouded by my own blood. I fired two shots in his direction, hoping to get lucky. There was a startled shout, a wild shot in return that whacked into the floor harmlessly, and the clang of a heavy metal door.

I lay there panting for a full minute, my gun arm still outstretched, my eyes half-blinking away the warm oozing from the gash just above them.

I rose to a sitting position, found the wall with my back, pulled out my handkerchief, and wrapped it around my head to staunch the bleeding. Then, like an old and stubborn dog with only one purpose in life, I got to all fours, then to one knee, and finally rose to my feet again, as determined as ever to see this through to the end.

I wasn't driven by the image of Shilly's mutilated body or the humiliation of having been duped by Shattuck. I kept going because I saw no other option. Only in Korea, decades ago, had I experienced such a seeming loss of choices, when, cold, starving, exhausted, and shell-shocked, I and dozens like me had held on to positions that could easily have been abandoned. Then, as now, retreat—or even common sense—hadn't appeared as an alternative.

The heavy clang I'd heard had not come from a door but from a large hatchway in the floor. I pulled it open by a ring mounted to a bracket and was thrown off balance by how easily it came away. It was counterbalanced by a weight below and stayed in whatever position I left it, which explained how Shattuck had vanished so quickly. He had already opened it before trying to blow my head off at the entrance, planning a quick escape.

Below me was yet another passageway, lined by dozens of thick, insulated electrical cables. It was narrow, cramped, and as black as night. I cautiously climbed down the short steel ladder at the edge of the hole and looked around. The tunnel was just six feet in circumference but was actually very cramped due to the bundles of cable. It extended in opposite directions, but whether for eight feet or eight miles, I couldn't tell in the dark. I did hear some noise straight ahead, however, along with a distant, reflected glimmer of light that died almost as soon as I'd noticed it.

I quickly looked around, hoping the absence of light was something the subway work crews were equipped to overcome, and found not a master switch or fuse box but six large flashlights strung together through their handles by a busted chain mounted to the wall, presumably some more of Shattuck's handiwork.

I took one of the lights, switched it on, and began to trot in the direction of the distant flicker I'd seen.

My momentum didn't last long. At the first corner, I came to an opening halfway up the wall of a large junction area, square, high-ceilinged, and fed by a dozen or so tunnels similar to the one I was in. A second steel ladder led down to the floor of this chamber. It was anyone's guess where that flicker of light had vanished to.

Dispirited, drained by the thought that all the effort I'd expended—not to mention the blood—had been for nothing, I climbed down the ladder for a last look around. It was unlikely, I knew, but maybe in his haste, Shattuck had left some sign indicating which tunnel he'd used.

The entrances weren't all at the same level. Some were flush with the chamber's floor; others were located atop high ladders near the ceiling. I checked them in order, working counterclockwise, flashing my light down each one, listening carefully, until I got to the tallest of the ladders, about fifteen feet up.

By this time, I'd lost whatever edge my nerves had been keeping sharp. The roller-coaster plane ride, the drenching walk through the storm, the street sign totaling Norm's car, the near-suicidal jump off the train, the hunt-and-go-seek with guns, all had pretty much done me in. I'd been battered, bruised, kicked, scraped, cut open, and shot at. I was beginning to feel like hell.

So I was unprepared, three-quarters of the way up the last ladder, gripping the railings with a gun in one hand and a flashlight in the other, to see Shattuck pop out above me like some evil jack-in-the-box, complete with a sinister grin, and jam his pistol square in the middle of my bandaged forehead.

"Hi there." His voice was flat and quiet—a serpent's hiss.

I was sitting at the foot of the ladder, my back against the rungs, my hands tied to the rails, my feet sticking out ahead of me. Shattuck rested cross-legged on my shins, his weight crushing my calves and causing my knees to spasm in agony. He played with his revolver—a brushed steel .357 Magnum—with a practiced nonchalance.

"It was Joe, right? Vermont Joe. You're not looking too good. You do put up a hell of a fight, though, for a man your age." He tipped my head toward the dim light to examine the burns left behind by his earlier muzzle flash.

"Nasty. What makes you so persistent?"

I didn't answer, nor had I said a single word since he'd caught me.

"Is it Shilly? Did it bother you what I did to him? He was a hypocritical prick. I knew about him from the old days— big on bringing medicine to the people, saying the Establishment was ripe for burning. He was just killing time, figuring out how he could cash in, especially after he got thrown out of the hospital.

He shook his head in wonder. "What a mind fuck, you know? Tracking me down after all those years, looking for a name for your skeleton. . . . Like a babe in the woods. You smarter now?"

I remained silent.

A furrow appeared between his eyes, and he leaned forward slightly, causing me to clamp my teeth against the jolt from my partly inverted knees. "I need to know what you've learned, Joe."

Through the pain and the fear, I knew he was telling me

the truth. Norm *had* shaken him off on our way to visit Penny Nivens at her fancy school, and the mobsters that interviewed her later obviously hadn't communicated their findings to Shattuck, which confirmed he was working alone and beginning to feel left out.

For all his seeming confidence, he hadn't gained any ground since he'd kidnapped Shilly. Which made me his one reluctant ally.

Nevertheless, I didn't want to answer his question, or reveal how little I knew. "What do you want after all this time? The money?"

His face tightened with emotion. "Don't sell money short, Joe. Money is power, when you use it right. And I want those who betrayed me—all of them. They stole my future with that money, and the hopes of everyone I would have saved. And when I find them, you'll think Kevin Shilly died a peaceful death."

I watched the swollen vein pulsing on his temple and the hard glitter in his eye. The intensity of his anger made me think of Alfredo Bonatto—his interest barely perceptible beneath a demure, discreet, almost bland exterior—the exact opposite of the firecracker facing me. I wondered whether I could get the two of them to keep one another off my back. Given my position, it was as realistic a notion as any, and perhaps a good way to keep Shattuck off balance.

"You may not get your chance. You and I aren't the only ones interested in this."

"What's that suppose to mean?"

"Shilly told you what he did for Pendergast, didn't he?"

"You mean putting in the metal knee?"

"Because the real one had been blown off by a mobster named Tommy Salierno."

Unconsciously, Shattuck leaned back slightly, easing the pressure on my knees. He sat there thinking for a while. Finally, he rocked forward, bringing his face close to mine and the pain to new heights. I couldn't swallow the groan that gargled in my throat.

"So the Outfit's in on it. Tell me, Vermont Joe, you think this buys you some slack?"

It wasn't the question I wanted to hear, but the leering quality he dressed it in cut through my fear. I was angered that he thought somehow he'd be able to walk away from all this—untouched and a winner. "I think it puts you in a worse position than I am."

The gun settled in his right hand and his index finger slipped around the trigger. "Yeah?"

He straightened slightly, slipping the pistol between us, so that our eyes met just over the front sight. The only light came from the flashlight lying on the floor, which dimly caught the gleam of sweat on one of Shattuck's hollow cheeks, his wide, unnaturally bright eyes, and the dull gray glow from the revolver's burnished barrel.

"You don't know shit about me. I'm the bear who's been hibernating for damn near twenty-five years, and now that I'm out, I don't give a rat's ass who gets in my way—you, or the Outfit, or the fucking National Guard. I'm real hungry, and the last thing anyone wants to do is to get between a pissed-off, hungry bear and his food."

His voice was a whisper, a farewell sigh, and I knew then that I'd miscalculated, that I'd allowed him to count me out of his plans. The pain from my legs melted away, along with the hope I'd been collecting and hoarding. I watched those dark, gleaming, too-wide eyes and felt nothing but weariness. He wouldn't survive in the long run—that was a given—but I knew now I wouldn't be a witness to his end.

Shattuck's thumb pulled back the hammer. I could see the vague outline of his mouth, still locked in its smile—friendly, comforting, supportive, or so I worked to make it, to remind me of the sweet things in life—a little something to take with me.

His index finger tightened slowly on the trigger, like a good shooter's should. The barrel didn't waver. His eyes narrowed slightly in anticipation of the explosion.

I closed my eyes.

And the hammer fell.

There was a sharp, brittle click, like the sound of teeth snapping shut, but louder and more painful.

Shattuck lowered the gun as my eyes reopened. The smile

widened but the voice remained a whisper—barely audible. "Shucks—must've forgot to reload."

And then he left me alone in the dark.

Chapter Twenty-eight

I spent the rest of the night and part of the next day in the hospital, getting stitched, X-rayed, medicated, poked, and questioned. I felt like a used car getting a wax job so that everybody around me would feel better.

Norm Runnion and his colleagues had found me a couple of hours after my brush with Shattuck's version of Russian roulette. They'd traced the train back to the littered platform, to the blood-spattered floor and the open hatchway just beyond, but found no sign of Robert Shattuck—only the well-supplied hideaway he'd been living in for the past several days, at the end of one of those infrequently traveled electrical tunnels.

They did find out about my and Runnion's involvement in chasing Shattuck down, however, which was enough to get me a ticket out of town on the next morning's flight and to put Norm in the hot water he'd gambled on avoiding.

Norm came by around midday, cleaned up and looking rested, sporting a bandage around his head similar to my own. With his beard, it gave him a vaguely rakish air—the aging pirate wearing a tie.

He sat in the chair facing the bed and propped his feet on one of the bed's lower rungs. "How're you feeling?"

"Like I was rolled in a cement mixer. They going to punch your ticket?"

"With three months to go? Not likely. They'll huff and puff."

He looked at his shoes for a moment.

"I'm sorry the Outfit connection didn't work out," I said.

He sighed. "Yeah—that would've been nice."

"I told Shattuck about their involvement."

He grinned at that. "No shit, really? He might be crazy enough to try something with them. That would be interesting."

There was another pause. "I hear you got until sunset to leave town."

"More like sunrise—earliest flight they could book. They filed an official complaint with my chief for willfully meddling in an ongoing investigation and for unprofessional and discourteous conduct."

"How's that going to sit back home?"

"They don't give much of a damn about what outsiders think. It's one of the advantages of provincialism."

"What about the case? Did you get enough?"

"I would've liked to chase down the University of Illinois connection between Pendergast and Fuller—put a real name to Fuller. A yearbook might've done that. Then interview anyone who knew them, find out why Fuller never appeared with David except in that one shot."

"Hell, I can check out some of that."

I shook my head. "I don't think so, Norm."

But he waved his hand dismissively. "Oh shit, Joe, don't worry about it—it'll give me a chance to use my contacts one last time. Believe me, the brass'll never know."

I nodded my appreciation. He stood up to leave, leaning over to shake my hand. "I better get back to work. This little stunt added about two feet to my paperwork. It was nice knowin' you."

I held his grip for a moment, spurred by an impulse that had hit me the night before, during my little chat with Shattuck. "There is one more thing, Norm—kind of a strange favor."

"Shoot."

"Is there any way you can contact Bonatto—ask him to meet me somewhere?"

He gave me a long look. "It's a good thing for both of us you're headin' out tomorrow. I can do it, but I can't guarantee they'll agree to it, and they'll want to set up it up themselves, in any case. They'll need to know where to find you."

"Same motel—I reserved a room for tonight."

He nodded. "All right, but only if you promise to tell me about it later."

I thanked him for his help and apologized again for the way things worked out. He brushed it off but paused at the door. "In the report, you said that after he tied you up, you and Shattuck talked for a while before he left."

"Yeah."

"He didn't do anything? I was thinking of Shilly, you know? It made me wonder. . . ."

I thought back to those last moments, staring down the pistol barrel, watching that smile, my despair trying to turn it into something hopeful. "No. We just talked."

Runnion nodded and left, obviously unconvinced.

It seemed unfriendly, after all Norm had done for me, but how do you tell somebody about something like that?

The old Navy Pier sticks out almost a mile into Lake Michigan—an ancient, crumbling artifact that the city is working to resurrect into some sort of tourist attraction. All of downtown Chicago lies like a jeweled crescent across the water from it—distant, stellar, and magnificently still, its distant rumble quelled by the gentle lapping of the waves against the pier's corroded cement sides.

I pulled into the near-deserted parking lot at midnight, as the phone call had instructed, got out of my car, and walked over to the pier's entrance—a gaunt and shabby brick building with an archway in its center and two six-sided towers on the ends. Its once imposing aura had been diminished by the restoration crew's efforts to beef up its failing frame—there were huge gaps where the brick had been torn away to reveal the original rusty I-beams. The whole structure looked like a dottering old lady whose sole remaining dignity had been removed along with her clothes.

I approached the chain-link fence that barred the archway and was met by a dark form separating itself from the shadows.

"You Gunther?"

"Yes."

"ID?"

I pulled out my identification and handed it over. A flashlight beam suddenly blinded me as the man compared my battered, bandaged face with the one pictured next to the badge. Satisfied, he unlocked the padlock on the gate and let me through.

"Walk to the back."

The "back" was actually another building like the first, only gaudier, with fancier towers and a pitched slate roof. It straddled the far end of the pier, a half mile away. It was dark also, but visible in the reflected glow from the city behind me, looking like a lost piece of castle that had floated out to sea.

I walked down the center of the wide concrete pier, as broad and as long as a runway. My footsteps clattered loudly across the cracked, potholed cement. Aside from the guard at the gate, I'd seen no one, nor had I heard any sounds from behind the compressors, generators, bulldozers, and other equipment that littered the pier's length. But I sensed them nevertheless, watching me, watching out for Bonatto, as silent and lethal as high-strung Dobermans.

I had no idea if the money originally had belonged to the mob, or to Shattuck, or someone else entirely. I didn't know if Pendergast, Fuller, and their mysterious friend had fled to Vermont as victims running for cover or as criminals on the lam. And who had killed Tommy Salierno? Pendergast, Fuller, the third guy, or Shattuck . . . ? Or had he been knocked off by his own people, whose interest now was in shutting up the witnesses?

I rubbed my tender forehead, the far pavilion getting much closer now. Whatever the truth, both my competitors and I had avenues to follow, none of us knowing which of the others would get to the prize first, and all of us relying in part on one another to give one of us the advantage.

At least that's how I was hoping it would turn out after tonight's meeting.

A second shadowy figure appeared from out of the dark and asked me to spread my legs and arms, a procedure they'd bypassed the first time. He checked me thoroughly and jerked his thumb toward the glass door leading into the pavilion. "The door on the left."

I entered a semicircular lobby, veered off to the left, and went through the indicated door.

What I entered was an enormous vaulted room, its hemispherical ceiling buttressed by a converging latticework of curved steel I beams that met at its apex high overhead. Strung along the lower edge of each of the beams, from the polished hardwood floor to where they all came together like a single muted burst of fireworks, were lines of tiny low-wattage bulbs. It was a concert hall, perched at the end of the pier, its floor-level row of windows looking out onto a cement promenade and the vast emptiness of the lake beyond. In the distance, to the right, the slow, red, rhythmic flashing of a lighthouse reminded me of a dying pulse.

"Over here."

I turned at the familiar voice. Alfredo Bonatto was sitting alone on a metal folding chair in the center of the stage, between the door I had entered and its mate on the other side.

I walked up to the stage, my footsteps loud on the polished floor. "Did the police department candid-camera crew follow you here?"

"Why is that a concern of yours?"

"My poking around has gotten a fellow cop in trouble. It would be better for him if his colleagues didn't know you and I were meeting."

Bonatto's heavy, sad face lifted slightly in a small smile. "You needn't worry. How are you coming with your little mystery?"

"What've you heard?"

He raised his eyebrows. "It means nothing to us. I was merely being polite."

I let him know what I thought of that. "I hear your boys were pretty polite to Penny Nivens—a little scary maybe."

He rose from his chair slowly, steadying himself by resting his hand on its back for a moment. Then he motioned to the stairs at the end of the stage and began walking toward them. "Let's step outside. It's a beautiful night."

I followed him through one of the double glass doors leading out to the promenade. The air was fresh and cool and clean, filled with the sound of lapping water and the occasional deep-throated bleat of a foghorn. The city, doubled in size by the mirror-smooth reflection, shimmered like a diamond-dusted cloud on the horizon. Not for the first time, I was struck by the absence of a sea's briny odor—the fundamental paradox of all the Great Lakes.

"I'd heard you ran into some trouble. You look as though you did."

I unconsciously touched the bandage on my forehead, which had been extended down the side of my face to cover the burns there. "That's part of the reason I wanted to meet with you."

Bonatto had placed both hands on the railing above the water and was staring at the view. "Ah."

"The man I was after is a sixties radical named Robert Shattuck. He tortured a Dr. Kevin Shilly to death trying to get information."

I paused. Bonatto didn't move for several moments, then looked at me in mock surprise. "I'm sorry—is that supposed to mean something to me?"

I pursed my lips in irritation. "You wouldn't be here if it didn't."

He looked away again. "Why are you telling me about Robert Shattuck?"

"I think you and Shattuck are after the same person, though for different reasons. There's not much I can do about that, at least not at the moment. But Shattuck's got a head start, seems to know who he's after, and now knows that person was last living in Vermont. I thought I'd slant the playing field a little."

"I don't think I understand."

"Shattuck's a loose cannon—the one who could cause the most damage. It's his treatment of Shilly versus your treatment of Penny Nivens, if you want. If I have to have either one of you dogging my heels, I'd just as soon it be you."

He chuckled softly. "So you want us to handle Shattuck for you? That's pretty good."

"He knows you're interested in all this, and he's not discriminating." I pulled Shattuck's mug shot from my pocket and handed it over.

Bonatto released his grip on the railing, taking the picture without comment. Finally, he turned to face me. "Where did you work before Vermont?"

"I saw action in Korea—did a couple of years of college in California on the way home. That's it. Why?"

He hitched his shoulders ever so slightly. "You have a peculiar way of doing business. I doubt we'll meet again."

He left me then, alone on the pier, to enjoy my last view of Chicago, my mind full of doubt and self-recrimination, my heart longing to get back home. This was not my town, and I had not navigated its waters well. Instinct had filled in where procedure and practice had been wanting, and that was rarely a good basis for sound police work.

I didn't know how my last chat with the locals would play out in the long run, but it couldn't be any worse than what Shattuck had done to Shilly. And now, if my guess was right, Shattuck was heading for my turf.

I therefore took comfort in one telling detail—Bonatto had left with Shattuck's picture in his pocket.

Part Three

Chapter Twenty-nine

Gail stood alone inside the Keene, New Hampshire, airport terminal, looking at me with wide, sad eyes as I limped through the double set of glass doors from the apron.

She reached up and hugged me tightly, without saying a word. I rubbed her thin muscular back with my free hand, enjoying the clean odor of her hair. When she finally stood back, she smiled unconvincingly and touched my cheek with her fingers. "What have you done to yourself?"

I raised my eyebrows, painfully aware of how I looked—bandaged, burned, nicked by dozens of glass cuts. "I think we better find somewhere else to vacation."

She laughed, if only for a moment. "Are you all right?"

For an instant, I thought back again to Shattuck's revolver hammer slamming home on an empty shell casing. "Sure. I might end up with a small scar from this one." I tapped the bandage on my forehead.

Gail took my arm and walked with me toward the exit. "I had such a bad feeling when you left here—almost a premonition. When Tony told me you were in the hospital, it was like hearing the other shoe drop."

I squeezed her hand and kissed her. "It's good to be back."

We left the terminal and stepped into the small parking lot.

"Tony came with me," she said, pointing.

Brandt came out of her car and greeted me, shaking my hand and staring into my eyes as if checking to make sure everyone was at home. "You look awful."

"Thanks."

"Did Shattuck do all that, or did the Chicago PD chip in?"

"That pissed, are they?"

He took my bag, put it into the trunk, and opened the front passenger door for me. "I don't think I'll be sending another of our finest over there anytime soon."

We got into the car, with Tony in back. I fished Pendergast's photo out of my coat pocket and handed it to him, along with the snapshot of him and Fuller at the Marquette fair. "That's David Pendergast on the left; Fuller on the right."

He looked at them carefully. "That anthropologist of yours was right on the money—Pendergast's quite the beautiful boy."

"Only skin-deep; I hear he was a nasty son of a bitch."

Gail had pulled into traffic and was headed west toward Vermont and Brattleboro, twenty minutes away. "We got the longitude and latitude on that chart."

"You're kidding." My incredulity was instinctive and immediately regretted. Gail turned and gave me a steely look. "I told you it would work—you never believed in it from the start."

Brandt, ever the politician, steered for a middle course. "So tell him the bad news."

Her expression turned rueful. "It's near New York City."

"Somewhere around White Plains/Mount Vernon," Tony added.

"Not exactly the boonies," I muttered doubtfully. I was having difficulty believing a fanciful, color-coded, hand-drawn chart of someone's stars could accurately yield up something as concrete as birthplace coordinates.

Brandt was much more accepting—or diplomatic. "No, it's not, but it is worth a look. By the way, I told your people to be at the station for an informational meeting as soon as we get there."

"There is something I ought to warn you about, Tony. I have a feeling Robert Shattuck will be showing up here, sooner than later."

I heard the stillness in the car.

"What does that mean?" Gail finally asked. "Who's he after? You?"

"Not specifically, although I think he sees me as the someone who can lead him to the person he's after. The three people who came here in '69 or '70 with those famous hundred-dollar bills did Shattuck some damage he never recovered from. Stole the money he was pinning his future on and ruined his dreams. He's been nursing that ever since—I think it's fair to say he's after blood.''

"Where did the money come from?" Brandt asked.

"I still don't know."

"He knows who this third person is?"

"I'm sure he does. His problem isn't who; it's where. I think that's where he hopes I'll come in—by leading the way—and his ego has it that he'll succeed even if I don't want him to."

"Maybe," Tony said thoughtfully, "or Shattuck could try forcing you to cooperate."

I saw him looking at Gail, who immediately grasped his point. After a few seconds' silence, she pulled off to the side of the road and put the brake on. She sat staring at the instrument panel before her. Her voice was neutral, almost cold, in an obvious effort to keep her emotions at bay. "Do you agree with Tony?"

"He does have a point," I admitted. "If Shattuck does come to Vermont, he'll be a complete outsider. He knows we'll be watching for him, and he doesn't have the connections or the hiding places he has in Chicago. He'll have to work hard just to keep out of sight—and try to make every shot count. If he finds out about the two of us . . ."

She nodded silently.

"I'd feel a whole lot more comfortable giving you around-the-clock protection," Brandt said to Gail, "or suggesting you take a small vacation."

She stunned me with her own alternative. "If I stayed in town, and the police protection was discreet, I could be useful getting this guy out into the open."

"I disagree," I blurted out, horrified at the idea.

"Why not? It's perfectly logical."

"This guy's not sane, Gail—"

Tony interrupted. "She does have a point, Joe. And we could control it so she wouldn't really be exposed."

"This is dumb, and it misses the point. What we need to focus on is the identity and location of the third man."

"From what you've told me, Shattuck'll do anything to gain an edge; it might pay to take advantage of that." Brandt turned to Gail. "You have call forwarding on your office phone?"

"Office and home both."

"So you could work out of your home?"

She shrugged. "For a while, I suppose. I do need to get out—show properties, that sort of thing. Plus, there's the board and my other activities."

"But for a few days? We could set you up at home and have the place covered while you posed as bait. You could tell people you had the flu."

I scowled at him. "Thanks a hell of a lot. One innocent person's already been killed because of this."

Gail said quietly, "By killing me, he'd be killing his leverage."

"That's rational—he's not." I turned from her to Brandt, who merely smiled and raised his eyebrows. The terror I had felt at Shattuck's hands was mine alone. I could try to impress them just how cold-blooded he was, but I knew the end result would be the same, and that only I would feel reduced by the experience.

All that was left, therefore, was to concede to her logic— reluctantly. "I hate this."

Gail smiled sympathetically, squeezed my hand, and put the car back into gear. "He probably won't even show up."

I didn't bother answering.

"There is another problem," she said after a while. "You better cook up something for the board explaining what Joe's been up to this last week. If they find out I knew before them, we're all going to feel the heat." She glanced over her shoulder at Brandt. "I don't know how specific you want to make it, but maybe you could have a little conversation with the town manager, and let him be your messenger."

He nodded. "Good point. I also need to update the state's attorney. I won't say anything to the selectmen about Shattuck or the stakeout—just that you were in Chicago, Joe, and stirred up a few wasps in the process."

* * *

The meeting Brandt had arranged with the squad had the elements of an awkward homecoming, prefaced as it was by the ritual number of jokes about my battered appearance, and offset by several quizzical sideward glances I was not intended to see.

"I didn't get all the answers in Chicago that I'd banked on," I began. "But I did get a few. I'm hoping that with the information you've been gathering in my absence, we'll be able to wrap this case up fast. And speed, unfortunately, is now of the essence. It turns out we are no longer the only ones interested in finding out who opened up on us with an M-16. For that reason, I want to stress that what is said in this room stays here. There will be no interoffice memos, no casual chats by the coffee machine, and no late-night pillow talk with wives or significant others. If anyone questions what we're up to, your answer should be we're trying to put a name to the skeleton and find the person who did the shooting. Don't tell anyone how we're progressing. Our advantages in this race are knowledge and speed. If we give those away, we lose. It's that simple."

"Who's our competition?" Ron asked.

I held up a mug shot. "This man—Robert Shattuck." I then passed it to Ron to make a tour of the table.

"That photograph was taken about twenty years ago, so age the face in your minds and add gray hair—last seen tied back in a ponytail. Shattuck is just over six feet, trim and fit—one seventy-five to one eighty—and fifty-five years old. He is armed and violent. These"—I tapped my bandages with my finger—"are the results of some of his handiwork. He's a dangerous man."

I held up the two shots of Pendergast. "And this is our skeleton—David Pendergast, born in Marquette, Michigan, aged twenty-nine when he died. From what I could find out, he was charismatic, reckless, manipulative—and also dangerous. Not unlike Shattuck. I'll have copies made of all these."

I leaned forward on the table, choosing my words carefully. "Mr. Shattuck knows who we're after—as far as I can make out, it's someone from his past—but he doesn't know where he's hiding. Which means Shattuck may end up, one way or another, depending on us to supply that information. If he does show up in Brattleboro, he should stick out like a sore thumb, so he'll probably act quickly and ruthlessly.

"He might try to get to me through Gail Zigman, since our friendship is common knowledge. If that happens, we hope to use that opportunity to lure Shattuck out into the open. The chief will fill you in."

Brandt didn't bother standing. In his familiar unemotional style, he told them of the plan he and Gail had worked up in the car. Gail would be under discreet guard at home, and would make outings only if absolutely necessary, and then always with a man on the floor of her car and another team tailing. The stakeout would be coordinated by the department's Special Response Team—our version of SWAT—of which both Ron and Sammie were members. Brandt told them there would be an SRT meeting following this one. Given my involvement with Gail, he added, it had been agreed that I would concentrate on the other aspects of the investigation.

Kunkle spoke up after Brandt had finished. "Why not just pull in our snitches and spread the word about this guy? It's not like he has a million places to hide."

I nodded in agreement. "We need to shake the bushes, but until we know Shattuck's in the area, the main thrust of this investigation should be to find the shooter. Again"—I raised my hand for emphasis—"the stakeout has got to be kept under wraps. Should Shattuck turn up, he'll expect a minor manhunt, but he may not think we're bright enough to set a trap."

I stepped away from the table and began to pace at the head of the room. "Mr. Dunn has kindly made available to us a list of former residents of so-called Hippie Hollow, dating back to the time of Fred Coyner's wife's death. The list is fairly extensive, and we don't know how many—if any—of them are still living in the area. But we need to find the ones who are and question them about Fuller, Pendergast, and anyone else who might have been with them. That means telephone directories, phone calls, the computer, and so forth. If you get a hit, follow it up in person and let me know as soon as possible. Remember: We want to do it right, but it's got to be fast, and it's got to be discreet. We don't want to tip our hand, so watch your backs, and take note of anything or anyone unusual.

"Our second job is to locate the subject of the astrology chart that was stolen from Fuller's house. We now know from an evaluation we had made of a copy of that chart that the subject was born at ten-fifty-five P.M., eastern standard time, on April 7, 1946, in the Mount Vernon/White Plains area of New York, just north of Manhattan. I know a lot of you are probably as skeptical about this as I am, but it is a lead, and we need to see if we can match a name to those statistics."

DeFlorio let out a whistle. "Christ. Does that mean we got to call every hospital?"

"No," Kunkle growled scornfully. "County or town clerks have those records, assuming they're cooperative."

Brandt stirred in his seat. "Actually, there may be an easier way—bypassing the clerks and the fees and the paperwork. When I took the FBI Academy refresher course a few years ago, I got friendly with a state police investigator from that area who might be able to help us out. Let me give him a call. If I make it sound urgent enough, we might get something in a couple of hours instead of waiting days for the bureaucrats to get stimulated."

I nodded my agreement. "Okay, that'll allow us to concentrate on the ex–Hippie Hollow residents. Sammie, you were the one who interviewed the old mortician at the Retreat, right?"

She paused in gathering her papers together. "Yes, for what it was worth—he was pretty far gone."

"He probably had an assistant back then. Maybe he or she might remember something."

Sammie reddened slightly, perhaps feeling I was finding fault with her. "I'll call and find out."

"Okay. If there is such a person, set up an interview ASAP. We can do it together."

I turned my attention to the rest of them, who were beginning to head for the door. "We'll reconvene here at sixteen-thirty."

* * *

Sammie stuck her head into Brandt's office a half hour later and announced she'd located the mortician's ex-assistant. I made my apologies to Billy Manierre and Brandt and joined her with a sigh of relief. The three of us had been discussing how to juggle the schedules of both the Special Response Team and Billy's three patrol shifts, and I'd been finding the process difficult to deal with objectively.

Roland Bennet—the name Sammie had gotten from the mortician—was part owner of the Chameleon Café on Flat Street, Brattleboro's one forthright gay bar. There was a large "Closed" sign in the window; Sammie pounded on the door as she'd been instructed on the phone, and in a few moments we heard rapid footsteps approaching from the inside.

Bennet greeted us like a long-lost aunt; he was expansive, gregarious, and utterly unfazed by our official status. "I apologize for the smell in here—too many cigarettes and too many bodies. You don't mind if I leave the door open, do you? I have a fan going in the back, but it takes forever without a cross current."

He ushered us through the small lobby to a twenty-foot oak and brass bar that lined one wall of the place and pulled out a couple of stools for us. He then circled behind the bar. "Can I get you anything to drink? Juice? Maybe a midmorning snack?" At the back of the large room, beyond a cluster of small tables and a door leading to the kitchen, the dance floor was being vacuumed by a young man wearing bib-top overalls and no shirt.

We both shook our heads.

Bennet looked me over. "So, you're Joe Gunther. I've seen you around—I just never put the name to the face. You wanted to talk to me about my days in the body business?"

I returned his smile, not knowing—or caring—if his slightly campy tone was natural or just for my benefit. "We understand you worked for Ed Guillaume in the late sixties, early seventies."

"That's right—I made 'em look good one last time."

"Do you remember making Hannah Coyner look good in 1970?"

He laughed. "Good God, no—none of them had names as far as I was concerned."

"She died of cancer. Her husband was Fred Coyner. He might've visited the parlor with two hippies—bell-bottoms, long hair." I laid the photos of Fuller and Pendergast on the bar.

Bennet took a long moment studying them, especially the one of David Pendergast. A slow smile spread across his face. "I remember this one. He took my breath away—God, that was so many years ago."

I felt Sammie, as conventional as most cops, struggling to maintain her composure.

"Do you remember anything specific? Anything he said or did?"

"Don't I wish. I never even spoke to him. I saw them through an open door. I worked mostly in the back; old Guillaume did the soft-shoe stuff. But I remember seeing this one and just staring—he was so beautiful."

"You didn't overhear anything?"

"No. It was always the usual claptrap, anyway." He held the picture in his hand like a star-struck movie fan. "That's amazing, seeing him so many years later."

I removed the photo gently and replaced it with Fuller's— the one that had been artificially "youthened." "How about him? Was he the other guy?"

Bennet made a face. "There was no other guy. It was a girl."

I turned in surprise to Sammie. "Was Guillaume sure about it being two men?"

"I wouldn't say he was sure about anything."

I looked back at Bennet. "Are you sure it was a girl?"

He crinkled his nose at me, hamming it up now. "I may not have much use for them, but I know what they look like."

"All right. Just at a glance, did they seem like a couple?"

He thought back, and finally shook his head. "It's hard— that long ago, but I don't think so." Then he smiled. "I was only really interested in him, you know?"

I gathered the pictures together and put them in my pocket. Bennet watched the last one go with an expression of regret. "Thanks, Mr. Bennet; you've been a big help."

He smiled again, back to hamming it up. "My pleasure. Come back when you're off duty sometime—and bring your friend in the photo if you find him."

I pushed Sammie out the door before she could explode.

Later that afternoon, Dennis DeFlorio called me on the phone, sounding slightly out of breath, as usual. "Joe, I've found somebody here who used to live on the buses, but he's not being too friendly."

"Where are you?"

"Putney—The Sourdough Bakery. This guy's one of the bakers, named Gary Schenk."

"I'll be right up."

Putney is about seven miles north of Brattleboro on the interstate, and is famous for its pride, its politics, and its dense population of artistic types.

The Sourdough Bakery bragged of twenty-year-old commune roots and was run by mostly underfed-looking, soft-spoken vegetarians. I found Dennis in the parking lot near the building's rear entrance, his fat, sweaty, meat-fed body looking particularly out of place.

"He's inside—refuses to talk to me."

"Okay. Why don't you wait in your car? I'll let you know what I find out later."

He didn't look unhappy with the suggestion. While others might have taken offense, Dennis took almost everything as it came—which had both its up and down sides.

The temperature inside the bakery was blistering, and as soon as I'd introduced myself to Gary Schenk, I moved the interview back outside, near a small corral containing the garbage cans.

Schenk was in his mid-forties, with long hair held in place by a colorful bandanna, and sporting a thick and handsome waxed mustache, obviously a source of some vanity. He was not overly happy to see me. "What do you guys want, anyway?"

"Detective DeFlorio didn't explain?"

"He said you were trying to find someone from the Hippie Hollow days. That was a long time ago."

"He show you pictures?"

Schenk scowled at me. "Look, I'm busy. I don't have time to play twenty questions. Why don't you go bother somebody else?"

I showed him Pendergast's smiling face. "Ring a bell?"

There was a long pause as Schenk looked at me, realizing I was not about to let him go until he cooperated. With an angry, exasperated sigh, he snatched the photo from my hand and glared at it. "Okay, I remember him. Satisfied?"

"What was his name?"

His mouth dropped open. "How the hell do I know? Dewdrop or Acidhead or Groovy or who the fuck cares. Nobody had real names back then. He was just a guy."

"Traveling with this man." I handed him Fuller's picture.

This time, he looked more carefully, taken aback by the calculated sureness in my voice. "Yeah. I remember them."

"And a girl."

He looked peeved again. "Look, if you know all this, why waste my time?"

"They keep mostly to themselves?"

"The girl and this one did"—he tapped Fuller's photo—"but the big guy got into everybody's business. Real pain in the ass. I was happy to see them go."

"Were you there when Fred Coyner blew out the bus windows with a shotgun?"

Schenk paused. "Man, that is ancient history."

"How did the big guy react to it?"

He scratched his head, for once giving the issue some thought. "He was really into it, wondering why the old dude did it. They all split pretty soon after that."

"Did they ever talk about where they came from?"

"Nope—they mostly hung together."

"They ever flash any big bills?"

Schenk laughed. "Oh, right—we all had loads of that. Look, I gotta get back to work."

He moved toward the back door.

"One last thing." I stopped him.

"What?"

"There were only three of them, right? Nobody else?"

"Not that I ever saw."

"Was the girl particularly fond of one or the other of the two men?"

"Jesus—you guys. She was hitched to the quiet one. The big guy was too wrapped up in himself."

On the drive back into town, I took advantage of the peace and quiet to mull over how the pieces were beginning to slip together. What Gary Schenk had told me amounted to the last sighting of a ship before it drifted off into the fog forever—bearing a mismatched trio with blood in their past and death in their future. My concern now was how to intervene before the fate of two of them extended to the third.

I closed the door to my office when I got back and dialed Gail's number. "How're you holding up?"

She let out a small laugh. "Fine, I guess. I keep thinking about this story I read as a girl, where some hunters staked a fawn in a clearing and then waited in the underbrush for the tiger to appear."

"How did it end?"

"You don't want to know. You having any luck?"

"It's early yet—we're making progress. You comfortable with the setup there?"

Her voice was cheerful, artificially so, I thought. "Oh yes—Marshall Smith is keeping me company in the house, looking like a one-man army; the others are somewhere outside. I can't see any of them, which I suppose is good."

"We can pull the plug on this, Gail."

Harriet Fritter poked her head into my office and whispered, "Line two. Norm Runnion."

I nodded silently. Gail's voice on the other end had resumed its firm footing. "I'm fine, Joe. You do your end; I'll do mine."

I let out a small sigh. "See you tonight?"

"There may not be room." She chuckled. "Give me a call."

I said good-bye and punched the blinking button at the base of the phone.

"You get your ass in a crack back home?" Norm's voice was comforting at the other end.

"I told you what Vermonters think of the big city. They welcomed me back with open arms. You been fired yet?"

"Not hardly. They didn't pin a medal on me, though. I dug around a little on the University of Illinois angle for you. Pendergast shows up, all right, but the one you call Fuller doesn't show up anywhere. I looked at the yearbooks, then I went to the admissions records to check on students who dropped or flunked out. There was nothing that fits, Joe."

I pondered that for a few seconds.

"Maybe the old lady in Marquette got it wrong," he suggested.

"Could be."

"Want me to chase down anything else?"

"No, Norm—you've stuck your neck out enough. Thanks."

"No sweat. Tell me how it turns out."

I put the phone down and looked up, to see Willy Kunkle, wearing a satisfied expression as he leaned against my doorjamb, his withered arm stuffed in his pocket like some odd piece of cloth the tailor had forgotten to remove from his jacket. "You look pleased with yourself."

"Shattuck's in town."

My heart skipped a beat and I sat back in my chair, feigning casualness. "Do tell."

"One of my snitches was approached at the Sky View trailer park by some guy wanting information on you. Apparently, he's been making the rounds with a lot of questions and a lot of money. It's a definite match with Shattuck's picture, all the way down to the ponytail. From what I was told, he's not being real friendly."

"Is it worth it to check out the Sky View?"

Kunkle shook his head. "He's long gone." He hesitated, a rare flicker of compassion crossing his face. "The guy'll screw up sooner or later. Someone'll tell us where he's hanging out."

I glanced at the wall clock, frustration and urgency mingling deep inside me. I thought back to Gail's cheerful farewell on the phone and realized only then how much I'd been hoping that for some reason Shattuck wouldn't appear. "Thanks, Willy. Keep me updated."

* * *

Fifteen minutes before our scheduled afternoon meeting, Tony Brandt walked into my office and placed a single fax sheet on my desk. "As promised. I asked my contact to get me every birth within twelve hours on either side of the time on the chart, just to be on the safe side. I'm afraid there're quite a few."

I glanced quickly at the list, running my finger along it to see if any of the entries jumped out at me. Halfway down, I stopped at the one name that instantly made complete sense of much that had been baffling us—including why no one had been able to connect Abraham Fuller to David Pendergast. "Did you look these over?"

Tony shook his head. "You find something?"

I twisted the list around so he could read it from where he stood by the side of my desk. I pointed out the name with my fingertip. "I'd been focusing almost exclusively on David. He'd been the natural leader of the three—the one best remembered, the only one with a record, the only link to Bob Shattuck. It was even his metal knee that got the ball rolling for us. I should've known to look more carefully into his background."

Tony read the name aloud. "Susan Pendergast?"

I was moving toward the door, seized by the importance of this discovery—and by the urgency to act on it quickly. "His sister, who ran away from home and was never heard from again. She was the only family he had left after his parents died. I should've wondered about that."

I pulled open the door and shouted into the squad room. "Sammie?"

She popped up from behind one of the soundproof room dividers. I gestured for her to join us, then closed the door behind her.

"You checked out Abraham Fuller earlier, right?"

She nodded, looking uneasy.

I showed her Brandt's list of names. "Susan Pendergast is David Pendergast's sister. She's got to be the connection between Fuller and her brother. She must have linked up with Fuller in Alaska, which would explain why he never cropped up when we were checking into David's activities in Chicago.''

"What about the picture of them together in Marquette?" Brandt asked.

"My guess is Susan brought Fuller with her to Chicago shortly before 1969, where they hooked up with David. And David must've brought Fuller up to Marquette for a visit, maybe treating him kind of like a brother-in-law." I turned to Sammie. "Did you find anything at all relating to Fuller in your digging—documents, bank records, credit companies, anything at all?"

Sammie shook her head. "I checked everything six ways toward the middle. The only Abraham Fuller I came up with that fitted the approximate date of birth was a kid I found in the town clerk's records."

I stared at her for a moment. "What kid?"

Sammie tugged at a strand of her hair. "I was looking through the birth certificates. For a second, I thought I'd hit the jackpot, but it turned out that Abraham Fuller had only lived a few days."

"You think that's our boy?" Brandt asked softly.

I began pacing the small room excitedly, using the two of them as a sounding board to the revelation that was burning brighter and brighter in my mind. "It's one of the ways you can establish a new identity, especially in rural areas, where few people bother checking into details.

"You find the grave or death certificate of an infant, assume his name, and put in a request at the town clerk's or wherever for a new birth certificate, claiming you lost yours. The clerk looks up the birth certificate on her rolls, which are kept separate from death records, issues a duplicate, and bingo— you're on your way to establishing a new identity."

"But I checked everywhere else," Sammie protested, "Abraham Fuller never did establish an identity. Besides, what's all that got to do with Susan Pendergast?"

I bolted for the door, Sammie's exasperated question ringing like a comfirmation in my ears. "Because," I said on the threshold, "if Fuller took on a false identity using that method, then Susan Pendergast probably did, too."

I strode out into the squad room and toward the exit, Brandt and Sammie hard on my heels, both of them now sharing my impatience to explore this new avenue.

As we moved rapidly down the hall toward the town clerk's office, I addressed the other part of Sammie's question. "I don't know why Fuller never went beyond just taking on a false name, but assuming he was wounded just after coming to this area, I'd guess he became so traumatized, he completely withdrew from life, which made a new identity irrelevant."

The young woman behind the town clerk's counter stared openmouthed as we marched by her to where the record books were kept in a back room. I handed out several of the large, heavy volumes to both of them.

Sammie was still perplexed. "What do we look for?"

"Those are death records from the 1940s. Eventually, we should compare them to something like the Department of Motor Vehicle records, see if we can locate a living, licensed driver who should have died fifty years ago. But right now, let's just look for anything that might ring a bell."

We moved quickly, spurred on by our hopes that we'd finally cracked the enigma—and that a single name might provide us with the answers we'd been seeking.

It finally did, but with none of the joy I'd been anticipating. For the second time in fifteen minutes, a name leapt out at me with the power of pure revelation. But this time, instead of the excitement of having my efforts rewarded, I felt only the frustration and anger at having been duped, almost from the start of this investigation. The name neatly penned on the page before me resounded with its owner's self-confidence and daring. Susan Pendergast had used Gail as a way to meet me, then had used my own prejudices to buy herself time.

I slammed the book down on the table in disgust, causing Tony Brandt to come over and glance down at the page. "I'll be damned."

Sammie looked up from her own scrutiny. "What did you find?"

"Wilhelmina Lucas—Billie for short."

Chapter Thirty

I sat alone in the office on the top floor of the Whipple Street house that Susan Pendergast, as Billie Lucas, had lived in and worked out of for the past twenty-odd years, conducting pottery classes, doing charts, and generally playing the expected role of the socially conscious, liberated woman she'd painted herself to be.

It was late—past ten o'clock. For the past five hours, we'd been combing the building for signs of where she might have vanished, for vanished she had. According to the friends and colleagues we'd contacted so far, she'd left in the middle of a meeting several days ago, purportedly to use the phone.

It was the completeness of her disappearance that nagged me the most. By now, we had poked into every square inch of the building. We had found bankbooks, business records, tax papers, personal correspondence, even love letters. In her bathroom and bedroom, everything was still in place, from her underwear to her toothbrush. Her car was still parked by the side of the house.

I had detectives and patrol units all over town interviewing people, rousting judges for warrants, going over phone and bank records, and analyzing the papers we'd found here. Photos and descriptions of her had been circulated all over the state, and to police departments, sheriff's offices, and state law-enforcement agencies beyond our borders. But somewhere in my gut, I knew it would all be for nothing, because I knew that it wasn't the police that had kept Susan's survival instincts sharp over the years—and would drive her now to burrow deep underground—but the threat of Shattuck's revenge.

Without a single shred of evidence, I was convinced Susan Pendergast was acting out the nightmare she'd kept bottled up inside her for two and a half decades. She was the last of three fugitives. After Abraham Fuller had died and David's bones were disinterred, she must have known her own anonymity was doomed, and her life become forfeit.

The question was, where was she now? From the time I'd arrived back in Brattleboro, I'd felt like a racehorse striving for the finish, trying to beat out a shadowy, unseen competitor. But now that I knew Susan was scared and running, how could I keep myself at the head of a race that had suddenly changed from a mad sprint to one of careful strategy?

I was sitting at the same desk I'd seen Billie typing at the first time we'd met. The lights were off now, and only the reflected glow from the streetlamps outside revealed the vague details of the room. Downstairs, I could still hear people moving about, checking and rechecking the contents of the house, frustrated that the policeman's adage that nobody vanishes without a trace was proving to have an exception.

There was a knock at the door and J. P. Tyler, who was heading up the search of the house, stuck his head in. "Anyone here?"

"Yeah."

He stepped inside, wisely leaving the lights off. He knew my moods. "We found a hiding place, kind of like Fuller's. Two M-16s and several boxes of ammunition, all .223 LC 67 stock."

"That it?"

"There's a small fortune in cash, too, the stolen chart, and a book."

"*The Scarlet Letter*?"

"Yeah. I was going to box it up for the Waterbury lab, but I thought you might like to take a look first."

I switched on the desk lamp and he walked forward, gingerly carrying a paperback hanging from a wire like a small piece of laundry from a clothesline, preserving whatever fingerprints it might have on it. He laid it carefully on the desk. I saw the title on the spine was roughly circled in a rusty brown—the dried blood from Fuller's pricked finger, just as it was on the photograph I'd seen.

"The inside cover," Tyler indicated.

I used my pen to pry back the front of the book. On the

inside, also scrawled in brown, was the message: "I burned it—Love."

"I checked the rest of the hiding place; there's nothing else—at least nothing obvious."

I nodded and let the cover fall back. "Does it look like anything was removed recently?"

He picked up the book again. "It's hard to tell, of course, but I don't think so."

"How much money?"

"Something like a half million, all in hundreds."

"Okay, J.P.—thanks."

He retired and I switched the light back off, remembering the fresh ashes and the match we'd found in Fuller's wood stove.

I burned what?

The intercom on the phone buzzed. I picked it up and gave my name.

One of the search team said, "Ron's on line one, Lieutenant."

I hit the blinking button. "What's up?"

"Couple of things I thought you'd like to know. I'm at the bank right now, going through her records—the manager's madder than hell, by the way, and said he'd let you know what he thought about us rousting people in the middle of the night—but what we've found so far is nothing. I took her IRS files from the house to compare them with these at the bank, and they match perfectly—same basic income and expenses. And we opened her deposit box, too—just some jewelry. I know she probably has other accounts under other names, but so far, it all looks regular as dishwater, so I don't know where she stashed her share of the money, assuming she has one."

"J.P. just found it hidden in the house—about half a million."

Ron digested that for a moment. "Then that makes sense. Something else came up a couple of days ago, when you were still in Chicago, kind of through the grapevine. You know the driver of that hearse that was shot up on the interstate? Well, he's still in the hospital, doing fine, but two days ago, one hundred thousand dollars was deposited anonymously into his account. I just called his wife and she confirms it. They didn't know what to make of it. You think it might have been Lucas?"

"Probably. Let me know if you find anything else."

I hung up and dialed Gail's number. I'd spoken to her earlier, when we'd found Lucas had flown the coop. She'd been stunned at Billie's duplicity, and perhaps a little hurt at the betrayal of trust.

This time, when I talked to her about the hundred thousand dollars, Gail was more philosophical—and supportive of her former friend. "It doesn't erase what she did last week—or whatever she might have done in Chicago—but it's got to work in her favor. It proves that the good things about her weren't complete lies."

I didn't debate the salving of one's conscience with other people's stolen money. After all, I, too, had taken an instant liking to Billie Lucas, and I had to admit that her gesture had been generous and thoughtful, especially considering the amount involved. Also, I wasn't so pure, either, when it came to protecting myself from Bob Shattuck. Like Billie, I'd taken protective measures. Hers had been amateurish, resulting in the injuring of an innocent man; mine, far more devious and subversive, had enlisted the mob, or so I hoped. Putting things in that light, I was in no position to judge another's desperation.

So I stuck to the task at hand, leaving unchallenged Gail's understandable loyalty. "You haven't come up with any ideas of where she might have gone?"

"No. I've been racking my brains, trying to remember if she ever mentioned someone or someplace that might fit, but she never did—never talked about her family, where she came from, or anything else private. She'd always turn the conversation around and talk about the here and now. She was so good at it, I never really noticed.

"I've been looking at that chart again, by the way. I'm pretty sure now it's Billie's. For one thing, it doesn't jibe at all with what she told you."

I made a sour face in the dark. "That figures."

"None of us thought to double-check it, since she was

the local expert, and we ended up focusing on finding the birthplace, anyway.''

I appreciated her not saying that my reluctance to deal with the chart from the beginning had fostered that lack of thoroughness. ''I don't suppose the damn thing says where she is now?''

''No, but it would've told you who she was much sooner, I think. Just using my own books and the little I know about chart reading, I picked up a few warning lights tonight.''

I wasn't sure I wanted to know. ''Like what?''

''The major personality trait isn't shyness at all, but a need for approval, even applause—the kind a community do-gooder might get. Also, the child-abuse emphasis doesn't involve the mother, but the father, who has all the typical trimmings of a military man. If you'd known that, you might've pegged her when you were in Marquette.''

''Oh, well,'' I muttered, by now thoroughly depressed, ''spilled milk, I guess.''

Her voice was sympathetic. ''I'm sorry, Joe—this must be pretty frustrating. Got any ideas?''

I reflected back on what I'd been pondering earlier, before Tyler had knocked on the door. ''I've got one—a long shot—but I need to bounce it off Tony first.''

''He's here—want to talk to him?''

''What're you doing there?'' I asked Brandt when he got on the line.

''I switched with Sammie. Gail said you had something on your mind. Why don't you come over? I think she's getting a little sick of seeing just us. You can give me a full update then, too.''

I agreed and headed out Route 9 into West Brattleboro. Gail lived in a converted apple barn on a hill high above Meadowbrook Road, an isolated but exposed spot, which is why Brandt had found it so suitable a place to trap Shattuck.

I was still some distance away when the radio burst to life with the news I'd been dreading since the drive from the airport. ''M-80 from 0-1—shots fired; officer down at Mead-owbrook Road, Zigman residence. All available units respond to seal the area.''

M-80, radio language for our dispatch, began handing out

assignments and coordinating approaches to shut off all exits from Meadowbrook, but I was no longer listening. The chorus of voices, the arcane ten-code synonyms, and the growing excitement crackling from the loudspeaker went by me like so much background music. I concentrated on driving as fast as I could, not giving a damn about anything other than getting to Gail in time.

The house was completely illuminated, like a lighthouse on a hill. I spun my tires racing up the steep driveway and ground to a halt behind Gail's car. Below me, unseen in the darkened valley, the distant howling of approaching sirens sounded like hungry wolves on the prowl.

The windshield to the parked car was shattered, and the side of Gail's house riddled by a string of bullet holes. The acrid smell of gunpowder lingered in the air. I bolted up the steps leading to the deck, the sense of dread so heavy on me now, it bordered on complete panic. I almost collided with Tony Brandt as he stepped through the shattered double doors at the top.

He placed his hands against my chest momentarily. "She's fine—not a scratch—in the kitchen," he said, then let me go by.

I found her leaning against the counter, staring at a slowly filling coffee machine. Her face was pale and drawn, but the smile and the relief it foretold were genuine. She turned, put both her arms around my neck, and gave me a fierce hug. "Christ, I'm glad to see you."

I pulled back enough so that I could see her face, my heart still pounding from fear. "Thank God you're okay."

"If I'd known what to expect, I might not have been quite so eager to volunteer."

I hugged her again. "What happened?"

Shattuck had apparently thrown all caution to the winds, appearing from out of the dark on foot and kicking in the glass front doors. All hell had then broken loose—from inside, where Tony had been joined for the night by SRT member Al Santos, and outside, as the perimeter guards had closed in.

Gail had never been exposed to any direct danger. The Special Response people had insisted that she sleep on the floor of her office, located on the uppermost of the house's several lofts, and Brandt had positioned himself on a landing just below the only set of stairs leading to her.

Al had not been so lucky. Stationed in the living room, with a view of the doors and most of the windows, he'd been the first to confront Shattuck, and had caught bullets in the right hand, the right earlobe, and through the fleshy inner portion of his left thigh, all delivered by a short-barreled, rapid-firing machine gun.

Al's presence, however, and his single misplaced shot, had done the trick—at least in preserving Gail's safety. Shattuck had quickly retreated, firing as he went, forcing the SRT members outside to dive for cover. Santos had ended up being the only casualty. The same careless bravado that had stimulated Shattuck to attack in the first place had also served him well in his escape. By the time the shooting had stopped, he'd disappeared back into the night.

The coffee maker finished its job as Gail reached the end of her account, and she began pouring out cups for the growing number of police officers who were now gathering around the house. Tony Brandt let her finish filling a tray and then suggested that the three of us get the hell out of there and let Billy Manierre and Ron Klesczewski coordinate the mop-up and search operations. "Given this crazy bastard's style," he concluded, "there's no guarantee he won't try again."

Since my car was hopelessly blocked in by now, we used Brandt's, which was discreetly parked on the street below, and drove directly to the Municipal Building. We decided Gail should spend the rest of the night at the police station and then go "on a vacation" to see her folks in New York City first thing in the morning. She had taken the whole experience well, but her willingness to be packed up and sent off without a murmur of protest told me how thoroughly she'd been shaken.

Back at the station, after settling Gail in, I pulled Brandt to one side. "Something occurred to me when I was at Billie Lucas's tonight. What do you think about using Katz and the *Reformer* to reach Billie—or Susan—to persuade her to come to us? Shattuck might've actually done us a favor. If we tell Katz what happened, Billie is sure to find out Shattuck is in the area, and realize that turning herself in is her only chance.''

Brandt nodded. "Okay. Let's make a couple of phone calls. Maybe we can convince Stanley to take one last bow before retirement.''

Stan Katz's resignation officially took effect in one hour—at midnight. As Brandt had guessed, however, the chance to go out with his byline under a front-page lead was more than Katz could resist. He promised to meet us at the newspaper's offices.

The *Reformer*'s night editor, Ruth Tivoli, a local woman and a career journalist with a reputation for integrity, was waiting for us. She was a holdover, as was Katz, from the *Reformer*'s better days.

She rose from her desk and came to greet us as we entered the building. "Hello, Chief—Joe." She eyed my face. "What happened? We've been listening to the scanner.''

"Is Stanley here?" I asked.

She pointed toward the distant coffee machine, where we could see Katz pouring himself a cup. He raised his eyebrows when he saw us and broke into a grin, "This, I've got to hear.''

Ruth gave him a baleful look. The four of us filed into a small conference room and settled around a table.

Brandt headed off Katz immediately. "Let me say something before you let fly." He then addressed them both. "Things have begun to speed up since we found that skeleton and turned Stanley into a war correspondent. We had information that an attempt might be made to kidnap Gail Zigman, and we took precautions to prevent that from happening. We were successful in that action, although one of our officers, Sgt. Alexander Santos, was wounded in an exchange of fire.

"The stimulus for all this activity is a robbery of sorts that took place some twenty-odd years ago in Chica . The three people involved fled to Vermont to assume new identities. I say 'of sorts' because we don't think the money was from a legitimate source.''

"What makes you say that?" Katz asked.

"We haven't established it for a fact, but we do know there were no complaints of a theft during the same time frame."

I had to hand it to Brandt. Over the years, he had mastered that bizarre bureaucratic ability to build walls out of words with the practiced aplomb of a mason—taking his time, refusing shortcuts, and saying only what he wanted to say.

"In any case, Abraham Fuller, which is not his real name, was one of those three. The second was the skeleton we unearthed. The third is still at large."

Katz opened his mouth to ask another question, but Brandt silenced him with a raised hand. "That survivor is running, we think, not because of us but because of the person who suffered the original financial loss—tonight's shooter." Brandt laid Shattuck's mug shot on the table. "His name is Robert Shattuck. His physical description and a brief history are on the back. You see"—he leaned forward for emphasis, perhaps hoping his body language would compensate for omitting that our discovery of the M-16s in Billie's house directly linked her to the wounding of the hearse driver—"we have no proof this third person was actually involved in any crime, but we do know he or she is in mortal danger from Shattuck. We are offering a safe haven, and we're hoping you will make that message clear."

Ruth Tivoli shook her head. "What makes you think a story in the paper will reach this person. Is he still in the area?"

Brandt let me answer. "We're working on the assumption that this third person will still be reading the paper, looking for news of the investigation." I slid a piece of paper across the table at them. "We've set up this telephone number as a kind of twenty-four-hour, one-person hotline."

"Who tried to shoot Gail? Shattuck?" Katz asked.

"We don't think that was his intention. It was probably a kidnap attempt."

"Why?"

"To tilt the deck in his favor," I answered. "With Gail as a hostage, he would have had someone to trade if we found this missing third person before he did."

"So you're offering sanctuary. Anything else?"

Brandt spoke up again. "If need be, a new identity. There's a strong chance there may be enough to interest the federal government in offering protection. What we really want is to save someone who did something dumb, but perhaps not criminal, a long time ago from being tortured to death by some crazy bastard bent on revenge."

A moment's silence greeted his calculated choice of words.

Katz had stopped writing and was looking at us quietly, perhaps reflecting back on similar instances when he and I had cooperated and had both come out ahead.

He turned to Ruth. "Let's do it. I want to ask a few more questions, but I think this looks good."

There was a knock on the door. A reporter poked his head in. "Someone to see Joe."

It was George Capullo, our night-shift sergeant, looking as uncomfortable in the newsroom as a cat in a dog pound. "We just found somebody named Gary Schenk, beaten up pretty bad. Claims it's your fault. I thought you might like a ride to the hospital."

We drove cross town to Brattleboro Memorial in the stillness of the night. The streets were devoid of life, and as empty as a huge abandoned factory, although I knew that somewhere, behind one of these silent walls, Bob Shattuck lay waiting, watching the clock.

"Where'd you pick up Schenk?" I finally asked.

"We didn't. The hospital called it in. He was brought in by ambulance from his home in Putney. Apparently, he'd worked the late shift at work, gone to a party after that, and was attacked as he was unlocking his front door."

"He live alone?"

"Yup."

That explained the timing, I thought. Shattuck had probably discovered Schenk by following either Dennis or me to the bakery where he worked, but he hadn't been able to move on him until he was by himself.

We found Gary Schenk on his back in a hospital bed, both his arms wrapped in plaster, his fingers strapped to aluminum splints, his split and swollen lips parted, revealing a row of broken teeth. George had outlined his injuries on the drive over—Shattuck had broken up his victim one piece at a time, finger by finger, arm by arm, like some oversized chocolate Easter bunny, no doubt fueled by his frustration at having missed Gail.

Schenk's eyes gleamed with hatred as he focused on me. "You prick."

The words were thick and slurred, but no less punishing. I turned to George. "He positively ID'd Shattuck's mug shot?"

George nodded.

I moved closer to Schenk. "We know who did this to you, Gary. It won't be long before we get him."

"Fuck you."

"What did you tell him, Gary? It might help us nail him."

"Leave me alone."

"You told him about our conversation? Was that what he wanted to know?"

"What do you think?"

"Did you tell him anything you didn't tell us?"

He closed his eyes, perhaps realizing I wouldn't take a hint. "I knew the girl was Billie Lucas."

I pursed my lips. That little tidbit wouldn't do Shattuck much good at this point, but it did mean he now had as much information as we did. "How?"

"I'd seen her around—I remembered."

"Did she know that?"

"No. I never liked her. Why bother?"

"But you felt a loyalty, nonetheless—when we came to talk to you."

"Sure—you're the pigs." The words were even less distinct; he was beginning to fade.

Old habits die hard, I thought. "Did you tell him anything about her other than her name?"

"That's all I knew."

"What about the two men we showed you?"

"You assholes . . ." He drifted off.

The nurse who'd been standing nearby took his pulse. "That's it—the injection's kicked in. He'll be out for hours."

George Capullo stood staring at Schenk for a while. "What a mess. Seems like overkill for the little he knew."

"I don't think getting information was really the point.

This poor bastard is more like a postcard—Shattuck's way of telling us he's still out there, still hungry, still capable of getting the jump on us.''

Chapter Thirty-one

I spent the rest of the night—what little there was of it—with Gail at the police station, in the darkened department gymnasium in the basement, stretched out on a couple of foam exercise mats. We were surrounded by barbells, a stationary bike, and a chrome-plated weight machine, all glowing dimly in the reflected red light from the exit sign.

We didn't sleep much, nor did we talk a lot. We mostly just lay in each other's arms and rested, our eyes tracing the half-seen maze of overhead heating and plumbing pipes that interlaced across the high ceiling. In the morning, she would be driven to the airport in a patrol car and I would be going after Shattuck again. This wasn't time we wanted to lose by sleeping.

Toward dawn—that quietest of hours—we removed each other's clothes and made love, risking discovery in exchange for an intimacy and a sense of peace we knew we wouldn't be able to regain anytime soon.

The rest of the morning was considerably less engaging. I managed the flood of information that had been stimulated by last night's search for Billie Lucas, kept tabs on the continuing investigations, and spent hours sifting through Billie's personal history. At the back of my mind, I knew instinctively that success lay less in what we were doing and more in the hopes that somewhere in this or some bordering state, the woman we were searching for was reading the *Brattleboro Reformer* and weighing her options.

Six hours later, around lunchtime, the waiting came to an end. The special telephone that had been placed on Harriet's desk began to ring. It was a direct line, bypassing our switchboard, and had a digital callback box attached to it to indicate the caller's number as soon as the receiver was lifted and a button pushed.

I was out of my office by the the second ring—and just as Harriet was about to call out my name. "Recorder on?"

She nodded.

I picked up the receiver. "Joe Gunther."

"This is Billie Lucas."

"Hi, Billie. Are you in a safe place?" I pushed the callback button. Harriet wrote the number down and passed it to Ron Klesczewski to trace. With any luck, a location would be pinpointed and a state police unit dispatched before the conversation came to an end.

"Yes."

"Do you know Bob Shattuck?"

"Is he the one you were talking about in the paper?"

"Yes. He's tracking you down. Shattuck worked over a guy last night, after the paper was being printed—broke both his arms and put him in the hospital just because he recognized you from the Hippie Hollow days. He's getting desperate and getting close. I don't know that we can stop him."

"I'm not counting on you for that."

"You have a plan for getting away?"

She didn't answer.

"Billie, the fact that you called me shows you're in doubt. Let's meet at least and discuss it."

"In jail?"

I decided not to tell her we'd found the M-16s. "No—your choice of setting. There may not be any jail in this. But you are in danger from a man who seems to have nothing left to lose."

There was a long, thoughtful silence on the other end.

"Can you tell me a bit about what happened—then maybe I can give you a better idea what I can offer."

"The Witness Protection Program the paper mentioned?"

"Could be."

"I doubt I've got enough to interest them."

"Try me."

She hesitated. "I don't know."

I tried visualizing the woman on the phone. When I'd met

her, she'd been in her home, in control, playing me like a violin. What I was hearing in her voice now didn't fit that at all. It had none of its earlier confidence. She sounded timid, tentative, even slightly bewildered.

"Tell me about the money. Who's was it?"

"It belonged to supporters of the Chicago Eight."

That startled me. "What?"

"The money was donated to pay for their legal fees. It wasn't so much for them specifically, but for the cause they represented—antiwar, antiracism. People with money were persuaded to contribute for the common cause. The Eight were merely figureheads."

"And the three of you stole it?"

A hint of anger crept into her voice. "Not like that, no."

"I'm sorry. There's a lot I don't understand here."

"Bob Shattuck had positioned himself to help channel that money, but he had no intention of it reaching anyone but himself. He wanted the money to create his own radical splinter group—a kind of Black Panthers for white radicals."

"How did the three of you fit in?"

Her voice filled with sadness. "Sean and I didn't know what David and Bob were up to. I mean, we knew about Bob's plans for the group—the two of them talked about it all the time—but we didn't know they were planning to steal the money."

"Sean was Abraham Fuller?"

"Yes—his real name was Sean Brady."

"Did David double-cross Shattuck."

"No. . . ." Her reaction was sharp and abrupt but almost instantly withered. "Well, yes—finally; I guess so. I don't think he planned it that way, but that's how it turned out. We were supposed to courier the money from one place to another. . . ."

"You, David, and Sean?"

"Yes. Sean and I were along almost as a lark. We were never heavily into all the politics—I tagged along because of David, and I guess Sean did because of me."

"When did you return to Chicago? I thought you'd run away to Alaska."

"I had—that's where I met Sean. David had asked me to come back."

"Were you and David close?" I asked dubiously.

"No, but he thought we should be together after our parents died. David and I were all that was left of the family, really. . . ." After a telling pause, she added. "David was pretty hard to turn down when he wanted something."

"What about Sean?"

"He liked David, at least at first. . . . They started out as friends—until after the robbery."

"He went with David to Marquette?"

She sounded surprised. "Yes—to show Sean where we'd been brought up. I refused to go."

"Was David in tight with Bob when you and Sean moved to Chicago?"

"Yes. They spent all their free time discussing politics, collecting weapons, reading radical literature. They used to practice martial arts together and analyze how to blend with the local population. They learned how to make weapons and bombs out of everyday items. It became a spiritual thing with them. They completely believed in themselves and what they were doing. All they needed was money."

I picked up her earlier narrative. "The night of the robbery, you and Sean were with David."

"Yes—he wanted us along for protection; it was a lot of money—almost a million and a half dollars. We had guns, but Sean and I still looked at it almost as a game. I was twenty-three at the time, and Sean was twenty-two, but we were more like teenagers. Dumb as dirt.

"We drove in a closed van to the stockyard district, picked up the money at the drop-off point, and were about to leave when these guys came out of nowhere and tried to hold us up. David went crazy. He had one of the guns—an M-16— and started firing before anyone knew what was happening. He killed one guy; Sean killed another in self-defense; and the other two took off."

"Was that when David got hit in the knee?"

"Yes. The man he killed shot him."

"Did you know who they were?"

"Not then. David told us later."

"What happened?"

"David was badly hurt. The knee was almost gone and he was in agony. Sean had fallen apart. He was crying hysterically. We got David into the van and to the nearest hospital we could think of. That's where he found this doctor who agreed to fix him up fast and not tell the police."

I interrupted her to keep up the pressure—a calculated risk. "I talked with that same doctor last week—just before Shattuck tortured him to death."

She stopped dead, and I worried I'd overdone it. "So David paid off the doctor with some of the cash?"

Her voice was slightly hesitant again. "Yes. We had two bagfuls. David kept a handful with him, just in case. He was ice-cold through it all. Once he'd paid off the doctor, he told us to disappear until he came to fetch us. We weren't to call anyone, see anyone, or go anywhere where people might recognize us. We left town, found a motel, and called him at the hospital so he'd know where to find us."

"Did you know what he was up to yet?"

"No. He told us after he escaped from the hospital. That's when he explained who those people were, and by then, he said, both Bob and the Chicago Eight people thought we'd stolen the money. If we came clean, either the Outfit or Bob would take us out. We didn't have a choice anymore, according to David. We had to keep running. . . ."

"How did the mob find out about the money in the first place? Did he know?"

"David figured either Bob had crossed him or the Outfit had heard about the transfer some other way and had decided to kill two birds with one stone—cripple the radical left and get a bunch of money in the bargain. But we never knew for sure."

I had a feeling I did know. Shattuck's reaction to the Outfit's involvement—assuming he hadn't been setting me up—indicated that Tommy Salierno, always hungry for the independent score, had somehow caught wind of the money coming in and had acted on his own. "So you came to Vermont," I resumed.

"Eventually."

"Billie, why did you stick together? Your brother had lied to you, betrayed your ideals, gotten you involved in murder and theft."

She came to a full stop, refusing to answer. It was clear I had entered an emotional mine field. I decided my best route now was the most direct one. "How did David die, Billie?"

"I've got to go."

I gave it up. "All right—never mind about David. You're the important one here, Billie. Let's get you under protection. I don't want you hurt."

There was some background noise from her end of the line, as if she was moving around. When she came back on, her voice was hard and bitter. "You bastard."

The phone went dead in my hand.

Chapter Thirty-two

The state police unit missed Susan Pendergast by seconds. They arrived at the address we'd traced—a general store in a village north of Rutland—and found the phone still warm. But there was no sign of Billie. They quickly checked the area around the store, called in extra units for a wider search, and came up empty-handed.

Two hours later, I was standing in Tony Brandt's office, staring out the window while he finished listening to the tape of my phone conversation with Billie.

He hit the OFF button on the recorder and sat back in his chair. "Well, that explains at least half of this case."

"Not the half that got us involved."

He thought back a moment. "Yeah. Must've hit a nerve, unless she just got distracted by the state police rolling up."

"I think something happened between her brother and Sean, and she still has a tough time dealing with it. Either that or she's guilty of more than just tagging along with a couple of bad boys."

"You mean she might've killed her own brother?"

"It's possible. Suppose David begins pushing his weight around, demanding all the money. Things fall apart, and blam—he shoots Sean—maybe Sean pulled a gun on him. Who knows? Susan implied things went sour between them. Anyway, Susan grabs a gun and shoots David. Susan buries her brother because Sean's too badly hurt to help; she hangs around to nurse Sean back to health; and then, unable to deal with all the guilt and emotional baggage between them, she and Sean split up—she to be reborn as Billie Lucas and he to become a hermit."

He shrugged. "It still doesn't tell us where she is now."

I thought about Susan being reborn, and about her not counting on us to save her from Shattuck. She had described David and Shattuck analyzing ways to blend into the local population. It occurred to me that although she'd been gone several days, she'd called us from near Rutland, only seventy miles away.

"I've got an idea," I told Brandt. "I think Susan—or Billie, or whatever the hell she's calling herself now—has a backup plan, another identity she's been saving for a rainy day. She was worried about the mob and Shattuck on the phone, but she didn't seem that worried about us, and she'd obviously planned an escape from that general store beforehand. This is not a woman running blind, Tony. I want to check the records again at the town clerk's."

The same clerk's assistant who'd helped us the day before watched me come through the door with obvious dismay. I remembered we'd caused her to stay open way past normal closing hours. "Sorry we loused you up yesterday."

Her eyes dropped to the counter. "It's okay."

I made my way back to the same oversized books we'd searched before. "This shouldn't take too long."

She followed me back and gave me a weak smile. "Would you like some help?"

I didn't want to pull in my people from the field, who were still out checking leads to Susan's whereabouts; accepting her offer might both speed things up and make her feel a little better about having her office invaded again. She also knew the records intimately.

I put her to work on the death records, while I combed the birth certificates. One by one, I called out the names of female children born in the mid-1940s, and she checked if there were any corresponding death dates. Each time there was, I gave the name to Brandt over the phone and he typed it into his computer, which was linked to the Department of Motor Vehicles. I was hoping we could conjure up another fifty-year-old ghost with an up-to-date driver's license.

An hour later, we struck gold with the name Marie Benoit.

It had been a long shot, and for a moment, I had difficulty accepting my luck. "You're shitting me. Where does she live?"

"Wheelock, Vermont—the Northeast Kingdom. I know that area; it's northwest of Lyndonville."

"Damn." I slammed down the phone, thanked the assistant clerk profusely, and ran back to Brandt's office.

With success came concern that we might lose our advantage. Neither one of us had forgotten what had happened to Gary Schenk, whom Shattuck had obviously found by putting a tail on either Dennis or me. Now that we were hoping we'd located Susan Pendergast, we didn't want to make the same mistake twice, nor did we want to involve another police department.

The solution turned out to be Al Hammond—the Windham County Sheriff. A seasoned politician, a lifelong law-enforcement officer—with several years in the state police and elsewhere—and, most important, one of Tony Brandt's best friends, Al was also the owner of a small single-engine plane.

Brandt and I broke out maps and phone books, looking for appropriate landing sites and ways to get from the plane to Wheelock. We didn't want to use another police agency to help us out. We were still smarting at the fact that a highly visible state police cruiser had tipped Susan to how close we'd gotten to her. If that was to happen again, it was going to be our fault alone.

We found an airfield just north of Lyndonville, and a friend of mine from Saint Johnsbury who was willing to have a pickup truck waiting for me—no questions asked. Departure was planned from the grass strip in Dummerston—between

Putney and Brattleboro—at 5:30 that afternoon, the soonest that Al Hammond could get away from his office.

Brandt escorted me out to the parking lot when I was ready to leave. "I wish I was coming with you."

I shook his hand, a formal gesture that belied my casual tone. "If we've done this right, I should be back by late tonight—with Susan Pendergast."

He merely pursed his lips. "You bring a gun?"

I patted my hip, under my jacket.

He pulled the department's cellular phone out of his pocket. "Take this, too. You get your ass in a crack, you can at least call in the cavalry."

The cumulative toll of the attack on Gail, finding Schenk beaten, and just missing Susan Pendergast—on top of very little sleep—had left me jittery and beat. Two hours of flying at several thousand feet above Vermont's soft, verdant mountains, following the broad, gleaming, sinewy track of the Connecticut River, obliquely lit by a sinking sun, did wonders to dispel the nervousness that had knotted up inside me.

The sun was just touching the hills by the time we landed at the Caledonia County State Airport, leaving a slowly fading golden light in its wake. I thanked Al for his help, then headed north on Route 122 in my friend's borrowed Ford 150 pickup truck.

A quick four miles later, I came to Wheelock, a pleasant clustering of houses lining both sides of the road for an eighth of a mile. I drove slowly, the ease of the flight replaced once again by apprehension and doubt. I pulled over in front of a house where an elderly woman was on her knees, fretting over an immaculate garden.

"Excuse me."

She looked up, pushing her glasses back in place with the back of her gloved hand. "Hi there."

"I'm looking for Marie Benoit. I hear she lives around here."

The woman smiled and jerked her head to one side, indicating the north. "The house at the top of the hill, just before you leave town, on the right."

"Thanks." I put the truck back into gear.

"She's not there, though."

"Oh?"

"Yup. Went to the circus."

"The circus?"

"Bread and Puppet, up in Glover."

I nodded. "Right—I've heard of it."

"They're having a big to-do—lots of people. Too much for me. Besides, I think those people are a little funny, anyway. Nice, but funny. Marie likes 'em, though."

"Have you known Marie long?"

"Almost twenty years now. Don't know her well, of course. She's not here very often, and keeps pretty much to herself, but she's a friendly thing—just private. You a friend of hers, as well?"

"I met her in Brattleboro. She said nice things about Wheelock."

The woman glanced back at her garden. "Well, I'm running out of light."

I looked at her for a moment, suddenly feeling cold and slightly ill. "You asked if I was a friend of hers, 'as well.' Was there someone else looking for her today?"

She straightened, again shoving her glasses back. "Yes. Came by about half an hour ago."

"Thin man? Gray hair tied back in a ponytail?"

"That's him."

I thanked her, drove to the top of the hill, pulled off the road into Marie Benoit's driveway, and switched on Brandt's cellular phone. If ever there was a need for the cavalry he'd mentioned, this was it—except that there wasn't much cavalry in this part of Vermont.

Brandt was still at the office, as we'd agreed earlier. "What's up?"

"Shattuck's already here—he's got a half-hour lead on me."

"Shit. Where are you?"

"Wheelock. Susan Pendergast has gone to the Bread and Puppet Circus in Glover—they're apparently putting on a big show. I need people—as many as you can round up."

I started the truck again and began driving as fast as I could up the road toward Glover, some eight miles farther on, cradling the phone in the crook of my neck. I could hear Brandt on the other end shouting instructions to someone in the background.

He came back on. "Joe—how did he do it?"

"I don't know, but I've got a bad feeling about it. Get hold of that clerk's assistant who helped us out with the birth records. I didn't give it any thought at the time, but when I was in there last, she seemed a little out of it—under stress somehow. Shattuck trained Susan Pendergast in urban guerrilla tactics. The town clerk's office would've been a natural place for him to start looking for her."

"I'll check it out. Keep that phone with you."

I drove as quickly as I could along the narrow, twisting road. The oddly named Bread and Puppet Circus had been founded years earlier as an alternative to traditional indoor theater. It was socially political in its rhetoric, loosely organized, and supported by volunteers and low-paid workers. It also staged its performances out-of-doors, both locally and in other parts of the world. What made it unique among other vestiges of early countercultural street theater, however, was its use of props. Bread and Puppet—which also made and sold bread to raise money—was famous for its papier-mâché masks, statuary, and "puppets," some of which were fifteen feet tall and carried on the ends of long poles by white-dressed attendants. The effect of seeing these looming, gaunt, often grim-faced giants high over the heads of the grass-strewn audience, with only the mountains and the sky as backdrop, was alternatively enchanting, mystical, unnerving, and downright ominous.

This, combined with the unique music and the unconventionally delivered social messages—along with the tough but savory bread—made it a very popular attraction. If the Circus was putting on an especially big performance, I expected to find hundreds of people in attendance.

I began seeing cars parked on the shoulders on both sides of the road a half mile from my destination. I continued on more slowly, unsure of the geography. I'd seen photographs of the circus and read articles about them, but I'd never actually been up here before. What also fueled my caution was a conviction that if Shattuck knew Susan Pendergast was here, he knew I wasn't far behind.

I passed a dirt road on the left with a "Bread and Puppet Circus" banner strung across it and then immediately came to a gathering of buildings by the road—a huge barn attached to a farmhouse on the right, opposite a rough shed and a couple of colorfully decorated but decrepit school busses. In front of the barn was a driveway with a prominent "No Parking" sign. I backed my truck in and killed the engine.

I got out and looked around warily. Up and down the road were hundreds of cars, vans, and trucks. And yet there was not a soul in sight.

I walked over to the barn, a gigantic three- or four-story whale of a building, weather-beaten and sagging, and pushed open a small side door marked "Museum." It was dark and silent inside. The ramshackle white house attached to one side seemed equally abandoned.

On the soft breeze, I heard the muffled thumping of distant drums. I crossed over to the dirt road with the banner. It, too, was lined with cars, and led downhill, curving to the right. The sounds of music—pipes, more drums, instruments I couldn't identify—had grown louder.

At the bottom of the curve, around a small outcropping of trees, I came within sight of a broad field, some distance off, that had been cut into the side of a hill years before—perhaps as an old gravel pit. Now, softened and disguised by grass and passing time, it had become a perfect amphitheater, its three green walls gently sloping toward the flat, circular "stage" at the bottom.

I stopped close by the trees, still under their protection, and surveyed the scene. The Bread and Puppet Circus was in full swing, its many members dancing and carrying their trademark towering puppets to the accompaniment of odd and exotic-sounding musical instruments. But they were facing the same way I was—directly into the crowd of well over a thousand people. If I continued the way I was heading, I would come out into full view of the crowd as I followed a well-worn trail that swept up and around the right side of the back of the amphitheater. For several minutes, I would be clearly visible to everyone watching the show.

I retreated up the road a short way and cut into the woods that bordered the left side of the amphitheater, hoping to come out above and south of the old pit, where my appearance would pass largely unnoticed. It was becoming darker—I guessed the half-light following sunset would be completely gone in about forty-five minutes—and I was becoming pessimistic about ever locating Susan Pendergast.

I was almost to my goal, but still in the woods, when the soft chirping of the cellular phone brought me to a halt. I pulled it out and answered.

"We found the assistant town clerk," Brandt said, his voice thin and distant. "She's dead."

"Oh, Christ." I was suddenly siezed with a violent anger, directed both at Shattuck's casual bloodthirstiness and my own inability to bring it to an end.

"She was at home. It looks like a broken neck. She probably told him what he wanted to know, and then he killed her so she wouldn't talk. I guess you were right about him staking out her office—maybe he'd already gotten to her and was holding something over her . . . coercing her somehow. If so, all he had to do was wait 'til we'd done his research for him, before driving up to Motor Vehicles in Montpelier for a current address, no questions asked. . . . Where are you now?"

"I'm just about to start searching the crowd. You got backup coming?"

"There was a domestic brawl somewhere in your general area. It's got almost everybody tied up, but they're trying to break people loose. They're moving as fast as they can, but they got to cover the distance."

"Have them block off the roads when they arrive. If they get here before the show ends, they should have everybody stay where they are. That's got to play to our advantage. And tell them to bring lots of lighting. It's going to be dark soon. And, Tony?" I added as an afterthought. "Get hold of Al Hammond at the LynBurke Motel. He was planning to spend the night there. Maybe he can help out."

"Right."

I switched off the phone and stepped out of the woods into the mowed swath that curved around the upper semicircle of the amphitheater. What I saw filled me with hopelessness and frustration—a thousand people, many of them with their backs to me, sitting on the grass, jammed together in a solid sea, amid the rapidly failing light.

I joined a fringe of people at the back who were mostly standing, many of them equipped with either still or video cameras. I walked up to an older man with several Nikons around his neck.

"Excuse me. Could I ask you a big favor?" I said in a low voice.

He looked at me with a startled expression. "Sure—what's up?"

I pulled my badge out and discreetly showed it to him. "My name is Lt. Joe Gunther; I'm from the Brattleboro Police Department. I'm looking for someone in this crowd. I know it sounds a little crazy, but I was wondering if I could borrow one of your long lenses so I could see better."

He stared at me for a moment, the smile fading from his face. "Are you putting me on?"

"No—I'm quite serious, and I'm running out of time."

Something in my voice or expression must have done the trick, because he bent down to the bag at his feet and came out with a monstrous telephoto lens that he quickly snapped onto one of the camera bodies around his neck. He then slipped it off and handed it to me. "It's the biggest one I've got. You're not going anywhere with it, are you?"

"Only along the edge here. Stay with me. If I spot the person I'm after, I'll pass you the camera and get out of your hair."

He nodded and stepped back slightly to give me more room.

I hefted the camera up to eye level and began scanning the faces of the crowd on the bank opposite me. Beyond them, across a distant, overgrown field, I could see the dimly lit top of the barn where I'd parked my truck.

It was an impressive lens—high-quality, one thousand millimeters, very clear. Even in this light, it functioned well, allowing me a distinct close-up view of even the most distant faces. As I moved from one person to the next, carefully sweeping from left to right, I began to feel more optimistic.

Given enough time and enough light, finding Susan Pendergast again became a possibility—assuming she was here at all.

Of course, hers wasn't the only face I was seeking, and I knew that if Shattuck was also searching for her, he, too, would be on high ground, studying the crowd. I had therefore begun my sweep with the people on the crest of the amphitheater.

That, as it turned out, was a piece of incredible luck, not for what I saw on that crest but in the distance behind it. Over the shoulder of one of the spectators I'd focused on, in the field separating the distant road from where we stood, I caught the blur of something bobbing up and down.

I refocused the lens. The bobbing turned into a man, his back to me, running toward the barn, a telltale ponytail swinging from side to side.

"Shit," I muttered, and handed the camera back to its owner.

"You found him?"

I didn't pause to answer. I was sprinting off as fast as I could, a good quarter mile behind.

I hadn't seen Susan, but the absolute certainty that Shattuck had beaten me to her was utterly clear to me. The quiet, almost unnoticed death of a backwoods hermit with a false name and a secret stash of money had led me here with fate's inexorable momentum. I had stood by in ignorance while Kevin Shilly had been cruelly murdered. Was I again too late to stop the murder of the one person left I had the power to save?

I discovered a narrow trail that cut through the field and the line of trees that bordered the road, making my progress better than I'd expected. Nevertheless, when I reached the road, it was empty.

I crossed the road to my truck, listening, my gun now in my hand, hoping for some sign to tell me where Shattuck had gone. Instinctively, as if drawn by its magnetic mass, my eyes went to the huge dark barn and to the museum door I'd pushed open earlier to look inside. I had closed that door behind me. It now stood open.

I went up the steps silently, pausing just outside, my back against the wall, trying to remember the layout I'd only just glimpsed before. Directly opposite the door was a broad set of stairs leading up to the museum; to the left was a gift-shop area, with bins full of prints, metal postcard racks, and various T-shirt displays. Beyond that had been three other doorways too dark to see into. To the right of the entrance was either a wall or another door—I couldn't remember.

I took a deep breath, gripped my gun with both hands, and swung inside, pivoting on my heel so that I ended up crouching at the foot of the stairs, my back against the wall, facing both the upstairs and the darkened gift-shop area. Almost immediately, I heard the single soft scrape of a foot somewhere above me.

I moved up the stairs slowly, my attention focused ahead, but also aware of any movement from beyond the gift shop. The wood beneath me was ancient, worn, and scarred, but solid and utterly silent, all the creaks and groans long ago beaten out of it.

The steps came up through the floor above, so that I had to crouch just below floor level and stick my head up quickly for a fast survey. What I saw was the source of dreams and nightmares—a huge, looming dark cavern of a room, columned and laced overhead by giant wooden support posts and beams—a classic monument of timber-frame construction, with bracing and counter bracing made of massive hand-adzed, tree-sized poles, linked in countless mortise and tenon joints. It was a structure of cathedral-like complexity, and all of it—the posts, the walls, the ceilings, and the two galleries lining the central aisle—was covered or populated with the papier-mâché manifestations of decades of whimsy-driven puppeteers. Masks of humans, clowns, animals, and demons hung everywhere; bodies made of sheets fell from enormous, pale, frozen-faced heads like stalactites; serried ranks of twelve-foot human forms, some with the faces of gargoyles, stood guard by the dozen; and everywhere, from every angle, row after tightly packed row of those large, dark, sightless eyes stared out at whatever passed before them.

Susan Pendergast, if she was here, had chosen well—this

was a place of confusion and befuddlement, of hope for the pursued and despair for the pursuer, where stillness and silence reigned, where movement meant revelation and death.

And yet move I had to if I was to finally thwart one man's twenty-four years of rage and save the life of a woman who'd made living an act of survival.

The two parallel floor-level galleries I'd noticed during my quick inspection were each separated from the central aisle by continuous three-foot-high wooden barricades, also festooned with decorative baubles, masks, and designs. Both galleries contained a variety of three-dimensional set pieces—frozen, puppet-peopled scenes of diners at table, animals at play, or simply a crowd of people gathered as in an audience. They were dense and layered and offered a protective maze of cover, assuming I could reach them.

I figured Shattuck knew I was here and that he was watching where I was hiding as carefully as he was searching for Susan. To try stealth to reach cover, therefore, was obvious folly. Dark as it was—and it was difficult seeing even the nearest wall in any detail—I would still be visible to anyone watching. An explosive entry, with a scramble to safety, seemed the only alternative. It also might destabilize Shattuck's stalking of Susan enough to give her an advantage of some kind.

I firmly planted my feet on the steps, rocked forward slightly, and launched myself in a sprinter's half crouch toward the three-foot barricade of the nearest gallery. I sailed over it in a dive, tucking my head in to land in a somersault, and crashed into a trio of puppets sitting around a small linen-covered table. I landed in a tangled sprawl amid hollow oversized bodies, a cloud of dust, and fragments of broken wood. Spurred on by the fear of a bullet, I twisted onto all fours and crawled as swiftly and silently as possible away from my calamitous landing site.

There was no bullet, however, nor any sound whatsoever. Stealthily now, I repositioned myself farther up the gallery, under the billowing skirts of a lady twice my height in Colonial dress, still hearing no more than my own quiet breathing. I rose slowly up the center of the puppet, alongside the central wooden pole on which she hung, careful not to touch the fabric surrounding me. Moving in slow motion, I pulled out my Swiss army pocketknife and, using the small scissors blade, meticulously and quietly cut a tiny window in front of my right eye.

Through this opening, I had a fairly broad view of both the gallery opposite and the barn's central aisle, as far as the gloom allowed. The problem was, of course, that unless something moved out there, I was confronted with only an army of lifeless, empty, oversized shells.

I didn't think Susan would give herself away; she had chosen this spot, and knew the value of stillness within it. Nor did I intend to move; I'd secured a near perfect observation post. The role of hunter was exclusively Shattuck's—it was his field to explore and his choice to risk exposure.

Or so I thought.

Far to the left, near the staircase, I saw something move— slightly, with no more urgency that the sweep of a clock's minute hand. I closed my eyes briefly to intensify their sensitivity to the dark. In the brief moment following their reopening, I saw the figure of a man in profile, shifting with the subtlety of a cloud's shadow on the moon. He was tall, lean, darkly dressed, his hair close-cropped.

Someone else was here beside Susan, Shattuck, and me. Instinctively, I realized the Outfit had risen to the challenge I had thrown down in Chicago.

Now there were two hunters, one prey, and me.

Never before had I played in a lethal chess game of this kind, where all the players stood apart, unallied, and potentially at risk from one another. I would later recall what happened next only in supercompressed bits of memory— like a series of blurred snapshots taken so close together that the action of one bleeds into the next.

It began with the cellular phone in my pocket going off like an alarm clock. Reaching for my pocket but still frozen to my small observation hole, I saw Shattuck materialize from the gallery opposite me as if from nowhere—a puppet come lethally alive. His legs were slightly apart and braced, his body gently curved, both his arms straight out ahead of him in a perfect shooter's stance, with his gun aimed straight at me. But the explosion, when it came, was from the left, and the accompanying white-hot muzzle flash revealed the shooter standing as a mirror image of Shattuck, his gun pointing at the first thing he'd seen appear, unintentionally saving my life. Behind him, just over his shoulder, I also saw Susan's startled white face among the masks on the wall near the stairs.

There was another blinding eruption, from Shattuck's skewed gun, triggered by the effect of the mobster's bullet passing through his head. In a second frozen image, I saw him twisted in midair, his eyes wide, his mouth open in surprise, the side of his head ill-defined and blurry, etched in crimson.

The two shots were a split second apart, and my reaction—stimulated by the knowledge that Shattuck had caught the first bullet only because he'd moved first, and that I was next in line—followed almost as fast. Realizing I couldn't fire my own pistol without the possibility of hitting Susan, I grabbed the center pole beside me, lifted the puppet off the hook on which it was hanging, and, running forward, tilted the whole thing like a knight's lance toward the shooter and threw it.

Now clear of the puppet's skirts, I saw Shattuck's killer diving to one side to avoid my missile, just as Susan dropped from the railing around the stairwell to the floor below. I was suddenly faced with a choice: to apprehend a fugitive I'd been after for days or to try to stop a contract killer who would next be gunning for me. After the smallest of hesitations, I chose Susan.

My choice was not as irrational as it first appeared. We were both after Susan Pendergast. If I could keep up with her, the man behind me was sure to follow, giving me, if I was lucky, another chance to deal with him.

Susan had cut right at the bottom of the stairs, into the gloom of the nearest of the three doorways beyond the gift-shop area. I followed, throwing the still-chirping phone to one side as I went, and blundered into her in the middle of a long, almost totally blackened hallway. She shied away from me, lashing out ineffectually with her fists.

"It's me—Joe Gunther. Goddamn it—cut it out."

She stopped at hearing my name, and I quickly grabbed her elbow and continued down the passage, which I could barely see was lined by crowds of puppets arranged like those upstairs. These, however, were all human-sized or smaller, since the ceiling was almost perilously low.

"Is there another way out?" I whispered.

I felt Susan shaking her head beside me. "I don't know."

We reached the end of the hallway and found a connector passage linking the three parallel galleries that fed into the gift shop. I propelled her into the middle passage and stopped, weighing our slim options, wondering when help would arrive.

Susan tried to shake free of my grasp.

"Stay put," I growled at her quietly.

"Why? I'm screwed either way."

"You are if he finds us. Why did you deposit the hundred thousand dollars in the hearse driver's bank?"

The question startled her, more because of where it was being asked than because of its substance. But it was a question I needed answered—to know, just for myself, the nature of the woman beside me and the extent of her guilt. I was forming a plan, but it risked allowing Billie to escape. I wasn't going to let that happen if I couldn't live with the consequences.

"Jesus Christ—I shot the man. It's the only good use that stupid money's been put to." She seemed to understand the debate going on in my head. I felt her hand grip my upper arm in an earnest plea. "I knew if you found me, Shattuck would, too. Destroying David's skeleton seemed the only way."

"You killed David, didn't you?"

She was silent for a moment. I knew that, ironically, the two of us held a momentary advantage over our stalker, who by now was reconnoitering the layout of the gift-shop area. Upstairs, there'd been one way in and out. Here, there were three. As soon as he committed himself to one of the passageways, the other two would be left open as escape routes. He was not going to move precipitously.

"To save Sean's life," she finally murmured, her voice seemingly sapped of energy. Despite the crimes she may have committed, I had never overlooked Gail's high opinion of her or my own first impression when we'd met days ago. Her politics and mine might not have agreed, but her commitment to the welfare of others—including the driver she'd inadvertently wounded—spoke well of her.

But I was to get no more. The luxury of time that our predator's caution had allowed us vanished with the loud squealing of wood scraping against wood.

Susan stiffened next to me.

"He's blocking two of the three doors at the other end," I said. "I expected that."

From the sounds, I could tell he was leaving the gallery we'd entered open for his approach, so I retraced our steps, speaking as we went. "You need to hide in this passageway—behind the puppets, in case he has a flashlight. Let him pass by, and then run for help. Police should be here soon, but they won't know where to look."

It was too dark to read her expression, but I could feel her eyes upon me as she weighed my trust in her against her well-honed instincts for self-preservation.

I gave her shoulder a squeeze, hoping I hadn't just staked my life on foolish sentiment. "Good luck."

In the dark, I felt her hand touch mine for an instant, and then she was gone.

The shooter had almost finished his handiwork, rearranging the tall, heavy counters in the gift shop in front of the other passageways. The last of his noise allowed Susan to hide herself somewhere down the passage. I waited in the narrow connector to the middle passage, peering around the corner.

The gunman did have a flashlight, held well away from his body so it couldn't be used as a reliable target in the dark, and he kept switching it on and off to further camouflage his location. Anticipating my scheme, he didn't proceed slowly and quietly as before, but began ricocheting from side to side, knocking over puppets and props as he went, ensuring that no one would be left hiding in his wake. His progress was now startlingly fast, brutal, and effective.

I had no idea where Susan had hidden herself, or how well. I only hoped that he would miss her in his own attempts to avoid becoming a target. But I also didn't know how well her nerves would hold up. To remain utterly silent and still, inches away from someone intent on killing you, was a bit much to expect.

Reluctantly, knowing I was reducing whatever plan I might have had to a roll of the dice, I pulled my gun from its holster and aimed at the ceiling above the flickering flashlight. I knew I couldn't hit him with such a shot, but I also wouldn't hit Susan by accident.

I pulled the trigger and dove to the side, out of sight. The responding shot was almost instantaneous, slapping into the wooden wall behind where I'd been standing.

I froze for a moment, not knowing if my opponent would stop to take stock or charge to take me off guard. He chose the cautious route, keeping his light off and his movements to a minimum. I felt comfortable now that as long as she stayed put a while longer, Susan could make it to safety.

The light flickered again for a split second as the shooter got his bearings. I retreated farther back into the third gallery and began looking for a good hiding place. I'd done what I could for Susan; now I had to find a way to survive.

The third gallery, like the others, was lined with puppets set in scenes. Moving as quickly as possible, I made my way down its length, to get a feel for the territory. At the far end, there was a grouping of figures dressed in costumes, one of which felt, to my blindly groping fingers, like knitted material. I pulled out my pocketknife again, sliced into the fabric, and pulled at its strands. As I'd hoped, it began to unravel, creating a long, thin string. I tied one end to one of the puppets and retreated with the other back up the gallery, hiding as best I could amid a cluster of figures draped in sheets.

Now it came down to patience, time, and luck. The crowd outside had to be breaking up by now, walking to their cars; the performers were no doubt converging on the house next door to clean up and get ready to head home. The man stalking me knew that. It had occurred to me that perhaps the best way out of my predicament was simply to empty my gun into the floor. But by now, I wanted him as badly as he apparently wanted me.

I stayed against the wall for what seemed like hours, my

gun in one hand, the piece of yarn in the other. The gunman had reverted to his earlier technique, where his progress became indistinguishable from the shadows around him. I had no idea which gallery he was prowling, or even, for that matter, if he hadn't already passed me. I had planned to let him do just that, pulling the string to distract him, thereby getting the drop on him. But that had all depended on knowing where he was. I began to sweat in the total blackness, covered by dusty sheets, my body sore and cramped.

Suddenly, I heard two sounds: one distant, from near the building's front door; the other far more important to me—a barely perceptible startled intake of breath, not six feet beyond me.

I was about to pull the string in my hand when the blackness around me disappeared in a stunning, blinding brilliance. The barn's lights had been switched on.

Blinking rapidly, shading my eyes with the hand that had held the now-superfluous piece of yarn, I stepped from my hiding place to face the man who had killed Bob Shattuck.

He was halfway down the passage, his right side to me, similarly surprised but already twisting to get off a shot, when I saw Al Hammond's face appear beyond him, above the tall counter that had been pushed up against the entrance. He was staring down the sights of a Winchester pump shotgun.

Simultaneously, we both yelled, "Freeze."

And miraculously, fighting his own momentum with instincts worthy of a cat, the man froze in a half crouch, his gun almost bearing on my chest.

"Drop it."

There was the hint of a smile then, the man opened his hand, and the gun fell to the floor with a dull clatter.

Outside, ten minutes later, with the side of the old barn flickering in the blue lights of four state police cruisers, I watched as the gunman, handcuffed but outwardly unconcerned, was helped into the back of one of the cars.

A state trooper—the sergeant in command—paused in his interview of me to watch the car drive off. "Cold-blooded son of a bitch, isn't he?"

I nodded. "How did you know to look in the barn?"

"Some woman came running up as we were checking the crowd, said she'd heard gunshots."

"She still here?"

"I asked her to stay put, but one of my men just told me she took off. Probably didn't want to get all tangled up in this."

I took a deep breath of the fresh night air, wondering where Susan Pendergast was headed now and what would become of her. She was certainly no saint, but if the world let her keep her secrets, she still had much to offer. I knew I'd do my part—she'd gained my respect and my vote for another chance. I'd drop the investigation where it was and let Brandt sort out the public relations.

Unfortunately, Susan would never know that for sure, any more than she'd know whether Bonatto now considered the slate clean or still wanted her dead.

It made me wonder how much longer she'd keep paying the price of freedom, and whether, someday, she'd ever question the value of all her efforts. I hoped, for her sake and for those who stood to benefit from her talents, that she'd keep on fighting.

"I don't know, Sergeant. Maybe she thought she'd done the best she could."